About the Contributors

MARK ANTHONY has written a number of novels for TSR, including his latest title, *Escape from Undermountain*. He has also contributed stories to collections set in the DRAGONLANCE®, FORGOTTEN REALMS®, and RAVENLOFT® settings. "People of the Dragon" allowed him the chance to make use of his anthropology degrees—and also helped to prove his theory that, for a writer, no knowledge ever goes to waste.

A resident of Mobile, Alabama, **LINDA P. BAKER** wrote "A Lull in the Battle" for her husband Larry, who provided inspiration by taking her to ice hockey games. Linda is also the author of *The Irda*, a DRAGONLANCE novel about the downfall of the ogre race, and a short story in *The Dragons of Krynn*.

JEFF GRUBB is an author and designer of role-playing games and collectible card games. He is the author of *Lord Toede* and the co-author, with Kate Novak, of the Finder's Stone Trilogy and *Masquerades* as well as the upcoming *Cormyr: A Novel*, with Ed Greenwood. He is currently working on the gnomish version of cold fusion. You have been warned.

J. ROBERT KING is the author of *Heart of Midnight, Carnival of Fear, Rogues to Riches, Summerhill Hounds,* two PLANESCAPE™ novels (so far), and numerous short stories for TSR anthologies. He is currently a househusband and new dad and loving it. In addition to cooking, cleaning, diapering, breadmaking and shipbuilding, King is at work on book three of his in-progress Blood Wars Trilogy.

A longtime role-player and aspiring novelist, **ADAM LESH** was first published, on paper, in TSR's *The History of DRAGONLANCE*. Electronically, Adam is the editor-in-chief of *Apocrypha*, a webzine on the Internet devoted to role-playing games. He looks forward to q   b i   day job really soon.

Co-author of two other short stories set in the world of Krynn, **TERI McLAREN** also co-wrote the DRAGONLANCE® novels *Before the Mask* and *The Dark Queen*. More recent work includes three books for *Magic: The Gathering: The Cursed Land*, the soon-to-be-released *Song of Time*, and its sequel, *Shadows of Time*.

ROGER E. MOORE is a Creative Analyst for TSR, working on licensing books for various product lines. He is the author of short stories in several TSR anthologies, and he has a soft spot in his heart for the DRAGONLANCE saga.

A Wisconsin native and longtime writer of TSR book and game products, **DOUGLAS NILES** boasts of the fact that, despite plot similarities between his story and the movie *High Noon*, he successfully resisted using the title "Do Not Forsake Me, Oh My Dragon."

NICK O'DONOHOE is the author of a number of DRAGONLANCE short stories for TSR, as well as the novel *Too, Too Solid Flesh*. He has published two Crossroads novels with Berkley Press: *The Magic and the Healing*, selected by the American Library Association as a Notable Book for Teens, and *Under the Healing Sign*. A third Crossroads novel is forthcoming in 1997.

Author and musician **JANET PACK** recently came out of the closet about being cat-dependent. Janet contributed music to TSR's *Leaves from the Inn of the Last Home* and *The History of DRAGONLANCE*, as well as Margaret Weis and Tracy Hickman's *Death Gate Cycle*. Her short story "Scourge of the Wicked Kendragon" appears in *The Dragons of Krynn*. Her stories also appear in *Fantastic Alice*, *CatFantastic IV* and *New Amazons*.

DONALD BAYNE STEWART PERRIN, Capt. (Ret'd.), Bsc, rmc, cfss, retired from the Canadian Army where he specialized in artillery computing. He is currently Vice President of the trading game company Mag Force 7. *Theros Ironfeld*, published in the spring of 1996, was his first DRAGONLANCE® novel.

CHRIS PIERSON first came to Krynn when he was 12, and is overjoyed that his first published short story is part of the DRAGONLANCE series. He works as a freelance writer and editor in Toronto, Canada.

KEVIN T. STEIN has a degree in English and has studied Shakespeare in England. Author of *Brothers Majere* and the short story "The Hunt" in the DRAGONLANCE series, Kevin's other works include *The Fall of Magic* (as D.J. Heinrich) by TSR, *Twisted Dragon* by Ace, and *The Guide to Larry Niven's Ringworld* by Baen. Kevin is a script consultant, and also has two screenplays optioned by a Hollywood production studio.

Co-author with Tracy Hickman of the latest best-selling DRAGONLANCE novel, *Dragons of Summer Flame*, **MARGARET WEIS** is currently working with Don Perrin on her next DRAGONLANCE book, *The Doom Brigade*. The novel continues the story of Kang and the draconians featured in the short story in this volume "The First Dragonarmy Engineer's Secret Weapon."

A resident of Louisville, Kentucky, **MICHAEL WILLIAMS** teaches at the University of Louisville. He is best known to readers of the DRAGONLANCE series for his poetry and novels, among which are *Weasel's Luck*, *Galen Beknighted* and *The Oath and The Measure*. His most recent novel, *Arcady*, will be published by Penguin/Roc in Spring 1996.

THE DRAGONS OF KRYNN

Edited by Margaret Weis and Tracy Hickman

THE DRAGONS AT WAR

Edited by Margaret Weis and Tracy Hickman

The
Dragons
at War

Edited by

Margaret Weis and

Tracy Hickman

THE DRAGONS AT WAR
©1996 TSR, Inc.
©2000 Wizards of the Coast, Inc.
All Rights Reserved.

Distributed in the United States by St. Martin's Press. Distributed in Canada by Fenn Ltd.

Distributed worldwide by Wizards of the Coast, Inc., and regional distributors.

Distributed to the toy and hobby trade by regional distributors.

Cover art by Paul Jaquays. Interior art by Valerie A. Valusek.

First Printing: May 1996
Printed in the United States of America.
Library of Congress Catalog Card Number: 95-62203

9 8 7 6 5

ISBN: 0-7869-0491-7
620-T08378

U.S., CANADA, ASIA,
PACIFIC, & LATIN AMERICA
Wizards of the Coast, Inc.
P.O. Box 707
Renton, WA 98057-0707
+1-800-324-6496

EUROPEAN HEADQUARTERS
Wizards of the Coast, Belgium
P.B. 2031
2600 Berchem
Belgium
+32-70-23-32-77

Visit our website at **www.wizards.com**

TABLE OF CONTENTS

Introduction
Margaret Weis

It is storyteller's night at the Inn of the Last Home. Tika began the institution in order to boost sales during those cold winter nights when people would much rather stay home near the fire than venture out into the ice and snow.

They became enormously popular and now, periodically, she and Caramon send invitations to the most renowned storytellers in Ansalon, offering to pay room and board if they come share their tales.

This evening, the Inn has a fine collection of bards.

Caramon stands up on a keg of ale to be seen over the crowd, and makes the introductions.

"First, I'd like to present the old-timers like me," Caramon says. "These friends date clear back to the time of the War of the Lance. Just raise your hand when I call your name. Tasslehoff, put your hand down. We have tonight: Michael Williams, Jeff Grubb, Nick O'Donohoe, Roger Moore, Doug Niles, Margaret Weis, Tracy Hickman . . . Where's Tracy?"

Caramon peers out into the crowd. There are shouts of laughter when Hickman is discovered wearing mouse-colored robes and accusing everyone of stealing his hat.

After the noise subsides, Caramon resumes. "A few of our bards this evening are making return appearances. Please raise your hands. No, Tas, that doesn't include you. I—Wait a minute! What's that you're holding in your hand? That's tonight's cash box! Tas! Give me that!"

General confusion. Caramon clambers down off the keg.

Tas's shrill voice rises in protest. "I was just keeping it safe, and a good thing, too! There's a lot of shady-looking characters in this crowd tonight."

"No, that's just Roger!" calls out Michael Williams.

When order (and the cash box) are restored, Caramon introduces the bards who have told stories here before: Janet Pack, Linda Baker, Mark Anthony, and Don Perrin.

"Finally," says Caramon, out of breath and red in the face, "I am pleased to introduce several bards who are newcomers to Ansalon. Everyone please welcome Adam Lesh, Chris Pierson, and J. Robert King."

The newcomers are warmly welcomed and advised to keep their hands on their purses.

Caramon bows to thunderous applause and returns to his place behind the bar. Tika makes a final call for ale.

Come, friend. There's room on this bench next to me. Sit down. Order a mug and be prepared to laugh and cry, shudder and shiver.

Tonight, our storytellers are going to talk about *The Dragons at War*.

Dream of the Namer
Michael Williams

I

The song of the high grass,
the twinned lamps
of the arcing moon,

the whisper of stars
and the darker moon
we must always remember—

these are the guides
on the first of the journeys
to a time past remembrance,

past the words for time
into the Namer's country
where we venture in dreams.

The time of the walking,
the Namers call it:
the time of the breath,

the forgotten time
when the lamps of the moons
wink out in an instant
and we steer by the dark

unforgettable light,
by the lost heartbeat.

It is the dream
of the Namers' time,
the convergence of visions,

when the moon and the wind
the strung bead
and the parables of sand

unite in a story
we do not remember
until we have traveled its country.

II

On the eve of the wars,
the signs and omens
bright as mirages,

I walked in a dreaming,
through an emptied country
bloodied with iron and sunlight,

and there in the dream
I asked three times
for the voice of the god,

and he came to me quietly,
a shimmer of smoke
at the edge of imagined country,
where the whispered truth rises,

and the words that you dream
are here and suddenly elsewhere.

It is the old voice
felt on the back of the neck,
the thing under reason and thought,

when out of the smoke of your dreaming,
out of the harbor of blood,
out of the ninth moon's drowning,

the dead rise   are rising
have risen   and speak
in the language of sparrow and drum.

And oh may the gods
believe in my telling,
in the dream I recount,

and may the long dead listen
in the wind-drowned lands
in the dust's generation

as I tell you the seventh
of seven visions,
the song of the dragon's wing.

III

First there was eye,
then night, then immutable north,
then the smell of the springbok
over the launched horizon,

and then I was walking,
over a dying plain

littered with rock
and immaculate bone.

Ahead in a cavern
of dazzled sunlight,

on the sunstruck and burnished
edge of the world,

the dragons, dark jewels,
a flicker of ebony wings,

a frenzy of beetles
feasting on carrion,

and I cannot tell you
in memory's dream,

whether the sight
or the seeing drew me

whether I went
of my own accord
or drawn like a jessed bird
hard to the falconer's will.

But what did it matter
when the dark thing ascended

in an old smell of blood,
of creosote and coal?

I looked to the sun
and I saw them in legion

wingtip to wingtip
in the western skies

and it was for this
I was brought to the summit,

it was for this
that I dreamed the philosopher's dream.

Sunlight under my riding
and an alien heartbeat,

the cold pulse of blood
like the waters' convergence—

on the back of the monster
the sunlight was dreaming to shadows

as the wings passed over
the dying world.

And out of the lifting heartbeat,
out of the drum and shadow,

a voice rose around me,
inveigling, caressing,

a voice indistinct
from my own in my dreams,

a voice indistinct
from the chambered shadows,

from a century's nursing
of venom and fire,

and all of my dreaming
had brought me to this,

had prepared me to ride
on the wings of the darkness,

and the voice of the serpent
I heard in the air

as she spoke to me
saying . . . saying . . .

IV

Do not believe
this is only beginning,
Oh do not believe
of my dark and interminable legions,
that as long as the heart
is a thicket of knives,
we will not prevail
regardless of knights
and their rumored lances.
I am telling you this

from the heart of the storm,
from the tumult of wings
at the edge of your vision.
Over the miles
of a dozen kingdoms
I hasten toward Huma
toward his forged
and impossible lance,
toward victory, though
the hot abysm of dreams
swells with a voice
that is telling me always
it will end in this age,
in expected convergence
of dragon and darkness,
of the plain appointed
and the point of the lance.
Oh do not expect
there is ever an ending,
for even the sunlight
that closes around me
masks a nation of shadows,
the sigh of the desert
drowns out the wails
of the buried and beaten,
and do not believe
this is changing,
that the endings are happy,
that the cycle of seasons
awaits an eventual spring,
that the sunrise riding
the wake of the darkness
is more than a mutual dream.

Oh do not believe
as I ride into battle,
that the battle is more
than an accident, formed
in the clumsy collision
of sunlight and shadow,
that a morning will pass
in an unending sunlight
without the dark brush of a wing.

V

And as I arose on the Lady's back,
the wake of her wingbeats
blossomed in darkness,
darkness surrounded me,
darkness expanding
and harvesting light,
and around us a tumult of wings
settled like ashes
in a winter of loss.
So circled the Lady
over plain   over sunlight
toward the knight and the lance,
and I clung to the darkness,
to the spiraling chasm
that swallowed my clinging hands
to the scale   to the flesh
to a cavernous nothing
that opened beneath and around me,
to a darkness so deep
that the shadows around it
paled to a grayness

a darkness devouring
all color   all light
a darkness entangled
expanding contracting
a pulse that I heard
in the walls of my riding veins.

As she flew toward Huma
I fell toward the heart
that was slowly becoming my own,
and there at the source
of stillbirth and scar
of the hunger of knives,
there at the source
of a failed mathematics
in the chambers of knowledge,
where the mind says
this   it is this   no this
as the damaged world
slips from the net of numbers,

Oh the heart of the Lady
was fractured ice
was iron   was fever
the sharp and insistent
hook in the flesh,
was famine   pellagra
the tedium of days—
all of it stirring
the waters of darkness,
all of it saying
you are here   you are here
you are home.

They tell you a story
of lances and daylight,
the old song of Huma
spreads over the desert of night
like a balm   like a blinding
like an old narcosis of dreams.
We remember the lance-wielder
waiting in history,
we remember the story
the thousand contractions
of light and the absence of light,
and it was the dream
of Huma the Lancer
from which we have never awakened.
Oh continue to choose
the bright lance-wielder,
the feigned historical morning
in exchange for the heart
you have veiled in the dreams
that your Namers make idly
and the centuries sing
through a long desolation of night,
as the old heart inhabits
the innermost moon
you must never   must always remember.

People of the Dragon
Mark Anthony

When the valefolk uncovered the old grave, they sent for me at once.

The warm winds of spring had rushed into the valley only seven days before, breaking winter's hard grip on the mountainous lands of Southern Ergoth. As always, I was thankful for the change of seasons. Though cool and even pleasant in summertime, the cave in which I had dwelled these last years was during the dark months a tomb from which no fire—be it mundane or magical—could fully drive the bitter chill. However, winter had finally fled, and I had cast back the leather curtain that hung across the narrow mouth of the cave, letting light and air stream inside to dispel the dank darkness within.

The cave was small, no more than five paces across and thrice that number deep. Despite this, it served me well enough. The floor was dry and sandy, and there was more than adequate room for my scant possessions: a cot of bent willow supporting a pallet woven of rushes, a rack for drying herbs, and a shelf to hold wax-sealed clay pots filled with oil, salted fish, and wrinkled olives. A small fire burned in a brazier in the center of the cave, while coils of smoke sought an escape through unseen cracks in the ceiling above.

Sitting on a threadbare rug beside the brazier, I examined a tiny mole skeleton that I had affixed to a piece of bark with pine sap. By nature I am a man of learning, and I have always been particularly fascinated with the way in which living creatures are put together. I always found that each animal I examined possessed features perfectly designed for its manner of survival.

The mole was no different. Its almost fantastically convoluted arm bone allowed attachment for the powerful muscles used in digging, and its sharp, pointed teeth were well suited to piercing the shells of beetles, which were its primary food. I dipped a feather pen into a pot of ink made from nightshade berries. Then, on a piece of stretched sheepskin, I carefully drew the mole's skeleton, noting interesting features as I went.

A shadow fell across the doorway.

I looked up in surprise. A thin silhouette stood in the mouth of the cave. The dark figure froze at my sudden movement, then turned to run.

"Wait!" I called out.

The silhouette halted but did not step any nearer. Setting down my pen, I stood and approached the door. As I stepped across the stony threshold from dimness to daylight, I saw my mysterious visitor fully: a boy, no more than twelve winters. He was clad in loose clothes of rough cloth, and he shifted nervously back and forth on his bare feet.

It was not uncommon for the valefolk to come to me. From time to time, one of them trod the winding footpath that led from the ramshackle village below, up through the grove of silver-green aspen trees, to my cave. Usually they came seeking salve for a cut that had turned septic, or herbs to ease a toothache, or a tea to help a barren woman conceive. To the valefolk, I was simply a hermit, a wise man who had shunned the outside world, and had come to the mountains to conduct his studies in solitude.

Mad, perhaps, but not dangerous. Of course, if they ever learned my true nature, the valefolk would certainly turn on me and burn me alive in my cave.

It had been five years since I fled the destruction of the Tower of High Sorcery at Daltigoth. Sometimes I still dreamed about the flames.

The mob had come sooner than any of us had thought. The Kingpriest had decreed all mages to be anathema, workers of evil, and magic itself to be heresy. But Istar was nearly a continent away. Daltigoth was on the western fringe of the Empire. We had thought we had time—time to finish our work in progress, to carefully pack away our books and journals, to travel to secret havens where we might resume our magical studies in peace.

We were wrong.

The edict of the Kingpriest had traveled across the face of the land like wildfire, ignited by fear, fueled by hate, sending up thick clouds of ignorance like dark smoke in its wake. When the throng surged through the streets of Daltigoth toward the Tower, brandishing torches and gleaming weapons, we did not fight back. To do so would have only damned our kind further in their eyes. Instead, we let them stream through the open gates to set ablaze centuries of knowledge and cast down our shining Tower in ruin.

I had been one of the lucky ones. I had escaped in the confusion with only small injuries, and had fled south from the city, into the mountains, to this remote valley where none knew the look of a wizard. Sometimes I wondered how many of my brothers and sisters had escaped the destruction of the Tower. If any had, they would have hardly recognized me now. Once I had been Torvin, Mage of the White Robe, a bold and dashing young wizard. These days I was simply Torvin the Hermit. I wore only drab brown, and had let my dark hair and beard grow long. I was still tall, but living as I did had left me thin, almost gaunt.

In all, I quite looked the part of a recluse. And to that, I owed my life. The valefolk were loyal and fearful subjects of the Empire. If ever they discovered that I was no mere hermit, but a worker of magic, they would brand me a heretic. And there is but one punishment for heresy—fire. It was not an easy life, always concealing the power that dwelled within me, denying who and what I was. Sometimes I wished that I could fly away on wings of magic, and escape the fear, hatred and ignorance forever. But until then, it was better to dissemble than to die.

Before me, the vale boy chewed his lip, his eyes wide with fright. I offered him my most reassuring smile. "Don't worry," I said in a gentle tone. "Hermits don't bite. That is, unless they're terribly hungry. However, you're lucky, for I've just eaten. There's still some soup in the pot. Would you like some?"

The boy stared at me as if I had just offered him a bowl of poison spiders. He swallowed hard, then finally managed to find his words, speaking in an urgent voice.

"My father sent me to fetch you. They've found bones. In the field, while plowing."

I raised an eyebrow in curiosity. "Bones?"

The boy nodded vigorously. "They found this with them. And more things like it."

He held out a small object, being careful not to let me touch him as I took the thing from his dirty hand. I turned the object over in my fingers, my excitement growing. It was a knife of stone.

The artifact had been fashioned from a piece of smooth brown chert. Flakes had been expertly chipped away from one side to yield a sharp cutting edge, while the other side was blunt and rounded to provide a grip. The knife fit easily, comfortably, into my palm. I knew at once that the last time it knew the touch of a human hand had been thousands of years ago.

It was not the first stone artifact I had examined that had been retrieved by accident from long burial beneath the soil of time. Many believed that such things were created by goblins or trolls, but that was not so. The makers of the stone knives and obsidian arrowheads and copper axes were not goblins. They were people. People who had lived a long time ago, before cities were raised, before horses were tamed, and before the secrets of working gold and iron were stolen from the dwarves. I know, for I have used the things they left behind to see through their ancient eyes.

"We were afraid to keep plowing," the boy went on, growing bolder now. "Scaldirk claimed it was an ill omen. My father said to come fetch you, that you could say what the bones were, and appease the spirits in them."

I knew nothing of the craft of appeasing spirits, but I did not tell the boy that. I clutched the stone knife tightly in my hand. "Take me to where this was found."

The boy nodded and turned to pad swiftly down the narrow footpath. I hurried after him. My cave was situated at the foot of the ridge that bounded the north side of the valley. In the center lay the rushing river near which most of the people dwelled, in stone houses with sod roofs. To the south, the valley narrowed, rising steeply in a defile that plunged deeper into the blue mountains. It was a pass—a way into the mountains—

though one that was never tread, as far as I knew.

The defile climbed past countless massive shoulders of rock, making its way toward white-crowned peaks that hovered like sharp clouds in the far distance. Though all must be dizzyingly high, one summit soared above the others: a great horned peak that seemed to rake the sky. "Dragonmount" the valefolk called it, after the horned summit. Or, at least, so I always supposed.

I followed the boy across open heath and patches of scree. At last we crested a low rise, and I saw the knot of valefolk. They stood in the center of a fallow field, clad in grimy garb of brown and gray, gazing at the ground. Gathering my robe up around my ankles, I approached across the muddy ground. White shapes protruded from the dark, freshly turned earth. I knelt in the broken soil, my breath fogging in the moist air. With growing excitement, I examined what the plow had uncovered. Carefully I brushed away bits of dirt, my wonder growing at the ancient objects before me.

It was a grave.

Looking carefully, I found I could see a faint line where the color of the soil changed, marking the edge of the burial pit that had been dug and filled in again so long ago. The skeleton was largely intact, save the legs, which had been disturbed by the plow. By the shape of the hip bones, the lack of brow ridges on the skull, and the smallness of the bony protuberance behind the hole of the ear, I knew this was a woman.

However, the caps on the ends of her arm bones looked only barely fused to the shafts, and her wisdom teeth, though erupted, were barely worn down. It was the skeleton of a young woman then, perhaps twenty when she died, no more. They had curled her body, knees to chin, like a child in the womb, returning her to the embrace of the world that had given her birth. Rusty red stained the soil, remnants of the ocher with which they had colored her skin.

By the grave goods, I knew that she had been a princess of some sort. Beads of jade and carved bone in the soil around her neck bespoke a necklace, though the strand that had bound it together had rotted away centuries ago. Copper rings still encircled her fingers, and an ivory cup lay next to her, along with a comb fashioned from antler. Such riches would have accompanied only an important woman into the afterlife. I imagined she had been a chief's daughter. Though more careful examination of the artifacts would be required before I could be more certain, my guess was that she had been laid to rest over two thousand years ago by a forgotten people who had dwelled in this valley long before the valefolk.

My concentration was broken as one of the men spoke. By the similarity of their smudged faces, I took him for the father of the boy who had been sent to fetch me.

"What think you, Torvin?" the man asked. Fear shone in his small, dark eyes. "I have never seen things such as these. Is it an elf?"

One of the other men, a squat fellow with bowed legs, let out a brash laugh. "Bah! There aren't no such things as elves, Merrit." But his laughter fell short on the cool air, and the others looked around nervously, making the sign against evil with their fingers.

I did not tell them that there were indeed elves. I had never been so lucky as to see one myself, or to travel to their secret forest cities. But I had learned something of elves in my studies, enough to know that they would never fashion such crude artifacts as these. Gold they worked, and crystal, not bone and chert.

I told the gathered valefolk that there was nothing to fear, that this was simply a grave, and that the bones within had belonged to a person no different than us. If her possessions seemed strange, it was only because she had lived so very long ago. My words seemed to reassure them somewhat. I instructed several of the men in the manner in which the bones and artifacts were to be removed, and explained I would bury them myself in a secret place, where the woman's spirit would disturb no one.

I did not tell them that I intended to study her first. They would not have understood my scholarly goals, and would have feared my interest in the dead.

As the men labored, I moved a short distance away. I sat upon an old stump and watched, to make certain they did not work too carelessly. That was when I saw it. An arc of stone protruded from the freshly turned soil near my feet, far too smooth and regular to be natural. I dug my fingers into the soil and pulled, freeing the object. Brushing off the heavy stone, I examined it in my hands.

The stone had been carefully ground into a half moon shape. One end was broad and notched, and could have easily been bound to a wooden haft with sinew or twine. The other end came to a point, like the end of a dwarven pick-axe. I had seen such artifacts before. It was an adze. No doubt this was the tool with which the grave had been dug.

A sudden impulse came upon me. It was dangerous. I knew I should wait until I was safely in my cave where none could possibly see me, but that would mean waiting hours. Besides, the valefolk were busy with their work, and were paying me no attention now. They would not notice. I wanted to know who the woman in the grave had been. What better way to learn than to see her through the eyes of the one who had dug her grave so long ago?

Cradling the stone adze, I turned my back to the vale-folk. Before I fully thought about what I was doing, whispered words of magic tumbled from my lips. A thrill surged through my body as the spell was completed. My fingers tingled against the stone as everything went white. I blinked, and when I could see again, it was through eyes that were not my own.

* * * * *

He stood upon the shore of a high mountain lake.

An icy wind whipped his dark hair from his brow and tugged at the aurochs hide he gripped around his shoulders. He was a tall man, and well-knit. Despite the harshness of the lofty heights where his tribe dwelled, his handsome face was smooth and unlined. However, the light in his pale eyes belied his years. He was no youth. He shivered, for beneath the red-furred hide he was naked. With nothing they had come to the Dragonmere. With nothing he would go. Such was the law of Parting.

The tribe had gathered before him, two dozen men and women clad in close-fitting garb sewn of deerskin. All of the People of the Dragon were tall, and like the man, all seemed strangely unmarked by time. Their proud, beautiful faces were hard and grim. But sorrow shone in their pale eyes. Behind the tribe, a great peak soared into the sharp blue sky. Below, its horned summit was mirrored upon the silver surface of the Dragonmere. While it was not so for the real mountain above, by some trick of the rippling waters, the reflected mountain indeed looked like a dragon stretching its horned head skyward as it spread its silver-white wings.

One of the tribe, a powerfully muscled man, stepped forward. Though ageless like the others, streaks of white marked his coppery beard and long hair, and instead of gray, his eyes were the color of old honey. He spoke in a voice as rich and wild as the wind. "Do you truly mean to do this thing, Skyleth?"

After a long moment Skyleth nodded, tightening his grip on the aurochs hide. "I love her, Tevarrek."

"It is a perilous love, and one that will sunder your path from ours forever."

"I know."

Tevarrek shook his head, his expression one of confusion and anger. "Many of the People seem to understand you, Skyleth. I think some of them even envy you your love. I cannot say that I do. I think that you're a fool. But then, I've always been the odd one here, haven't I?" His voice became a sneer. "Is she so beautiful then, this creature of the valley tribe?"

A fleeting smile touched Skyleth's lips. "She is beautiful, yes. But it is not for that I would go. I know as well as you how fleeting a thing is human beauty."

The two locked gazes. At last Tevarrek let out a deep breath. "Once you descend beneath the Barrier, you will never be able to return. Do you accept this fate, Skyleth?"

Skyleth hesitated only a fraction of a heartbeat before speaking the words. "I do."

Tevarrek reached out and snatched the aurochs hide from Skyleth's shoulders, hurling it upon the ground.

"Then go! Go, and never return to this place again!"

Though he had chosen this fate for himself, the harsh words struck Skyleth like a blow. With one last glance at the faces of the People—his people no longer—he turned and ran along the shore of the lake. The cold bit at his naked flesh like a wolf, and sharp rocks sliced his bare feet.

At the far side of the lake, a stream poured forth to rush down a rocky defile and begin its long descent over moss and stone to the hazy green valley far below. Skyleth started picking his way down the steep defile. In moments the lake and those standing beside it were lost to sight. He blinked the stinging tears from his eyes and did his best to focus on the treacherous path before him.

After perhaps an hour he skidded down a slope of loose scree, then came to a halt. Tendrils of fog drifted over the stones before him, coiling around his legs. A bank of dense gray fog clung to the mountainside, stretching without break or gap in either direction. He had reached the first misty edges of the Barrier.

Skyleth did not understand the magic that had created the Barrier. It had been conjured centuries ago, in order to hide the People from the world after the Dark Time, when the rest of their kindred had been either slain or banished from the land. After the Dark Time, those scant few of the People who had remained had ascended to the Dragonmere, and they had forged the Barrier so that none could climb up from the valley below to discover them. Only so long as the world did not know they dwelled here, among these lofty heights, were the last of the People of the Dragon safe.

Skyleth did not allow himself to glance back before he braced his shoulders and stepped into the Barrier. At once the chill fog closed around him, transforming the world to swirling silver. Shivering, he stumbled downward, making his way by touch only. Time and again he slipped, skidding down the rocky slope. Once he fell, cutting his hands on sharp stones. At last the fog brightened. Dim shapes appeared around him: a dead tree, a jagged spur of granite. Yes. This was the place where he had first glimpsed her, like a lithe shadow in the fog. Ulanya.

What fate, he wondered, had caused them to dare venture into the preternatural fog on that same spring morning, she from below, he from above? He did not know. All he knew was that when he glimpsed her slender shape in the mist, he had known at once that he loved her. That day they had parted at the meeting of fog and light, beyond which he had dared not tread. Thrice more they had managed to come upon each other in the mists. And at the last parting, they had agreed it would be their final one.

Heart pounding now, Skyleth lunged down the slope, heedless of the skittering stones beneath his bare feet. The fog thinned, then all at once tore to tatters around him. Halting, he blinked against the brilliant sunlight. He had passed through the Barrier.

A voice spoke, as clear as water over stone. "Skyleth. You did come."

At last his vision cleared. A willowy young woman stood before him, eyes as brown as her deerskin clothes, hair as black as the obsidian knife at her hip. She held a silver wolf pelt toward him. He stumbled forward and found himself wrapped in warm fur and her soft embrace.

He shuddered against her. The hoarse words ripped

his raw throat. "I can never go back, Ulanya."

She held him more tightly yet. "Then come with me, to the valley. Our hut is waiting for us."

Finally his trembling ceased, and he nodded. Only then did he remember the gift he had brought her. Against the tenets of the Parting he had hidden it against the nape of his neck, beneath his long hair. He reached back, unbraiding the strands that bound it in place. The object came away in his fingers, and he held it toward her: a large ring of ivory, carved with flowing designs. It was very ancient, and one of the greatest treasures of the People.

Ulanya gasped in delight, and at his instruction slipped the ring over her arm. The pale ivory gleamed against her brown skin. He smiled. Later he could reveal to her the armband's secret. For now, it was enough to see it grace her body. He kissed her, and when that was done they started down the mountainside.

They had gone but a few steps when a cold gust of wind rushed down from the peaks above. A finger of mist reached out from the gray wall of the Barrier, coming between Skyleth and Ulanya. Suddenly she was lost to him. Panic welled up in his chest.

"Ulanya!" he cried.

For a terrible moment there was no answer. He stared blindly into the billowing mist. Then a cool hand slipped into his, gripping it tightly.

"I am here."

The wind changed direction, blowing the fog back toward the Barrier. His heart settled in his chest. This time he did not let go of her hand as they started down the slope, and soon joy rose again within him.

Yet all the way down to the valley below, Skyleth

could not quite forget how the chill fog had come so suddenly between them.

* * * * *

"Torvin? Master Torvin?"

The world spun around me in a blur of colors, then came to a sudden, wrenching halt. The valefolk had ceased their work at the grave, and several of them now gathered around me, concern written across their simple, windworn faces. Always before, when I worked the spell of past-seeing, the visions gleaned from the focal object were dim and muted, like events seen through frosted glass and heard through thick layers of cloth. But this had been so clear, so real. The images still shone in my mind—fragmentary, yes, but almost brighter than my own memories. Never had I experienced anything like this. I gripped the curved adze tightly.

"Master Torvin, be you well?"

I looked up. The coarse voice belonged to Merrit, father of the boy who had fetched me from my cave. I was definitely not well—my head throbbed in the wake of the interrupted spell—but I needed to allay their fears. I managed to gain my feet, though a bit shakily.

"It's nothing," I told them. "A passing dizziness, that's all. One last touch of the winter fever. But I should return to my cave."

My explanation seemed to satisfy them, and Merrit grunted in agreement at my words. He explained that they had finished excavating the grave, wrapping the bones and artifacts in an old blanket, and that two of the others had already started off for my cave with the bundle. Leaving the valefolk to return to the spring plowing, I made my way slowly across the barren fields and back up the winding footpath to my cave. By the time I at last stepped across the stony threshold of the cave, there was no sign of the men who had come before me. However, the bundle they had brought lay in the center of the floor.

I set down the stone adze, which I had been unwilling to leave behind despite its weight, and lit a fire in the brazier with a thought and a word. Even this small spell resulted in a sharp throbbing between my temples. Heating water, I brewed a bitter tea of willow bark and rose hips. I drank this, and though I was not hungry, ate a bit of flatbread as the sparrows sang the evening away outside the entrance to the cave.

By the time night had fallen, the tea had done its work, and the pain in my head had receded to a manageable drone. I moved to unroll the blanket, wondering if the bones or artifacts had been broken in the unearthing, or if the valefolk had taken care as I had instructed.

I paused. Turning, I gazed at the stone adze resting beside the brazier. It would be foolish to try the magic again so soon, perhaps even dangerous. All the same, I was filled with a sudden desire so strong that I knew I could not resist it. I wanted to know more of his story. Skyleth. Why the desire was so overpowering I did not know. After all, this was a man who had lived and died over two thousand years ago. How could it possibly matter what had happened to him? Yet somehow it did. Perhaps it was simply that I knew what it was to be an outcast.

Sitting cross-legged, I lifted the curved head of the adze into my lap. My fingers slid across the smooth stone, as if they could feel the memories imprinted within. I drew in a deep breath, hesitating. Then the words of magic fell from my lips like water.

* * * * *

Their daughter was born in the depths of winter.

Ilinana they called her, which meant Child of the Sky in the language of the valley. For though she had her mother's obsidian hair and nut-brown skin, her eyes were like none ever possessed by a child born into the valley tribe. They were gray-blue, the color of the winter sky, just like her father's.

The birth had not been easy for Ulanya. For three days she had writhed in pain within the hide-walled hut. All the while, the tribe's wise woman had cast black looks at Skyleth, as if the wizened crone believed this was his fault. In the end there had been much blood, but the wise woman had worked her craft well, for both mother and daughter had lived. Though the child was strong, and soon thrived, the experience had left Ulanya weakened.

For over a moon she was unable to leave the hut, and for several moons after that she could do little save sit where they had placed her, wrapped in warm furs. However, by summer Ulanya's strength had returned. And if the shadows had not entirely fled the hollows of her cheeks, then at least they were not so easy to see under the brilliant sun.

Though at first the tribe had been wary of Skyleth, even fearful, in time this too seemed to change.

The day Ulanya had led him into the circle of domed huts—tall, gray-eyed, and naked save for the hide she had given him—the tribe thought she had found a spirit creature on the high mountain. In answer to their fear, he had used a stone knife to cut his arm, showing them that he bled red blood just like any man. Unlike the others, the tribe's chief had been not fearful, but angry. Ulanya was his only daughter, and he had forbidden her to bond with this stranger. However, at this a fierce light had shone in her eyes. She had grabbed Skyleth's hand and had led him into their waiting dwelling. It was a woman's right to take what man she chose into her hut.

For many months the tribespeople shunned Skyleth. Then, in the spring after Ilinana was born, the chief's youngest son fell into the river, which was white and swollen with the melting snow. The boy would have drowned except Skyleth, doing what no other dared, dove into the icy waters and pulled him out.

After this, things began to change. The tribespeople, if not accepting of Skyleth, at least no longer seemed so fearful. He showed them good places to lie in wait for the shaggy red aurochs and taught them how a longer bow made their stone-tipped arrows fly farther and with more power. Ulanya's eyes glowed warmly as she watched him do these things, and the rest of the year the days slipped by happily.

That winter Ulanya fell ill. However, by the time the spring winds rushed down from the mountains, the sickness had passed, and Skyleth soon forgot it. Ilinana was walking now, and learning to speak, and so took most of their attention. Then, one evening as green summer gave way to golden autumn, Ulanya told Skyleth that she was with child again. He kissed her and held her tightly in his arms.

"You are everything to me, Ulanya." He murmured

the words like a prayer.

She smiled, but said nothing in reply, and only brushed his cheek tenderly with her fingers.

Three days later she was dead.

The child had been ill-made, the wise woman said. It had passed out of her body, and in so doing it had torn something deep inside. It had happened quickly. Skyleth had been out hunting. By the time he reached their hut, Ulanya was already gone.

He dug the grave himself with a stone adze. They had laid her on a blanket beside it, adorned in beads and fine leathers. Skyleth knelt and kissed her still lips. Then he slipped off the ivory armband he had given her. "You need this to fly no longer, my love," he whispered, placing it around his own arm.

Ilinana was crying, calling out for her mother, but none of the women would comfort the child. Skyleth picked her up, and she quieted as he held her in the crook of his arm. Many of the tribe cast dark looks in his direction. Their goodwill toward him had died with Ulanya, and now their faces were again filled with fear and suspicion. Ilinana they might have accepted, but for her pale eyes, which forever marked her as different. There was nothing left here for either of them.

As the others lowered Ulanya's still body into the ground, Skyleth lifted his eyes to the horned peak that loomed over the valley. A strange thrill coursed through him. He had been forbidden to ever return to the lake. But not Ilinana. The People of the Dragon were her people now. Only they could show her who she really was. Tevarrek had said it would be impossible to go back. But for Ilinana's sake he had to try.

As the others wept, casting the first handfuls of dirt into

the grave, he walked away, holding Ilinana tightly in one
hand while the adze slipped from the other to fall to—

* * * * *

The vision shattered.

I gasped as my eyes flew open. For a long moment I
stared at the adze; then I let it slip from my fingers. It
had no more memories to tell. The throbbing between
my temples was not so fierce this time. Perhaps the tea
had had some residual effect. Or perhaps I was growing
accustomed to the power of the images.

I knelt beside the bundle the men had brought to my
cave and unwrapped the folds of rough cloth. Ivory
bones glowed in the firelight, and copper glinted bright
red. So it had indeed been Ulanya in the grave. A damp-
ness trickled down my cheek, and I wiped it away.
Strange, that I should weep for one I never knew, who
was lost thousands of years before I was even born.

Standing, I moved to the back of the cave. To the
casual eye it seemed only a narrow shadow cast by a
spur of rock. I knew otherwise. Lighting a candle, I
squeezed through the narrow crevice and into the
cramped space beyond. Resting on a stone shelf was a
cedar trunk. I lifted the lid, and a sweet, dusty smell rose
upward. Here I kept the things I dared not let the valefolk see: crisp parchment scrolls, vials of colored glass,
and clay jars filled with unguents and powders. These
were my own artifacts, the tools of magic.

I ran my fingers over the fine white cloth of my neatly
folded robe. Like Skyleth, I wondered if I could ever go
back. To the Tower, to my studies. But what would I find
if I did? I did not know. Maybe the same thing Skyleth

found, if he ever returned to the Dragonmere. If. There was no way I could ever know. Unless . . .

Even as the thought occurred to me, I knew I meant to try. I readied the things I would need—food, a water flask, and my walking staff. Then I spent the rest of the night arranging Ulanya's bones upon the blanket, and arraying the grave goods carefully around her. When I returned I would give her a proper burial once again. For now, this would have to do.

I set out in the gray light before dawn to climb the pass to the lake. As I crossed the valley, I saw that the valefolk were already stirring, beginning the day's hard labor. Near the huddled gathering of stone houses I came upon Merrit. He gave me a curious look. It was not usual for me to come to the village, especially at so early an hour.

Merrit bid me greeting, then rubbed his hands together. "Did you bury the bones, Master Torvin?"

"Yes, yes," I lied, annoyed at this delay. "No spirits will trouble you today, Merrit. Now haven't you plowing to do?"

He ducked his head, then hurried away, but not before casting a sidelong glance in my direction. Had I not been so preoccupied, I might have been disturbed by the suspicion glinting in his small eyes. Instead I continued on my way, to the south end of the valley. Here began the narrow defile that rose upward, past rampart after rampart of raw stone, to the horned peak—the Dragonmount. The mountain loomed above me, stained crimson with the first light of dawn. I started climbing.

The going was not easy. Life in a tower and a cave had not well prepared me for extreme exertion, and soon I was gasping for breath. I struggled up the steep slope, my boots slipping on loose scree. Realizing my walking staff was worthless, I cast it aside, and began using my arms as much as my legs to propel me upward. As I went, the air grew thinner, feeling like a cold knife in my lungs.

Just when I was certain I could continue no longer, the steepness of the slope lessened. The pass broadened into a long valley whose rounded bottom told me it had been carved out by glaciers long ago. New green grass carpeted the floor. I made my way more quickly here, stopping only occasionally for a mouthful of water or a bite of food.

At last I reached the end of the green valley. Turning around, I saw that I had come much farther than I had guessed. The vale where I dwelled lay far below, muted with haze and distance. Turning back, I craned my neck. I could not see the Dragonmount now. It is a strange trick of mountains that they are more easily glimpsed from farther away than close up. However, I knew it was not far.

I decided to rest for a few minutes before the final ascent. Nearby was a broad, flat rock, warm from the sun. I sat upon it, ate some dried fruit, and sipped water. At last I stood to go.

That was when I saw them, scattered around the base of the boulder. I picked one up. It was a small flake of flint, thick at one end, thinning to a sharp edge at the other. Someone, long ago, had paused at this place just as I, and had fashioned a tool of stone, probably a knife. The scatter of flakes was the detritus, like the shards of stone chipped away from an artist's sculpture and left upon the studio floor.

I stared at the flake of stone in the palm of my hand,

wondering. Could it be? Few had ever come this way. I gripped the flake tightly. There was but one way to find out. I let my mind go dark as I murmured the now-familiar words of the spell.

* * * * *

His strong legs flexing, Skyleth ascended the last few rocks, then came to a halt. Before him stood a billowing wall of gray mist. The Barrier.

Ilinana squirmed restlessly in his arms. Her small legs wished to run. But not here. He gripped her more tightly and ignored her cries of protest. A tendril of fog reached out and brushed against his arm. He recoiled at its chilling touch, then caught himself. Ilinana's only hope lay beyond the Barrier. Bracing his broad shoulders, he stepped forward. The mist closed silently around him.

Instantly he could not breathe. The grayness seemed to fill his lungs, choking him. He heard Ilinana crying, but the sound was distant and muffled, even though he could feel her tiny form clinging to him in fright. He held her more tightly yet, and the mist seemed to thin slightly, allowing him to draw in gasping, labored breaths. They were barely enough to keep him alive, but that was all he needed.

Dizzily, he tried to move forward. The mist parted around him only reluctantly. It was like pressing his way through half-frozen mud. The damp air clung to him, dragging him down and back, so that he could barely move his limbs. However, Ilinana's arms waved wildly in distress, unhindered by the mist. He hunched over her. The fog parted around Ilinana like water, and he was able to make some progress in this manner, like a leaf floating in the wake of a canoe.

Without Ilinana he would not have been able to move ten paces into the Barrier. But the geas of banishing that lay upon his shoulders did not mark her. She was like a key, and with her he was able to stumble onward, chewing and choking on the unnatural mist, his powerful limbs struggling against the invisible magics that resisted him.

At last Ilinana's crying turned into a soft whimper. Skyleth's head felt strangely light. The mist swirled wildly around him, and he wondered if he was going mad. His thoughts grew dim and hazy. He stumbled on a slick, unseen rock and fell to his knees, cutting them. Just then, a sudden gust of wind whipped past, blowing the mist into tatters that scudded along the rocky ground. Before him, suddenly revealed, lay a gray-green slope stretching toward high peaks above. Behind him, the wall of mist melted away onto the cool air.

A sob escaped his throat. He buried his head in Ilinana's soft, dark hair. Sensing the importance of this moment, she fell silent, gazing at the mountains with wide blue eyes.

At last Skyleth stood. They were both hungry and needed food before making the final ascent. He found a rabbit that had wandered into the edges of the mist and become dazed. He dispatched it with a swift blow to the back of the neck, then took it to the broad, flat boulder where he had left Ilinana. With practiced swiftness he chipped a knife from a piece of flint and used it to cut up the rabbit. They ate the meat raw, then rested for a time.

Before long Skyleth rose. Ilinana had fallen asleep, and he took her gently in his arms. He bent over her and spoke in a low whisper. "Come, my love. Let us go home."

Then he started up the pass once more.

* * * * *

I reached the lake at sunset.

My lungs burned as if on fire, and my legs trembled from exhaustion. However, I did not stop to rest. Skyleth had made it past the Barrier. The visions gleaned from the cast-off flakes of stone had confirmed it. But what had happened after that? Was it truly possible for an outcast to return? I had to know.

I gazed at the lake and gasped in wonder. A great coppery dragon lay beneath the crystalline waters. It was the reflection of the horned peak, of course, colored by the setting sun. Yet so eerily real was the image in the water that, for a moment, my heart jumped, and I half-feared, half-hoped that the dragon was indeed a real, living creature. But dragons were a myth, and it was simply a trick of light and water. I turned from the lake and began searching. There had to be something here— some relic from that time long ago.

Perhaps it was simply chance that led me to the right place, or perhaps it was some impossible connection that had been forged between us. Regardless, when I scrambled up a jumble of boulders to gain a better view, one of the rocks shifted beneath my feet. Unable to catch myself, I tumbled down into a dim hollow below.

He was slumped against a stone, exactly as he had lain two thousand years ago while drawing his last breaths. I think I would have known it was him no matter what. The bones were yellow and brittle with time, and many were broken and splintered. However, just looking at them I knew they had belonged in life to a man tall and proud in bearing. Any last doubts were shattered by the ivory ring that still circled his arm.

Strangely, I felt as if I had just come upon an old friend after long years of parting. Perhaps, in a way, I had. Separated as we were by the millennia, somehow our lives—our fates—had become tangled together. My hand shook as I reached out and slipped the armband, his gift to Ulanya, from the old bone it encircled.

"Forgive me," I murmured. And I knew that I was indeed forgiven.

For a long moment, I gazed at the intricately carved circle in my hands. Then, one last time, I used my magic to see through another's eyes.

* * * * *

He stood upon the shore of the lake. The tribe had gathered before him, their mute faces troubled. One stepped forward, a massive man with coppery hair. He spoke, his voice a perilous rumble. "You have brought death upon us, Skyleth."

Skyleth shook his head fiercely. "No, Tevarrek. I've brought hope." He held Ilinana out before him. The tiny child gazed silently at the other man, her round face calm.

"There is no hope in that abomination," Tevarrek snarled. He thrust an accusing finger at the ivory ring around Skyleth's arm. "First you steal our most sacred treasure. Then you give the gift to one who should never have received it in order to make this . . . this thing." Disgustedly, he waved a hand at Ilinana. "Now, with her help, you have destroyed the Barrier. It is only a matter of time until we are discovered. We must flee, though where we can go now, I do not know. Wherever it is, be sure you will not be coming with us."

"I don't care about that." Skyleth took an urgent step forward. "Just take Ilinana with you. That's all I ask."

Rage colored Tevarrek's cheeks. "Never! She is not one of us."

"Yes she is!" Skyleth implored. "Look at her eyes!"

Tevarrek did not even glance at the child. "It is my decision, and I say she will not come." He started to turn away.

"Then I challenge you."

A gasp rose from the gathered people. Before Tevarrek could reply, Skyleth set the child on the ground and spread his arms. He thrust his head back and let out a fierce cry that echoed off the mountains. Tevarrek spun back around, staring in fury. A spasm rippled through Skyleth's body. His muscles writhed beneath his skin, bulging impossibly, tearing his clothes to shreds. With strange speed his body grew, and as it did, it began to change, shifting into a new form. All at once the man Skyleth was gone. In his place, a great silver form leaped upward into the sky, spreading vast metallic wings, cocking a horned head back on a sinuous neck to let out a trumpeting cry.

A silver dragon.

Exhilaration filled Skyleth as his wings pumped, lifting him higher and higher above the lake. He reveled in the feeling of air against his shining scales. It had been five centuries since he had donned this, his true form. Not since the last Dragon War had he known the joy of flight. At the end of the War, the one mortals called "Huma" had banished all dragons from the land with his shining, magical lance. At least, so the legends of the mortals told. But a few of them had escaped the lance by assuming human form, and they had come to this place, to hide from a world where dragonkind no longer belonged. Now that hiding was over.

Skyleth spun in midair, nearly drunk with the sensation of flight after so many years without it. A cry of fury from below snapped him back to his senses. On the ground Tevarrek spread his arms wide. His form shimmered. Suddenly, in his place, a massive dragon with scales of bronze launched into the air. Red-gold wings beating, the bronze hurtled toward the silver with deadly speed. Skyleth knew he was outmatched by the larger dragon, but the challenge was Ilinana's only hope.

As the tribe below watched, the two dragons circled each other over the lake. Without warning Tevarrek reversed direction and lunged. Skyleth countered, but a fraction too slow. The bronze's claws traced a hot line of pain across Skyleth's flank. Beating his wings frantically, Skyleth managed to fly beyond the other's reach and then he wheeled around. For a confused moment he did not see his foe. Then a rushing sound from above reached his sensitive ears. He craned his serpentine neck upward, then cried out. He had forgotten much in his years as a human. Moving through air was not the same as moving on flat ground. But it seemed Tevarrek remembered more than he.

The bronze was diving.

Skyleth had forgotten the advantage of height. While he had fled, Tevarrek had soared higher into the sky. Now the larger dragon folded his wings back, plunging downward with fatal speed. Skyleth arched his back, beating his wings, but he knew there was not enough time to get out of his enemy's path.

Just then, movement below caught his eye. Skyleth glanced down for a split second. A tiny form stood beside the lake, waving small arms, reaching toward him. A pang of love and sorrow touched his heart. He knew what he had to do. There was no escape for him. It was her freedom that mattered now.

He snapped his neck back up. Tevarrek was almost upon him. The bronze's eyes glowed with deadly golden light. His sharp teeth were bared in an expression of victory. Skyleth tensed his wings, then flew upward to meet his foe. The fury in Tevarrek's eyes turned to surprise. This was not the action he had expected. They hurtled toward each other head on. Tevarrek spread out his wings, trying to change his course. It was too late.

With a sound like thunder, the two dragons collided in midair. Crushing pain coursed through Skyleth's body. He ignored it, digging his claws and teeth into Tevarrek, heedless of the other's slashing talons. Tevarrek writhed wildly, trying to free himself, but it was no use. He could not spread his wings wide enough to remain aloft. In a tangle of silver and bronze, the two dragons plummeted downward. For a moment their mingled cries echoed off cold stone. Then, as one, they struck a jagged outcrop of stone, and all was silent.

Skyleth knew at once that Tevarrek was dead, and that he himself was dying. He could not move his body, and his mind felt as light as a bit of thistledown floating on the wind. A shadow appeared before his eyes. He realized it was one of the People. She held Ilinana in her arms, and the child gazed at Skyleth without fear or recognition. Of course, he thought dimly. She does not know this form. With the last of his will, he concentrated. His broken body blurred and shrank. Now it was the form of a bloodied man who lay upon the rocks, naked save for the ring of ivory that still encircled his arm.

"We must go now," the woman said. Sadness shone in her pale eyes.

A single whispered word escaped Skyleth's throat. "Where?"

"I think that we will leave the world," she answered. "We will join the others. As we should have long ago."

Ilinana reached out a small hand, brushing his blood-smeared cheek. Then, holding the child, the woman turned to walk toward the rest of the People.

A moment later Skyleth blinked. The woman was gone, and all the People of the Dragon with her. The shore beside the lake was empty. But, reflected in its surface, two dozen magnificent silver forms soared into the sky. With them rose one much smaller shape, spreading tiny, shimmering wings. Smiling, Skyleth watched as they flew into the deepening twilight until, at the last, all grew dark.

* * * * *

It was for the reflection in the lake that they came here, but it was not for the reflection they were named. I knew that now. Dragons were not a myth after all.

At dawn I left the lake. The night had been long and cold, but I had feared trying to descend the pass in the dark. Part of me had been reluctant as well—reluctant to leave him behind. It was like leaving a part of myself there, lying beneath the cold stones. I slipped the ivory armband into the pocket of my robe. This much I had at least. With one last look at the silvery Dragonmere, I turned and started down the mountain.

I saw the smoke when I was still high above the valley. It rose upward in a thin blue line, though from this distance I could not discern its source. I continued to pick my way down the rocky slope. As I did, an unease steadily grew in me, though I could place no name upon it. I began to move faster.

By the time I neared the bottom of the pass, I was running headlong, heedless of the treacherous slope. At last the walls of rock fell away to either side, and I found myself in the familiar landscape of the valley. I raced across half-plowed fields. The land was eerily empty. There was no one in sight. Despite my weariness, I ran up the winding footpath that led through the aspen grove to my cave. Rounding the final bend, I came to a sudden, breathless halt. At last I knew the source of the smoke, and of my strange unease.

They had set fire to my cave. Blue-black smoke poured out of the entrance, rising sluggishly to the sky. Stunned, I stumbled forward, but the fierce heat drove me back. It was too late. I knew everything was gone. Ulanya, the artifacts. My scrolls, my books, my white robe. I stared numbly at the billowing smoke. I did not feel angry, nor sorrowful, just strangely empty.

Branches snapped behind me. Shadows stepped out of the forest, into the clearing before the cave.

"So, you've come back."

Slowly, I turned around. It was Merrit. A dangerous light smoldered in his small eyes. He gripped a pitchfork in his meaty hands. A score of valefolk stood behind him. All wore looks of hatred and suspicion. And all bore some sort of weapon, be it axe, spade, or wooden club.

Merrit took a menacing step forward. "We know what you are."

I said nothing. I could not take my eyes off the pitchfork in his hands.

Merrit went on, his voice a low hiss. "Selda came to your cave this morning to have you see to a toothache. She found the bones that you said you had buried. They were all laid out, like some sort of spell. She fetched us, and we searched your cave. We found everything—your foul potions and accursed books of evil magic. All this time you've lied about what you are. But you can't hide from us anymore . . . wizard."

He spoke the last word as if it were poison. I could not help but wince at the loathing in his voice. I took an involuntary step backward, toward the smoke-filled entrance to the cave. As one they stepped forward, mirroring my movements, raising their weapons. They meant to kill me.

"You don't understand," I murmured softly. It was not a protest, not a denunciation. It was simply a fact.

"I understand this, wizard." A terrible grin split Merrit's face. "I understand that you're going to burn, just like the Lord of Istar said all heretics must burn." He gestured to the others. "Into the cave with him!"

In a way I was glad that the long charade was over. Like the People of the Dragon, I could hide what I was only so long. I reached into my pocket and pulled out the ivory armband. The valefolk pressed forward, brandishing their weapons. The heat of the fire scorched my back. For so long I had wished to be free of the fear, free of the hatred and the ignorance. Now, at last, that time had come. I shut my eyes and slipped the ivory ring onto my arm, to be my own funeral treasure.

The voices of the valefolk receded into the distance. They were shouting now, though it seemed to me the sounds were those of fear, not bloodlust. The heat of the fire vanished, and cool air rushed over me. My body felt strangely smooth and sleek. Radiant power surged through my veins. It was a glorious sensation. Was this what it was like to die?

I opened my eyes, and I knew at once that I was not dead. Somehow the valefolk were below me now. They dropped their weapons in fear and scurried into the forest, looking for all the world like frightened mice. Even as I watched, they grew smaller, and the smoky entrance of the cave receded into the distance. The tall aspen trees looked like pale twigs.

Higher I rose, and higher, feeling a power and a freedom that I had never known before. The valley faded away into the haze, and soon a horned peak loomed before me: the Dragonmount. I looked down, and at last I understood the power of the armband, and the nature of the gift Skyleth had given Ulanya.

Once again I saw a great dragon reflected on the surface of the Dragonmere: silver wings beating, graceful neck outstretched, eyes gleaming like sapphires. Only this was no trick of light and water. This dragon was real. I could never go back. But I could fly free.

Opening my mouth, I let out a trumpeting cry of joy, and my heart soared even as the wind lifted me higher.

Quarry
Adam Lesh

The stench of elf filled the ancient red dragon's nostrils. It did not register immediately in his slumber-filled brain, but when it did, Klassh jolted awake, every fiber of his being on full alert. Still, he did not move. Any movement on his part would disturb the mountainous pile of gold, silver and gems on which he rested. Keeping his breathing regular, Klassh slowly half-opened one eye and scanned the triangular Great Hall, looking with satisfaction on the enormous hoard he had collected over the centuries, until he found the elf. The thief was alone, crouched in a far corner, working on the lock of a long, thin box, which the dragon had never seen before. Near that corner of the room, Klassh also noticed a concealed door—now open—that he had not known was there.

"Damned dwarves," the dragon said to himself. "They can never have enough back doors and you can never find them all."

Fully awake now, Klassh realized that the elf smelled slightly off—like bad fish. Studying the elf, the dragon noted the broad shoulders, tall, wiry frame, and silver hair.

"Half-elf, most likely," mused Klassh. "Probably won't taste good. The half-breeds never do."

Strangely, although well armored, the thief wore only an empty scabbard at his side. The burnished elven chain mail had leather strips woven through the rings to dampen much of the noise of the metal. A hooded gray cloak was thrown over the elf's shoulders, out of the way of his hands as he worked.

The irritated dragon watched the elf as it diligently applied itself to the lock. Like a stalking cat not ready to alert its prey, the dragon remained perfectly still.

Click. The lock opened.

Klassh quickly closed his eye again as the elf checked to see if the dragon had heard the noise. Satisfied that the beast still slept, the elf threw back the lid. Klassh opened his eye again, watched as the elf drew forth a magnificent glowing broadsword that fairly sang with enchantment. The dragon was stunned by the realization that such an artifact had been in his possession and he'd never known it!

The elf quickly sheathed the sword and started slinking toward the open door, completely ignoring the other fabulous treasure lying literally at its feet. Klassh sent a gout of flame flaring at the elf. It must have been watching, however, because he managed to dodge the fire by ducking behind a pile of blackened plate mail and scorched bones, the remains of foolish knights who had dared to challenge Klassh. The flame ignited some moldering tapestries and a few wooden chests, filling the hall with smoky light.

The dragon had long ago learned that his enormous form was not well suited to negotiating the glittering dunes of precious metals, gems and trinkets heaped high throughout the room, so Klassh muttered a word of magic.

The dragon stifled a cry of pain as his neck contracted and his torso folded in on itself. Once his great mass had shrunk by a quarter, his head and limbs reshaped themselves to a feline form. Flaming red hair sprouted all over his body, most thickly on his head and neck, where a large silky mane grew. Smaller, but sharper, claws protruded from his paws, glistening in the shadowy firelight.

Now with a cat's agility, the dragon gathered himself, let out a thunderous roar and leapt with tremendous strength toward the elf's hiding place. Gold and silver flew through the air as he landed gracefully on the floor and bounded over the armor. Alighting on the far side of the pile, Klassh saw the elf scurrying to a more protected position among the gleaming heaps of treasure. It slipped out of sight behind a stack of wooden chests.

The dragon followed the elf, sniffing the air, hoping to use his feline sense of smell to detect the thief. Unfortunately, the acrid reek of the burning tapestries blocked out all other odors; the smoke also made it difficult for Klassh to see farther than a few feet ahead.

At last, the dragon found a trace of the elf's fetor in an opening between a few of the chests. Pawing away at the crack, his claw caught on a piece of cloth. With a triumphant roar, Klassh attempted to yank the elf out of its hiding place. The dragon had hold of the elf's gray cloak, now singed and stained with soot.

The dragon heard a creak from above. Klassh looked up too late to see the pile of chests crashing down on him. The elf was nowhere in sight. The chests knocked Klassh to the ground, pinning his forelegs. He tried to free himself, but could not gain the leverage.

As the fires began to die down and throw heavy shadows throughout the Hall, Klassh changed form again. Pain wracked his body as his form altered and flowed, legs and arms merging with his torso. The debris shifted and settled. He used his serpentine form to slither out from under the chests. As he emerged from the wreckage, he spotted the elf. The thief faded into the shadows near a large pile of coins.

Unable to maintain the limbless snake form for too long, the dragon shifted and reduced his size again, forcing his head, limbs and torso to approximate a humanoid form.

Though now about the size of a large ogre or small hill giant, Klassh could never be mistaken for either one. With tough, red, reptilian skin, flashing red eyes, and huge muscles rippling throughout his torso, arms and legs, he looked more like a demon from the Pits than any Krynn-born creature. Breathing heavily and momentarily weakened by the multiple transformations, Klassh surveyed the chamber.

Klassh strode toward the heap of coins where he'd last seen the creature. As always, when in human form his senses were dulled and sluggish. He could smell nothing but smoke and fire. His efforts proving fruitless, the dragon stalked toward the dwarf-made door, intending to guard it against the elf's escape.

Metal scraped on stone. Klassh ran to the large pile of weapons—leftovers from the dead knights. A sword fell to the ground. Rounding the pile, the dragon found nothing but a large gem near the fallen sword. Realizing this had been yet another distraction, Klassh turned to look at the secret door. He spotted the elf making a break for it.

Kicking the sword, Klassh sped toward the door. The elf made a flying leap into the opening. The dragon lunged and managed to wrap a scaly hand around the elf's ankle. The elf pitched forward. Klassh twisted the elf around in midair and hurled him away from the door. The thief flipped like an acrobat, and landed gracefully. It drew its magical shining sword in one smooth motion.

Klassh scooped up the fallen sword and advanced. Whirling the blade in a dizzying series of figure eights, the dragon, still in human form, engaged the intruder. For a few minutes, the combatants parried and thrust, testing each other's mettle. Dancing out of the way of a thrust, the elf delivered a deep, painful slash to Klassh's left leg. The dragon howled in pain. Klassh lost control of his form, polymorphing back to his original shape. The elf dashed for the portal.

The dragon sighed in relief from the strain of holding the humanoid form. He turned just in time to see the elf clear the doorway. Breathing another flame blast lost Klassh precious seconds and was ultimately a waste of effort. As the flame flowed down the corridor behind the elf, the intensity of the heat destroyed the tunnel's already decaying support structure and it collapsed in on itself. That way was blocked. Klassh would have to use the front door.

Launching himself through the once-grand entrance, Klassh took to the air with a mighty thrust of his wings. With powerful strokes, he climbed rapidly into the stormy skies. The first rain was in progress after a brutally dry summer. Ordinarily, Klassh enjoyed an autumn squall, which cooled the heat generated by his fiery breath. But today he was oblivious to the shower. Soaring upward, he caught a strong thermal and relaxed his wings, gliding upward in ever-tightening concentric circles.

As he reached the apex of the updraft, now hundreds of feet in the air, Klassh looked below and spotted the elf moving down the mountainside. The dragon's ire had cooled now, but he was annoyed with himself for not

establishing mental contact with the troublesome thief.
Klassh possessed a Pendant of Mind-Seeing stolen long
ago from the elves. Once Klassh locked onto the elf's
thoughts, it could not escape. Now that Klassh had a clear
line of sight, it was just a matter of a few seconds.

. . . *ready yet,* the thief was thinking.

Contact!

FEAR!

Delicious terror flooded Klassh's brain as he read the
emotions of the fleeing elf. The intoxicated dragon did
not even realize he had lost the thermal and was
descending until the feeling intensified and he noticed
the elf looking skyward. It had spotted the dragon and
was scrambling for cover. Klassh pulled out of his dive
and flew upward.

Klassh concentrated deeply and once again entered
the frightened elf's mind.

FEAR!

Once again, the elf's utter panic flooded the dragon's
brain, but this time he probed deeper, and managed to
extract a name: B'ynn al'Tor. Attempting to push even
further into the elf's mind, the dragon found the way
blocked. Its brain was locked up tight behind the barrier
of his panic.

The elf dodged skillfully through the rough terrain.
The green had mostly gone from the landscape, replaced
by the spectacular reds, oranges, yellows and browns
that pervaded the mountains in the fall.

Shortly before the First Dragon War, the dragon had
come to these mountains to find a home. He had been
pleasantly surprised to discover a dwarven stronghold
nestled near the very top of one of the highest peaks.
Although Klassh loathed all mortals, he reserved his

most deep and abiding hatred for dwarves. He had greatly enjoyed clearing them out and making their great hall his lair. He spent most of his time now at what the dwarves had once called Cobb Hall.

The elf was now descending a rather steep and slippery slope. The sparse growth at this elevation, compounded by the drizzling rain, must have made the footing precarious.

No longer in any rush to kill the intruder, but rather in a mood to deal some pain to the creature before finishing it off, the dragon, mostly hidden by the storm clouds, flew over the elf at a great height. Cresting, he dropped, using the mountains to conceal his descent. Only a hundred yards from the elf, who was still picking his way carefully down the mountain, Klassh quickened his descent and flew rapidly toward his quarry. As he passed over the elf, only a few yards above, the great blast of wind spawned by his furiously pumping wings blew the elf off-balance.

The elf might have recovered, if the gust had not also triggered a small rockslide. It fell hard, rolling down the hillside, battered by the wet, rocky surface as well as the loose stones falling on and over it.

PAIN! FEAR! HUMILIATION!

Well pleased, the dragon soared upward, basking in the emotions coursing through the elf's mind. The joy of the game was upon Klassh and he was not about to let it end too soon.

Klassh circled and swooped down again.

The elf crawled painfully behind a boulder. The dragon warmed to the chase. The doomed elf had proved remarkably resourceful and entertaining so far.

The thief had managed to crawl into an outcropping

of boulders that supported a flat rock, forming a protective shield against the dragon's attacks. Stymied from direct assault, Klassh lit on the shield rock, adding his considerable weight to the precariously balanced stone.

FEAR!

The elf's terror spiked sharply, but he had nowhere to go. The dragon gave the elf a few minutes to relax, then shifted his weight. The stone ground against its supports, sending showers of pebbles and dust down on the wounded elf.

FEAR!

As Klassh expected, the elf's fear rose to a crescendo, filling the dragon with sweet music. Just before the shelf collapsed, Klassh lifted off.

As he rose, Klassh was aware that the elf had started to move again, but when the dragon circled around to look, he could not see the thief. Squinting his eyes, scanning the area near the elf's recent hiding place, the dragon spotted the elf moving toward a sharp drop-off.

Swooping down, the dragon buffeted the area with his wings, stirring up a small dust storm. The elf ran toward the cliff and jumped off.

Startled, the dragon rose into the air and swung around to see what had happened.

A small ledge projected from the face of the cliff, leading to a cave in the cliff face. The cliff blocked the sun, casting its huge shadow across the cliff's face. The dragon could not readily tell the size of the cave as he flew past, but he would not permit the thief to get away this easily and spoil his fun. Klassh could not land on the thin ledge, so he circled around and dove directly into the cave.

Klassh transformed in midair. He passed through the

cave opening, the outspread feathered wings of his griffin form easily slowing his headlong flight. When he landed, a sharp pain lanced up through his rear leg, nearly causing him to lose control. Looking back, he saw that the wound given him by the elf in the great hall had festered.

Returning to his natural form, Klassh licked at the wound, and tasted the residue of magic. The intrinsic curative powers of the dragon's saliva quickly overcame the remaining traces of magic and the wound began to heal, though it still stung.

Klassh's eyes adjusted to the gloom and he knew for certain that he had found another dwarven structure, which looked as old as Cobb Hall.

"Twice-damned dwarves! Busy as beavers they are," Klassh muttered.

Some avian creatures had obviously claimed the place as their nest. Two large eggs sat in the middle of the largest pile of refuse. The dragon gulped the eggs casually as he explored the chamber.

Fortunately, the senseless dwarves liked to build big, as attested to by the huge opening right in front of the dragon, which was just big enough to accommodate his bulk. The elf's trail was clearly marked in the dust by footprints on the stone floor.

As Klassh moved through the dry corridors, the dust swirled about him, sticking to his wet skin, obscuring his vision, stinging his eyes and choking his breathing. He was no longer enjoying the game as much.

"The thief will pay for this," Klassh vowed. "When I get my claws on the elf, it will wish it had perished in my first flame blast. I will chew it slowly, savoring its fear and anguish."

Suddenly, the footprints vanished. Looking closely, Klassh peered through the dust. The footprints started again a few feet away.

Klassh continued.

A pit sprang open beneath him, but it was far too small for his great size.

"Ha! Stupid dwarves!"

The dragon slithered on.

FEAR!

Still unable to penetrate the shield of the elf's panic, Klassh contented himself with monitoring the creature's emotions and reading the odd stray thought that slipped through.

Must keep moving . . . dusty . . . following my footprints . . . trap . . . Such were the elf's terror-ridden thoughts.

Shortly, Klassh came upon another gap in the footprints, but the dragon did not even slow down. He felt something very sharp prick his side. But the pain quickly subsided, so the dragon ignored the wound and kept moving, trying to catch up with the elf.

Suddenly Klassh's skin began to itch. The joy of the hunt was definitely gone now, replaced by anger and irritation. Klassh desperately wanted out of these stale corridors. When he caught up with the elf, the dragon was inclined just to roast the thief with a fire blast and be done with it. He would retrieve the gleaming sword from the elf's charred corpse, then go to a nearby mountain lake and relax in its deliciously cold waters.

His pleasant thoughts were interrupted by another sharp prick in his side. He again ignored the wound, but at the third stab, he snapped and let out a bellow of annoyance and pain.

A wave of nausea swept over Klassh. His body and head began to ache violently. The itching on his skin increased tenfold, as if his skin was trying to crawl off his body. He lost control of his limbs and sank to the ground.

"Poison! Thrice-damned dwarves poisoned me!" Klassh roared.

He thrashed his tail. His stomach twisted. His head pounded as if a stone giant were hitting him with a hammer, and then darkness swam before his eyes. For the first time in his long life, Klassh passed out.

* * * * *

The dragon came to slowly. His body ached, his head still pounded and his stomach roiled, but his system was fighting off the powerful poison. He had no idea how long he had been unconscious. He could no longer feel the thief's emotions or hear its thoughts. Losing consciousness had severed the magical contact.

The dragon heaved himself up onto his feet. It took Klassh a few more minutes to get his bearings and find the elf's footprints in the dust once more.

Consumed with his own misery, Klassh did not notice the dust beginning to thin and the footprints starting to mix with others. He did not hear voices emanating from a passageway before him until he turned a corner and ran into a small group of goblins. The goblins froze for an instant, and then burst into complete panic, dropping everything they were carrying, running about, tripping over each other, and gibbering in high-pitched voices. Klassh lunged forward and snagged one by its jerkin.

"How do I get out of here?" he roared at the hysterical creature, who immediately fainted dead away in his grasp.

Tossing the goblin to the side, breaking its neck as it hit the wall, Klassh grabbed for another one and tried again, with the same result. The goblin passed out.

"Can't even answer a simple question," Klassh grumbled.

Giving up on that strategy, Klassh followed the largest concentration of goblins. It seemed probable that they were heading for the exit. But he soon discovered, when he came to a dead end, that the goblins were rushing about in a blind panic. Loathe to waste one of his powers, but aware that he was now hopelessly lost, Klassh grabbed another goblin and cast a calming spell over it.

"I will not hurt you. Lead me out of here," Klassh commanded.

The dragon cleared the way with his flame, frying anything in his way. The now-calmed goblin led the dragon through a series of seemingly endless corridors until they reached the exit. The sky had darkened since he had entered the cave. Rain now fell from the sky in a torrent.

The exit was halfway up the cliff face. Looking down, Klassh saw a strange contraption that looked like a wooden platform attached to a number of ropes. It moved along the face of the cliff next to a series of openings in a vertical line on the cliff face. He could see the elf through the sheeting rain, working the ropes.

"Thief!" screamed the dragon, launching himself out of the opening and into the sky, inadvertently knocking the goblin out as well. The goblin remained calm. It did not even scream as it fell to its death on the rocks below.

Klassh spread his wings, hearing them crack and snap,

the joints flexed themselves, and started to climb
ward. The cool rush of air on his face and the wet
latter of raindrops on his body helped to clear his
ad of the last remnants of the poison and sickness.
ith a terrific sneeze, he blew the dust from his nose,
en circled downward toward the wooden platform.

The elf on the platform had just reached the next
ening when Klassh painted it with white-hot flame.
e platform caught fire instantly. The ropes holding it
sintegrated. Leaving a flaming trail, the fiery wreck-
e crashed down to the rocks and landed near the hap-
ss goblin's body.

Klassh spiraled down and landed near the burning
in. He examined the debris closely, but could not find
y trace of the elf, any of its belongings, or the pur-
ined sword.

"Dwarf entrails! The thief must have managed to get
to that opening!"

It took Klassh nearly an hour to find a small, dis-
ised cave—an egress from the tunnels nestled at the
ot of the mountain near a vale. The glade offered
enty of cover with a forest beyond. An ideal spot for
a ambush.

Klassh found a sturdy ledge on the mountain and lay
wait for the elf.

* * * * *

Klassh was not disappointed. An hour later, the rain
d eased. The elf poked his head out of the cave.

Focusing his concentration on the elf once again, the
agon strove to reestablish the mental link.

Where is the dragon? the elf was wondering.

The thief had his answer. He saw Klassh on the led
Fear.

The elf's emotions once again flooded into t
dragon's head, but they were not very satisfying. T
dragon still could not penetrate deeply into the el
mind.

The thief advanced again, moving quickly but silen
through the glade, using trees and boulders to hide.

Fear!

The elf moved faster now, running full out for the r
ative safety of the forest. The thief would be well hidd
if the dragon chose to fly above the trees. Despite I
fury, Klassh was loathe to use his flame on his beauti
forest. He rose into the air, went into a steep dive, a
laid down a line of fire between the elf and its goal, ca
ful not to let the flames get too close to the trees. T
dragon pulled out of his dive a few feet from the grou
climbed into the sky, and swung around.

The elf continued running as fast as he could direc
toward the flames, not slowing at all. With a leap,
dove right through the fire. A golden shimmer su
rounded the elf's body as he passed unscathed throu
the flames, rolled deftly to his feet, and dashed into t
forest. The elf continued to run through the spars
outer growth until he reached the heavy canopy, a
then vanished inside.

"Thief," Klassh spoke and this time felt the word pe
etrate the elf's mental block.

Surprise. Fear.

"Thief. Elf," the dragon continued. "I know you c
hear my thoughts. I can feel your fear. You think you a
safe within the forest, but I will burn it all to the grou
destroy every last tree, plant and creature to get to yc

Give yourself to me. Since you have been a worthy adversary, I promise you a quick death."

Go to the Abyss, the elf responded.

"Come now, elf. I know your kind well. I have fought you for millennia. You would not let all this forest be destroyed just to buy yourself a few more moments of life."

Silence from the elf.

"B'ynn al'Tor," Klassh said smugly.

SURPRISE.

"Yes, thief. I know your name. I know your family as well. The House of Tor is well known to the Dragons. We have always regarded your family as a powerful adversary. How far you have fallen. A mere thief, not worthy of the name of Tor."

SHAME.

. . . am worthy . . . the elf thought.

"No, you are not worthy," Klassh said sternly. "A worthy Tor would not resort to sneaking into my lair through a back door, running away, hiding in dwarf-made tunnels, and skulking around in a forest, which I will burn down around your ears if you do not give yourself to me."

SELF-LOATHING.

. . . foolish . . .

"Yes, you are very foolish, young elf. Do you not know who I am? My true name you will never know, but I have been known to the world as Klassh, most ancient and powerful of dragons."

SURPRISE.

"Surprised?" Klassh laughed. "You should be. Takhi-sis herself released me from my earthen tomb, and as she requested, I have kept my freedom hidden from the world so that I may be more effective in aiding the new generation of dragons to conquer Krynn. I tell you this now since I know that, one way or another, you will die before the day is out."

Silence.

"No response, B'ynn al'Tor . . . half-breed?" Klassh snickered.

SURPRISE. SHAME.

"Yes, I know everything about you, Tor. Half-breed. Outcast."

Klassh fabricated a story. He still could not fully penetrate the elf's emotional barrier, but the dragon knew enough about elven society to improvise.

"In the great hall I smelled the human in you. Crossbreeds are not welcome in proper elven society, are they? So they kicked you out and you became a common thief. The black mark on the proud House of Tor."

The elf trekked cautiously through the forest. The dragon could see from above that the area of the forest the elf had entered was actually a narrow band of trees. The forest was sliced through by a deep, wide ravine, like a half-healed scar in the yellow-red autumn skin of the earth. The trees ran nearly to the edge of the ravine. The elf would not be aware of its blunder until it was too late.

It would only take a few minutes for the elf to reach the gorge.

"I tire of the chase, outcast, so what is it to be?" Klassh demanded. "Do I burn down the forest, or do you give yourself up? Come now, what do you, a half-breed, have to live for?"

ANGER.

. . . wife . . . child . . .

"A wife and child. Now that is something to live for . . . and perhaps die for," Klassh said. "If you cause me to burn down my forest, I will not only destroy you, but also your family. I will track them down, thief. I will kill them slowly. I will savor your child's taste in my body. Then the mother. Her I will swallow whole and let die in the raging fires in my stomach."

OUTRAGE!

"You must realize by now, thief, how tenacious I am," Klassh continued. "It does not matter how long it takes, I will find your family and kill them. Perhaps I will instruct some of my brethren to seek especially those of the House of Tor. Perhaps I can wipe that noble house that has survived for millennia from the face of Krynn, purge it utterly from the world. Gone. Forgotten. All because of you, the half-breed that dared to challenge the might of Klassh."

GUILT.

"You can save them, B'ynn al'Tor. Just give yourself to me now and your death will suffice."

. . . *lies!* thought the elf.

"I do not lie. I am a dragon of my word. Just come forth, and I will spare your family and the House of Tor. Just you need die to satisfy me. Just you."

No!

The power of the elf's reply astounded the dragon, but Klassh let it pass. In a moment, the elf would leave the protection of the trees and find the ravine blocking its path. Klassh looked forward to the overwhelming despair that would flood from his quarry at that time.

The dragon was to be disappointed.

Bursting from the trees, the elf saw the canyon. Instead of stopping, it ran more strongly than before.

The thief was going to attempt to jump it!

HOPE!

Sensing something amiss, the enraged dragon decided to end the game. He went into a powerful dive that would take him right into the gorge at the point where the elf was about to jump. If flame could not touch the thief, then tooth and claw would do.

The elf jumped over the edge.

Klassh swept over the edge of the chasm, saw the thief grab a rope and swing out and away from him. Klassh hurtled past, completely missing the elf. The dragon crashed into the thick brush and trees that lined the sides of the ravine. Desperately trying to free himself, the dragon heard a crashing sound. He was suddenly being pummeled from all sides. Rocks and dirt fell past his head. Klassh realized that he had been tricked. Then he felt a blow on the side of his head and all was dark.

* * * * *

Klassh awoke, unable to move. He was having trouble breathing. His eyes focused on the elf, now sitting on a boulder just a few feet from the dragon. The elf held the glowing sword across its knees. Klassh tried to move, discovered that he was nearly buried under tons of dirt, rocks and stones. The weight of the debris was slowly crushing the life from him. He tried to muster up a blast of flame, but it caught in his throat.

"How . . .?" Klassh whispered.

In reply came the strong mental voice of the elf.

You were tricked, dragon. It is as simple as that. The terrible and mighty Klassh was tricked.

"Mindspeak? You have it?"

Yes, Klassh, and I have always known who you were; I have the gift. That is why you couldn't read my thoughts freely. In fact, though you didn't know it, you read only the thoughts and emotions I allowed.

"Who . . .?"

I truly am B'ynn al'Tor, half-breed son of the House of Tor, but my story is not as you supposed it. The elves are more enlightened these days and realize the strengths that the human-elf pairing can produce. Many of us are recruited to special assignments, for which our combination of superior strength, constitution and agility make us ideal. I am a Dragonsbane, a killer of dragons.

"Never heard . . . of you," Klassh muttered.

None of your kind ever will. We leave no trace, just a dead dragon, killed by accident. It has done wonders to demoralize the dragonarmies. That's right, Klassh, B'ynn al'Tor continued. *I came to kill you. Once I locked my mind onto yours, you didn't have a thought I didn't hear. You never made a move I didn't anticipate. I fed you the emotions and thoughts you wanted to hear. I played you like a fish, reeling you in, then giving you some slack, until the final yank lured you into my trap.*

"How did you know about the sword?"

The sword is the Blade of Tor, an ancestral heirloom lost during the Kinslayer Wars. The same dwarves who gave me the secrets of Cobb Hall also informed me their ancestors had recovered the blade and hidden it in the great hall.

Silence from the dying dragon. Just the ever-slowing breath pumping in and out of his tortured lungs.

Nothing to say, dragon? B'ynn al'Tor asked. *Goodbye then. You will die shortly and I will go on to kill many more of your brethren.*

The elf watched as the dragon's eyes slowly closed for the last time, and he waited for a few hours to be sure Klassh was dead. Satisfied, B'ynn al'Tor, Dragonsbane, turned and climbed back up the ravine, never looking back.

* * * * *

In another century, Dunstan Van Eyre, student of Astinus, would write about the Dragonsbane:

During the Third Dragon War, a secret group of highly trained elves and half-elves was formed. It was chartered to hunt down and kill important dragons. The members were remarkable warriors and magi. They were Dragonsbane. Schooled in the physiology and psychology of their prey, the Dragonsbane used stealth, deception and consummate planning to eliminate the dragons one by one. They left no trace, ensuring every death looked like an accident. Though they operated for decades and though the dragons must have had suspicions about the many accidental deaths of their brethren, the dragons never uncovered any evidence of their existence. This sage only learned about them by accident, from a descendant of arguably the greatest Dragonsbane of them all, B'ynn al'Tor.

The motto of the Dragonsbane was: "One Dragon, One Bane."

Rumor has it that they still operate to this day.

Glory Descending
Chris Pierson

The summer wind bore autumn's faintest chill as it snapped the castle's blue-and-gold pennants. The knights on the castle walls wearily stamped their feet, squinting across the Solamnic plains toward the southeast. Always the southeast. One bold squire had been heard to say that if an army came upon the keep from the northwest, it could knock down the wall and be taking tea in the outer ward before anyone noticed. On learning about the jest, the boy's master had sent him to muck out the stables for his loose tongue. Good humor had been scarce in the keep for some time: the coming war with the Highlords had seen to that.

Still, Sir Edwin couldn't help glancing to the northwest with a grim smile as he emerged from the building that had once been the castle's chapel. That was before the Cataclysm, before the gods had turned their backs on the world. He shook his head as he marched up the stairs to the keep's high inner wall. The joke, he knew, had been harmless: though the knights were surrounded by the enemy, they knew there was no danger from the northwest. That wasn't where the bulk of their foe's army was concentrated.

The southeast, however, was a different matter.

Not that there was anything yet to see that way, either; the scouts had gauged the army at several days' march away, and Castle Archuran yet stood in the army's path. Still, there were dire rumors among the troops. Some even said the dragons had returned, darkening the skies with their wings as they had done in Huma's day.

Most of the knights scoffed at this notion, but Edwin's face darkened as he considered it. His fellows put little stock in the old legends, but he had long believed, at risk of being branded a fool, that many of the tales were true. Edwin honored the memory of Huma Dragonbane, though few others did these days. If Huma was real, then so were the dragons—and where were they?

Edwin wondered if the answer to that question mightn't come all too soon.

He looked down the wall's crenelated length. At last he spotted the figure he sought, standing near the Southeast Tower. The man stood rigid, his back to the castle wall, his blue cloak whipping in the wind. The other knights gave him a wide berth as they paced the battlements, none pausing to exchange comradely greetings or banter with the down knight. Edwin sighed and started toward the knight, singing a few verses from an old Solamnic war song as he went:

To Hanford came the Hooded Knight,
   With cloak of gold and steed of bay,
His sword a-flashing silver-bright,
   A-thirsting for a wyrm to slay.
The Lord of Hanford welcomed him,
   For woe and grief were his domain:
The dragon they named Angethrim
   Had long since been the townsfolk's bane.
For many years the wyrm had flown,
   His breath afire, his jaws oped wide,
Thrice monthly when the red moon shone;
   Those few who stood against him died.

Edwin had never been much of a singer, but what he lacked in talent he more than made up for with zeal. The other knights smiled and saluted as he passed. It did his heart good to see them cheered so, when grimness was the order of the day.

There were many more verses to the song, and Edwin would have sung them all, but the dour knight silenced Edwin with a glance. That man was not cheered by the song; rather, he stiffened at the young knight's approach. Edwin stopped a respectful distance away.

"You do no one any favors, speaking of dragons so," the knight said.

Edwin shrugged. "'Tis but a song, brother, to raise the men's spirits."

"It sows fear," returned the knight. "Let the dragons remain children's stories."

"But what if—" Edwin caught himself, but not in time.

With a rattle of armor, the brooding knight turned away from the plains and glared angrily at Edwin.

The young knight endured his brother's piercing gaze for a moment, then looked away.

"You were about to say what if the rumors are true?" stated the older knight, his face drawn into a scowl, as usual.

Edwin looked at him in surprise. "Yes, brother, I have considered it. 'Rumors rarely blossom without the seed of truth,' so the saying goes."

The older knight glanced back at the barren plains. "But even if there *are* dragons among the foe, what good does it do to remind the men? They're nervous enough as it is. Putting dragons in their dreams only makes things worse, whether the dragons are real or fancy. I want an end to such nonsense!"

Edwin bowed his head, stared fixedly at the flag-stones. "Yes, Derek," he said wearily. In his thirty years, he'd said those words more often than he could recall.

Lord Derek Crownguard turned his head, then laid a gauntleted hand on Edwin's arm. "I don't mean to be harsh, brother," he said. "This war wears on us all, and I worry for the men's morale. Too much talk of dragons could break them." He paused, glancing up and down the wall to make sure none could hear. "Ofttimes, I wonder if Lord Gunthar's men haven't been spreading those stories with just that in mind."

Edwin nodded, still staring past his brother. It was well known that there was more love between knights and goblins than between Derek Crownguard and Gunthar Uth Wistan. Both had long desired the coveted position of Lord Knight of the Knighthood, and the years of rivalry had built up a wall of stone between them.

Their political maneuvering was like a great game of khas, a game that was a favorite with Derek. Edwin had never much cared for khas, or for politics, but he understood that with Castle Crownguard facing imminent siege and Lord Gunthar—the nominal head of the High Council—presumably safe on Sancrist Isle, Derek was on the verge of losing the game. Edwin had the unhappy feeling—though he tried to rid himself of it—that losing at politics meant more to Derek than losing his family's castle and possibly his own life.

"Has there been word from Sancrist?" Edwin asked.

Now it was Derek who looked away. His shoulders slumped slightly, though only Edwin saw this. The fury in the older knight's eyes, though, was plain to any who looked his way. "None," he snarled softly. "Gunthar must surely know our plight. He's holding back, hoping I will fail!"

"You do him an injustice!" Edwin said. "How can you think that?"

Derek looked at his brother sharply. There was no missing the unspoken accusation in the question: Derek would have done the same by Gunthar—if not worse—were the tables turned.

"He would do anything to keep me from becoming Grand Master," Derek growled. "Even withhold reinforcements. But it won't work." He stared back at his castle, eyeing it as if it were a rook on a khas-board. "Mark me, the day will come when Gunthar rues all he's done to thwart me."

They stood on the battlements together, neither saying more. Strangers were often amazed to discover that Derek and Edwin Crownguard were of the same blood. Derek was serious, dour and brooding, while Edwin's brow was clear, his eyes bright and guileless. "Naivet," some called behind his back.

In olden times, it had been the custom that a lord's firstborn son became his heir. His second son, with no lands to inherit, often entered the priesthood. Of course, there had been no priesthood since the Cataclysm, but it was a standing joke among the knights that Edwin may as well have been a cleric. Besides believing the ancient tales, he spent much of his time in the old chapel, where—he claimed—he found inner peace.

Derek scoffed at this notion. He would have never tolerated such behavior in anyone but his brother, and he had always hoped Edwin would grow out of it. Now, looking at Edwin—so blissfully free of the burdens lordship had placed on Derek—the older knight realized that Edwin would never change. And though some snickered at Edwin Crownguard and called him simple, Derek sometimes wondered if what others took for Edwin's naivete wasn't instead a clarity of vision Derek himself had never possessed.

"Ho! Look to the plains!"

The cry came from a young Knight of the Crown atop the tall Northeast Tower. He pointed afield. Derek, Edwin and the other knights turned and stared in shock. For a moment, all were silent, then one of the knights cursed softly.

"Virkhus and his legions preserve us," Edwin whispered. His fingers touched Trumbrand, his ancient sword.

Derek said nothing; he only stared toward the cloud-dotted horizon.

In the distance, black and curling with the chill wind, a thick plume of smoke had begun to rise.

* * * * *

By midday, Castle Crownguard's inner ward was filled with refugees, most terrified beyond words. Eventually, the knights found a man not maddened by fear, and brought him to Derek in the keep's Great Hall.

"Linbyr of Archester, a tanner," heralded Sir Winfrid, the seneschal. He motioned for a portly, balding man to enter the hall.

Derek looked up from the great war table, with its map of Solamnia and markers representing the knights and the assumed locations of the Highlords' armies. As he studied the peasant in the ruddy firelight, he twisted one tip of his long brown moustache between his fingers.

Linbyr stared back scornfully.

Unused to seeing such contempt in a mere commoner, Derek flushed with anger. "Don't stand there wasting my time! Out with it," he growled. "What ill befell you and your fellows?"

Linbyr was grim. "What ill? I'll tell you, my lord," he said, his voice thick. "We trusted your kind to protect us, that's what ill."

Derek half-rose, balling his hand into a fist, then checked himself. He couldn't let himself be baited; it was beneath him. Still, he spoke with enough rage to give Linbyr pause. "What do you mean by that?"

Linbyr cleared his throat. "What I mean, my lord"— he sneered disdainfully—"is that the armies of the Dark Queen have sacked Archester."

Derek scowled. "Impossible. Such a thing would never happen with Castle Archuran protecting—"

"Castle Archuran has fallen as well."

Derek was so shocked, he let the interruption pass. He caught his breath. "Lord Aurik?" he asked.

"Slain, my lord, along with his men."

Derek sat back in his seat. Lord Aurik had long been one of Derek's greatest political supporters. He had also been a friend, a formidable warrior, and an eminently honorable man. That he and Castle Archuran could have fallen was unthinkable. Derek had never heard of a siege so short. "What treachery wrought this?"

"No treachery, my lord," said Linbyr. His voice had at least softened with compassion for the fallen knights, but this pity only further inflamed Derek's temper. "The armies overran the castle."

Derek snorted. "In a thousand years, Castle Archuran's walls have never been breached, by siege or sorcery."

"That's as may be," Linbyr said, "but they crumbled like clay before the dragons."

Derek looked away, clenching his fist. So it had come true. Edwin's song had come true. He knew it was irrational, but he felt like laying the blame for the dragons on his brother.

"Yes, my lord. Dragons," repeated Linbyr. "Out of the songs of old. The knights were too busy dying to defend our poor village." He shook his head. "And to think we believed they could keep us safe from harm."

With that, and without asking leave, Linbyr turned and left the hall. Derek made no move to stop him.

One word kept echoing in Derek's head. *Dragons.* Dragons had thrown down the walls of Castle Archuran, had slaughtered Aurik and his men, had dealt yet another blow to Derek's aspirations.

Carefully, he reached out and plucked the marker representing Castle Archuran from the map.

"My lord?"

Derek looked up from the table and saw Sir Winfrid in the doorway. The old seneschal's face was drawn with worry.

"Well? What is it?" Derek snapped, rather more harshly than he'd meant to.

Winfrid was well used to his lord's temper, and if he was stung at all by Derek's curtness, he gave no indication. "A rider approaches from the northwest, my lord," he said. "His shield bears the Knight's Crest."

Oddly, the first thought that occurred to Derek was that the joking squire had been wrong: the sentries *were* looking to the northwest, after all.

"A messenger from Lord Gunthar, do you think?" he asked.

Winfrid shrugged. "He nears the gates. The archers are standing at ready, my lord, lest it be a trick."

"Good," Derek said. "Let's see what this is about."

He followed Winfrid out of the hall and across the inner ward. Edwin was there, fussing over one of the villagers, a young woman with a bloodied leg.

Derek didn't spare him a second glance. Edwin had a knack for healing the sick and injured. He knew herb lore and how to set broken bones. People said his presence alone made them feel better. Derek thought it all nonsense. Neither his brother nor the frightened, exhausted villagers were foremost on his mind.

He and Winfrid went into the gatehouse, then climbed up the watchtower stairs. At the top, bowmen crouched between the merlons, arrows nocked. Derek peered past them, down the road that led to the castle's stout gates. A rider was approaching at a gallop, and his gleaming shield bore the kingfisher, rose, sword and crown of the Solamnic Knights. His armor was swathed in hunting greens, hiding his identity. The rider, nearing the gates, reined in his frothing chestnut horse. He glanced behind him furtively, as if expecting pursuit, then tried to climb out of his saddle. His legs gave out, and he fell to the ground with a crash and a muffled curse.

Derek watched the knight thrash on the ground. From the looks of him, the knight had seen hard fighting of late. That wasn't a surprise: the hills were rife with enemy outriders, and the roads were dangerous for a lone horseman to travel. The knight pushed himself to his knees, then yanked off his visored helm. A shock of red hair spilled onto his shoulders. The man's face was pale, and a thin trickle of dried blood had crusted on his chin, but there was a glint of laughter in his eyes as he gazed up at the watchtower.

"Hail to you, old friend!" he called up to Derek. He broke into a coughing fit—he had plainly been riding hard for some time, and was winded. "A fine day for a ride in the countryside, what?" he wheezed when he found his breath. His red moustache curled above a toothy grin.

Derek was amazed. The green cloak, the red hair, the irrepressible good humor: he knew only one such knight. "Aran?" he called as the man staggered to his feet.

"The last I knew," returned the red-haired knight. He glanced behind again—it seemed more reflex than conscious action—then back up at the watchtower. "I don't suppose you'd mind raising the gates and letting me in?"

* * * * *

Derek descended to the bottom of the watchtower and started toward the castle gates. Two young squires preceded him to offer their assistance in helping Sir Aran Tallbow walk. Aran was doing his best to shoo them back. "Get away," he grumbled. "I've just ridden halfway across Solamnia. I can make it to the bleedin' courtyard on my own."

"Take his horse," Derek ordered the squires. "See she's rubbed down, fed and watered. And brush the burdocks out of her mane." Nodding and bowing, the squires took the animal's reins from Aran and led the horse through the barbican into the inner ward.

Aran Tallbow, Knight of the Crown, looked Derek up and down, then limped forward wearily. "It's good to see you again," he said, grinning despite his soreness.

from long hours in the saddle.

Derek stepped forward and clasped Aran's arms, coming as close to smiling as he ever did. "It looks as if you've seen hard times," he said.

Aran winced, grimaced. "Had a spot of bad luck near Owensburg," he said. "I ran afoul of a hobgoblin patrol—never seen so many of the buggers—and had to shoot my way through." He shrugged off the quiver he wore across his back and opened it; he was down to his last two arrows. "It was close, mark me. I rode old Byrnie hard the rest of the way. I was afraid I'd break her."

"She'll be all right," Derek assured him. "But what brings you here in these troubled days? It seems an odd time to be calling on old friends."

Aran chuckled, shouldering the quiver again. "That it does, but here I am. I was at Castle Uth Wistan when the messenger arrived with your call for reinforcements. I asked Gunthar if I might be sent here."

Derek stepped back, rubbed his hands with pleasure. "Then Gunthar *is* sending help!"

Aran's smile vanished. He scratched the back of his neck. "Well, not as such, I'm afraid. I'm all he could spare."

"Damn him!" Derek spat, and struck the wall with his mailed fist. Metal rang against stone. "The fool! Doesn't he realize—" He stopped short, looking around to make sure none of his men had witnessed the outburst.

Aran regarded his friend with concern, then smiled again. "I didn't say I was the only one coming," he said. "Before the Council withdrew, I cornered Alfred MarKenin and had a word in his ear. I told him how grateful you'd be, as Lord Knight, to those who helped you when you were in need. He agreed to send a company of Knights of the Sword, without Gunthar's knowledge. They'll arrive from Solanthus within the week, and you'll never guess who's leading them."

Derek blinked, taking all this in as he swallowed his rage. "Not Brian Donner," he said.

Aran flashed his broadest, most disarming smile. "All right, so you *did* guess." He clapped Derek on the back. "We three, together again, what? It'll be just like when we were young, newly dubbed and spoiling for a fight."

Derek nodded. In his head, he was already sizing up the khas-board and contemplating his new strategy. "Thank you for this, Aran," he said.

"It was no trouble, old friend," the red-haired knight returned. He glanced around the gatehouse. "Edwin around?"

"He's in the inner ward. Seeing to those in need."

Aran laughed. "Some things never change. Not that I'm surprised. Still dreaming of following in Huma's footsteps, is he? Well, maybe he'll have his chance."

Derek frowned. "This is no time for jokes."

Aran started to say that he hadn't been joking. The dour look on Derek's face silenced the knight.

"I'm going to say hello," Aran said, turning to go. "Then I think I'll have a lie down. You wouldn't believe how I ache. I'm not as young as I used to be. We'll have a feast tonight, to welcome me, what?"

Derek nodded, and Aran went into the castle. Though he was tired and sore, the red-haired knight still had a singular ease to his gait—the same ease he'd had many years ago, when they'd been questing-brothers with Brian Donner. Derek turned to dark thoughts. It had been a day full of bad news: first Linbyr's tale of dragons—unconfirmed as yet, he reminded himself—and now, at last, proof of

Gunthar's refusal to reinforce Castle Crownguard.

"So, you think you can win by leaving me unde-
fended before the enemy," he whispered to the shadows. "You think you can sacrifice me like a cleric in a
khas match. Pray you're right, Gunthar." He curled his
fingers into a fist. "Pray you're right."

* * * * *

"I fear our hospitality is not what it used to be," said
Edwin as Aran Tallbow helped himself to a slab of roast
boar.

Servants bustled about the Great Hall, keeping
flagons filled with warm, dark beer. Bread, cheese and
summer fruits lay scattered about the great dining table,
scarce compared with peacetime feasts. Edwin gestured
with his knife at the other knights who had assembled
for the meal. "Most of us have grown accustomed to
porridge and salt pork by now."

Derek, who had hardly spoken since the first bread
had been broken, glared at his brother. "Edwin, be still."

Aran chuckled around a mouthful of meat. He quaffed
his beer and shook his head, his red hair bouncing mer-
rily. "No fear, Derek," he said lightly. "I've been through
sieges before. At least you're not reduced to eating rat
meat. Why I remember a time when—"

He stopped. No one—except Edwin—was even
politely pretending to listen.

Aran glanced around the table and shook his head.
No matter how he tried to brighten the mood, these men
seemed determined to be gloomy. Well, they had every
right—or so he was forced to admit. He'd looked at the
map table before the feast. Castle Crownguard was all

but surrounded. The hobgoblins that had caused Aran so much trouble were coming down from the north. And there was, by all accounts, a sizable army on the way from the south, an army that had razed Castle Archuran. Derek had learned that much from the peasants, before they'd set out to take their chances in the hills. He warned them that they were not likely to survive long in the wilderness, but they'd been adamant about not wanting to stay at the castle.

What worried Aran most, though, was his host. Derek had always been serious—ill-humored, even—but now he was dark and ominous as a thundercloud. Aran wasn't looking forward to seeing the lightning strike.

"How many knights can we expect to aid us, Sir Aran?" asked old Pax Garett, Knight of the Sword, who had been one of Derek's father's closest friends. He stroked his steel-gray moustache. "And when will they arrive?"

Aran cleared his throat awkwardly, setting down his knife. "Um," he said, "twenty or thirty, provided they don't lose any on the way. And they'll be here in five or six days—again, assuming all goes well."

"Twenty or thirty!" Pax returned, shocked. "Five or six days! By the Abyss, man, that's not enough! What does Gunthar think he's doing?"

"Gunthar's doing nothing," Derek growled. All eyes turned to him. "He sits in his castle, hoarding his troops rather than committing them to the front."

Aran shook his head. "Not so, my lord. Truth to tell, there are few knights left on Sancrist. Barely enough to hold the High Council. Most are fighting at Vingaard and Solanthus. Gunthar expressed his regret that he couldn't help—"

"Bah!" Derek snarled. "He and his men are probably laughing at us even now! He's done this deliberately, to get us out of the way. To get *me* out of the way." His eyes gleamed in the hearthlight. "In fact, it wouldn't surprise me at all to hear he'd made a deal with the enemy—cast us to wolves, while he goes free!"

All noise in the hall stopped. The knights stared at Derek in shock. Aran lowered his gaze to his plate.

"Brother!" Edwin reprimanded. "You don't mean that!"

Derek blinked, glancing around the room, then rubbed his anger-blotched forehead. "I'm sorry. I didn't mean that," he said wearily. "But Gunthar's left us virtually helpless to bear the brunt of the enemy forces."

"There's little here for the enemy to be interested in— no offense, Derek," Aran responded. It was true enough. Whereas the Crownguard family had once been one of the most powerful in Solamnia, Lord Derek now had little domain. The family's prestige had long been in decline, and only years of careful, constant maneuvering had brought the seat of Lord Knight within Derek's grasp.

But now even that was beginning to come apart, and the realization made Derek jab the table with the tip of his knife. "They will attack," he said.

"But *why?*" demanded Aran. "What use is there? Even Lord Alfred wasn't sure why he should draw troops away from Solanthus to send to defend Crownguard, when the enemy can simply pass us by and attack rider targets."

"They'll attack us," Derek replied, his gaze steady, "because they can win, and quickly."

"They have dragons," Edwin added.

This time, even the servants stopped and stared. Derek flashed a hot glare at his brother—he hadn't told the others of Linbyr's tale yet. Not that his telling was necessary; they'd all heard the rumors. This was the first time the news had been spoken aloud. Pax and the other knights looked stricken.

Aran broke the silence with a hollow laugh. "Dragons! Oh, ho!" he cried, trying to pass it off as a joke. And, indeed, he did not believe it. "You've developed quite the wit, Edwin! Hasn't he, Derek?"

The other knights weren't laughing. Aran glanced sharply at his old friend. "Hasn't he, Derek?" he repeated, more urgently.

Derek poked at the cold meat on his plate. "My brother speaks aright, for all of his bluntness," he said harshly, taking a gulp of beer that tasted like dirty rainwater to him. "The dragons slew Aurik and his men, and leveled Castle Archuran. One and all the survivors told the same tale."

Aran blew a long sigh through his lips. He knew now why the quiet conversation that had buzzed at the table throughout the feast had been so forced and half-hearted. Now, at last, he realized how desperate Derek truly was. He laid his knife aside—his appetite had fled him—and stared up at the rows of gleaming shields that hung high on the walls of the hall. Each bore the crest of a Crownguard, marked with the sigil of a Knight of the Rose. The Tallbows were a less noteworthy clan, but Aran understood the pride Derek took in his heritage. That heritage was doomed now, meaningless.

"What's this, then?" rumbled Sir Pax, thumping his fist on the table. "Gloom in the face of honorable death? Surely these aren't Knights of Solamnia all about me, brooding over their flagons that they might face a dragon in worthy battle!"

That cheered the other knights somewhat, but when the feast was done, they dispersed quickly, off to stand the night watch on the battlements. Before long, only Derek, Edwin, and Aran remained, sipping brandy at the map table.

"How long before the armies arrive?" Aran asked at length, shaking his goblet so the golden brandy sloshed around its edges.

"The villagers said the enemy drove them part of the way here, then withdrew near the Axewood," Derek answered, pointing to a small cluster of trees on the map. "Their supply wagons will have to catch up, but I suppose we'll sight them two days from the morrow."

"Then Brian's company likely won't arrive in time," Aran said flatly. "We can't count on using anything more than we already have."

"The defenses have been raised," added Edwin. "We'd be glad if you would command our archers."

Aran nodded. "I was hoping you'd ask. I'd be honored. With your leave, Lord Derek, of course."

Derek nodded and grunted absently. It went without saying that Aran, one of the finest archers in Solamnia, would lead the castle's bowmen. But Derek's mind was elsewhere. "What do you know of dragons, Aran?" he asked.

"No more than you, I'm afraid—perhaps not even that much, at that. Just what the nursemaid told me when I was a lad," the red-haired knight replied. "They're big, scaly, scary, and they eat bad little boys for lunch."

He chuckled, and Edwin smiled, but Derek continued to brood. Aran sighed and shook his head. He swirled the brandy in the glass. Brandy sloshed onto his fingers. "Confound it, Derek! What do you want me to say? I didn't even know they existed before tonight. I certainly don't know how to *kill* one of the blasted beasts! Huma needed the dragonlance, if you believe the stories. You don't have any of those lying about in the armory, I trust?"

Derek glared at him, didn't respond. Aran scowled and sucked brandy from his knuckles.

"The Hooded Knight only needed his sword," Edwin said quietly.

"Damn it, both of you!" Derek yelled suddenly. "The Hooded Knight is a fairy story! And so is Huma!"

"And what are the dragons, brother?" Edwin asked. "Fairy story? Real? You're not so sure anymore, are you?"

Aran had heard this argument before, many times. Edwin believed the old stories. His heroes were Huma and Vinas Solamnus and Berthel Brightblade. Derek had always ridiculed his brother for this. Derek believed only in himself. Aran knew the argument could last long into the night. He opted for a strategic retreat.

"I'm afraid the ride here wore me out," Aran said, and feigned a yawn. "I'll retire now, by your leave, my lord."

Derek waved him away, his flinty gaze still on Edwin. Aran made an apologetic face at the younger knight, then rose and left. He shut the door as quietly as possible, but it still boomed like a thunderbolt in the cavernous silence.

* * * * *

After Aran's departure, the two brothers sat in stony silence. Edwin endured his brother's glare as long as he could, then looked down at his hands, folded in his lap.

"I—I'm sorry, Derek. I didn't mean—"

"Yes, you did," Derek said coldly. "I'm a fool for not believing every song a bard ever played. Is that it?"

Edwin cringed. "Brother, please . . ."

"No, no." Derek sneered, waving his hand. "You're right, of course. There *are* dragons among the enemy. You'd best run along, find the Hammer of Kharas and forge yourself some lances, so you can save the world."

"Stop it, Derek!" Edwin pushed his chair back and stood, his finger shaking as he pointed at his brother. "I've had enough of your mockery. I'm not a child any more. I don't want to be Huma, Derek. I just want to *believe* in something. Can't you see that?"

Derek stared at Edwin, his eyes dark, his hands balling into fists under the table. This time, though, Edwin met his brother's glower with defiance. Derek's gaze turned to glittering ice, and he shook his head. "Very well, *believe* in something," he said. "Believe in the dragons. And, since they're coming, we must send a man on to Vingaard to warn the knights there."

"Aye, that's good thinking," Edwin agreed. He stopped suddenly as he realized what his brother was saying. "No, Derek. Surely you wouldn't—"

"I mean it, Edwin. I want you to go."

"But this is my home! I can't just leave—"

"If the dragons come, you'll *have* no home," Derek continued. "We will die, one and all, like they did at Castle Archuran. The Crownguard name must not fall. You have a wife, safe in Vingaard. I do not. You must sire an heir, so the family may carry on." He paused, his lips becoming a firm line. "And you must go before Lord Gunthar and accuse him of having part in my death, and those of my men."

Edwin slammed his fist on the table. "So that's what this is truly about!" he yelled, his trembling voice ringing all the way up to the rafters. "If you can't be Lord Knight, you mean to shame Gunthar out of it as well! You've played this damned game for power so long, you can't see anything else! Not even your own honor!"

Derek was not accustomed to such defiance. He stared at his brother in amazement.

"Send another lackey on your errand, brother," Edwin continued. In thirty years, he had never spoken to his brother with such anger. "I won't be a pawn on your khas-board." With that, he turned and left.

Derek stared after him until the fire in the hearth began to gutter out. If only it were as simple as Edwin imagined, he said to himself. How fine it would be if Paladine would drop by and save the day. But Paladine wasn't coming. Not now. Not ever.

Gunthar's refusal to send reinforcements was all part of a plan, Derek decided finally. Gunthar had sapped the hope from Derek's men, turned Derek's brother against him, and consigned the Crownguard family to the ashes. All to keep Derek from ascending to his rightful place.

Snarling, Derek hurled his crystal goblet against the wall. It trailed an arc of golden brandy behind it, before it smashed to flinders against the flagstones. Derek sat quietly, gazing intently at the glittering shards. He sat for hours.

Plotting his next move.

* * * * *

By dawn the skies above Castle Crownguard were

heavy with storm clouds the hue of unpolished armor. The lands to the southeast were hazy with approaching rain, and the wind had turned from vaguely chilly to damp and cold. The men on the walls clasped their halberds with shivering hands and lowered the visors of their helms against the slashing wind. No one sang now. Few spoke. The castle's scouts were reported missing. They had been due to return from patrol several hours before, but not even the sharpest-eyed sentry had yet seen any sign of them. With the storm coming and the enemy army not far behind, hopes that they would ever be seen again dwindled hourly.

By morning's end, rain lashed the castle walls, and some of the more callow squires were talking of following the folk of Archester into the hills. The knights quickly silenced such talk, but not even the harshest reprimands could lift the shadow of dread from the young men's eyes. Sir Winfrid ordered the watch at the postern gate doubled to prevent desertion, and the worst cowards were locked away to keep them from sowing fear throughout the keep.

Derek was furious when he discovered the dissension, and took special note of each culprit's name—if, somehow, he was spared, he swore to bring up their cowardice before the High Council. None of them would ever be knights, if he had any say in the matter.

That wasn't the worst of it, though. Derek had discovered that his brother had gone to the old chapel to hold vigil in the old custom. Some of the younger knights wanted to join him. It was sacrilegious folly, and Derek considered putting a stop to it. But Edwin's angry words from the night before still stung. Derek reluctantly left his brother to his fancy.

Derek Crownguard was in a dark mood when he left the map table in the Great Hall to inspect the castle's defenses. At the top of the keep's high inner wall he found Aran Tallbow sitting alee of a wooden canopy, patiently whittling a shaft of wood. Aran's fine longbow rested beside him, its string covered to keep it dry. He looked up when he heard the rattle of Derek's armor.

"A fine day to you, my lord," he said with a wry smile.

Derek glowered. He did not return the greeting.

"You don't need to make arrows, Aran," Derek said, crouching beneath the canopy and wiping rainwater from his face. "We've enough to last the winter, if needs be."

Aran shrugged. "You know me, Derek. I'd sooner wear another knight's armor into battle than loose a shaft I didn't fletch myself." He stuck a green-dyed feather onto the arrow with a dab of glue from a clay pot. "Any word of the patrols?" he asked, plucking a second feather from his deerskin pouch.

Derek shook his head. "Perhaps they sought shelter, to ride out the storm."

Aran finished with a third feather, then started fitting a broad steel head onto the shaft. "You don't believe that," he said. He tapped the arrowhead to make sure it was secure, then eyed the finished shaft critically. "You've got bigger problems if this wind doesn't let up, though. Your archers won't be able to hit a blasted thing."

Derek grunted. "Neither will theirs."

"Small help that'll be when their siege ladders go up." Satisfied, Aran slid the finished arrow into his quiver, which was already half full. Without pause, he took up his knife and set to carving another shaft. "Seen Edwin lately?"

"He's in the old chapel."

"Praying to Blessed Paladine? I hope he gets an answer."

Derek glared at the knight. Aran grinned. "You could try enjoying a joke now and again, my friend."

Scowling, Derek shook his head and looked away. Aran had always been good at hitting close to the mark, be it with arrows or words. Derek had the awful feeling Edwin *was* praying to the old gods. That was the last thing he needed!

Derek turned and gazed across the castle's inner ward. At the Great Hall, several servants scrambled to cover a window whose shutter had been torn free by the storm. Sir Pax and Sir Winfrid were deep in conversation near the Northeast Tower. A footman chased his cloak as the wind bore it across the courtyard.

A dark shape appeared in the sky, plummeting toward the castle from the east. Derek caught his breath and touched Aran's arm. The red-haired knight stopped whittling and looked skyward.

"What in the Abyss?" he asked, then his eyes widened. "By Huma, hammer and lance!"

The object was—or once had been—a man.

The body struck the keep's western wall with a sickening thud, and fell onto the roof of the granary. Several knights dragged the body down to the courtyard. By the time Derek and Aran arrived, the corpse lay out on the cobblestones, covered by Sir Winfrid's deep blue cloak. Aran cleared a path through the crowd, and Derek stepped up and pulled back the shroud.

Derek looked on the body. It was one of the scouts—that much was sure from the garb—but the face was too battered to tell more. Numerous slashes had torn the man's flesh, as if he had been mauled by the claws of some animal. The slashes were long, deep. The talons that had made them must have been as sharp as spearheads.

Despite his best efforts, Derek shuddered as he covered the body again. "Take him into the chapel," he said with forced calm. "Return to your posts."

Reluctantly, the men began to disperse. Derek turned and marched toward the gatehouse.

Sir Winfrid hurried to catch up. "My lord!" he called.

Derek stopped and turned. "There was something else, my lord," the seneschal said, proffering a wet roll of parchment. "A message affixed to the body."

Derek took the parchment without a word, then turned and walked into the gatehouse. Aran followed him. Once he and Aran were sheltered from the storm, Derek unrolled the message and held it up to catch the torchlight. The ink had run in the rain, and a smudge of blood marred one corner, but the words were still legible. To Derek's surprise, the script—written in a sure, flowing hand—was in fluent Solamnic:

> "To the lord of this castle: Look on your own death. Surrender. The Dark Lady."

"Well, now," Aran said, with an awkward, forced smile, "that's that, what?"

* * * * *

It didn't take long for word to spread.

The enemy was coming and given the choice between dragons and the hobgoblin patrols that roamed the surrounding hills, the servants, squires and footmen chose the latter. The knights at the postern gate held valiantly against the terrified men and women who sought to flee Castle Crownguard. In the end, Derek ordered the Knights to stand aside rather than risk a riot. By dusk, only the knights and a few brave commoners remained. And, while news of the Dark Lady's warning strengthened many knights' resolve, some of the younger ones were starting to lose their nerve.

As night came on, the storm grew more fierce. The wind howled. The cloud-wracked sky blazed with lightning, and thunder shook the castle's very stones. Aran gave up working on his arrows in disgust and turned to polishing his sword. Derek stalked the inner wall, keeping the knights heartened. He found a few of them missing from their posts. He thought they had deserted.

"My-my lord," said Sir Pax. "They've gone to the old chapel."

* * * * *

Edwin knelt within the chapel, his head bowed, his ancient sword Trumbrand clasped in his hands. The men had laid out the scout's shattered body on a bier. Edwin had never once moved, and if he saw the corpse, he gave no sign.

The young knights crept forward, glancing nervously at one another. Edwin did not look up, did not even move as they knelt on either side of him. His eyes were closed, his breathing slow and deep, his lips parted slightly.

"Give me a sign," he prayed, beseeching whatever powers might harken to his voice. "I am not afraid. I will do what you ask. Just give me a sign that I am not alone."

Over and over he repeated his simple plea. The prayer filled his thoughts, staved off hunger and weariness, suffused him with peace and calm. He had come to the chapel often in his youth, when he could steal away for an hour or two without Derek noticing. He had knelt there, keeping vigil as Huma and Vinas and the Hooded Knight did in the tales. Sometimes, he had thought he had felt something, but he had never been sure. Now, he prayed more fervently than ever. Dragons—*real* dragons—were coming. But if dragons were real, that meant that Huma might have been real as well. And then, that meant—he trembled at the thought—that Paladine was real!

"You must be tired, young man."

Edwin caught his breath so suddenly, he nearly choked. He opened his eyes and stared in wonder. There was nothing there. He glanced to either side. The young knights who had joined him in his vigil dozed where they knelt.

"I said, you must be tired, Edwin," said the voice again.

The voice came from behind him. Wincing as he moved joints stiff from hours of motionlessness, Edwin half-turned to see who had joined him. Behind him stood Pax Garett, and there was compassion in the old knight's face. He rested a gauntleted hand on Edwin's shoulder and smiled kindly.

"S-Sir Pax!" stammered Edwin. "Why have you come? Is something the matter?" He started to rise, his brow creased with worry, Trumbrand ready in his hand. "Are we under attack?"

"No, no," Pax said. Gently but firmly, he pushed Edwin back down. "Nothing so bad as that. I just needed to get out of that accursed storm for a while." He glanced over his shoulder at the chapel's closed door. "And I had to speak with you, this night." He reached for a flask on his belt, unstopped it, and took a deep draught. Wiping his grizzled mouth, he handed the flask to Edwin. "It's only water, I fear," the elder knight said. "My old heart burns these days if I drink anything stronger."

Edwin took the flask and drank thirstily. Knees creaking, Pax crouched down beside him.

"Why have you come to see me?" Edwin asked. "Surely my brother—"

Pax shook his head. "Your brother has enough to worry about." He fixed Edwin with a piercing gaze.

"I knew, soon or late, this day would come," Pax said. "And," he added, his expression growing fond, "in a way, I'm glad it has. You were always special, Edwin. So few believe the tales these days. When I was a lad, there were some who scoffed, but they were few. Now, times have changed. Men think the stories are fancy, that Quivalen Soth and Rutger of Saddleway were just artful liars."

Edwin nodded. He'd heard as much—from Derek and others—all his life. "Then . . . the tales . . . they *are* true?" he asked slowly, his voice hushed.

Pax smiled, gave a short chuckle. "Who's to say?" he replied. "I wasn't around to see Huma take the field against She of Many Colors and None, or the Hooded Knight ride out to battle Angethrim. But then, I've never seen a dragon, either. Some of the tales may be false, some true, some both. What does it matter? All that's important is the believing. I could never make Derek understand that, but you"—Pax patted Edwin on the shoulder fondly—"you always knew. Keep believing, Edwin, and one day the bards might sing about you."

Edwin's gauntleted hand reached out, grasped hold of the older man's. "What about you, Pax?" Edwin asked at length. "Will the bards sing about you?"

Pax chuckled again, but his eyes were wistful. "I doubt it," he replied. "In the tales, there aren't many dragon-slayers who've seen eighty summers. But you never know, do you?" Wobbling slightly, he pushed himself back to his feet and laid his hand on Edwin's forehead. "Keep believing, young man," he said, and walked away.

Edwin looked to the bier, toward where Paladine's altar had once stood. He was surprised to see the first gray light of dawn beginning to shine through the shutters on the narrow windows behind the bier.

A loud, rattling cry sounded from the window, rousing the other young knights from their dazed slumber. Edwin caught his breath. The shutters had blown open. On the sill perched a kingfisher, its blue feathers glistening with rainwater, its head angling this way and that as it studied the knights. It opened its beak to utter its harsh call again, then it was gone, flying out the window with a flash of blue wings.

Edwin nodded quietly to himself. "Thank you," he whispered, and smiled.

* * * * *

Morning came, a pale shadow. The knights watched and waited, most in hopeless despair. Even old Pax, who stood sword-in-hand near the Northeast Tower, looked weary and preoccupied. Once more, there was nothing to see upon the storm-lashed plains, hour upon hour. Gloomily, Derek told Aran things could scarcely get worse. Then at midday, the storm ceased.

The wind slackened enough for Aran to take up his bow once more. The rain turned to drizzle, and the inky thunderheads gave way to brighter overcast. The knights peered edgily to the southeast, the tips of their halberds quivering, expecting to see the dark shapes of the foe's armies marching across the plains. Derek, who had come down to the inner ward to speak with Winfrid, touched his sword and eyed the sky warily. Aran, at the Southeast Tower, fitted an arrow onto his bowstring and waited.

The chapel door opened. Edwin stepped out, blinking in the light. His armor, shield and sword gleamed in the muted daylight. Behind him, squinting like newborn rabbits leaving the warren for the first time, came five young knights. Derek turned and glowered at them.

"I was right, Derek," Edwin said. The serenity in his voice made the older knight's scalp prickle. "I was right to believe the tales. Pax told me."

Derek scowled. "What are you talking about?"

"Paladine gave me a sign in the chapel last night," Edwin repeated. "I was right, Derek—I understand that now."

"Stop this, Edwin," Derek snapped, irritated and embarrassed. "You're talking nonsense. Get those men back to their posts. I'll discipline them later."

"But—"

"*Now,* Edwin!" Derek shouted. He turned away. After a moment, he heard Edwin heave a quiet sigh and march off, the five young knights following.

"What do you suppose *that* was about?" asked Sir Winfrid.

Derek shrugged. "Maybe he fell asleep. It'd be just like Edwin not to know the difference between a dream and—" He stopped, seeing Winfrid's gaze shift. "What is it now?"

"Your brother," Sir Winfrid answered. "He's going up into the Northeast Tower."

Derek swore silently. He turned just in time to see Sir Pax step aside as Edwin and the five young knights— Edwin's knights, to all appearances—marched across the inner wall and entered the tall tower. They emerged at the top of the spire and raised their swords. The rest of the men watched, fascinated, as Edwin took his place beneath the Crownguard banner that flapped atop the tower.

"The damned fool," Derek cried, Edwin raised Trumbrand to his lips and kissed its hilt.

And a nightmare dropped through the clouds.

The dragon was huge, almost half as long as Castle Crownguard was wide. Its scaly body, borne on tremendous, azure wings, gleamed like an enormous, flawed sapphire. Wickedly curving claws flashed. Eyes as red as the fires of the Abyss stared from its death mask face. Row upon row of swordlike fangs jutted from its gaping maw. Its great, serpentine tail trailed behind it.

The knights dropped their weapons and fled.

Sir Pax roared with fury as the younger men scattered, casting aside swords, halberds and shields to flee the monstrosity that glided over the castle. Fear, strong and otherworldly, swept down from the dragon, turning stalwart men's knees to water and their minds to thoughts of death. Only a few remained, among them ashen-faced

Pax, and Aran, who watched the dragon with stunned amazement. In the courtyard, Winfrid was paralyzed by the wyrm's baleful gaze. And even Derek, who had never buckled to fear, who had, in his younger days, stood with Aran and Brian Donner against ogres, sorcerers and worse, quailed and froze beneath the waves of magical fear that crashed over Castle Crownguard.

Only Edwin, standing with his men atop the Northeast Tower, appeared to be unaffected. His back was straight, his stance firm.

The dragon circled. Derek tried vainly to make his legs move. Half of him screamed to get out of the beast's sight; the other half wanted to charge up to the Northeast Tower, to save his brother. Instead, Derek did nothing. Beside him, Sir Winfrid lost his own courage and bolted for the shelter of the gatehouse. Derek didn't notice.

Finally, the wyrm pulled straight up, into the clouds, and vanished. Aran let out a tentative cheer. He fell silent as a horrific scream, loud as thunder, tore the air.

Mouth gaping wide, its wings folded back, the dragon dove down like an arrow. It streaked straight toward the Northeast Tower. Toward Edwin. He watched it, unflinching. And then Derek heard something strange. Something he couldn't believe. His brother was singing!

"To Hanford came the Hooded Knight,
    With cloak of gold and steed of bay,
His sword a-flashing silver-bright,
    A-thirsting for a wyrm to slay."

Edwin raised his sword. The great blue dragon sucked in a breath. A bolt of lightning flashed.

The levin-bolt struck Edwin's sword. Sparks leapt from his armor, showering all around. A brilliant flash blew Castle Crownguard's Northeast Tower apart.

"Edwin!" Derek yelled, throwing an arm up to shield his eyes. He heard the dragon shrieking, flames crackling, flagstones raining down into the courtyard. Then all of these were drowned out by the roar of the tower crashing to the ground. A stone chip slashed across Derek's cheek, drawing blood, and he squinted furiously, willing his eyes to focus. He concentrated on a great blue blur—it had to be the dragon—as it soared above him and up toward the sky. The rush of air from its wings knocked Derek flat, sending him sprawling onto the cobbles. By the time he staggered back to his feet, the great blue blur was nowhere to be seen.

All was quiet. The air stank of ozone.

Derek stared up at the cloud rack. The dragon was gone, of that much he was sure, for the dragonawe no longer clutched at his heart. His gaze shifted to the ruins of the Northeast Tower.

All that remained was a heap of rubble, much of it turned to glass by the lightning strike. Through the gap where the spire had stood, Derek could see the Solamnic plains. The Crownguard banner—Azur, a crown d'or—lay smoldering atop the heap.

* * * * *

Four of the young knights' bodies were found amid the rubble. The fifth, and Edwin, were still missing, and the knights continued to dig. Falling rubble had smashed through the slate roof of the Great Hall, crushing Derek's map table and all its carefully arrayed markers. Oddly, though, the old chapel, which had stood beneath the tower, was unscathed. The knights bore their slain brethren inside and arrayed them, mercifully swathed in white shrouds, beside the dead scout. They spoke no prayer, nor sang any hymns for the dead.

Derek stood alone in the chapel in the dim half-light, his eyes on the bier. The thought that his brother was dead worked its way into his brain. Though they hadn't found the body, no one could have survived such a blast.

Behind him, the chapel door creaked softly open. Derek didn't turn. Footsteps approached, and Derek recognized his visitor by the rattle of arrows in the man's quiver. "My fault, Aran," he said tonelessly. "I should have stopped him."

Aran Tallbow had nothing to say to this. He shifted from one foot to the other, his armor clanking softly.

Derek turned to face him. "You have news," Derek said flatly. "Out with it!"

The red-haired knight shook his head. "Winfrid and I have assessed the damage. The walls are beyond repair. A well-ordered army could press through the breach within a day, whatever we did to block it."

"Then it's over," Derek said, and sagged wearily against the bier. "Though the siege has not yet begun, Castle Crownguard has fallen."

A knock fell on the chapel door. "Enter," Derek called. The door swung open, revealing Sir Winfrid, looking haggard. Like most of the knights, he was ashamed to remember his flight before the dragon.

"They've found another one of the knights," Winfrid said. "Not Edwin," he added, seeing Derek's eyes spark. "A Sir Rogan Whitemantle, Knight of the Crown."

"Whitemantle," echoed Derek. He tried to put a face

to the name, but couldn't. "Have him brought in here
with the others after they dig him out—"

"But, my lord," Sir Winfrid said, "he still lives."

Derek and Aran exchanged shocked glances, then ran
for the door.

* * * * *

Sir Rogan was still alive, but whether that was good
fortune was open to debate. His legs were crushed. His
back was broken. His face was burned, his hair and
moustaches scorched off the skin by the dragon's lightning breath. His head lolled weakly from one side to the
other. Each breath came as a wet rattle, and blood
welled on his seared lips.

"He asked to speak with you, my lord," said one of
the knights.

Derek and Aran picked their way through the rubble,
joining the small circle of knights who had stopped trying to patch the sundered walls long enough to comfort
their dying fellow. "Sir Rogan," Derek said, crouching
down. He wrinkled his nose at the stench of charred
flesh. "I am here. What did you mean to tell me?"

"My lord," Rogan wheezed. His wide, glazed eyes
flicked toward Derek. His voice was no louder than a
whisper, and Derek and Aran had to lean close to hear.
"Your . . . brother . . ." He moaned. Aran quietly clasped
the young knight's hand, then looked at Derek.

Derek's face was flat, emotionless. "What about
him?"

"He stabbed the dragon . . . through . . . the neck,"
Rogan gasped. "He didn't let go . . . didn't let go . . ." He
sucked an agonized breath through his teeth, squeezing

his eyes shut. He didn't open them again. "Just before the tower . . . fell, I saw the . . . dragon flying away. He . . . Edwin . . . was still . . . holding on to . . . his . . . sword . . ."

He let out a long, slow breath. His arm went limp, and his hand slipped from Aran's grasp.

"Rest," Aran whispered, laying a hand on the dead knight's forehead. He looked up at Derek hopefully, but his friend's expression had not changed. "What do you think?"

Derek shook his head. "Delirious."

"Probably." Aran stroked his red moustache thoughtfully. "You're right, of course, Derek. Still . . ." He regarded Derek carefully.

"No," Derek said, and there was no missing the finality in his tone. "My brother is dead, somewhere beneath this." He waved his hand at the blasted stones piled around them. "This isn't one of the old tales, Aran. Men don't fly away, clinging to swords stuck in dragons' throats. My brother believed those songs all his life, and they led to his death. I won't have him become another tale, based on the ravings of a dying man."

Aran pursed his lips as if he meant to argue, but then he saw the fierce look in Derek's eyes, nodded, and lay Sir Rogan's hand on his stilled breast. "We can waste no more time in a fruitless search. This will be my brother's bier."

Derek rose and brushed off his cloak. "Put this man in the chapel with the others," he bade, nodding at Rogan's body. "Then stop digging. Assemble the men." Glowering, he turned his back on the dead knight and walked away.

* * * * *

Two hours later, Castle Crownguard stood empty. Once mighty and impregnable, it was now just another smoldering ruin on the Solamnic countryside. The knights left behind what they could not carry on horseback, including the bodies of the scout, Edwin's five knights, and Sir Pax Garett.

Derek had found the old veteran dead on the floor of his chambers. Some of the knights whispered that, unable to face his flight before the dragon, Pax had taken his life according to the old custom. Derek soon put a stop to that rumor. Pax had been an old man, and the dragon's otherworldly fear had simply finished what age had begun. His heart had burst, that was all.

The ride west was slow and perilous. Aran rode ahead, on point guard, an arrow always nocked on his bowstring as he watched for signs of hobgoblin ambush. Sir Winfrid brought up the rear, his gaze flicking back toward the castle long after the wooded hills blocked it from view. All the knights eyed the skies nervously, watching for screaming blue death to descend upon them, but the sky remained clear as a summer's day, though the autumn chill in the wind seemed to have come to stay.

Lord Derek hardly spoke a word, and the men let him be. He had, after all, lost brother, home and holdings in one stroke. Whatever black mood he was nursing, he had earned it. Still, one young Knight of the Crown who caught a glimpse of his lord's eyes during the ride remarked to his fellows that Derek's mien was not that of a man beset by rage or grief.

"He looks," the knight observed, "more like a man at a khas table, thinking about his opponent's last move." The knight did not speak of what else he had seen, hough: it wasn't right to speculate that the gleam in our lord's eyes might be that of nascent madness.

As it happened, there was no hobgoblin ambush. The nights rode two days and nights along the Solanthus Road without seeing anything more threatening than a quirrel. Then, on the third day, Aran rode back to join he main party. The knights reached warily for swords nd maces, but Aran waved them off. He pulled up efore Derek as Sir Winfrid rode forward to join them.

"What news?" Derek asked in a voice raspy from disuse.

"A company of knights on the road ahead," Aran eplied. "Brian Donner rides at the fore."

"Our reinforcements," muttered Winfrid bitterly.

Derek nodded, his lips tightening. "Ride on."

* * * * *

Soon after, the knights of Castle Crownguard met the ompany of Sir Brian Donner, Knight of the Sword. The einforcements numbered no more than twenty, and)erek raved in impotent fury at the sight of how few nen his call for aid had mustered.

Not that it much mattered, he told himself, when he almed down. They were too late to be of any use, any-vay. Then he glanced at them again, and thought twice. 'erhaps, he told himself, measuring up the khas table nce more, they will be more useful than a whole regi-nent. He turned the thought over and over in his mind, nd every time he considered it, his foul mood bright-ned just a bit. By the time Brian Donner hailed them nd spurred his gray stallion ahead of his company to ,reet them, Derek Crownguard was feeling almost civil.

"My friends!" called Sir Brian, his silver-shot, blond

moustaches curling above a warm smile. "'Tis meet tha we three should be together again."

Aran rode up to Brian, and the pair clasped arms Long ago, before Lord Kerwin Crownguard's death Derek, Brian and Aran had quested together. They ha seen more exploits than any could remember, unti Derek had left to assume the mantle of lordship over hi family's fief. The reunion robbed Aran of speech. Dere came forward next, and gripped Sir Brian's gauntletec hand. He might have even smiled, had Brian no frowned toward the men of Castle Crownguard an cleared his throat roughly.

"But, why have you not awaited our arrival at you keep, my lord?" he asked.

Aran looked away, his brow darkening. Dere announced proudly. "There is no need," he said. "W broke the siege, and I am now sending my men north t Vingaard Keep, to aid her defenders. I ask you to do th same."

Sir Winfrid stared at Derek in shock. "M-My lord?" h stammered.

Beside him, Aran's jaw went slack.

Derek turned to look at the two, and Aran flinched a the sight of the peculiar glitter in Derek's cold, blu eyes. "I'm telling Sir Brian about our defeat of th enemy army and their dragons," Derek said. He turnec back to Brian. "It was glorious! My men fought bril liantly, and finally the enemy disengaged. I suppos they decided Castle Crownguard wasn't worth th effort. They won't dare molest it again."

"Derek . . ." whispered Aran.

Derek turned in his saddle and stared piercingly a the red-haired knight. "What?" he demanded.

Aran drew himself up in alarm—the glitter in Derek's eyes had turned into a blaze. "N-nothing," Aran murmured, cold dread gnawing at his stomach. "It will wait."

"So you were victorious," Brian said. His eyes flicked nervously between Derek and Aran.

"Aye!" Derek roared, swinging around again. "They ran from the sight of us! We broke their spirit, gave them reason to fear the Knights of Solamnia!"

Brian nodded hesitantly. He glanced back at Derek's knights again. Some of them were acting restless. Derek's words had carried back to them.

"What—" Brian began, then faltered.

Derek looked at him sharply, and Aran glanced quickly away.

"Wh-what became of Sir Edwin?" Brian asked.

Derek's left eye twitched, just once. Brian tried not to notice.

"Lost, in honorable battle, along with Sir Pax Garett," Derek answered hollowly. "They fought valiantly, but 'tis war, and men die. Perhaps," he added, his eyes narrowing to glinting slits, "they wouldn't have, if your men had reached us sooner."

Brian flushed. "M-My lord, we've ridden as hard as we could—"

"No, no, it isn't your fault, my friend," Derek said, and rested his gauntleted hand on Brian's shoulder. "It's Gunthar's. He has betrayed us, betrayed the whole Knighthood. His inaction cost us dearly, and he shall hear of it. You, Sir Brian, will travel with Aran and myself to Sancrist, where we will tell the High Council of my triumph and Lord Gunthar's deceit. Then," he added, his face splitting into a grin that made Aran shudder, "then I shall be Lord Knight!"

* * * * *

They rode on. When the road forked, the knights continued north, following Sir Winfrid. They did not speak of the battle of Castle Crownguard, then or ever. Except to tell how Edwin Crownguard, standing atop the Northeast Tower, had died defending his home.

Derek, Aran and Brian turned south. When they were well away from the others, Brian could no longer contain the question that boiled within him. "My lord," he asked, "what *truly* happened at Castle Crownguard?"

Derek turned slowly, his saddle creaking, and fixed Sir Brian with a glittering stare that could have bored through steel. "Victory," he said. "Glorious victory. And one day, the bards will sing of it."

Brian glanced at Aran, who shook his head. The message in the knight's worried eyes was clear: *Ask no more.*

Brian sucked pensively on his lower lip, then shrugged. "If that is your wish, my lord," he said, and looked back toward the dusty road.

None of the three said anything more that day.

A Lull In the Battle
Linda P. Baker

Lashing rain on the ragged slate roof.

Thunder from the heavens, punctuated by bright slashes of lightning.

The clunk of earthenware mugs on the bar as boisterous voices called for more ale.

The smack of flesh on flesh as one of his men backhanded another.

Shouts of derision. Cries of support.

The smashing of broken furniture.

This was the relaxing respite from battle.

To Laronnar, First Captain of Second Company in the Dragonarmy of the Dark Queen, the respite from battle was neither restful nor relaxing.

He stood, and his chair crashed to the floor. The sound didn't merit a notice in the bedlam of the tavern.

With three quick, irritated strides, he was beside two men grappling together. He grabbed each by their collars and used the momentum of their struggles to crack their heads together. As both reeled, he snatched the dagger from the hand of the smallest one and drove it into the table. The blade stuck there, quivering in the smoky light.

"No fighting," he said quietly, ominously.

He glared at the comely barmaid, tall and red-haired. She was the cause of the fight. It was the second such fight he'd broken up over her.

"No more fighting." This time, the words were for her.

The smaller of the two men meekly recovered his dagger. The other mumbled an apology.

Laronnar stomped back to his chair, so sure of his anger, of his control over his men, that he didn't hesitate to turn his back on them. With his foot, he righted the chair, slammed it into place, and sank into it. He motioned for the red-haired barmaid to refill his mug. He was in no mood for barroom brawling. Not when Second Company should be out fighting the enemy instead.

His plan had been working beautifully. Just as he'd predicted, the contingent of humans and dwarves who were guarding the port town of Lenat had been taken completely by surprise when Second Company swooped in from over the water. They must have appeared to be an attack direct from the dark gods, arrowing from out of the fiery afternoon sun.

The troops of Paladine had fled Lenat in disarray, heading for the safety of the nearby foothills. Laronnar's squad had been about to cut them off when the storm came. The rain had stung like needles, the driving wind had caught in the wings of the dragons and sent them careening through the sky. Had Laronnar been in command, they would have continued to fight regardless.

"So close," he muttered for the twentieth time since he'd entered the bar, taking a gulp of ale. "We were almost upon them!" He glanced at his lieutenant, Haylis, sitting across the table from him, then up at the red-haired barmaid who was pouring more ale into his mug.

Haylis grinned at him over the shoulder of the plump, pert woman who was perched on his knee. His dirty blonde hair was perpetually rumpled. It stuck up in tufts, giving him a malicious, devilish look despite his affable grin.

"Forget it, Captain," he urged, laughing as the woman tried to wriggle free of his grasp. "We took the town. We'll get the Warriors of Light tomorrow."

Despite the weight of the woman on his lap, Haylis lifted a booted foot, planted it on the hip of the red-haired barmaid and shoved her toward Laronnar. "Enjoy the lull."

More by reflex than desire, Laronnar caught the barmaid as she stumbled toward him. She fell into his lap, balancing the pitcher of ale so well that she spilled not a drop. Her lips were pursed, whether in mock anger or real, Laronnar could not tell. Nor did he care. She was the spoils of the victors.

She tried to rise, but he held her close, pressing his face into the riot of waist-length red curls. She smelled of smoke and ale and spice—better than anyone with whom Laronnar had come into contact for several months.

Perhaps Haylis was right. There was, after all, nothing Laronnar could do about the battle until the storm blew over and his commanding officer decided they could sound the recall. He might as well loosen up.

The Striped Monkey Tavern was the best of a sorry lot in the port town of Lenat, but it was better than some he'd seen. The tavern was lit with sputtering candles, smoky torches and one huge fireplace that gave off a sooty light and the scent of damp wood. The heavy oak bar gleamed with the shine of generations of elbows, and the plank floors showed the scarring of many boots. The ale was bitter, but plentiful, and while the barmaids weren't overly friendly, they were at least too frightened to be openly hostile.

The **L**-shaped common room of the tavern was filled with troops—a mishmash of human, ogre, and draconian, all celebrating in high spirit. Noisy. Unwashed, smelling of battle and blood. Rapaciously trying to down as much ale as possible, to attract the attention of the barmaids before the storm blew over and the battle was renewed.

"Here now." Laronnar snuggled the red-haired one closer, caressing the pale skin of her upper arms, halting her wiggling attempts to escape. "I'm the captain of this ragtag band. You'll not do any bet—"

The front doors of the Striped Monkey slammed open, admitting a gust of rain and cold wind scented of the sea. The torches guttered in their tarnished brass sconces. A woman near the door squealed in mock dismay. A silvered, honeyed male voice entered the door ahead of its owner. "It was a glorious battle! There we were, hovering above the forest, the tops of the vallenwoods tickling my dragon's belly . . ."

Laronnar froze. The red-haired barmaid started, rose when his grip around her waist loosened. His fingers bit into the soft flesh of her forearm as he yanked her back to his lap, cursing softly.

The voice of Dralan, Laronnar's commander, continued, "We were waiting for the elves when they burst from cover of the forest. They were so intent on ambush . . ."

The words, spoken in a tone both deep and masterful, made Laronnar feel as if he'd bitten down on slivered glass. "Bastard," he murmured under his breath. "My plan!" Trying to ignore Dralan's voice, Laronnar caught the barmaid's ruffled collar and tugged her closer.

Across the table, the woman on Haylis's lap was cooing like a dove in mating season. Evading Haylis's kiss, she slipped her arm from around his neck, dislodging his grip. "Is that the Commander?" she breathed. "He's handsome. And so elegant!"

In response to her words, Dralan tossed his cape back over his shoulders, revealing the shining steel-gray dragonscale armor that molded his muscular form and the medallion, supposedly a gift of Takhisis—Queen of the Dark Gods—which glittered gold and emerald on his broad chest.

"Oh . . ." the woman sighed.

As Laronnar glared across the table, the barmaid on his lap regarded him speculatively. "He *is* very handsome," she agreed.

Her soft, appreciative voice made Laronnar want to slide his fingers around her slender neck and squeeze until a less irksome sound was forced out.

Dralan, of royal blood and majestic bearing, was everything Laronnar would never be. Tall, broad-shouldered, imposing. Black-haired and handsome. His blue eyes and rich voice had the ability to attract any woman he chose, and his demeanor gained him the respect and trust of every man he met. Dralan was a gentleman, well-bred, stylish, educated, a favorite of the Dragonlady who led their army.

The Dragonlady did not even know Laronnar was alive. Had she met him on the street, she would not have glanced at him twice for all that he was as tall as Dralan and as strong.

Dralan's piercing, sky-blue gaze noted the interest of the two women. He bowed first to Laronnar, his first captain, managing to make a simple gesture of greeting both elegant and scornful, and bestowed a smile on the red-haired female perched on his lap.

"Kaelay!"

So that was her name.

Dralan held out his hand. Without a word, the red-haired beauty slid off Laronnar's knee.

Laronnar caught the tail of her apron and tried to yank her back.

This time, she refused to be detained. Slapping playfully at his hands, she sashayed away. She glanced back over her shoulder, laughter sparkling in her green eyes. "After all, it was the commander's strategy that won the day. I want to hear the rest of his story."

Laronnar scowled and started to rise. "That was *my* plan!" he hissed under his breath.

"Captain!" Haylis cried, jumping to his feet before Laronnar could stand. "I'll get us another drink!" He snatched up the pitcher and poured what was left into Laronnar's mug. Then he loudly demanded more ale.

For a moment, Laronnar hesitated, half out of his seat, his gaze locked with Dralan's. The commander's eyes were open wide, curious, ready to allow Laronnar to back down, ready to meet any challenge. The retinue of human and draconians surrounding Dralan regarded Laronnar with obvious hostility.

A feverish thrill rushed up his back, made the hair on the back of his neck stand erect.

"Let it go, Captain," Haylis whispered, his back to the crowd at the door. "Do you want to be skinned alive? Or worse? You know the Blue Dragonlady favors him."

The words penetrated, but not for the reason Haylis mentioned. Laronnar, with his straight brown hair and eyes his own mother called 'mean brown,' did have one talent the commander would never match. No one was more brilliant, more devious, in planning a battle. Dralan had so far claimed Laronnar's success for his own. It was the reason Dralan tolerated him.

And the reason Laronnar tolerated Dralan was because of the promise he had made. Dralan had promised him that, this time, a quick, successful campaign in Lenat would merit a mention of his prowess to the Blue Dragonlady. This would, Laronnar was sure, bring him the career opportunities he desired.

For that chance, if for no other reason, he must hold his tongue, must disguise his hatred and jealousy. With effort that must have showed on his sharply angled face, Laronnar forced his anger down, pulled it back into a constricted knot in his belly.

Feigning disinterest, Laronnar picked up the mug of ale and upended it. The bitter liquid, thick as oil, seared his throat. Haylis tapped him lightly on the arm, urging him to sit.

Dralan's voice boomed out again, calling for drinks, and became fainter, a mere annoying buzz, as he was drawn to the bar by the throng of sniveling, obsequious sycophants. Several voices clamored to buy him a drink if he would only continue his "fascinating tales."

"Of deeds that are not his own," Laronnar muttered, but the anger stayed in check, simmering. He shrugged and sat. Planting one booted foot firmly on the wooden plank floor, he shoved his chair onto its back legs and hooked the other foot around the rungs. The chair thunked against the wall, but amidst the noise and revelry of the crowded tavern, the sound went unnoticed.

Breathing an audible sigh of relief, Haylis, too, sat and

rocked his chair back.

Laronnar glared at his commander, who stood with his arm around the red-haired barmaid. "One day that draconian lizard who serves Dralan will find our illustrious commander with a dagger in his throat."

"Shh!" Haylis leaned across the table, glancing about to be sure no one had heard. "You should be more careful."

Laronnar glowered in the direction of the bar. Kaelay was waving the patrons away to make space for the commander. Soldiers and townees alike obeyed her without hesitation, stepping back.

The woman smiled at the commander as she handed him a flagon. Dralan turned his back on the crowd around him, admirers and aides forgotten. With greedy hands, he tucked her against his side and bent to whisper in her ear.

Laronnar snorted with disgust. "I wonder whose ideas he's claiming now."

"Was that really your idea, tricking the elves out of Silvanesti by leaving an ogre picnic party in the field?" Haylis said, trying to divert his friend's thoughts.

Laronnar forced his gaze away from the gorgeous woman who appeared to be devouring every false word. He took several healthy gulps of ale before slamming the flagon down on the table so hard that the little ale that was left sloshed over the rim, spattering the grimy tabletop.

"It was!" he declared. "As was the plan we used to take this stinking port."

"Coming in over the water, that was your idea?"

"Yes. And it was working, too. Not that it will matter if we sit here drinking and whoring until those damnable knights regroup." Laronnar glared around the bar, said loudly. "It was *my* plan. Have any of you heard otherwise?"

The port of Lenat was located on a jutting peninsula bordered by the Khurman Sea on the northeast and Bay of Balifor on the southwest. Although smaller than Port Balifor, which was across the Bay, Lenat would make an excellent staging ground for the army of the Dark Queen. Silvanesti, the elven stronghold, was less than one hundred and fifty miles to the south; only two hundred miles southwest was Sanction. Seizing this port had indeed been a splendid idea.

Laronnar's idea.

"No," Haylis said, a touch too quickly. He slapped his friend on the shoulder. "We'll be back in the field before you know it. The knights won't have the wits to regroup. Not after the scare we gave them."

Haylis's attempt at placating Laronnar only deepened his suspicions, but the warmth of the ale was beginning to take effect. His voice was nonchalant, a bit slurred as he spoke. "A thunderstorm is no excuse to break from the battle."

The wind sounded as if it might tear down the wall against which he leaned. He could hear the rain striking the plank walkway outside the tavern.

"No matter how ferocious," he added suddenly.

"You are not enjoying the ale, my lord?"

Laronnar started as a shadow blotted out the room and its boisterous patrons. His hand was already on the hilt of his sword when he realized the soft voice was that of the lovely red-haired barmaid. He relaxed, his hand slipping casually back to his thigh. His gaze, heavy lidded and sluggish, raked her from the tip of her head to the leather boots peeking from beneath her tunic.

Kaelay was magnificent. The cloud of red hair, so fiery that it made her pale skin seem as white as the sands at the edge of a bay, framed her face and shoulders. Her ivory tunic molded to the sweet curves of her breasts. The cloth was fastened on her shoulder with a plain wooden brooch, and the soft folds seemed precariously close to coming loose.

From hips to knees, the blood in Laronnar's veins quickened.

The woman deftly filled his mug. She swiped at the wooden table with a ragged cloth not much cleaner than the dingy floor. "I could not help but overhear. You would prefer to be about on such a wet night as this? I've heard that rest is good for the morale of the troops."

Laronnar mumbled, "It's good for the pocketbook of your master." He caught her arm and smiled—a slow, inviting smile that eased the sting of his sarcasm and made no attempt to disguise his interest.

He rubbed his thumb across the smooth, soft flesh of her wrist. She lowered her gaze to his caressing fingers. For a moment, Laronnar imagined he saw annoyance on her flawless face. Then she smiled at him, and his breath caught in his throat.

She bent down. Her lips were close. . . . "As I was saying, Kaelay"—Dralan's deep voice cut through the clamor and chatter surrounding them—"I saw at once that the sails of the vessels would give us the cover we needed."

Kaelay straightened. She glanced back over her shoulder at Dralan, then back to Laronnar, then back at Dralan, trying to make up her mind.

"We were already so low, gliding across the waves, I could taste the sea on my lips."

Dralan's smooth voice decided her. With a rueful little smile, she turned away.

Anger simmering, Laronnar allowed her to slip her hand free without a word.

Ignoring the calls for ale, Kaelay worked her way through the crowded tables to where Dralan stood, his back turned, one elegantly booted foot resting on the footrail.

Laronnar fumbled for his mug. He brought it to his mouth and drained it. Droplets of ale ran down his chin and dripped onto his white shirt. "Not this time," he vowed, rising.

Haylis rose as swiftly, grabbed his arm. "Captain! No! She's just trying to make you mad. If she had her way, we'd all kill each other. It would save the warriors of Lenat the trouble."

"I was already mad," Laronnar growled and strode away before Haylis could stop him. He caught up with Kaelay just as she edged closer to Dralan.

"The wind is quite different over the water . . ." Dralan was saying.

"Here now." Laronnar grabbed Kaelay's arm and pulled her toward him. She smelled of spices and malt and smoke. "You don't want to waste your time listening to his lies!"

Kaelay laughed, loudly enough to draw Dralan's attention, and tossed her long hair back over her shoulder. "Is it a waste of time to listen to your commander?"

"You're drunk, Laronnar." Dralan pushed between the two of them. His knuckles dug into Laronnar's breastplate. "The lady doesn't want to waste her time with you."

The anger he'd been repressing for far too long flared

in Laronnar, white-hot and corrosive. He tried to step around Dralan, fingers curled into fists.

Dralan blocked his way with an immaculate boot. He pressed his fist harder against Laronnar's chest. "I suggest you leave, Captain. I was just telling the ladies and gentlemen about my victory today."

My victory! Had Dralan thrown lava on Laronnar, he could not have better fueled his anger.

"That was my plan and you know it!" Laronnar's voice was low, barely controlled. "You said that this time—"

"That's enough, *Captain*." Dralan stressed the rank just enough that Laronnar understood his message. Much more easily than he had risen through the ranks, he could fall.

He could barely think through the rage and sense of injustice he felt. Dralan had never intended to honor his word. Never intended to give Laronnar credit.

Dralan regarded him with narrowed, laughing eyes.

Challenging his commanding officer in front of a tavern full of supporters was desperation. But Laronnar didn't even try to pull back, to cool the fury churning inside.

Suicide, said an inner voice through the wrath.

He glanced at Kaelay. Just the barest tip of her pink tongue snaked out and moistened her lips. The pupils of her eyes were so dilated he could barely see the brilliant green.

Suicide. He was beyond caring. "The plan was mine!" Laronnar shouted. The words ricocheted off the high ceiling, came back to him, more satisfying than a victory on the battlefield. He felt suddenly, abruptly, as sober as if he'd not had a drop of ale in a month. "All the plans were mine!"

Dralan's face transformed slowly, went from laughing to dangerous and nasty. Silently, deliberately, he placed his hand on his sword hilt.

"You've probably never planned a battle in your career." Laronnar jeered. "Oh—except maybe the time you ambushed those gully dwarves!"

Though his face was rigid and pale with anger, Dralan extended his hand, offering a handshake.

"Come, Captain," said Dralan coolly. "You know the rules."

Laronnar knew the rules. He enforced them for Dralan. Brawling wasn't permitted among the troops under Dralan's command. Dralan considered brawling uncivilized. But a dispute could be settled with a gentlemanly duel.

Laronnar sneered at the proffered handshake. It might masquerade as the gesture of a gentleman, but it was an old trick—shaking the hand of an opponent with feigned gentility while checking for a hidden weapon. Keeping his gaze warily on his commander, Laronnar pulled out the cestus that he wore looped over his weapons belt and worked it onto his hand.

Made of stiff ebony leather, the top part of the glove was reinforced by steel mesh, elven made, as delicate as a spider's web, as strong as chain mail. Razor edged spikes studded the knuckles.

With quick, deft movements, Laronnar slid what appeared to be a long dagger from its scabbard and flicked away the fake wooden hilt. What remained in his hand was a strong steel blade, three hands long, notched at the hiltless end. He jammed it into a slit in the glove, sliding it into a sheath along the top of his hand.

The metallic clicks were audible. The blade glinted blue in the torch light, as Laronnar flexed his hand, seating the glove onto his fingers. With deliberate slowness, he opened the catch that held his sword belt and allowed the weapon to drop.

Predictably, the gaze of everyone in the tavern, including Dralan, followed the fall of the sword to the floor.

Laronnar slashed inward with the blade that protruded from the back of his hand. His movement was sure, expert, so fast that Dralan stumbled back against the bar as the blade flashed past his face.

The commander recovered quickly and pushed away from the rail. He drew his sword. Pushing aside the draconian who was hovering at his elbow, Dralan stepped into a fighting stance. The crowd stumbled backward, clearing a space for the combat.

The two touched swords, gently, each testing the other's blade. Steel rasped against steel. Through the cestus, the song of the two blades danced across Laronnar's skin, skittered along his bones.

Laronnar attacked. Grasping his gloved hand with the other, he swung the blade at his commander with all his strength.

Dralan ducked out of range.

Laronnar allowed the force of the swing to wheel him completely around, used the momentum to carry him into another slashing sweep. Dralan met the blow, and their swords connected, clanged in the air with the booming peal of bells.

As Dralan swept back, his sword caught the wing of one of the hovering draconians. The knife-sharp edge sliced through the leathery webbing and green ichor prayed from the wound. The draconian howled in pain and was dragged back out of Dralan's path by a fellow lizard man.

The gawking crowd shoved and pushed away from the path of the fight. The two men danced back and forth parallel to the bar, their blades flashing and ringing as they met. The men cheered, enjoying the entertainment, not caring who won.

The cries of encouragement gave Laronnar strength, and he attacked with even more fury.

In the face of such power and speed, Dralan fell back. He parried each swing, but just barely, as he retreated. He dodged below a vicious slice, leapt into a chair and up onto a table. The table tottered dangerously beneath him. His sword slashed downward with alarming speed.

Now it was Laronnar who dodged, parrying a blow meant to split his skull. Now it was he who retreated out of range of Dralan's expert swings.

Dralan leaped down off the table, almost on top of him, and for a moment, the two men grappled hand to hand, swords waving dangerously in the air about their heads.

"I warned you," Dralan snarled. "Now you'll learn to heed your betters."

Laronnar saved his breath for the fight. He released his grip on Dralan's forearm and grabbed his neck. The bigger man gasped as Laronnar's thumb dug into the softness at the base of his throat.

Dralan crouched, then reared, shoving with the weight of his body. His grip torn away, Laronnar's fingers dug bloody furrows in Dralan's neck.

The two men circled, both gasping for breath.

Dralan shifted his sword to his left hand, wiped at his neck with his right. His fingers came away smeared with blood. He cursed, then attacked. His bladework was beautiful, a dance of agile feet, deft arm movements, the silver blade flashing in the candlelight.

Laronnar stumbled, fell backward across a table. Dralan struck, bringing his sword up high and straight down for the killing blow. Laronnar barely had time to twist aside. The blade whistled past his ear, thunked into the table where his head had been. Wood chips sprayed his cheek and neck.

Laronnar rolled off the table and crawled away on hands and knees. Dralan pursued, roaring with laughter, tossing tables aside as if they were mere branches instead of heavy oak trestles.

Laronnar came up fast, sword raised over his head as a shield. The tip of Dralan's sword sang along the edge, grazed Laronnar's hand and drew blood. But Laronnar was on his feet, backing away.

Dralan grinned, eyeing the blood dripping from his opponent's wrist. "Surrender, Laronnar. Perhaps if you grovel enough, I'll spare your life."

Laronnar feinted right, then rolled left across a table, then another, and came up facing Haylis, who, like Dralan's aide, was shifting to stay near his captain. In his hand, Haylis held the belt and sword Laronnar had dropped near the bar.

As Dralan charged, Laronnar snatched at the parrying dagger Haylis carried on his belt. Misunderstanding what his captain was trying to do, Haylis surged forward, offering the sword, and tangled the leather belt and his feet with Laronnar's.

Stumbling, Laronnar grabbed his lieutenant by the

houlder and twisted away. Dralan's sword slid into
Haylis's back.

The young man jerked in Laronnar's arms, gurgled
nce, and went limp, his expression mystified, aston-
shed. His blood poured out over Laronnar's arm.

"Bastard!" Laronnar snarled at Dralan.

The commander, his sword still buried in Haylis's
ody, was as surprised as his victim. "But I didn't—"
Dralan gabbled.

Laronnar thrust his fingers into Haylis's weapons belt
nd shoved the body into Dralan's arms. The dead
weight yanked the belt free, and Laronnar scrambled to
afety with it clutched in his fingers.

By the time Dralan freed his sword, Laronnar had
what he wanted—Haylis's dagger. For good measure,
e had also snagged the lieutenant's deadly little hand-
eld crossbow and shoved it into his belt.

Dralan saw the dagger and sneered. A dagger was a
ackup weapon, a thief's weapon.

Laronnar grinned, parried Dralan's first blow with his
lade. Laronnar had a little surprise in store for his
rainless commander.

So contemptuous he was almost nonchalant, Dralan
wung again. Laronnar deflected the swing with dagger
nd sword. As Dralan toyed with him, Laronnar shifted
lightly, leading his enemy back toward the open floor.
aronnar stepped into the aisle. Free of obstacles, he
ttacked with his bladed fist, swinging viciously outward, deliberately leaving his left side open.

Dralan stepped into the trap.

Laronnar lifted his left arm and thumbed the jeweled
utton on the dagger's guard. The two narrow parrying
lades sprang away from the center blade. Laronnar

trapped Dralan's bright and shining sword in the thre
blades of the dagger. Sparks flew. Metal sang agains
metal. The dagger slid halfway down Dralan's blade
Laronnar twisted, putting his weight behind it. Th
snap of the blade was a crack like lightning in the sud
denly quiet tavern.

Dralan cursed and flung the hilt of the broken swor
at Laronnar.

Laronnar swung into motion, dropped the dagge
and slashed with his right hand. He swung his blade
fist in a tight half-circle.

The blade caught Dralan on the shoulder as h
tumbled backward. The sharp edge bit through leathe
and cloth and skin. Dralan fell, clutching his blood
arm.

Laronnar slashed downward, gloved fist grasped i
his left hand. At the last moment, Dralan rolled side
ways. Laronnar's sword cut through empty air wher
Dralan had been, slammed into the heavy oak planks
Laronnar fell to his knees. Dralan kicked.

Pain exploded through Laronnar's head as the com
mander's heavy boot connected with his face. The forc
of the blow tossed him backward. His hand crumpled
beneath him.

Laronnar groaned and tried to roll to his feet. H
could taste blood on his lips, on his tongue, and h
focused on it, on the sickening, coppery flavor. Clutch
ing his head, he managed to push up on his knees and
elbows. Regaining his balance, he saw Dralan being
helped to his feet by Kaelay.

The draconian aide was holding Dralan's dropped
sword, giving it to the commander.

On his knees, Laronnar drew Haylis's small crossbov

from his belt and fired.

There was a sound from the tavern patrons, like the rising and falling of the wind, as the draconian fell backward through the rickety doors of the tavern, the crossbow quarrel protruding from his forehead.

Rain and cold salt wind whooshed in through the demolished doors. Shuffling and pushing, the patrons crowded near the door, shifted back along the walls, loath to leave the fight, loath to get wet while watching it.

Dralan, chest heaving, stood dumbfounded for a moment. He stared at his dead aide and at the long sword, glinting dully on the boardwalk, still clutched in the draconian's fist. Dralan looked at Laronnar. "Two good men have died because of our quarrel. Let us end this now," he rasped, hand extended, palm up. "Honorably."

Laronnar forced himself, by will alone, to stand. The cold air snuffed the candles, whipped the torches, leaving the room in flickering semidarkness. The chill helped to clear his head. He nodded in agreement and extended his hand—the gloved hand.

Something in his face, or his eyes, gave him away.

Dralan wheeled away, falling toward his aide's body.

Laronnar hooked his fingers in the back of Dralan's armor and dragged him into the tavern just as the commander grabbed the lizard man's sword. Using the steel-augmented glove covering the back of his hand, Laronnar struck the back of Dralan's head.

He could tell by the way Dralan lurched and slid down in his grasp that the blow had stunned him. But Dralan maintained his grip on the two-handed sword, dragging it with him.

Laronnar swiped at Dralan's exposed neck with the

spikes, raking the side of his head. Dralan roared like a wounded animal, threw himself forward. His weight tore his armor from Laronnar's fingers.

Dralan righted himself and wheeled drunkenly to face Laronnar. Blood was streaming down the side of his head, spreading across his white collar. He clutched the draconian sword in his hands.

Dralan struck, but his grip on the sword was clumsy, his vision impaired. The blade hit Laronnar's ribs, and he went down. The next blow was better aimed and the tip of the blade slashed into his thigh. Laronnar gulped in air. Pain shot up his leg.

The pain gave him fear. The fear fed him strength. Laronnar kicked out with his good leg. The sword flew out of Dralan's hands, and Laronnar crawled away, clutching his bleeding leg.

Stumbling, Dralan scrabbled for the sword, found it, and came after his enemy. He tried to turn the heavy sword, to correct his grip on the huge pommel. Pausing, he swiped his sleeve across his face, to clear the blood from his eyes.

Laronnar scooted back. He still held the crossbow. His fingers fumbled for the quarrels on his belt. They were all gone—lost in the struggle!

Laronnar upended a table, crawled behind it and tried to pull himself up. His leg burned like it was on fire. And he could hear the scraping of Dralan's approach.

Then he felt a soft hand on his arm, urging him to remain where he was. He wheeled to face the red-haired barmaid, Kaelay, smiling sweetly and smelling of spice. Not a hair was mussed, but her tunic was smeared with blood across the breast where she had helped his commander to stand.

"Let me help you," she said, and her voice carried the music of rushing wind.

"What game is this you play?!" Laronnar snarled. He dropped the useless crossbow and clutched a broken chair leg like a dagger. "Revenge for the taking of your paltry little town?"

"No game, my lord. I will help the one who can best help me in return." She went to her knees beside him.

"First you help him, then me." Laronnar tried again to stand. The sound of scuffing, booted feet on the plank floor was very near.

Laronnar fell, and she caught him.

The heavy sword suddenly clanged down on the table edge, right above his head. Wood chips and splinters flew.

Ignoring the twisting pain in his thigh, Laronnar pushed himself to his feet. He swung the chair leg. It whistled in the air just inches from Dralan's face, and he lost his footing. The heavy sword slid from the edge of the table, its tip thunking on the floor.

While Dralan struggled to lift the sword once more, Laronnar wheeled on Kaelay.

"Bitch! You try to distract me!" He slashed at her as he had slashed at Dralan. "If you kill us all, more will come to take our places."

More nimbly than his commander, she dodged. "I will help the one who would help me in return," she repeated. Her sweetness was gone, replaced with venom and fire. She slapped her hand down on his, clutching his fist, and uttered a single, incomprehensible word.

Laronnar gasped. A noxious, smoky glow flared from

the joining of their hands. It stung his flesh like the barbs of nettles.

Kaelay uttered another word, then released his hand so abruptly he reeled. In place of the chair leg, where the warmth of her hand had covered his, was the little crossbow, loaded with a quarrel and cocked.

Her quick intake of breath alerted him. He wheeled to meet Dralan, who held the draconian sword, gleaming, in his hands.

Laronnar stepped forward and pressed the loaded crossbow to Dralan's chest. Laronnar pulled the smooth trigger of the bow.

The little quarrel, only a hand long, exploded Dralan's heart, just as Dralan's sword hit Laronnar's shoulder. Pain spangled out and down, but it was amazingly mild.

Laronnar watched surprise, then anger, flit across Dralan's face. Watched Dralan's dead fingers slide off the sword. Watched as Dralan slipped to the floor. Heard the sword rattle as it fell off his shoulder and hit the table edge, then the floor.

And Laronnar was still standing!

Cautiously, he moved his chin just half an inch to the side, just half an inch down, shifted his gaze to his shoulder. No blood. No torn flesh or bloodied bone ends. The sword had not cut him! How—?

He turned to Kaelay. She had moved away and was standing alone among the jumble of tables near the door. She smiled and shrugged, the movement tugging the soft tunic across her breasts. Then she turned away.

Before he could go after her, a rousing cheer went up from the soldiers who had remained in the bar. They rushed Laronnar, grabbing up his numb hands to shake them, pounding him on the back in congratulation.

* * * * *

Laronnar stepped out of the inn and breathed deeply of rain-freshened salt air. The call to battle had been sounded. The lull was over.

In the evening sky, the twinkling of the night's first stars glinted off puddles of water on the rough boardwalk. The street before him was a mire, so empty and quiet that he could hear the sound of the sea, the creaking of the ships at water's edge.

He had won! He was commander now. His heart still thudded with the quick pulse of battle, of exhilaration and pride. His wounds burned. His shoulders ached. He was stumbling from exhaustion, but he didn't care. His ears rang from the shouts and toasts to his new title: *Commander* Laronnar.

He spread his arms wide to embrace the coming night, the coming battle. Now all he had to do was find the green-eyed wizardess who had helped him win the duel. He could make good use of such power.

In the darkness of the sky above him, a dragon circled, once, twice, then swooped low and landed with hardly a sound. Not his fierce blue dragon with its black button eyes. The commander's dragon, Char.

A savage, treacherous creature, all grace and power, malevolence and majesty, Char had been ordered to partner with Dralan by the Dark Queen herself. The huge creature lifted its feet gracefully, stepped across the muddy street.

Laronnar watched the dragon warily.

Had she come to congratulate him? Or kill him? Suddenly gone was the pulsing exhilaration of battle, the joy. His breath caught in his throat.

Across her shoulders and chest, Char wore an elegantly tooled leather riding harness and a saddle decorated with braid and gleaming jewels. A band crisscrossed the broad, scaly expanse of her chest. In the center of it, embossed in metallic threads in five colors, was the symbol of the Dark Queen, a five-headed dragon.

"It was a fair fight," he croaked. He swallowed visibly, but no moisture came to ease the dryness in his mouth and throat. He went to one knee before the huge creature. "Ask any of them! Don't kill me!"

"Death." Char rumbled deep in her broad chest, her voice both bantering and sarcastic. "Is this what you expect in return, Laronnar? I said I would help the one who would help me."

Laronnar lifted his gaze. He stared into sly, shining eyes, as emerald as the spring grass of the plains. He smelled spice and smoke. He forgot his fear of being crisped where he stood.

"You—!" He gasped.

"My lord?" She took one huge step forward and lowered her left leg, extending it for him to climb up.

"It was you!" he exclaimed, then realized he was staring at her with his mouth foolishly agape. He took a steadying breath. "It was you who helped me! You who—"

She inclined her head. Yes.

"Why?"

"Perhaps I was tired of Dralan. Perhaps I thought him too . . . honorable," she said softly.

The sweet malice in her tone sent a shiver, half fear, half pleasure, down Laronnar's spine.

"Perhaps I judged you more worthy." The huge dragon turned her head side to side, regarding him as one would examine some species of bug under a light.

Laronnar stretched to the limit of his height and bowed, never taking his eyes from the dragon. "Thank—"

Char's snort halted the formality. "The man who fights on my back must be merciless. Without scruple. Without honor. So fiendish even his own mother would hesitate to turn her back on him."

She leaned down, craning her thick neck until her glowing green eyes were level with his. "Be warned. I have ambition to be more than the leader of a small company in my mistress's army. You will go the way of Dralan if you fail me."

Laronnar settled his helmet down over his head, snapped the faceplate into place.

He stepped up onto Char's thick foreleg and vaulted into the saddle on her back. "We have a battle to win!"

With a thrust of her powerful legs, Char leapt into the sky and spread her enormous wings to catch the crisp salt air.

Proper Tribute
Janet Pack

"Weak-minded human." Bronze dragon Tariskatt's scathing baritone boomed in Lyndruss's ears the moment the muscled warrior slogged onto the muddy field where Sky Squadron mounts awaited their riders. The scaled beast scented the air, making clear he found a distasteful odor in the rain. "Drunk again."

The war against Takhisis and her minions for domination of Ansalon was approaching its zenith. All fighters of all stations had answered the desperate call to arms. All races fought, if not side by side, then army beside army. It was a time when even a hand scythe was welcomed as a weapon. A good dragon and rider team was invaluable, especially if the pair had as much battle experience as did Tariskatt and Lyndruss. Unfortunately, their hatred for each other reached as deep as the roots of the Kharolis Mountains did into the heart of Krynn.

The fighter flushed hot even in the cold rain, his muscles twitched with anger. His hand, holding the dragon's harness and small saddle in an oiled bag, clenched to a fist, his blunt, scarred fingers stabbing through the leather. His partner always seemed to know the words that would irritate him most. Tariskatt was adept at getting in the first verbal thrust, especially on mornings when Lyndruss had a hangover. His dragon's grating voice worsened the fighter's throbbing headache and further soured his prickly nature.

"You drink, human, because you are afraid," said the dragon. "You drown your cowardice in ale."

"I try to drown your stink in ale," said Lyndruss.

The dragon's sulfurous stench, tainted by old blood, was overwhelming in damp weather. Lyndruss forced himself to walk closer. Tariskatt's tail twitched a little. Reading his partner's signs, the human readied himself for an attack. Anything could happen. Despite his hangover, the fighter prepared to dodge slashing horns or savage teeth.

He did not drink to drown his fear. Lyndruss did not get staggering drunk, as did some other fighters. He drank to take the edge off blood-ridden memories, and to be social.

He had always, since childhood, detested dragons. He hated everything about them—their arrogance, their smell, their sarcasm. And now here he was, riding a dragon in the war against Takhisis. The fighter's mouth tightened in a half-smile as he considered the sudden and peculiar twists life could take.

The gray rain spilled down his cheeks and chin like cold tears. Lyndruss would much rather skewer this ice-hearted beast with a dragonlance than ride him into battle. Lyndruss took another step toward his duty.

A tiny motion brought the human to full alert. A muscle over the dragon's left eye arched, making one of the protrusions on his forehead stand almost erect. The movement usually happened before a swipe from the razor-sharp claws. Lyndruss already bore several scars.

Lyndruss braced himself, kept walking.

The dragon's chill eyes held the warrior's blue ones. Tariskatt's tail thumped the mud a little harder.

The fighting skills Lyndruss had picked up in his

travels both helped and hindered him. At first General Sharrid had given him high rank and the command of a ground force. Two years ago the general had persuaded Lyndruss to abandon that in favor of training with a young copper dragon. It soon became clear that the human fighter needed an older mount, a match for his own experience. And when Sharrid named a man to lead the air squadron, Lyndruss had been the logical choice. The only dragon available with enough expertise, however, had been acid-tongued, human-loathing Tariskatt.

Lyndruss complained about his mount to everyone, especially to General Sharrid. The commander told him that at this point in the war he had no choice but to pair the enemies. They must do their best with a bad situation. No one understood how it happened, but gradually their battles with each other enhanced their work as a team. Once in the air, they learned to use their mutual enmity as a sharp lance against a mutual foe.

"Moth," snarled Tariskatt, tail lashing now. "Come to my flame."

"Yellow snake," Lyndruss returned, holding his ground.

He kept both eyes on the dragon, bending his knees more and digging his boots into the mud. The big bronze never accepted the dragonlance harness without a fight, and the warrior was almost within range to cast the leather strips attached to the saddle and dragonlance mount across the animal's shoulders. He changed his grip on the leather bag, ready to yank it open and throw at the first opportunity.

Tossing his head to one side, the dragon suddenly changed direction and lanced a long horn straight for

Lyndruss. Incisors gleamed and parted as Tariskatt opened his mouth to bite.

The human dodged, slipped in the mud, reestablished a foothold, and dove beneath the bronze's chest under his right leg. The massive jaw tore into the slimy earth where the fighter had stood. Rolling, Lyndruss pulled the harness from its bag and threw the buckle end and the saddle over the thickest part of Tariskatt's neck. Ducking, he managed to evade scything claws. The warrior dashed from beneath the dragon, just as Tariskatt lowered his ungainly body into the muck, intending to flatten the human. Lyndruss grabbed a gleaming shoulder scale and swung himself upward. Pulling the harness straps together, the fighter fastened the buckle one-handed. He dropped back down into the mud.

The dragon's head turned toward him. Lyndruss sped away until he was out of range of the teeth, claws, and tail of his battle partner. He turned to the dragon, panting.

"Not bad," he crowed.

Insolently, Tariskatt lifted a claw. A muddy rag hung from it, the same color as the saturated dirt beneath his feet, but showing a bit of dark red the hue of Lyndruss's tunic. Tariskatt dropped the distasteful rag and cleaned his knifelike claws fastidiously on a nearby boulder.

Lyndruss looked at his torn tunic.

The dragon had snagged loose material above the fighter's left hip. A little deeper and Tariskatt might have rent a mortal gout of flesh from his body.

"You worm!" Lyndruss taunted, to show he wasn't unnerved by the close call. "You deserve flaying alive. Boiling oil should be poured into your nose and down your throat, and carving beetles set between your toes—"

"Silence!" ordered a familiar voice.

Lyndruss turned. "General Sharrid!"

The tall older man crossed his arms over his chest. His prematurely white hair, pulled into a braid at the back of his head, gleamed against the gray rain. "Stop that talk!"

The warrior straightened, saluted. "But—"

"Humans," snorted the dragon, shifting restlessly. "There's neither a good meal nor a competent rider in this camp."

The commander's eyes shifted from dragon to man and his mouth tightened. "Some day your hatred will come between you in the skies. One or the other will make a mistake. Then I'll lose both of you. Our forces are shrinking too much for me to allow that. Understand me. You're leaders. I want no more fights, no more insults. It's lowering morale." He stared from one to the other and back, his eyes blinking against the rain. "Answer me."

"Yes, sir," the warrior replied reluctantly.

"I understand human language," rumbled the dragon. "And insect as well."

The general ignored Tariskatt, took one step toward Lyndruss, and lowered his voice. "By the way, I hear the draconians have called in reinforcements and their best airborne team. You'll face Zanark Kreiss and his red dragon."

"Curor Bonebreak?" The dragon pounced on the information like choice prey. "A worthy opponent."

Sharrid laid his hand on Lyndruss's armored shoulder. "I dare not delay this battle for weather. Be wary. Clouds and rain can make things tricky, as you well know."

"Thank you, sir, but I—"

Tariskatt rumbled a warning.

"Uh, we—can handle them," Lyndruss amended, the general's eyes on him. "We have before."

Tariskatt looked into the clouds, impatience and boredom showing in the tilt of his head and the tension in his body.

Shaking his head, the general stepped back a pace. "The good gods ride with you."

"Thank you, sir."

Lyndruss shivered. Foreboding crawled up his back as a runnel of rain wormed its way beneath his leather armor. He expected an insult from his battle partner, but for once the bronze remained silent.

Battle approached and though neither admitted it, this was what each lived for.

* * * * *

Tariskatt dove into a dense cloud bank. Raindrops stung Lyndruss's skin. His eyes fought to penetrate layers of murk, but grays upon grays were all he could see.

They were suddenly clear of the low clouds, diving directly for a scout dragon and its young human rider caparisoned in the blue and gold of Takhisis's armies. With a roar Tariskatt took the smaller beast from above, dropping his impressive weight in perfect position against the middle of the enemy dragon's neck. Tariskatt's huge claws reached, clamped, and held. Floundering, the scout dragon desperately pumped the air with its wings, trying to match the war dragon's great speed as he surged upward. After a short desperate time of trying to keep up, something snapped like a large breaking branch in the scout dragon's neck. Lyndruss's mount let go. The Dark Queen's dragon folded and fell, accompanied by terrified screams from its rider.

"Huh," complained Tariskatt. "The crowd."

They were now joined by six other pairs of fighters, the entire compliment of the Sky Squadron. The dragons formed a loose wedge behind Tariskatt and Lyndruss, staying well away from their unpredictable and inflammatory leader. Several times the group circled the soggy battlefield where foot soldiers were gathering into formations, then winged off through the rain looking for battle.

Tariskatt's wingbeats increased suddenly, throwing Lyndruss against the back of the saddle again as the bronze spotted something. He attacked at full speed. The rival dragon, a black, howled and met him with outstretched claws as its rider brandished his sword. Lyndruss crouched behind the dragonlance, watching for an opportunity to use the weapon.

"Right," the warrior shouted to the bronze, seeing a weakness open in the black's defense. "Right, quarter roll!"

Tariskatt wasted no time. Ducking beyond raking talons, he plunged almost underneath their enemy. This set the human's weapon in the perfect spot. Lyndruss drove the metal-tipped shaft through the enemy's scales and deep into the chest of the black. The dragon howled, surprised at the mortal wound, and tried vainly to latch its teeth onto Tariskatt's neck.

Sinking, the rival dragon only managed to catch its talons in the top of one of the bronze's chest plates, loosening it. Tariskatt grunted and backwinged, gaining a little altitude. Rapidly weakening, the black's wingbeats slowed and faltered, its eyes glazed. The shaft of the dragonlance snapped as the bronze rose and their enemy dropped. Lyndruss saluted as the black and his dazed rider plummeted.

Tariskatt suddenly writhed, the shock of a surprise attack vibrating throughout his body. Lyndruss gasped and clutched the hilt of the useless dragonlance, sharing his mount's stun almost as if they were one entity. After what seemed a very long moment of silence, the bronze bellowed, whirling, to face Curor Bonebreak and a grinning Zanark Kreiss.

Lyndruss cursed. The enemy had used their moment of euphoria and relief after the kill to the best advantage possible. It was a trick from which he should have guarded them, a trick he himself had warned the rest of his flight squadron about only a short time ago.

"We finally meet," yelled Kreiss through the hissing rain. "I've heard you might make decent sport."

Not bothering to reply, Lyndruss considered their situation. He knew Tariskatt was wounded, but he dared not take his eyes off the deadly pair before him to find out how badly. He glanced around, searching for help. The rest of the fighters were engaged in their own battles. He and his partner were on their own.

Feeling naked without the dragonlance and knowing he and his mount were now very much on the defensive, the warrior pulled off his back scabbard, drawing the hand-and-a-half blade. He grimly prepared for a battle of wits and short weapons.

Still showing a good deal of strength, Tariskatt banked abruptly and flew into a thick cloud to gain time. He made two tight turns to throw off their opponents, and winged back to the battle.

Lyndruss had hoped for more surprise. Kreiss and

Curor had made nearly the same maneuver. The enemy only had to swing three-quarters of the way around in a tight circle before the dragons clashed. No more than a dozen heartbeats passed while the warrior settled into his saddle, howled his battle cry, and readied his sword.

Roars and slashes with teeth and claws. Wind whipping across wing leather. The dragons grunted in their efforts to outmaneuver one another, augmented by the commands of their riders.

Tariskatt wheeled for a strike. Lyndruss knocked away Kreiss's spear with his blade and made a feint he couldn't hope to follow up because of his dragon's rising wing. His enemy brought his two-handed weapon around quickly for another pass, the long sharp blade slicing across the bronze rider's upper arm. Lyndruss felt the heavy hide of his boiled-leather armor part, hot blood cascade down his arm. It wasn't a deep wound, but bad enough. Lyndruss set his mind against the pain and readied his hand-and-a-half again as the dragons twisted and grappled.

Kreiss made a series of shallow slashes along Tariskatt's near wing just to irritate the dragon. They weren't serious, but blood loss from cuts such as those could change the course of battle as a dragon tired. Lyndruss had to get rid of his opponent's spear and even the odds.

"Up, Tariskatt! Now!" The warrior urged his bronze partner upward with all of his soul. Turning slightly away from the red, the big metallic-hued dragon beat against the rain for altitude. Speed and a little distance opened the tiniest opportunity for Lyndruss and his sword. He timed his blow between his own mount's wingbeats, leaning out of the saddle and cutting down on the red wing. Lyndruss had hoped to break the bone. Instead a deep ragged gash opened, spewing red droplets that looked almost black in the dim light.

Curor howled and broke off, shearing into a cloud. The bronze followed him closely and attacked, causing the red to turn again. His tattered wing gave him less maneuverability. Kreiss poked at them with his lance, exactly what Lyndruss wanted. Watching his timing, the warrior held his blade until the last instant. With a mighty downstroke he severed the pole a few inches from its silvery head. Cursing, the enemy dropped the useless wood, pulled his own sword, and urged his mount to attack. The dragons met with a deafening crash.

The battle continued until the bronze heaved with exertion and his rider felt giddy. Neither pair of fighters dared call a halt to breathe. Neither dared to give away the slightest advantage to his enemy.

"This day will belong to the dragon with more stamina," thought Lyndruss grimly, hacking at Bonebreak's legs. "Let that be you, Tariskatt." One of the red's claws glanced across his forehead, leaving a shallow cut before the warrior could parry. He shook blood from his eyes and fought on.

The wily bronze pulled out his most devastating attacks and his best feints. Curor matched them with his own inventive strategies. The dragons were as equal a match as the two warriors on their backs. The humans shouted instructions and slashed at one another as their mounts bowed, lifted, and grappled in the mid-sky dance of death.

The bloody froth on his dragon's lips and the faltering effort in his wingbeats finally told Lyndruss the truth.

Today would not belong to him and Tariskatt. Nor could any days in the future. Zanark Kreiss's broad smile showed that he knew where victory lay.

With a bellow loud enough to shake the sky, the bronze gathered himself, winged away, turned suddenly, and made a mad dive toward the red. Far too late to change the plunge into anything else but an all-out attack, Lyndruss lifted his sword with a numb arm and assessed the closing distance with hot, dry eyes. He figured the time of collision precisely right. The warrior realized too late what this assault would cost his partner.

"You damned worm!" he howled. "Are you mad? Don't—"

Seeing his danger, Curor labored for similar speed. The dragons came together with shattering force. One of Bonebreak's claws caught in the loose scale on Tariskatt's chest. Lyndruss saw the hideous gleam of delight in the dragon's eye as the red ripped and scythed until unprotected flesh glistened.

With equal satisfaction, Lyndruss stabbed deep into the red dragon's eye and braced himself as the beast jerked his head back, bellowing. Tariskatt took advantage of the reaction and raked all four feet down, down and down over mutilated scales on Bonebreak's belly. Curor howled as his own red drops fell among the rain. He broke off abruptly, veering for the relative cover of thick clouds, leaving the metallic dragon and his rider masters of the sky.

"Down, easy," ordered Lyndruss as Tariskatt shuddered, trying to reset his wingbeats to normal speed. They faltered. The dragon had no strength left. His wings stopped, sending them into a steep dive. Mind sagging with the pain of his wounds, Lyndruss prepared himself to die. Closing his eyes, he commended himself and his excellent fighting dragon to Paladine.

A jerk made his eyes open on gray, always gray. They were flying again. The motions were uneven and still aimed groundward, but their angle was much more gentle.

"What are you doing?" his rider yelled.

The silent dragon labored on, blood speckling his rain-shined scales.

"What are you doing? Tariskatt! Answer me!"

"Landing," the bronze finally gasped, voice rusty with effort.

"You don't have the strength. We'll go down together."

"No."

Communication cost the beast much in energy. Lyndruss gritted his teeth, knowing he could do nothing to change his partner's mind. The only thing the warrior could do now was ride the rest of the way, and hope.

Their landing was hard. Tariskatt tried his best to backwing them, but the effort proved too much for his remaining strength. He crashed, breaking both front legs with cracking sounds that sent splinters of agony through Lyndruss's soul. The impact widened the wounds in the dragon's chest as he skidded. With a grunt of pain Tariskatt lay where he had fallen, unable to move.

Lyndruss sliced through the waist straps of his harness with his sword and tossed the weapon to the ground. Sliding down the beast's shoulder, he hit the mud at a run and came to a stop at Tariskatt's head.

The brilliance of his partner's eye was already fading

as the dragon's lifeblood stained the puddled rain. Lyndruss could only watch, caught in a welter of unfamiliar emotions. He felt desolate, at a loss as to what to do, and frustrated there was no way to save the great bronze.

"Our fight will be remembered in songs," the dragon whispered. It almost seemed as if he was trying to comfort the human.

"Only winners make songs," Lyndruss replied savagely, kneeling in the mud beside the horned face that had suddenly become as precious as life to him.

The one metallic eye the fighter could see blinked once, far too slowly. "You're a good rider, human. Don't let it go to your head." Tariskatt's chest heaved one last time. His eye closed, he shuddered. The bronze dragon lay completely still.

Lyndruss felt a great, tearing pain. A scream surged through his mind and through his lungs. Raising his face to the heavens, he roared the dragon's name again and again and again. The best friend he'd never realized. The dependable partner. The great intellect so unlike his own. Only his dragon, who had known and understood his strengths and foibles as no other ever had, mattered.

Frustrated, Lyndruss stared into the skies, watching the battle that, for him and his partner, was over. Lowering his head, the fighter stumbled through the rain toward a cliff rising at the edge of the plain.

The top of that cliff burned in Lyndruss's mind like a beacon. The warrior climbed the rain-slick height, bruising his hands and knees. He welcomed the small pains that pushed through his dulled senses.

Staring at the battlefield carnage below, lit by a lurid sun setting between two banks of thunderheads, Lyndruss realized what he wanted most. To die with such a great dragon warrior as Tariskatt would have been an honor. But the last act of that crazy beast had been to save him, the human rider he loathed.

Was the final wish of Tariskatt's dragon-centered mind to die without a human on his back? But Lyndruss *had* been on his back, ridden the dragon down, been the only witness to the great beast's demise and his parting words. A compliment. Had the two of them used hate to cover other, more unfamiliar emotions?

Desolation swept his soul. Lyndruss felt cheated by the dragon, an enemy turned friend suddenly gone. He felt cheated by life. He desired release from his mortal body with every fiber of his being.

His eyes dropped to the edge of the cliff on which he stood. All he had to do was step into the fading light, already dim enough to hide the base of the sheer stone wall and the talus that littered its foot far below. So easy. So final. He raised one foot over the void.

So wrong. The warrior threw himself backward, shaking. After fighting Takhisis's army for many months with Tariskatt, he couldn't, no, *should not* make his last act wasteful.

A slow smile stretched his mouth, his blue eyes flamed as a thought arrowed through his mental agony. Quickly he turned away from the brink. He skidded recklessly down the same slope he'd lately climbed, taking small boulders, bushes, and showers of gravel with him.

His new sense of purpose glowed as brightly as Tariskatt's bronze scales. There was a way for Lyndruss to take final advantage of his skill, as well as honor the dragon. He ran back to the battlefield and began stripping weapons from the dead, collecting as many as he could carry. Distributing them about his body took some time, but the fighter didn't care. Everything had to be within easy reach—hung from thongs laced through holes punched in his leather armor, his belt, wherever he could find space. It no longer mattered if the heavy leather was ruined. Soon he would not need it any more.

Lyndruss rested for a moment after he'd finished. Then, with his usual thoroughness, he checked the positions of the knives, maces, swords, bows, and arrows he now wore. The fighter began walking toward the largest enemy war camp in the area. He would sneak in under cover of darkness, taking out sentry after sentry. Then, just at the right moment, he would fling himself into the midst of the draconians and the Dragon Highlords, yelling his new battle cry.

His would be a proper tribute to the best companion he'd ever have. Lyndruss planned to take many of Takhisis's minions with him into death, shouting the great bronze dragon's name.

Tariskatt would thunder once more among his enemies.

Blind
Kevin T. Stein

Dragons . . . are free to choose among the alignments
of the gods.

The Creation of the World

"Cheats," Borac muttered under his breath. Turning away from
his four companions, he pretended to reach into a riding
bag. From under the gaze of the men sitting cross-
legged at the foot-table, Borac slid off the bottom quarter of the card deck and palmed them in a strong grip.
The rest he tossed into a nearby cookfire.

"What game next?" Tynan grunted, drinking deeply
from a flask. When one of the others tried to grab the
bottle, Tynan scowled and swung the flask into the
man's nose. The man yelped more in anger than pain
and reached for his sword. A threatening look from
Tynan cowed the man into submission. He wiped at his
bloody nose.

Borac used the distraction to run his thumb over the
edges of the cards. Under his sensitive fingers, he could
feel that half were marked at the edges. He sneered and
threw the remaining quarter into the fire, shaking his head
in disgust. This time, he didn't care if anyone saw him.

"What's your problem?" Tynan demanded, pulling
out a handful of dice from inside his battle-worn black
riding armor.

The smoke from the camp's fires mingled with the
stink of sweat and unwashed bodies in Borac's nostrils.

His companions were among those of the most unwashed, with the exception of Captain Tynan, who at least had enough self-respect to clean himself after every sortie. But his general appearance was ragged, like a beggar who had stolen his clothes from a soldier found lying in a field.

"Cheats and liars, boasters and braggarts! I hate you all," Borac said. "You have no honor nor respect for a better man."

Tynan glanced at his companions, winked. "If there were another *man* sitting at the table things might be different. All I see is you, Borac!"

Borac clenched his fists so hard the leather of his gloves creaked above the general din of the camp. He had come to this point many times during this war, when he wanted to kill the men with whom he was forced to fight. His muscles strained tightly beneath his immaculate jet black clothes. He rose slowly, carefully, to his feet.

"You, Tynan," Borac stated coolly, pausing, taking a deep breath with each word, "are so . . . *lucky* . . . to have the Dark Queen's alliance."

Borac could smell their fear, all except Tynan, who was too drunk to be afraid. Tynan's expression dropped to bored neutrality.

"Live with it." he muttered and took another pull from the wine bottle. When he was done, he looked sidelong at the man with the bloody nose, who now held a greasy rag to his face.

"I've more respect for this idiot," Tynan said, jerking his thumb at the man. "He takes what he wants—or tries to. All you do, Borac, is whimper like a woman about fairness and the Alliance."

"The Alliance is the only thing keeping you alive,

Tynan," Borac returned. "I'd like to kill you myself."

Tynan sneered. "Go ahead . . ." The other men shrank back, away from the pair. Borac hesitated, fists clenched. Tynan drank from the bottle and rattled the dice.

Borac's hands unclenched. "You don't deserve the honor."

Tynan laughed raucously. He opened his hand and let everyone see the dice, shook them loudly till they all got the idea, pulling out their own. They all made a point of not meeting Borac's gaze. They picked their favorites by color and pips. After Tynan's first roll, they shouted, money changing hands quickly, losing dice picked out among the winners.

"Afraid to fight, eh, Borac?" Tynan said without looking up from his throw. He laughed harshly at his companion's misfortune and scooped up the coins from the little table.

"You talk of 'honor' and 'respect.' You demand it." Tynan looked straight into Borac's eyes. "We earn it."

Borac stared back, his muscles slowly relaxing. He let his face go slack.

The men laughed and good-naturedly cursed Tynan. Their eyes reflected back the light of the fire. Tynan threw his dice. From the bounce of the purple die, Borac saw that Tynan's dice were loaded.

"Cheat . . ." Borac said again, softly.

Tynan ignored the comment, taking his dice and money from the table. He raised his hand for another throw. Borac spat on the table before the dice fell.

The center of the table dissolved. Borac's spit turned the wood black.

"Humans! Fools and liars," Borac shouted.

The men at the table yelled in fear, scrambling away

from their places on the ground. "Damn you, Borac!" Tynan yelled. "I'd like to kill you myself! You'd better be thankful for the damned Alliance!"

Borac flexed his muscles once, his clothes vanishing into the growing darkness of his flesh. He could feel the comfortable magic of the amulet tht gave him human form. He spread his wings against the night, his gaze cutting the darkness, his vision clear.

The Queen of Darkness forced he and his kind to follow the terms of the Alliance, the alliance of dragons with humans. But he did not have to like it—or them.

* * * * *

"I just get to sleep and the commander wakes me," Tynan grumbled, hauling a saddle onto Borac's wide back. He expertly tightened the straps that slid across the black dragon's chest. "Says you've got another 'secret mission.' "

Borac said nothing, letting his chest relax enough for the man to make the necessary adjustments. He kept his eyes forward, his head resting on his front claws, staring at nothing.

"What's your secret mission this time, huh? If there *is* one!"

"It's been reported that the enemy has gained a cleric of Mishakal. He's healing their wounded. The general wants the cleric dead," Borac replied, voice grating.

"Oh, yeah?" Tynan woke up a little. He shrugged. "So how do we find this cleric?"

Tynan's favored weapons were javelins, and he kept a brace on either side of himself, over twenty in total. He also kept a short lance mounted on the saddle in a wide, static guard, a duplicate of the lance and guard used by the enemy. The man was obviously waiting for an answer.

Borac remained silent. The lance and guard reminded him of the cursed dragonlances, and that only made his mood that much darker. He did not care to answer any of his rider's questions.

Tynan strapped his sword onto his side, the sword he often said was enchanted to slay the weak and bring victory to the strong. Using a simple spell, Borac had found no magic on the blade, or on any of Tynan's other possessions. The man was all brag and smoke.

With a final check of his armor, Tynan drew the black leather hood over his head to protect his face against the abrasion of flying in the dust and cold, then donned his dented helm. Borac glanced back briefly, remembering every blow Tynan had received on that helm, every battle and every campaign. And in each, he had seen the human give no mercy to the fallen, no quarter. He cared nothing about the men he had slaughtered until the drinking started at the end of the day. Then the stories of his own prowess never ceased.

"I know what you're thinking, Borac," Tynan rumbled from within his helm. He pulled himself up by the horn of the saddle, dragging the straps uncomfortably across Borac's chest. When he had settled, putting his feet in the stirrups, he swung the lance into a neutral position and took hold of the reins that led to the harness around the dragon's muzzle. "I know what you're thinking, and I don't care. You just keep quiet. I'll treat you like any other horse."

Tynan pulled hard on the reins, forcing Borac to lift his head. Borac took to the air, keeping his fury to himself. Over the sound of the rushing wind, Tynan called,

"You're working with us, now, dragon! For *our* side. And that's where you'll stay."

* * * * *

"Pull up, damn you!" Tynan bellowed through the smoke, letting loose another black javelin as he twisted around in the saddle, a favorite stunt. Borac attempted to act as commanded, but could not find room to maneuver. A silver dragon above him converged with another swooping in from the left.

Tynan's javelin caught one of the silvers in the wing. It hesitated in its aerial lunge long enough for Borac to draw his wings in a moment, then unfurl them to their full span, catching the air and forcing himself higher. The first dragon shot past in a move Borac considered very immature. The dragon's rider was forced to clutch to the saddle to avoid falling off.

Tynan was kicking Borac frantically in the sides, pointing downward. With a quick glance around the aerial circus to ensure that he was in no immediate danger, Borac ignored Tynan's commands. The dragon opened wide the pit deep within himself, where his anger and bile lived and seethed. The taste on his long tongue was dark and thick, and when the acid left his jaws in a gout, he felt as if he spit out all his hatred for Tynan, for Tynan's friends, for all humans.

The acid splattered the silver dragon and its rider. Borac kept himself aloft, ignoring Tynan's continued commands and kicks, watched as the silver wings of his enemy were eaten away by the acid. The dragon, a young female, screamed as she felt herself dying from the attack. Unable to keep herself in the air, she spiraled downward. Finally, losing all capacity for flight, she dropped. Her body punched a hole in the wall of smoke, then vanished.

The dragon's rider screamed in pain and terror, screams that ended abruptly.

Borac rose higher into the sky, flying through the smoke. He guessed he was the oldest, most experienced dragon in this sortie. There was little to fear. Amidst the turmoil, however, they'd seen nothing of a cleric.

Tynan cracked Borac on the side of the head with a javelin tip, knocking the dragon from his reverie. "I gave you a command!" Tynan yelled. "I expect to be obey—"

Tynan's words were cut off in a gurgle of pain, his chest was pierced from behind by the bright silver tip of a dragonlance. The weapon tore through Tynan's body and struck Borac in the head above his eye ridge. Borac shuddered with pain, twisted his head to remove the barbed tip of the dragonlance. Another silver dragon, older and very experienced, had risen among the clouds and battlefield smoke to catch its enemy unaware.

The fiery agony of the dragonlance stripped Borac of all sensibilities. He dropped from the sky, a great black stone, agony driving consciousness away, instinct taking control. Ground and sky shifted dizzily as Borac continued to fall, assured that his foe would not follow him down such a steep, insane path. Tynan's lifeless body, harnessed in the saddle, jolted and jounced. Borac was glad Tynan was dead, wished them all dead. He wished for the ground to swallow him whole and lay himself to rest. To be free of this pain. . . .

* * * * *

. . . Borac faded back into consciousness. He lay crumpled against the hillsides where the battle between the forces of good and the armies of evil continued to wage. He was too weak to fly, and was aware that the fall had broken . . . something. He could not feel anything except the burning in his head.

The dragonlance had penetrated the bony plating around his left eye. He could barely see through his right eye, his left was almost blind from blood.

Weakly, Borac lifted his bloodied head. Tynan lay nearby. He had landed on his head; his neck snapped, his body at an odd angle. Borac felt nothing. Survival. That, now, was all that mattered.

There were many other dead soldiers nearby, from both sides. Borac felt himself slipping back into darkness. He needed a plan. A moment's panic overwhelmed him as he reached out his magic to touch the amulet. At first, it did not respond and he feared he might have lost it. Then, the magic worked.

Borac willed himself to the shape he wore among humans—broken bones of his wings became broken fingers, bruises and cuts scarred new flesh. His left eye burned with pain. Pulling himself with his few good fingers, he crawled over to one of the fallen soldiers of the enemy. He removed the man's clothes, donned them quickly, working around the pain, the agony. Then the blackness returned, fell harshly to crush him. . . .

* * * * *

Movement. Borac was jostled awake.

"He's alive!" someone whispered.

"Quiet!" a second man commanded. "Listen."

The wound over his eye continued to pulse blood, but now the eye was bandaged with a strip of cloth. His other eye was closed. He recognized the smell of humans.

A moment later, another man moved near Borac's right. "I hear nothing!" he said. There was the sound of sword scraping against shield, a rattle of armor, and shuffling dirt. "I'm going to try to find our company."

"We're not going anywhere!" the second man, perhaps the leader of these men, said. "A black dragon fell near here!"

The smell of human fear brought Borac closer to consciousness. He attempted to rouse himself further, unsure whether these men had penetrated his disguise, even clothed and in human form. They might be suspicious if they recognized the insignia on the uniform he had stolen. Borac clenched his teeth, letting himself feel the comfortable swell of acid within his belly. It brought some measure of relief. If he needed, he could revert back to his dragon body and kill these men in an instant, even wounded as he was.

"That dragon's around here, I tell you!" said the third man nervously. "I *feel* it. Can't you?"

Borac kept his face slack and his eye closed. He could hear them shiver in their armor, and they stank of terror.

"I'm going," the third man said. "The battle has turned! If we don't escape now, we'll never find our company!"

"What of the dragon? And this wounded man? We can't leave him here."

Borac waited for an answer.

"We'll bring him along. You go ahead, scout the way," the leader finally replied. "We'll follow."

Another sound of rattling armor, and the scout was gone over a ridge. Borac felt himself being shifted, his head propped up under something softer than the ground, probably a bedroll. "Let's try to find a couple of spears and make a transport for this man. We'll take him back to camp and pray to Mishakal her cleric can do something to save that eye."

A cleric. A cleric of Mishakal. Borac almost laughed at the irony. He, the perfect assassin, a dragon, wounded, disguised as a human, and dropped at the feet of the man he had orders to kill.

He almost laughed, but when they lifted him, the pain overwhelmed him. He dropped back into darkness. . . .

* * * * *

". . . slaughtering everyone!" Borac heard. "The wounded and the living!"

Borac stirred from his darkness and slowly opened his good eye. The pain had subsided somewhat, though the memory of the dragonlance was like a fresh stab reopening the wound.

"We've rested long enough!" the leader said. Borac eyed his rescuers. It seemed all the men were cut from the same cloth, each about the same height, the same size. Their white uniforms were tattered and their armor damaged, links missing from chain mail and plates dented by mace-blows. They wore their helms and had their weapons ready.

The leader gestured toward Borac, then bent to Borac's side. "It would have been easier on you if you had stayed asleep," he said. "Are you up to being moved?"

Borac said nothing. His muzzy thoughts wove themselves into the realization that this man and the others were risking their lives to save him. If he had heard this tale in a bar, he would have laughed derisively. He didn't feel like laughing now.

"Let's go," the leader commanded. They lifted Borac from the ground and carried him out of a small depression in the side of the hill where they'd been hiding. Two of six men pulled the transport made of a blanket and two spears, while the others surrounded him, weapons ready. There was a feeling in Borac's heart like no other he had felt in his long years. These men were actually *cooperating*, working together to save what they thought was one of their own. He wondered if they played dice.

The soldier to Borac's right suddenly toppled over, two arrows piercing his chest. The leader deflected a thrown spear with his shield. Before the first soldier dropped to the ground, a unit of fighters from the Dark Queen's army charged down the side of the hill. Their battle cry cut the air and seemed to penetrate straight into Borac's wound, making him wince.

"Sorry," one of the stretcher-bearers said as they laid down the transport as gently as possible, though quickly. They ran forward to meet the attackers.

The sound of battle raged in Borac's ears. The fight was evenly matched in numbers, but his rescuers were fatigued and demoralized. The leader had lost his white cassock to a long sword's cut that also drew a line of blood across his stomach. He fought on.

Behind him, from out of the trees, an archer raised his bow, arrow aimed at the leader's back.

Borac slowly raised his right hand. He spoke a spell of death with his human lips. The archer crumpled to the ground.

The leader never noticed. He locked blades with the enemy, pushing strongly until he broke free of the stalemate. He drew another blade from his belt, holding his broadsword one-handed.

With a swift short sword parry that left his opponent's guard open, the leader withdrew his broadsword from the chest of his enemy. The other man dropped to his knees. The leader raised his sword high above his head and cut viciously down, the wounded man barely parrying. With a cry and another swing, the leader finally killed his man.

"Where's that archer?" the leader cried to his men, using a foot on the dead man's chest for leverage to dislodge his sword.

"Here, sir. He's dead, sir!" one of the others reported. "Funny. There's not a mark on him."

"Just as well, then," the leader said as he knelt beside Borac. "Everything all right here?"

Borac looked the man in the eye. He saw concern, compassion. These men were sincere in their effort to get him to their cleric. On the Dark Queen's side, Borac knew he would have been left for dead long ago, abandoned. No honor, no courage. Cowards. And cheats.

"South," Borac whispered.

"What?"

Borac licked his lips. "Go south, not west."

The leader hesitated, staring at Borac. Then, to the others, he said, "We'll stop here awhile to gain our bearings. We can't afford another ambush. I want *all* of you to scout a half hour in *all* directions. We'll meet back here afterward."

The leader watched his men dash off across the field and hills. After a moment, the leader said, "You should be safe here for now. They'll be back soon to take you to the healer."

"I'm . . . a scout," Borac managed to say. Moving his jaw sent slivers of fire into his head.

"South," the leader repeated thoughtfully. Standing, the man checked his wounded stomach. Borac could smell that the cut wasn't deep. "Is there anything you need?"

Borac said nothing, slowly shaking his head. He felt himself slipping away.

The leader nodded once, stared a moment longer, then walked away, disappeared among the trees. Borac did not regret choosing the target of his spell; the leader would have been killed in a cowardly manner. Borac let out a deep breath and closed his eye, listening closely for the approach of the returning soldiers.

* * * * *

. . . Borac cursed the race of humans. It had been more than an hour since the others had left. He wondered if the fools had gotten themselves killed, picked off by marauding troops. He cursed them again for stupidly splitting up their strength rather than just forging ahead.

Borac tried to raise himself, but he was still helpless in the grip of the dragonlance's fire. His head dropped back onto the stretcher and he almost retched from the pain.

"Humans!" Borac cursed them all in the name of his Dark Queen.

Then, with a great groan, Borac lifted himself to a sitting position. He shifted his weight and got his legs under him and tried to stand. Growing faint, he fell over.

Someone caught him. "You've got to stay down."

It was the voice of the leader, come back from his scouting. Borac let himself relax, let himself be laid out again upon the stretcher.

"Where were you thinking of going?" the man asked. "Looking for us?"

Borac attempted to speak, but could only draw deep breaths to keep the pain at bay.

"We weren't gone that long. And you were right. We would have walked into the camp of the Dark Queen's army if we'd headed west. We've got to head south. Pick him up again," the leader commanded to the others. "He saved our lives. Let's do the same for him."

* * * * *

The words of the leader echoed in Borac's thoughts as the men carried him back into their lines. The forces of good were not yet routed but their retreat was in full effect. Those lightly wounded were being tended by physickers so they could return to the field and protect those too hurt to move themselves. Borac saw cavalry riding out to form a vanguard.

Borac was amazed at the cooperation and trust among the soldiers. No whips cracked, no threats, no drunken rowdiness. There was respect, discipline, friendship . . .

"We'll leave you here for now," the leader said. "We've got to return to the field."

With a wave, the man commanded his soldiers to lower Borac to the ground, placing him in front of a large white tent. The leader saluted once. "Perhaps we'll have the honor to stand with you in the field," he said. Then he and his men were gone, off to fulfill their duties.

An old man stepped out of the tent. His blue robes

156

were well kept, but his long white hair and beard were ragged and uneven. He knelt down beside Borac and carefully lifted the bandage over the wounded eye.

"Are . . ." Borac began, careful to keep his dragon's hate from spilling forth with his pain. "Are you the healer?"

The old man looked startled, either by the question or by something else. "Me? No! But he'll be with you shortly. I'm here to help keep your mind off the pain. Dice?"

Reaching into a pouch, the old man pulled out a handful of dice. Borac closed his eyes. This compassion was too much for him to bear. He was a mature dragon and had seen a great many things, but this . . . these humans were almost not credible.

"Come, come. I see you have your own dice. Risk a throw."

Borac reached into a black velvet bag and removed his own handful of dice. He motioned for the old man to throw. Borac watched carefully, very carefully, the spin of each die, the bounce . . .

"What are the stakes?" Borac asked.

"Life," said the old man.

Borac looked up, startled and wary.

The old man laughed. He held up a handful of coins.

The old man lost the first throw. And the third. Borac won five times, and twice they tied. The pain in Borac's head subsided, and he reached up, pulling the bandage away from his head. The bleeding had not quite stopped, and his vision was clouding.

"Did you see a black dragon on the field?" the old man asked, tossing a few coins to Borac.

Borac took the coins and added them to his stack. He shook his head.

"It is said that dragons are made from the essence of Krynn itself," the old man muttered, almost to himself. "I wonder if they can change from good to evil, from evil to good?"

Dice clattering on the low table, Borac let out a short breath. "I do not doubt it could happen."

Borac caught sight of a blue glow coming from a pendant that hung around the old man's throat. The sight in Borac's left eye was nearly gone.

"If you kill me now, dragon, you'll lose that eye," the old man said. "Join us! Give me your word you'll not turn back to evil and I will heal you!"

Borac's thoughts washed from one memory to the next, of the honor, courage, fairness he had seen in this army and the cowardice, mistrust, and cruelty he had witnessed in his own. With his fading sight, he peered closely at the medallion hanging from the old man's neck. It was a Medallion of Faith, with the symbol of Mishakal.

Borac stared at the medallion a long, quiet moment; the sound of the army's retreat was far in the background, but loud enough for him to hear.

His own army would have left him for dead, gladly. This one had saved him, but now they demanded something in return. That was the way of humans. Though their traits were different, they were still the same. And he, a dragon, was above them all.

Borac sighed, once tempted, now resigned. His dragon's hate bubbled slowly from his lips. He spit at the Medallion of Mishakal, burning it away from the chain.

"They'll find no trace of your body," Borac snarled.

As he pulled the old man into the tent, the sight in his eye fled forever.

Nature of the Beast
Teri McLaren

Falon, the chief scribe of Outpost Twelve, was having a very bad day.

"Pardon me for one moment, please. Blot, see to that fire! It's all smudge and no heat. My feet are freezing!" Falon shouted to the dirty-faced inkmaker, who spilled a pint of bubbling, jet black pigment across his hand in startled response.

"All right, gentlemen, shall we begin again?" The chief scribe rubbed his forehead and tried to focus his smoke-stung eyes on the two hunters before him. "I apologize. As you can see, I have a lot on my mind. Now, Kale, is it? Yes. You tell it this time. Edrin, you just be quiet until he is finished."

"But, sir—"

"I said be quiet. You have been shouting and my ears hurt. Go ahead, Kale."

"Well . . ." Kale began, his words barely audible. "We was up the mountain after bighorn and, uh, well, we hadn't seen nothin' all day but a half-eat carcass, and it was gettin' cold and late, so me and Edrin here said to Rilliger, let's go on back down, have a couple of pints down to the inn, ain't doin' no good anyway. But Rilliger had him a new knife, and he wanted to stay. Said it was maybe a bear got the dead sheep and we could get him instead, so we stayed, me and Kale over by a big rock and Rilliger at the edge of the clearin'. And then next thing, they was this big ol' dark shadder come over us, an' a real bad smell kinda like somethin' had died about last week, an' I hollered to Rilliger, 'Hey, Rilliger, that ain't like no bear I ever seen, take cover,' and Edrin said, 'I'm in!' but Rilliger . . . didn't answer." Kale paused, his face red from the effort of so many words and few pauses for breaths.

"And that's when you heard—" the chief scribe prompted.

"We heard something flappin' way overhead, 'bove the cloud cover, and then it got s' cold all the sudden we couldn't hardly move, but I saw an old cave 'hind us an' we run to ground there, and then it got dark, and we stayed `til mornin', shivered up together, half froze with no fire, and when it got light, we hunted for sign of Rilliger, but he was . . ."

"Gone. Just gone! No tracks atall!" cried Edrin, unable to hold back, his booming voice cracking with pain.

Falon nodded, at last getting the story straight.

"You say there was a bad smell? And a shadow passed over you? And there was a sudden coldness? Did you notice a lot of ice in the air?"

Kale and Edrin nodded, the two big hunters shuffling uncomfortably in the tight quarters of Falon's one-room scribal outpost. Falon understood that closed-in feeling. He was a big man himself, and he had been shut up in this room for five years, day in and day out, gathering information for Astinus's Bestiary, with only Ander and Del, his assistants, and the dwarf Blot, his latest inkmaker, for company. But just one more entry complete enough for the Bestiary—something like, say, a rare white dragon—would put him in the spacious offices of the Palanthan library itself. Where they had warm rooms. And the finest inks. And the smoothest vellum. The best of everything. This was the chance of a lifetime. The day had suddenly improved.

"Sir?" Edrin stepped closer. "What d' ya suppose it was got Rilliger?"

Falon raised his bushy gray brows and did his best to look concerned. "Gentlemen, at this point, without making an observation, I just don't know. You hadn't had a spot of grog on the hunt, now had you?"

Kale's face clouded with anger as he shook his head. "Sir, Rilliger's gone. We was his friends. We come a hard day's ride out here and we're asking f' yer help. Somethin' big and bad up there on our mountain, and we need to know the nature o' that beast. If it could take Rilliger, it could take anyone."

Falon nodded sagely. "Of course. My thoughts exactly. I'll put my best man on it. You gentlemen go on home now, and stay off the mountain until you hear from us."

Kale and Edrin moved silently out of the rough-hewn doorway, each of them ducking his head under its low beam. Falon turned to the corner of the room, where Ander, his most talented assistant, had been inking in the careful drawings of a drabfowl he had made a few days earlier. The bird had shown itself to be surprisingly colorful, despite its name.

"Ander . . ."

"Sir?" Ander answered, his eyes never leaving his work.

"Ander, have you been listening? Of course you have; you are a trained observer. So your training should have just told you that I have a very dangerous job here."

"Yes, sir. It sounds to me like those hunters ran across a dragon, very possibly a white from the location of the attack site. Although I've never heard of one this far north,

Mount Valcarsha is in the highest part of this range. It's cloaked in perpetual winter even at the halfway point," said the assistant scribe, mixing his inks to achieve the exact shade of the drabfowl's autumn crest feather.

"Well done, Ander. My conjecture precisely. You will then appreciate that I must send the man most able to complete such a difficult observation. I have chosen you," Falon replied.

Ander finally raised his head and faced the chief scribe. "Me, sir? But I just got back from the field! I still have to finish out these rough sketches. It's Del's turn to go out this time."

"He won't be back from the settlement for another week. And don't worry about your unfinished work. I'll take care of that for you. Anyway, there is a promotion in it this time for you, Ander. I thought you might like coming back from this one with the title of full scribe on your record. You are only one beast away from that, I see. Just one short," Falon observed as he ran his finger down a blank sheet of vellum.

Ander blinked at the chief scribe in disbelief, his quill poised in midair. "Do you mean that, sir? It's been so . . . long. I had almost given up hope."

Falon grinned capaciously. "Of course I mean it. Yes, I know things have moved, um, somewhat slowly for you here, but this is your big chance. Who knows, someday you could even have my job—after I've been sent up to Palanthas, of course. But that's not important right now. What is important is this white dragon. Oh, and Blot will go with you, for company and protection."

Ander remained silent for a long moment, marveling. An ice dragon . . . *his* contribution to Astinus's great book.

It was the chance of a lifetime.

"I'll do the outpost proud, sir." Ander smiled, his face glowing as he put aside the sketch of the drabfowl and began to stuff his pack with waybread and cheese, chalks and drawing tablets.

Falon motioned to Blot, who was lurking behind the coal bin, having just showered himself with an even darker coating of dust than usual. "You will give me the regular report . . . and a bit *more*, this time, Blot. Include a final sentence, please. A summary. This is a *special* case."

Falon winked. The dwarf's dirty face split into a slow, broad smile.

"As you wish, sir. A final sentence." He chortled.

* * * * *

Mount Valcarsha lay an arduous two days' journey from the outpost. Ander and Blot moved through the autumn-splashed countryside at a quick walk, meeting almost no one on the winding, uphill road. In fact, the only person they saw was a red-haired shepherdess who walked with them for a short time, showing them where to find fresh water and giving Ander a fairly complete visual description of the beast.

"Shiny. White. I couldn't see the head when it flew over, but its tail was long and thin, curling and looping at the end as it took the air. I'll tell you, sirs, that was the most frightened I've ever been in m' life. And the thing has got a good six of m' sheep in the last month!" she complained.

Ander drew a sketch as she spoke, adding the details as she remembered, and then showed her what her words had drawn.

"That's it! That's what I saw!" she exclaimed. "So what is it?"

"Just an educated guess, but I'd say it was a 'draco albicanus,' or a white dragon. Thanks for your excellent help," he called as they left the girl standing, awestruck, in the lane.

* * * * *

Another night of sleeping on frost-hardened ground and a day of cold rain later, they reached the base of Mount Valcarsha. Ander crouched low to the moist ground, blew hard upon the footprint in front of him to clear it of leaves, then took out his tape to measure the odd shape. "—twenty-four inches long, and about six inches deep, claw marks at the end of each of three toes. Blot, it looks like I was right. We've got a dragon up here somewhere. Nothing else makes a print like this. Look."

The dwarf stood peering over Ander's shoulder and nodding. "Yep. Dragon. Chief's gonna like this. Say, now that you got the print, and those drawings you did of what that shepherdess saw, how much more do you need for the entry?"

"Well, we'll need to get our own sighting, to do it right. Even better than that, though, would be some verifiable piece of physical evidence," Ander replied absently, sketching the print's shape upon his tablet.

"Let's go, then." said Blot, impatiently staring up the steep mountainside.

Half a day of hard climbing lay in front of them if they were to scout the territory the hunters had described. He fell in behind as Ander led the way for a long while through the bare twigs of lowland scrub. A little farther up, the scrub gave way to a thick evergreen forest, the early morning light breaking in hard shadows through its blue-green needles. Blot marked the path well.

He planned to be coming back down it alone.

* * * * *

Several hours and a few hundred feet later, they came upon a small clearing, the tall bordering pines split and shredded like kindling, the sheep's carcass still frozen in the glittering snow where it had been dropped.

Ander eased off his pack, sniffed the air, and listened. Not even the normal sounds of the winterbirds and the snow-tunneling rodents broke the eerie silence.

"This is where it happened, Blot. Look—there's where the dragon must have caught Rilliger."

Ander pointed to the scattered snow. Sure enough, only two sets of deep, hurried prints led away from the drift, while one more set stopped dead, as though the owner had simply taken flight. Blot squirmed as he eyed the dead bighorn, then looked skyward and thought about the hapless hunter.

"Hadn't we better find shelter? I mean, it's getting dark. And windy. What if the dragon comes back here?" the dwarf said nervously, his words carrying straight up the mountain.

"Yes, you're right." said Ander, looking up into the steely clouds. "I had hoped to be finished by now and back down to the valley. I don't like the look of that sky—could be more snow's on the way. The hunters mentioned a cave . . ." Ander said, searching the mountain's gray, ice-rimmed face until he saw a small, darker

165

shadow. "I think I see it."

A few minutes later, Blot struck a flint to some gathered kindling and fed a couple of larger windfallen
branches into a warming flame while Ander reviewed his
notes in the mouth of the narrow, high-vaulted cavern.

"Think we'll see the dragon before nightfall?" asked
Blot uneasily.

Ander smiled thoughtfully. "I don't think we'll have
to worry about that. Look at these walls—see how the
algae is scraped away and hangs in great wide sheets?
There are no bats hibernating in here either. And that
smell! Whew! It has to be coming from farther back in
the cave system. Blot, I think we're camping in one of
the back tunnels of the dragon's lair itself."

"The lair itself?" Blot's face turned pale beneath the
dirt and his scruffy beard.

"From the way the signs read, I'd say all we have to
do is explore a little farther here while we wait out the
storm. Then we can go back down."

"Explore?" Blot swallowed hard. "You mean, actually
go into its nest?"

"Relax, my friend. You can stay here by the fire if you
like while I have a look about the back of the cave.
There's waybread in the pack; help yourself," said
Ander, clapping Blot companionably on the back. "You
know, this is my big chance for a promotion; I can't let
Falon down. He's been helping advance my career in
this little nowhere place, and I owe him the very best
entry I can make. And, Blot, you know—I imagine that
he will do something nice for you, too. Before you came,
I used to be inkmaker, and then I got to be assistant
scribe after Del. Perhaps you'll advance when I do—
Falon will need another assistant scribe then. There

would be two more coins a week in it for you, too. And it's a much better job—you won't have to do all the dirty work!" Ander laughed, taking one of the smaller branches from the fire. He shook the thin coating of ash away to reveal its glowing heart, tucked his collecting bag into his belt, and started into the cave system.

Blot said nothing as he huddled closer to the small fire. But as Ander disappeared through the narrow crevice, he quietly unsheathed his long knife and followed, his face set into a dark scowl. The dwarf had business to conclude, and the sooner the better; just passing through a place where a dragon had been gave Blot the shakes.

He moved as quietly as he could behind the assistant scribe, the red glow of Ander's dim torch bobbing several feet ahead. Blot followed that glow through several ever-narrowing turns, the air in the cave growing more and more foul with the odor of decay, the walls and floor more slippery with unseen ice. A few yards into a suddenly wider tunnel, Ander's smoking branch threw its flickering light up the high vault of the passage, showing thirty-foot-high ice columns and row upon row of frozen stalactites, glittering like thousands of needle-sharp teeth, ready to rain down on them at the slightest disturbance.

And then the torch revealed something else.

Blot's stomach lurched as the faint light fell upon the source of the stench. The third hunter, or what was left of him, lay in a heap in the bottom of a great sinkhole, the most recent of many unfortunate victims. Blot could make out the bones of a moose, the skull of a bear, the jutting, crossed incisors of an ogre, all covered with the shed of large white scales.

Ander stood for a moment at the edge of the dark pit, unwilling to disturb the dead man. At last he knelt over the foul oubliette, and tenderly covered Rilliger's ruined face with a fold of the man's cloak. Ander reclaimed for Rilliger's friends the new knife that his stiffened hand yet clutched, and then gingerly picked a bright, diamond-shaped scale from the heap and placed it in a collecting bag.

This was the moment Blot had waited for—Ander had his physical evidence. Now Blot could finish his own work. He carefully raised his dagger, preparing to carry out Falon's orders. The final sentence. As long as Ander kept his back turned, it would be easy, he reminded himself. Just walk over and do it, push him into the pit with the hunter, blame it all on the dragon, and get out of there with the bag and the measurements. It would be easy.

It would be easy if he weren't so scared.

As Blot clutched at the wall to keep from fainting, he dislodged one of the long icicles. Its slight clatter was followed by a threatening chorus of eerie crystalline music. Ander lifted his head sharply at the sound, but did not look Blot's way as he tried to locate its source. Instead his eyes were fixed on the cave's north wall, as if he had heard something else. Then Blot heard it, too.

The click and scrape of claws, dragging something heavy.

Suddenly the cavern filled with a smell so foul that Blot's eyes watered uncontrollably and the hair inside his nostrils seemed to singe with every breath he took. He faltered, wiping his face, but had no time to recover before a noise shook the mountain and brought some of the shining crystalline ice daggers raining down upon their unprotected heads. His eyes tightly shut, Blot flattened himself against the wall while Ander dove for cover under a jutting rock. In a moment or two, the shaking stopped.

Fighting the dragonfear, holding the collecting bag over his head, Ander stood up, turned on his heel to leave. He stopped dead in his tracks in surprise. Blot stood a foot or two away from him, knife raised, a look of pure terror frozen upon his face.

"Shhh . . ." cautioned Ander, breathing a sigh of relief and pointing to the cavern roof. "Another loud noise and the other half of this mountain could come down on us." He stepped over a wide crevice and hastened to Blot's side. "You startled me for a moment there, but thanks for backing me up. We've got to get out of here! I found a scale, and the mystery of poor Rilliger's fate is solved. But I think we should leave now. The dragon's returned home!"

Blot slowly lowered the knife, his chance gone. But then Ander edged past him, moving down the tunnel, his back again vulnerable. From the north wall, the click and scrape of claws.

There was no time to lose. Blot raised the knife and took a step toward the torchlight, lunging for Ander's back. But the would-be assassin slipped on the ice-slick floor. Blot's feet went out from underneath him and he toppled backward into a deep crevice.

Ander turned at the sound of falling rock and ripping fabric.

"Blot! Are you all right?" Ander called softly, dodging a low-hanging lancet of ice. He held the sputtering torch out a few feet away from him, trying to find the inkmaker in the absolute darkness of the tunnel.

"Down here!" cried Blot, his voice muted and full of pain.

Ander bent to the sound. Holding his torch over the crevice, he discovered Blot three feet below, hanging over the grisly oubliette, held fast by one leg. He clutched at the other shin, a dark streak of blood beginning to ooze from his trouser.

"Hold on, Blot, I believe I can still reach you. Just don't move. And stay quiet," whispered Ander. Planting the torch into a crack in the cave wall, he lay down on the cold grit of the floor. Mercifully, the sounds coming from the north wall now seemed to be those of the great beast feeding. Ander leaned forward as far as he dared. Reaching down, he caught hold of Blot by the grimy shirt collar and pulled the dwarf up and over the edge.

"Put your arms around my neck!" Ander ordered. He lifted the dwarf upon his back and dashed through the corridor, back toward the fire and safety.

* * * * *

"There—that will do until we can get you to a proper healer," said Ander as he finished wrapping Blot's leg. "It's needing stitches sure enough, though. I know it must pain you."

"You have no idea." said Blot weakly.

"But, thank Gilean, the storm has moved off." Ander pointed to the mouth of the cave, where a bright beam of the afternoon sun glittered off the new dusting of snow. "There's enough light left to get down the mountain if we hurry. And I think we had better take this chance. The dragon's probably occupied with her kill now, but who knows how long before she notices us."

"I'm ready," said Blot, wincing as he tried to stand.

"Let me carry you," Ander offered. "We can leave everything but the tablet and the scale."

Blot nodded, unable to refuse, unable to meet Ander's eyes.

* * * * *

The trip down was quicker by far, and by far more uncomfortable. Because the dwarf outweighed Ander by at least thirty pounds, the journey was something of a miracle. Blot's leg throbbed and pounded with every step Ander took over the rough country, and the snow turned to rain as they descended into the tree line. Then Ander stumbled and they both slid the next hundred and fifty feet down a deep ravine, shaving at least an hour off the walk but also some three inches of skin from Ander's shoulder.

Blot passed out somewhere along the rocky slide, the deep gash on his leg reopening. When he regained consciousness, the leg had been rebound and Ander was carrying him through the last of the pine forest in labored silence, concentrating on the ever-darkening path before him. Sure enough, just as the sun set, the ground leveled out into a warmer, drier, wider way.

Blot looked back at the snow-shrouded peak of Mount Valcarsha, hardly believing he was alive. Not only had Ander brought him out of the dragon's lair, he had risked his life again and again on this steep trail to carry him safely down the mountain.

Blot began to rethink his mission. For all the time he had worked and slaved and hauled and done his master's bidding, Falon had never done one single thing for Blot. For a year now, Falon had been all grand talk and no action—continually telling Blot they would go together to Palanthas. The truth of it was that Falon didn't even take Blot along when he went to the inn for a mug of ale. Blot touched the unbloodied dagger at his belt.

Ander eased Blot onto the ground and stretched, his aching muscles glad for the relief. "Hold on, my friend. I saw the tavern's lights as we came down. It won't be long until we reach a fire and some grog. As I recall, the healer lives in the back of the inn. Say, Blot, you're very quiet. Is the pain worsening? You've lost a lot of blood."

"No . . . no. I'm just thinking is all," Blot muttered. "I can make it to the tavern."

"Then let's go before I stiffen up and we are both stuck here for the night," said Ander, lifting the dwarf back over his shoulders for the short walk to the inn.

* * * * *

A couple of hours later, Blot's leg was stitched and the healer had gone to her supper, leaving the dwarf with a warning about keeping the wound clean. Blot sat with his feet propped before a roaring fire, his belly full of stew and a tankard of grog in his frost-reddened hands.

"Ander . . ."

"Yes, Blot?" The assistant scribe put the last touches on a drawing of the white scale, closed his tablet and waited for Blot to finish his thought.

"I have something to tell you."

"Did you have enough stew? Is your tankard empty? I'll call the host."

"No, I'm fine, thanks. Ander, I tried to kill you."

"Once again, please, Blot? That sounded like you said you tried to kill me." Ander laughed uneasily.

"You heard right. I did try to kill you. That's why I lost my balance and fell. Falon ordered me to do it. He's been stealing your work for years now, taking credit for it so that he could get a soft job back at the Palanthan library. The white dragon was going to be his moment of triumph. I was supposed to kill you, take the entry back to him, and then he'd get his promotion. On all the work you've done. Falon erased your name and put down his own. No one even knows about you at the main library, Ander. Falon wanted to make sure they never did."

A long moment passed before Ander could speak.

"I see. And . . . you would have done it? You really would have killed me up there?" Ander fought hard to keep his voice from trembling.

Blot stared into his tankard. "You were supposed to have been a casualty of the dragon's wrath."

"All the time it's taken for me to advance. Falon's sealed dispatches to the library. *This* assignment. It all makes sense now. And you knew. And you were ready to leave me up there." Ander sighed.

Blot did not reply. There was nothing to say.

Ander moved to the window and looked out into the windy, wet night. Finally he spoke, his voice a little stronger. "Blot, there is one thing I still don't understand. After all this, why did you tell me? There would have been other chances to carry out your orders. Tonight, as I slept. Tomorrow, after we left the inn. Anywhere on the trail home."

At last Blot found his own words, a kind of strength returning to him as he spoke them. "I couldn't do it,

Ander. After I fell, you could have just left me there in that dragon's pit the way I was going to leave you—I've never been so scared in all my life. But you brought me here, paid for my food and the healer. I never had a friend before. So I had to tell you. Even though now you'll hate me." The dwarf looked miserable.

"I see." Ander returned to the table, sat down, and stared a long time into the crackling fire. "Well, Blot, where does this leave us? You know that Falon will not let this pass. If we go back together, he'll have to find a way to kill you, too."

"I know. I didn't figure to go back at all. I'm tired of doing Falon's dirty work."

Ander shook his head. "That won't work. He'll only come after you. You know that. And if I go back alone, he'll still have to try to kill me to get his promotion. What are we going to do?" Ander drummed his fingers lightly on the oaken tabletop, his sketches and notes spread before him.

They sat looking at one another for a few bleak moments. Finally Ander spread his hands wide across his fine work and took a deep breath. "Blot, there's nothing for it. You'll have to go back alone, and give this entry for the Bestiary to Falon, and let him do with it as he will. It's the only way everyone stays alive."

"But you'll never be a full-fledged scribe then!" Blot countered.

"No. But I'll be alive, and so will you. And that's better, given the choices," Ander replied, almost laughing.

"Well . . ." Clearly, Blot had no better idea.

Ander gathered the papers and handed them to his erstwhile assassin. "It's all right, Blot. I hope to see you again someday. Watch your back."

* * * * *

" '. . . and in summary, with the aforementioned measurements and illustrations, the mysterious beast can be irrefutably identified as the rare white dragon, as is evidenced by the collected specimen of one scale. By its size and shape, the scale is presumably from the anterior thorax of a female dragon. Accurate composite drawings can now be made.' Nicely done, Blot. This is just what I needed!"

Falon read Ander's words and held up the filmy white scale Ander had retrieved. Through its hazy translucence, the dingy little outpost copy room almost looked like the grand library at Palanthas. Falon could almost see himself standing in the warm, brightly lit southern wing, lecturing to aspiring apprentices while his assistants sharpened his quills and tidied his desk. Only one question remained.

"Blot?"

"Yes, sir?" said Blot, sullenly.

"You took care of Ander, did you? As per my instructions?"

"He'll not trouble you again, sir," Blot replied tersely. "I'll be going now, sir, to take back the horse."

"Yes, of course. You can pack my bags when you return. And then, Blot, I have a special task for you. As a reward for your faithful service." Falon smiled, his beady eyes following Blot to the doorway.

Blot could almost feel the knife enter his back as he limped away. The dwarf quietly shut the sturdy oaken door behind him, pulled himself onto the innkeeper's pony and headed down the road, a different road than he usually took.

Falon shuffled the papers together neatly, sat back in his rickety chair. He held up the dragon's scale again before the sharp ray of sunlight pouring through the outpost's one window and began to laugh heartily as the scale shimmered and sparkled in the bright ray. The thing seemed to have a life of its own.

Far away, a deep rumbling shook Mount Valcarsha, and a dark shadow passed overhead as Kale and Edrin walked their traplines in the valley.

* * * * *

Ander turned from the window and signaled to the tavernkeeper that he was ready to move on. He had been on the road a week, and this was his fifth inn. He took a long pull on his last tankard and stared out into the night. Time to travel under the cover of darkness.

"That'll be one steel, sir," said the tavernkeeper, handing Ander his bill.

"Going out this time of night, sir?" asked a voice behind him.

Ander's weary face broke into a grin. "Blot? What are you doing here? How did you find me? And you've . . . *changed*." Ander blinked, amazed at how clean the dwarf looked.

"I'm a fair tracker, remember? I've been on your trail for days. There is strange news."

"What are you talking about, Blot?" said Ander incredulously. "What about Falon?" His face grew dark with suspicion. "Did he send you after me?"

"Falon's gone," replied Blot casually.

"Gone?"

"And the old outpost, too. After I delivered your

entry to him, I returned the horse to the innkeeper, and when I came back, the place was totally flattened, absolutely destroyed. Nothing left standing. Everything covered in frost. Lot of folks spotted the dragon flying out from the mountain and some said they heard the explosion from seven miles away. You never saw such a mess, Ander. Gonna take a lot of work to rebuild the outpost. Innkeeper, another tankard, please."

Ander shook his head in amazement.

"But I've saved the best for last, Ander. Look what I found in the rubble. Everything is here, except for the scale." Blot held out a tablet, its edges still coated with gleaming frost.

"That's my entry—my observation on the dragon!"

Blot broke into a huge grin. "So it is, Ander. And now there's nobody to head the outpost."

"So . . ."

"So, don't you see?" Blot took a big gulp of grog and slapped Ander on the back. "Looks to me like Outpost Twelve is in need of a new chief scribe. I'd say you've just been . . . *promoted!*"

Even Dragon Blood
J. Robert King

It was the early days of the War of the Lance. So early, most people in Ansalon didn't even know there was a war. The town of Sanction knew, though it liked to pretend it didn't. The afternoon sun still hung, swollen and bloated, above Sanction's steaming harbor. The two at the bar were as drunk as if it were closing time. Aside from a half-asleep bartender, they were alone in the small wood-smelling place.

The two had been strangers when they walked in. Now, after a few pints of dragon blood ale, a few fifths of highlord hooch, and more than a few steels passing hands in a friendly card game, the two were thicker than thieves. Which was what one of them was.

The thief—a short stout man with a balding head and a beard like soot smeared across his chin—dealt another card to his besotted companion. Another card from the bottom of the deck. "Your luck will turn any moment now, my friend."

The tall man beside him nodded. His piercing brown eyes blinked. "It's got to. You've nearly cleaned me out. If I don't win something back, I'll have to walk out on Martha and the triplets, for sure." It was a standard loser's line.

The two slid into intoxicated silence as they studied the cards that jittered in their hands and blurred in their eyesight. The soot-jawed fat man gritted his teeth in a smile that might have been apprehension, or ecstasy.

"Something's coming for you, my friend. Your luck is changing."

The lean man glanced up and saw the inadvertent fulfillment of his companion's prophecy. Something *was* coming for him—something in a steel scroll case carried in the hands of a young man. He was a dark-haired youth, wearing the stern face of a stripling who wants to prove himself at his assigned task. He wore, too, the grim livery of the Blue Dragonarmy, with its occupation forces in Sanction.

If the fat man were less drunk and less recently rich from sharping his companion, he would have held his tongue in the presence of any representative of Ariakas's army. But he was both. "Your luck has changed, looks like," said the thief, and he gestured to the messenger standing in rigid attention behind his companion. "But for the worse."

"Kith Krowly of East Waverly Road?" the young man asked, his eyebrows drawn in a serious line. "You have just been conscripted into the Blue Dragonarmy, in the service of Highlord Ariakas. Here are your orders."

Kith reached for the scroll case, his thin hand trembling even more than it had when he had first seen the terrible cards dealt him. He took the case, goggled for a moment at the forbidding wax seal that had been stamped with Ariakas's own ring, and then solemnly opened it. A rolled piece of parchment slid forth, and he held it closer to his chest than he'd held his cards. He squinted down at the page, and read.

To the Esteemed Kith Krowly of East Waverly Road,
From Highlord Ariakas,
Greetings:

*It is your distinct honor to abandon your current
enterprise and report immediately to the Northern Army
Encampment on the plaza of the Temple of Luerkhisis.*

Kith looked up, frowned a moment at his bald companion, and said, "You're right. I've got to go."

A pudgy-fingered hand clamped onto Kith's arm.
"Let's see your cards first."

With no sign of his former reluctance, Kith tossed
down a whole lot of nothing, not a crown or a digger
anywhere in his meld. The fat man's tight grimace
turned into a broad smile as he showed his winning
hand: three gold crowns and two silver. His corpulent
fingers snapped up the coins before him.

Kith watched in what might have been dazed disbelief. "Thank you for the entertainment, my friend—"

"Jamison's the name," the fat man replied, and he
scraped the last of his coin pile into his bulging purse.
"Remember it."

Kith repeated the name, nodding. "Jamison, yes.
Jamison. I thought I'd finally found you. My true name
is Bulmammon, Aurak assassin. Don't write it down.
You'll have no need of remembering it."

Jamison raised his astonished gaze in time to see
Kith's sword descending. It was the last sight he saw.
The sword cleaved through bone and muscle. Kith
snipped the purse strings dangling beneath a loose
hand. The sack dropped, was caught short by Kith's
darting hand.

Gasps of breath from the messenger and the barkeep,
and the taproom went deadly quiet. The young man
took another step back, and a third, until he ran up
against an empty table.

Kith tied the purse of gold to his waist. Turning, he glanced at the shaken youth. "Oh, come now," Kith sneered. "You were told I was an Aurak assassin, weren't you?"

The young man nodded a stunned confirmation.

"You were told I was the best, right?" Kith continued.

Another nod. "Absolutely the best. That's what Colonel Armon said." He added lamely, "It's just . . . I've never seen an Aurak draconian before."

Kith gestured with irritation. "So stop shaking like an elf maid who's seen a spider! You've seen one now."

Somewhere in midsentence, the assassin had ceased to be a tall, lean human. He had transformed, changing into an imposing, gold-tinted draconian. Toothy jaws snapped once. A riffle of pleasure ran from the tip of Kith's snout, shivered his distinctive red coxcomb, and rippled down a leather-plated back, all the way to the tip of the creature's muscular tail.

"Well," he said, his voice deeper, coldly reptilian, and dangerously sober, "Ariakas said immediately. Let's go."

The Aurak's clawed hand snagged the youth's unchevroned sleeve and brusquely propelled him toward the door. As the pair made its exit, Bulmammon grinned at the barkeep. "It'd be best for you to get a mop and a shovel and forget what you've seen."

The man nodded eagerly and scurried away to comply.

Outside the tavern, in the dusty slum street, Sanction's ever-present tang of sulfur and steam hung in the air. The draconian strode rapidly up the sloping road, his tail tip sending a snake of dust coiling into the sky.

The young messenger was having a difficult time keeping up with the Aurak. He broke into a run. "Master

Krowly, don't forget. I was ordered to accompany you," the messenger said, panting.

"Master Krowly does not exist anymore. He was a yokel I killed so that I could take his shape and hunt down Jamison. My name is Captain Bulmammon, elite assassin for Highlord Ariakas. What is your name?"

The last time Bulmammon asked for a person's name, the person ended up in two hunks of meat on the floor. The youth's hand fell to the oversized dagger he wore conspicuously at his belt.

"Karl," he said warily. "I am Private Karl Baeron."

"Private Baeron," the draconian snapped, "your orders are to accompany me. My orders are to report immediately. I'm responsible only for my own compliance."

Private Baeron flushed at the rebuke. An uncomfortable silence fell between the two. Uncomfortable as far as the private was concerned. The messenger tried to make conversation. "Is Bulmammon your family name, or your personal name, Captain?"

"I have no family," the Aurak replied curtly. "No friends. One cannot be an assassin otherwise."

"Perhaps I would make a good assassin," Karl stated. "I am an orphan."

A sidelong thrust of the draconian's long snout brought razor-sharp teeth snapping in front of Karl's face. The draconian was amused. "How many men have you killed, Private Baeron?"

"None yet, but I've put in for transfer to the Solamnian front," Karl returned defensively.

The Aurak's tone was bone-cold. "I killed before I was three hours old. I came from a defective egg. My fellow hatchlings and I were deformed—puny, weak, missing a digit on our hands and feet, born with red coxcombs on our heads. The others were crushed under the heels of the priests who had made us. I hid in the pile of bodies and waited until only one guard remained. He was using a pitchfork to clear off the dead. I killed him, my first kill, before I was three hours old."

Bulmammon grinned. "From that moment, I knew what I was born to do. To kill. To torment and terrorize and kill. I thank the priests for teaching me that. I thank Ariakas for paying me to do it."

Reaching a bridge that spanned one of Sanction's many rivers of lava, the draconian and the discomfited messenger crossed over it. The private winced at the uncomfortable heat that radiated from the stone bridge. The draconian took no note whatsoever. He was looking ahead, beyond the bridge, into the stone-paved plaza of the Temple of Luerkhisis. In the plaza clustered the tents of Ariakas's encamped army. Among the flapping folds of canvas moved other draconians similar to Bulmammon. Compared to him, however, these others seemed dingy and somehow . . . common. Instead of gold-glinting scales and sleek wingless bodies, these draconians were brassy and bewinged. They dawdled about their assigned tasks. Interspersed with these reptilian troops were human mercenaries, minotaur warriors, and even a few chained ogres—Ariakas's brute squads.

The golden draconian paused at the apex of the bridge.

"Over there, Captain Bulmammon," said the private. "There is the colonel. There, by those shock troops."

Bulmammon's eyes shifted to where the young man pointed. Near the bridge stood eight draconian warriors, their scaly hides looking gray beneath the ashen sky of evening. Their wings moved in sullen fanning motions and cast deep shadows over their snapping-turtle heads. The draconians each bore a notch-toothed sword and wore metal-plated armor. One carried mountain-climbing gear—stout ropes and grapples; odd equipment for a winged creature.

"Sivaks," Bulmammon said, the single word expressing his contempt for his cousin draconians. "I hope this doesn't involve Sivaks."

With that, the Aurak strode down the arched bridge and onto the cracked stone plaza. All hesitation gone, he stalked up to the human colonel as though he would walk right through the man and on to the temple. As it was, the assassin halted half a pace too close to the colonel, forcing the man to hop backward like a spooked bunny.

"Blue Dragonarmy Assassin, Captain Bulmammon, at your service, Colonel Armon. What are your orders, sir?"

The colonel quickly recovered his composure, though his tight white face went a little tighter and a little whiter beneath his short sandy hair. He moved around the assassin and gestured toward the Sivaks, whose eyes watched the pair with avid interest.

"This is your strike team," Colonel Armon said. "Eight of the best Sivaks we've got. I want them returned—all of them." He shook his head. "No pleasure killing this time, Captain Bulmammon. I can't afford it."

The Aurak grunted. "I will return to you as many as are not killed in the completion of our mission, Colonel. Now, as to that mission . . ."

"You will lead these warriors toward the North Pass. Just before you reach it, you will see a large oak with a rope dangling from its lowest branch. A deserter was hanged there five days back. I left him as an example, but the body has disappeared. The rope is severed fifteen feet off the ground. The patrol that noticed the corpse's absence found a trail of trampled ground and claw marks—big claw marks—leading back to a cave. A lookout posted to watch the cave mouth reported seeing a maimed dragon—"

"A dragon? You want me to assassinate a dragon?" Bulmammon roared in disbelief.

"It is only a young dragon, and one of its wings is shredded. A young gold. Apparently we killed the mother some time back. We've only just discovered the wyrmling now. It's not a great threat, but why let it live to become one?" The colonel paused and seemed to consider. "And, no, Captain, I don't want you to assassinate the dragon. Highlord Ariakas wants you to. The orders come directly from him. You are to use the mountaineering gear to climb down into the cave, find the dragon, and slay it. The ropes will also help you drag its head back here."

"Let me go it alone, sir," Bulmammon said. "These Sivaks will only get in the way."

The colonel shook his head. "They go with you. Those are also the Highlord's orders. The Sivaks, and Private Baeron."

"Private Baeron?" Bulmammon scowled. "What do I need a puny human tagging along for?"

"Highlord's orders. Set out immediately. Good hunting, Captain."

Bulmammon snorted.

* * * * *

Captain Bulmammon set a breakneck pace, intent on reaching the North Pass above the Temple of Huerzyd before daylight had completely quit the sky. The private kept up, stride for stride, though sweat glistened on his face. The Sivaks marched afterward in heel-pounding double-time. They crossed the bridge and charged through the slums, the sound of their footfalls clearing the streets for blocks ahead of them. As they pushed past the Temple of Huerzyd, the last sliver of sun shone on the western Newsea. It was dark when the team began the winding climb toward the North Pass, but the red glow of the harbor volcano gave them as much light as did the sun.

The path they traveled was an uneven dirt trail studded with footworn rocks. It climbed steeply through switchbacks and past basalt outcrops. Blasted plants clung here and there on the volcanic mountainside.

The group marched onward, silent except for the scrape of scales on stone.

They crossed a saddle of eroded sand and climbed from basalt to granite. The peaks ahead were not volcanic, were older, rounder. Scrub brush gave way to trees—oak and ash and fir—that glowed so red from the calderas below that they seemed to burn. Captain Bulmammon led his troops into the shadow-dark woods.

Private Baeron drew his belt dagger. The blade flashed inexpertly in his hand, as though he'd used it for nothing but shaving—and didn't even need it for that. Bulmammon grinned and shook his red-coxcombed head. This human—an assassin!

Emerging from the tortuous trail through the woods, Bulmammon led the squad through a mountainside meadow and onto a promontory, which afforded a view of the fiery city behind them. In the center of the grassy knoll stood a huge oak beside the trail, its limbs splayed.

Bulmammon halted so suddenly that Private Baeron nearly ran full into him. Baeron swerved as the draconian's head swung around and fixed a red eye on him. "Put that dagger away, Private! You're liable to hurt yourself!" As the young man resheathed his dagger, Bulmammon turned back toward the tree. Behind him the Sivaks snarled and snapped among themselves.

Bulmammon spent a moment studying the tree, and the rope that dangled loosely some ten feet above his head. Slowly he turned and scowled at his troops.

"There is a traitor among us," he rasped.

Though no Sivak made any apparent motion, a susurrus of protest and disbelief ran among them.

Furious, Bulmammon advanced on the soldiers. He reached the nearest subordinate and seized the grapple ropes wound in bandolier-fashion around the creature. He shook the draconian, and wrenched the ropes free.

The Sivak glowered. "I did nothing, sir!"

Bulmammon did not seem to hear. He walked away from the line of draconians and toward the huge oak. With a flip of his clawed hand, he flung one of the grapples up over the stout hanging-limb, and kept walking. The line paid out from his hands and the grapple whistled over the branch. The hooked end arced down, caught short on the rope, and whipped rapidly toward Bulmammon's head.

He caught the hook. Iron rang against iron-hard scales.

Bulmammon turned back, faced his task force. In one hand, he held the grapple by its stem. In the other, he held the loose end of rope, allowing the line to uncoil behind him with each step. "One of you is plotting my death." The Sivaks looked at each other, then back at the Aurak. Oddly, they made no protest. It was Private Baeron who intervened. "Sir, that's nonsense!"

"Shut up, Private!" Captain Bulmammon studied the faces of the Sivaks. They were studiously blank, soldiers following orders.

Suddenly, the grapple clutched in Bulmammon's claws swung out toward the fifth Sivak in line. Its barbed tips slid easily beneath the Sivak's belly scales, sliced into a meaty gut. The snapping-turtle face of the Sivak showed nothing, not even surprise, until blood streamed from beneath his beaklike upper lip. The others snarled and growled, fell out of ranks, moving away from their slain fellow.

Captain Bulmammon hauled on the free end of the rope. The line went taut up to the bough, and then beneath the bough, yanking the impaled lizard forward across the grassy ground. In moments the twitching corpse of the soldier was being hoisted, lurchingly, into the air.

Private Baeron stared, openmouthed. As he drew the line in, Bulmammon explained. "After all, Private, to catch a fish, I have to bait my hook."

Once the shivering form hung a good fifteen feet into the air, Bulmammon crossed to a nearby tree stump and knelt to tie off the loose end of the rope.

Dusting off his hands in satisfaction, Bulmammon turned and issued orders. "You two, take up posts fifty paces to the north. You two, the same to the south. You three, take the west. The private and I will remain here. Watch for signs of the dragon. When it comes to take the bait, close in. I'll blind the creature with a magical flare—look away when it goes for the bait, or you'll be stumbling blind—and then I'll rope the beast to the tree trunk. It'll be spraying fire, certainly, but it won't be able to see, or to burn the rope without torching itself. Move in, then, and attack with swords. Any questions?"

The Sivaks were already melting into the darkness. Bulmammon watched them go, then hefted the second grapple and its length of line. He headed for the oak's trunk.

Private Baeron accompanied Bulmammon. As they neared the grisly corpse hanging from the tree, the private slowed, then stopped altogether. He stared in astonishment at the bloody corpse. Lambent light illuminated the face.

Karl gasped and looked at Bulmammon. The private squinted, and blinked, and rubbed his eyes. He stared back at the corpse. "Captain?" he cried. "Captain, why has the traitor turned into you? It has your face!"

Bulmammon was hooking the second grapple into the tree, about five feet off the ground. With patient preoccupation, the Aurak assassin uncoiled the rope, laying it in a large loop on the ground beneath the body. He circled the tree again and threaded the rope across a low branch.

Karl's gaze shifted between the face of the dead Sivak above and the live Aurak below. They were the same, right down to the distinctive red coxcomb.

Bulmammon laughed, a clicking, scissoring sound. He finished his preparations by covering the loop of rope with kicked dust, and then he paid out the free end as he backed toward their sentry position. "It's an old Sivak trick. They take the form of their slayer for three days after they die, so the murderer can be found, or so they can demoralize the killer's friends and kin."

Private Baeron followed the Aurak into the red gloaming. "What good does that do, sir?" the private asked.

"Despair and grief make you weak. You do stupid things," Bulmammon said. He settled into position behind a brush-shrouded boulder.

"Like I said, it's better to be connected to no one."

Karl looked at the slowly swaying corpse, and the black pool of blood forming by drops beneath it. A shudder ran through him. "It's a good thing you discovered the traitor, before he ruined the mission."

"He was no more a traitor than I am," said Bulmammon. "Now shut up. The dragon will have smelled the meat by now."

The sound of something large moving through the forest was followed by an interval of silence, as though the dragon had stopped, was checking to see if anyone was around. They heard two brief snorts. A small cave mouth on a nearby slope briefly glowed with fire. That was a warning. Most creatures would be wise enough to flee a dragon, even a wounded baby dragon. Few would try to trap and kill one.

"When it goes for the body," Bulmammon whispered to the private, "I will set off a brilliant flash of magical light in its eyes. Keep yours turned away. Then, I'll tie it up with the rope, cinching the beast to the trunk of the tree. Are you a fast runner?"

"I've kept pace with you, Captain," replied the private.

"Once the creature is held tight, you take the rope from me and run it around the dragon as many times as the rope will go. Got that?"

Private Baeron nodded.

Then it came, the shuffling rumble of something large and injured picking its way through the scrub plants and down the slope. By the sound of it, the dragon moved slowly, both wounded and watchful. This baby dragon might have been starving and maimed, but its desperation would make it all the more dangerous—a cornered beast.

The sound of the approach grew nearer; the throb shook the mountain. Then, from around a black brake of briars, the wounded wyrm appeared. First came a taloned foreleg, its sinews tight with pain and its claw curled in a ball. That leg was not made to bear weight, but it had done so for some time now, perhaps compensating for a wounded haunch. Into the puff of dust sent up by the foot came the murky outline of a hunger-ravaged breastbone, and another foreleg, this one drawn up beneath the shadow of a gaunt shoulder blade. Above the breastbone, a serpentine neck curled, holding the head up among the shadows of the stars. The moment-glow of fire within the beast's belly, licking up past gullet, tongue, and teeth, pierced the darkness above the shoulders.

As it moved forward, it cast a spell, seemed to drag the shadows along with it.

"A simple obscuring glamour," noted Bulmammon. "It will not stand up to my blinding light."

The dragon limped toward the tree. Using his night vision, Bulmammon watched his ring of Sivak pickets slowly tighten around the beast. The Aurak's breathing slowed, a true predator lying in wait for its prey, and he laid a scaly claw on the tense arm of the private. "Wait. Not yet."

They watched as the magic-shrouded monster sidled

toward the dangling corpse. Its fog of darkness could not conceal its starved and miserable state.

"The ropes will hold it," Bulmammon muttered in assurance to himself. "The ropes will bind it to the tree until dragonfire has ignited the whole hilltop. It will light its own pyre."

At last, the slack-skinned creature was beneath the dripping corpse. It sat down in the dust, lifting its foreclaws from the ground as it craned its neck. The obscuring darkness around it extended upward to envelop the corpse. The rope and the bough shuddered once under terrific weight.

"Not yet," said Bulmammon, his claws digging into the young man's flesh.

The bough shook twice more, and then sprang loose, whipping two severed cords into the air. The sound of crunching bone filled the air.

"Now!" the assassin cried.

Bulmammon kept his tight grip on Karl's arm, nearly yanking the private off his feet as the draconian bolted forward. In his other claw, the draconian held the end of the grapple rope. In moments, the draconian and the messenger had crossed halfway to the dragon.

Within the shadow, the chewing stopped, and wide intelligent eyes turned toward the two attackers.

Bulmammon gasped out a single arcane word, and with a blue-white pop, a lightning-bright ball of energy flashed into and out of existence around the dragon's head.

Captain Bulmammon shut his eyes. When the pop was over and darkness swooped back in upon the hilltop, the draconian swung around. He glimpsed, for one moment, the starved head of the baby dragon. It hovered in white-eyed shock, the half-masticated corpse of the Sivak hanging in its open mouth. The dragon's prickly ears stood upright, and its foreclaws were balled in terror. Fire licked between the dragon's teeth.

Bulmammon halted, yanking the private backward. A hot sizzling roar belched out into the night. Dragonfire. If Bulmammon hadn't stopped him, Private Baeron would have been in the burning heart of the blaze. Then the fire was gone and the captain darted forward, dragged the private with him.

They rushed through air that a moment before had been flame and was still crackling sparks. In five strides, Bulmammon reached the tree and yanked the rope up around the dragon. In two more, the rope whipped tight against the tree. Karl hauled on the line like a longshoreman.

The stunned and panicked dragon scrabbled to flee, but the rope about its waist cinched it into the tree trunk. Bulmammon pulled harder, beginning a tight orbit around tree and dragon both. He dragged on the line, groaning with each pull.

A belch of dragonfire ignited the bare boughs of the oak tree. Bark snapped and fell in smoking streamers around the draconian and the private. A hiss escaped as some of those sparks sank into the golden scales of Bulmammon's neck. He pulled all the harder on the rope and finished his circuit of the tree, wrapping the thrashing dragon in two tight strands. Then, suddenly, the captain stopped.

"Take it," Bulmammon growled, and thrust the rope end into the private's hand. "Keep circling the tree. Take it!"

Karl grasped hold of the cord, and once his hands were tight upon the hemp, he started to circle the tree.

He'd completed one circuit by the time the Sivaks converged with their swords and began hacking at the flailing dragon.

Bulmammon stood back, pleased with what he saw. The dragon writhed in terror, struggling against the cords. When the notch-toothed blades of two Sivaks lanced through its sinewy side, the dragon sent a fireball down after the scrambling, scurrying foes. The Sivaks ran clear, but the private almost stumbled into the rolling flame. He fetched up short enough to save his clothes, if not his eyebrows. When the wall of flame recoiled, the private ran on. He finally reached the end of the rope, having wrapped the dragon beneath four cords. The first two Sivaks charged back in, and two more came with them.

With troops like these, the assassin might not even need to strike any but the killing blow.

Swords rang in the fire-charged air and gleamed in flashing glory as they bit into the dragon's flesh. Roaring in agony, the infant dragon spat out a column of flame that set the branches overhead ablaze.

The kill was going just as Bulmammon had planned.

A flare sagged down from the orange-hot teeth of the dragon and swept down among the Sivaks, engulfing two of the four. Their black forms danced in crouched and jittering terror as they burned alive.

More Sivaks darted in, hewed and hacked, and danced away from the dwindling flares of dragonfire that splashed out toward them. Two of the Sivaks ran from opposite sides and struck as one, lopping off the infant wyrm's foreclaws. One of them paid for this prank, though. He slipped in the blood that jetted forth from the stumps, and was then blasted away to ash by a ball of flame that cauterized those stumps.

The dragon swung its blind head, driving back the attackers and pouring the last of its fire into a ring around it. The grasses of the hilltop flared into a brilliant orange wall of flame, which marched slowly outward from the tree and the wounded beast. The blaze pushed back the messenger and the two able Sivaks, and even Bulmammon. The dragon spat twice more, then its breath was finally spent, its last defense gone.

Bulmammon drew his sword and charged through the wall of flame. He experienced a moment of agony, then only stinging, searing scales, and he was inside the blackened ring of grass between the wall of flame and the dragon. Charging for the creature's throat, Bulmammon jabbed. He was flung back by a sudden thrust of the smoldering snout.

"Who slays me?" the infant dragon rasped, gray tendrils of smoke rising from his teeth. "Who slays me?"

Bulmammon was already on his feet, sword lifted before him. He crouched, ready to leap aside if there was more fire in that dragon gullet. "I have slain you. I—Captain Bulmammon, an Aurak, the greatest assassin of Highlord Ariakas, wearer of the red coxcomb—I slay you." He raised his sword for the killing blow and then stopped.

The dragon bowed its great blind head. Between the singed ears, there stood a red ruff that was the exact match of Bulmammon's. They had both been born of gold dragon eggs, both born with the coxcomb deformity. They were brothers, kin.

So what? Bulmammon raged, angry at himself for hesitating. The neck of the dragon was within a sword swipe of gushing out its life, dousing the fires and painting the hilltop in blood. But still Bulmammon did not move, could not move.

Sudden motion all around him. A Sivak soldier plunged through the grassfire, his armor limned in burning as he hurled his sword against the scales of the dragon. Another smoldering warrior followed after and cruelly split open the creature's shoulder.

Bulmammon glanced from his blade to the two Sivaks, slicing away in bloodthirsty glee, and then to the head-bowed dragon and the coxcomb that crowned them both.

One of the Sivaks motioned to the assassin. "The dragon's defenseless. Have some fun before the kill. You've earned it!"

Captain Bulmammon yet paused. Why? What stayed his three-fingered claw now, which could never before be stayed by any force in heaven or hell? A crimson coxcomb? No. The *sign* of the crimson coxcomb. It meant that there had been one other survivor from his star-crossed and slaughtered brood.

Bulmammon glanced again at his sword and noticed that it was freed. He could move and he did so, swinging his sword to lop the head from one of the Sivaks. The body collapsed, and the head rolled in the soot at his feet. His own face stared up at him in shock. In a daze, Bulmammon lurched past the dragon's haunch and swung his blade again, decapitating the second soldier. His nictitating membrane closed in reflex over his eyes as blood sprayed across him, searing like fire.

Turning, Bulmammon lifted his blade and brought it down one last time. He cut the ropes that bound the dragon to the tree.

"Live, Brother. Live, if still you can."

The assassin turned. He walked slowly away, unhurried and insensate, into the fire.

Even dragon blood was thicker than water.

He emerged from the fire, vaguely feeling the flames burning his livery. It was done. He had shied once from the slaughter, and would shy ever again. His life as an assassin was finished.

And so he did not even turn to fight the private, who leapt upon him. . . .

*   *   *   *   *

"Someone get him a rag and some water," Ariakas ordered. He gazed at the blood-soaked young man, standing at attention before his desk.

"I take it your mission was successful, Private Baeron?"

"Bulmammon was a traitor, just as you had suspected. Yes, sir. I killed him with this knife." The young man tossed the clattering blade onto the Highlord's desk. "Oh, and his kin is dead, too."

Ariakas leaned back in his seat and nodded his head. "Good. Of course, Bulmammon's demise leaves an opening in the ranks. I'll be needing a replacement for him." He paused, gesturing the private toward a nearby chair. "You have no family, do you, Karl? Good. It's time we talked of your future."

Boom
Jeff Grubb

"This is a gnome story," Wing Captain Moros exhaled, pinching the bridge of his nose with his index and forefinger. "Am I right?"

The lumbering sergeant gave a shrug of his massive shoulders, accenting the motion with a nondescript grunt. Ever since Moros's dragonarmy entered this accursed valley, everything had been a gnome story.

"One of the little rats wants you to favor him with an audience," stated the sergeant.

Moros exhaled another sigh. *Favor him with an audience.* The sergeant must be repeating the gnome's exact words, because the human subordinate was normally unable to speak more than seven words without an epithet, slur, or curse.

That was one of the more insidious problems with gnomes. After a while, it was far easier to just agree with them than to let them continue talking. Even before Moros entered into the Dark Queen's service, he had heard the stories of this soldier or that merchant who tried to get the better of gnomes, and whose body was later found in innumerable easy-to-carry pieces. Moros considered the gnomes to be the prime dangers to his army in the valley, and had ordered his men to give them a wide berth.

Not that they were malicious, mind you, Moros thought grimly. Were they outright rebellious or treacherous, he could ship the lot into slavery in the mines with an easy conscience. Had they shown even the slightest hint of darkness in their hearts they could be guided, channeled, even enslaved to serve the forces of Takhisis. But these gnomes were—well—oblivious. They could kill you, but it would be done accidentally, apologetically, and worst of all, cheerfully.

The wing captain wished silently that he was in a more secure position, like on the front line of battle, alone, facing a battalion of heavily armed elves. Anything but having to baby-sit an encampment of gnomes.

Moros gave a tired wave and the sergeant departed out the swinging door. A brief burst of bright autumn sunlight painted the gloomy interior of the tavern. Outside, an unseasonably oppressive heat lay over the valley like a blanket, reducing all activity to a crawl. The local inn was the only building of any importance within ten miles. Moros took it as his command post, ensconcing himself in the cool shade of its common room.

Gnomes—why did it have to be gnomes? Moros had gone from leading the army's spearhead to being trapped in a quiet backwater behind the front. And now Moros's superiors were asking questions. Nasty questions about the size and amount of the customary tribute. Nastier questions about rooting out potential spies and traitors among the native populace.

Couldn't those dunderheads in command realize that the safest thing to do with gnomes is ignore them?

And the war had been going so well up to this point! Moros commanded a few hundred human troops supported by a heavy brigade of ogres. Those ogres, backed up by Moros's own mount, the blue dragon Shalebreak, were usually enough to scare the towns and villages in their path into surrendering without a fight.

Perhaps the war had gone *too* well, because they quickly outstripped the other wings of the army. While other detachments ran into this clutch of Qualinesti or that pack of kender, his unit pressed far ahead. Word came for them to wait for the other parts of the army, but Moros always wanted to grab one more objective, one more chunk of land. The reports of this valley sounded ideal—primarily agricultural, situated near a minor crossroads, the only buildings of consequence being a cluster of whitewashed structures with high-peaked, thatched roofs. One of those structures was the inn that currently held Moros like a trap held a rabbit.

It had been a good campaign, Moros reflected wistfully. There was a bit of a battle, enough to impress the local humans into swearing fealty to their new masters, a suitable roof provided for his benefit (with a prodigious amount of ale), and a reasonable rest period as the remainder of the army caught up.

Then they struck gnomes, and everything went south.

None of the locals had mentioned the gnome encampment at the far end of the valley, across the stream. No, they swore their fealty and went back to getting in their crops. Only later, when he heard thunder from the far end of the valley, when he saw the blackened remains of the patrol come staggering back into camp, did Moros have the first inkling that there was trouble.

The inn's owner now waddled over to Moros's table. He was a human, kin to the farmers who held treachery in their silence. A slow, ponderously fat man, he swayed like a round-bottomed doll. Only his eyes, deep in the folds of his flesh, belayed his comic appearance. His eyes were as cold and hard as steel marbles. Moros could feel the man's resentment boiling behind those eyes. Moros's army had driven off business, damaged some buildings, even arrested a few of the innkeeper's clientele. Now Moros spent his days lolling around here, in the common room, reviewing reports and sucking down the inn's prized ales during the day, consuming the top-shelf liquors in the evening.

The idea that his presence irritated the innkeep almost brought a smile to Moros's lips. Almost.

The innkeep plunked down a frothy ale in front of the wing captain, and wordlessly nodded. Moros returned the nod in lieu of any payment, and the innkeep made his slow, waddling way back to his place behind the bar. He returned to polishing his mugs with a stained cloth.

Moros played with the idea of declaring the innkeep an enemy of the dragonarmies, and having him dragged off to work the mines. On reflection, he chose not to. This whale of a man would not last ten days in the pits. And besides, with the innkeep gone, Moros would have to fetch his own ale. The locals were needed to bring in their crops, and the gnomes . . . He'd just as soon stay away from the gnomes.

His ogre troops, of course, had wanted to go charging into the gnome encampment at once, but cooler heads prevailed. Moros, on Shalebreak's back, went out to "obtain the gnomes' surrender," as he had put it.

The far end of the valley, across the stream, was a greasy smudge on the landscape. As Moros and the dragon neared, he could hear the sound of gnomish industry. Coming closer, he saw between two to three hundred gnomes, all engaged in banging and clattering and ripping and rebuilding and all sorts of other tasks that made Moros tired just watching them.

No—he wanted nothing to do with gnomes.

What cinched matters was the fact that most of the gnomish encampment was built into a set of burrows and caves tunneling into the limestone foothills. Narrow, interlaced passages that a gnome force could use as a redoubt, surviving a siege for weeks or months.

And then there were the devices that littered the ground in front of the burrows—a massive tangle of wood, metal, and rope, broken by open patches used as smithies or assembly areas. Here were the remains of many gnomish inventions. Moros guessed that ninety of them had never worked at all, and nine of the remainder did something totally unexpected. But the one out of a hundred that did work might be enough to give the dragonarmies a fair fight.

And the dragonarmies of Takhisis hadn't gotten this far relying on fair fights.

Moros's instincts had been right, however. Shalebreak's presence was enough to convince the gnomes to surrender. They agreed to stay in their part of the valley. The dragonarmies, for their part, would leave the gnomes alone, and demand only a small tribute. At the time, Moros believed he had won his greatest victory without losing a man.

Now, weeks later, sitting in the inn, half-drained mug in hand, he was less sure. The gnomes had stayed in their burrows. The farmers had brought in the crops. The other units of the dragonarmy had arrived—and passed Moros by. His ogres were stripped from him for a push to the south, and half his human regulars were removed to handle an insurrection farther north. The remainder of his fragmented army was settling down or a long occupation. Discipline was lax and desertion was becoming a problem. Many of the men had helped the farmers get in their harvests, and were now thinking less like soldiers and more like civilians.

Moros had not sworn allegiance to the Dark Queen to become a military governor of some forgotten valley, but his masters refused to reassign him and Shalebreak. Instead, they complained about the amount of tribute and number of prisoners, the frequency of his reports and their content (when nothing happens, and you tell them nothing happens, they get peevish about the lack of progress, Moros mused sullenly). He was already in a bad mood and now this—a gnome.

Another burst of invasive sunlight heralded the sergeant's return. The most evil gnome in the world trailed in his wake.

Moros had never seen an evil gnome before, and had not even considered it a possibility. To him, and to most of his fellow soldiers, gnomes were like kender—playful, small creatures only two steps up from vermin. They had a nasty tendency to blow things up, but never intentionally. Gnomes were simple creatures, and were harmless if left alone.

The gnome that padded in behind the sergeant, though, was different. Dressed in baggy pants and a linen shirt with a black cotton vest, the creature had a reptilian shuffle in his walk, and a serpentlike glare in his eyes. The gnome rubbed his hands together incessantly. He wore a heavy overcoat draped over his shoulders like a cape, which accentuated the squat gnome's already-pronounced stoop. It was as if he kept his evil in his deep coat pockets.

This evil gnome was like a rabid bunny, or a chipmunk possessed by spirits of the Abyss. Moros was intrigued. A malevolence clung palpably to this gnome.

Looking at him, Moros thought that there might be hope for the gnomish race yet. He had heard of hobgoblins, even draconians, performing acts of kindness and charity on occasion. Those were aberrations from the norm, so why not an evil gnome?

The wing captain motioned to the chair opposite and the gnome clambered up. He did not sit, however, instead leaning forward, palms flat on the table, his eyes boring into Moros's face. He seemed to be calming the rest of his body and forcing all of his nervous energy through his eyes.

"Name?" said Moros.

"Boom," said the gnome.

Moros blinked. "Boom?"

The gnome drew in a tired, deep breath, almost like a reverse sigh. "Boom-master-the-great-and-glorious-the-one-who-harnesses-the-force-of-the-blast-and-plies-the-dark-secrets-unknown-to-men . . ."

Moros waved off the rest of the gnome's name with a shrug. The gnome quieted, resuming his deep stare at the wing captain.

"Boom, then," said Moros, "What do you have for me?"

"A weapon," said the gnome, his eyes practically glowing with eagerness. "A weapon capable of destroying all those who oppose you."

Moros arched an eyebrow. He had not expected the gnome to come offering anything destructive. Such a device, if real, would smooth over the troubled waters with command, and perhaps get him out of this abysmal posting. Still, most gnomish weapons tended to be huge, fragile, implosive, and impractical.

"Show me," he said.

The gnome pushed a hand quickly and deeply into his right-hand coat pocket. Moros saw the sergeant's hand stray to his sword hilt. Across the room, the innkeeper ceased his mug-polishing.

The gnome pulled out a small object and laid it on the table. The innkeeper craned his thick neck to get a better look. The sergeant relaxed, drawing his hand away from the weapon.

"It's a rock," said Moros. "As a weapon, I think it's been done before."

"It's a very *special* rock," said the intense little creature. Moros wondered if the gnome ever blinked.

The wing captain picked up the rock. It looked fairly unremarkable, even as rocks go. It was a grayish-brown lump of the type found at the bottom of every stream within ten miles. A small sliver of the stone had been scratched away from one side, and revealed more grayness, broken by occasional flecks of grainy black.

"What does this 'special' rock do?" asked the wing captain, turning it over roughly between his fingers.

The gnome giggled, a high-pitched whinny. "It explodes. Boom."

Moros froze and bobbled the stone, almost dropping it. The gnome giggled again.

"Don't worry, that one won't blow up," said the small creature. "I have to refine it—like iron ore is refined to produce steel—in order to create the explosive material. I call the unrefined rock Gnomite. The enhanced, final product would be called Plus-Gnomium."

Even so reassured, Moros set down the stone carefully. He waved the innkeep to bring the twisted gnome an ale. The wing captain noticed that the innkeep approached the table with all the caution usually used for encountering venomous porcupines, then set down a mug with the care of a safecracker.

"Do you have any of this material . . . refined?" asked Moros, almost dreading the answer.

"They didn't believe me, the fools," said Boom suddenly, ignoring the question. He grabbed the mug and emptied about half of it in one gulp. Moros nodded at the innkeep to keep bringing more ale.

"They?" prompted Moros.

"I am not one of these country tinkerers," said the gnome haughtily. "I hail from Nevermind itself, the great citadel of the gnomes. There I was known as a genius, as a visionary, until I told them of Plus-Gnomium and its power. The cowards took my work from me, and cast me out. It took me years to find this place, where Gnomite was abundant, and more years to recreate my confiscated notes."

The gnome leveled a hard stare at Moros. "Understand this, human. They took me away from my work. Do you know what happens when a gnome is prevented from pursuing his life's work?"

It twists him, apparently, thought Moros; bends his soul in on itself until it collapses in a intense ball of hatred. That would explain the gnome's frenetic spasms and nervous glance, his unblinking eyes.

"So this exploding material is already in the hands of the gnomes of Nevermind?" the human asked. Surely if the gnomes had a super-weapon, they would have used it by now.

The fidgeting gnome shook his head. "They don't know how to make it work. It is harmless in their hands.

My notes have likely been misfiled, and my prototype has probably been turned into a lamp or something." He giggled again, and Moros was reminded of metal claws scratching on a chalkboard.

"You said the rock would not explode unless refined. Now you're saying that the refined product won't explode either?" Moros was too weary to hide the tired tone in his voice. This was just another gnome pipe dream—all moonbeams and guesses.

"Let me start again," said the gnome, picking up the rock with one hand, and draining the mug with the other. "When you cut this rock in two, what do you get?"

Moros shrugged. "A smaller rock?"

"And if you cut that in two?"

"A smaller rock still."

"And if you keep splitting the rock in two?"

The mild pain in Moros's head was starting to blossom into a full-fledged ache. "Eventually," said the wing captain, "you'd get a piece too small to cut, a piece that would be smaller than the blade you're cutting it with."

"Good, good," said the gnome. "Now assume you have some type of vorpal weapon, a sword of amazing sharpness, that can cut anything, no matter how small the fragment. What then?"

"I suppose," said Moros, "you would end up with flecks of dust."

"And if you split the flecks of dust?"

"Smaller dust?"

The gnome nodded in enthusiastic agreement. "At some point you'll come to the smallest possible particle of the rock. If you cut this, it will cease to be a rock entirely. I named this smallest particle after the smallest member of the pixie family, the atomie."

The ache was reaching its tendrils through Moros's brain, curling behind his sinuses. "What happens then?" he said.

"You split the atomie in two," said the gnome.

"And?"

"Boom," said the gnome, cackling and leaning back. He grabbed the second mug of ale the barkeep had brought and downed it twice as quickly as before.

Moros made a growling noise. "So you have a material that causes an explosion only if you have a sword of amazing sharpness to cut it with. Now, why do I need such an explosion if I have a sword of amazing sharpness in the first place?"

The gnome held up both hands, a sour-milk look on his face, "That's background. I want you to understand what I am saying."

"Background," muttered Moros, and looked at the sergeant, who was staring into space. It was clear the subordinate had stepped out of the discussion about the time they began cutting things that were too small to cut.

The innkeep set another foaming mug down before the gnome, recovering the empties with a single swipe of his massive hand. From the innkeep's face, Moros assumed that the fat human understood something of what the gnome was saying.

Which put him one step ahead of the wing captain.

The gnome ignored the reactions of the humans and grabbed at the newly proffered mug. "Now, you're right, it's very difficult to cut something into so many pieces that it gets down to the atomies. In fact, some materials provide new homes for atomies, preventing them from flying off into space. But other things, like the metal refined from the hunk of Gnomite here, aren't as well held together as others. Their atomies are loose, unstable, and easier to cut."

Boom the gnome pulled what looked like a small insect from a shirt pocket, and set it on the table. "Another device of mine." He beamed proudly. "It lets out a chirp whenever it consumes an active atomie, one that has escaped from rocks like this."

The gnome flicked a switch on the insect's back, and it let out a bored chirp. After a few seconds, it emitted another metallic chirp.

"Watch what happens when I bring the rock near it," said the gnome. "It will become more agitated, more eager to consume atomies."

Indeed, as the gnome brought the rock near the insectoid automaton, its antenna pivoted and the chirps became a clatter of clicks, finally melding into a dull, humming buzz that rattled Moros's teeth and drove spikes into his already-aching brain. He motioned for the gnome to cease the demonstration.

The nervous gnome smiled a lopsided grin and shoved the insect-device back into his pocket. It continued to click eagerly. Boom slapped his pocket, hard, and the chirping ceased.

Moros harrumphed. "So you have an unstable rock and an eager counter of atomies. How does this make a weapon?"

The gnome drained the remainder of his third mug and smiled. "These stray atomies act like a sword of amazing sharpness, cutting off more atomies from unstable surfaces. The refined Gnomite metal, Plus-Gnomium, is oozing with stray atomies which, if brought into contact with more refined Plus-Gnomium, find more stray atomies, until the entire pile of material ignites from all these atomies bouncing around and—"

"Boom," finished Moros.

"Like links in a chain, the reaction continues until the atomie pile is consumed in a fireball." The gnome glowed, as if lit from within by stray atomies.

Moros scowled, picked up the rock again, and said, "How big? The blast, I mean? Let's say we take a pound of your refined Plus-Gnomium and set it off outside the inn, here . . ."

He stopped because the gnome was giggling. "If we set it off right outside, this entire building would be vaporized by the blast, reduced to its component atomies and scattered to the edges of the world. There would not be enough of you left to fill a snuffbox."

Moros fought the pounding in his head and said, "All right, then at the creek at the bottom of the hill . . ."

"The inn would still be caught in the crater from the force of the blast. Your bones would be mixed with the flaming earth, and turned to steam by the power of the blast."

"Well, then, across the creek, near the gnomish settlement."

"The firestorm sweeping outward from the blast would fry the inn and all its inhabitants about one second after detonation," said the gnome matter-of-factly. "There would be ninety-eight percent fatalities among the gnomes in the first seconds of the blast."

"Fine. At the far end of the valley, then."

The gnome tapped a pudgy digit against his lips for a moment, then said, "You might avoid the firestorm, but the wind from the blast would level this place, reducing the timbers to kindling. And, of course, if you were watching it, it would be like looking at the sun. Your eyes would be reduced to molten pools in their sockets."

Moros was suddenly aware that the innkeep was standing next to him, with another ale for the gnome. The man's knuckles gripping the mug's handle were white.

"Thank you," said the wing captain pointedly. The barkeep set the ale down sharply, then retreated. "How big a blast are you talking about?" Moros asked the gnome, trying to get down to specifics.

"Given a pound of material, I'd estimate about a half-mile across for the crater itself, with the firestorm spreading up to four to six miles across. And, of course, the land itself would be blasted and barren for a few human generations to come."

"A few . . . generations," said the wing captain slowly, taking in what the gnome was proposing. This was no wizardly fireball, no cunning battlefield tactic, no simple siege engine. This was pulling a piece of the sun to Krynn in a single second and letting it blaze its way across the surface of the land. If true, Plus-Gnomium was a weapon that could bring the last rebellious elves and humans into line.

If true.

But who would detonate the bomb? Gnomish timers were horribly unreliable. Perhaps a suicide unit? No one could hope to outrun the effects of the blast. Even a dragon would be unlikely to outfly the fireball, or survive the effects Boom was describing. Involuntarily Moros looked toward the door, toward the stables that billeted Shalebreak. Could he bear to see his mount incinerated, even if it meant defeating an enemy army?

Could any Dragon Highlord?

And the cost of such an attack on the land! What general in his right mind would lay waste to a place for generations? How would people eat? And what good was a land without people? Even keeping Plus-Gnomium in the armory would be folly, because it could be stolen, or—worse yet—duplicated.

If it worked at all. Could you base an entire military campaign on a gnome's promise?

Moros shook his head.

"I'm sorry, Boom," he said, trying to let the crazed gnome down gently. "But I don't think your idea meets our present needs. I'm sure that your reasoning is very sound, but the whole idea of cutting tiny rocks and small faeries producing big explosions sounds like so much moonshine. I mean, I have great respect for your obvious personal talent, but gnomes in general, well, you know . . ."

The wing captain's voice trailed off.

The gnome's face had the complexion of a ripe turnip. The gnome's eyes were wide and white against the purple background of his apoplectic face. The gnome's entire form shook, vibrating with rage. Moros feared the twisted little creature would ignite in a small fireball all his own.

"Of course, I can file a report with my superiors, and if they are interested . . ." Moros began, but it was too late.

The gnome shot a stubby arm forward, accusing finger pointed at Moros. "You're just as bad as the fools at Nevermind! Wrapped in the past, afraid to see the future! But this time, I'm ready for you!"

The twisted creature's other hand shot into its left coat pocket. It pulled out a cube the size of a man's fist. The cube was smooth and reflective on all sides, and had a thick, grayish rod jutting from the top. The end of the rod was flattened into a grip, like that of a key.

A pound, the gnome had said. This looked as if it might weigh a pound . . .

"I built a working prototype!" cried the gnome. "I can prove my theories are fact!"

He pulled the key from the box.

Moros dove beneath the table, as if a slab of oak would protect him from the promised explosion. As he fell, he saw the innkeep dive behind his bar, and realized both of their actions were futile in the face of the coming fireball. The sergeant, thick-headed and only half-comprehending, was charging toward the gnome, figuring the creature had lit some type of grenade.

The bomb did not go off.

Ignoring a sharp pain in his shoulder, Moros pulled himself to his feet. The sergeant and the gnome were wrestling in the center of the common room. The sergeant had three feet of height and one hundred twenty pounds of mass on the small creature, but the gnome fought with the strength of the insane. The sergeant's face was already gouged with deep scratches, and the mad gnome kept slipping out of his grasp.

Across the room, the innkeep was slowly recovering as well, his wide face appearing cautiously behind the counter. Between him and Moros were the brawling man and gnome, and the scattered contents of the gnome's pockets—gears, bits of string, notepads with pages half-torn out, the mysterious rock, chewed-on pieces of chalk, and the insect-automaton.

The insect-automaton, which eagerly counted atomies, was active again, and chirping loudly. The chittering increased with each passing moment.

The sound made the wing captain freeze. More noise meant more spare atomies were in the area. As far as Moros could remember, this meant that the Plus-Gnomium was already caught in the reaction the gnome had described, the chain of events leading to an explosion. The atomie pile was starting to ignite.

They weren't safe. The cube-shaped bomb was about to go off.

Moros looked frantically around the room. He could find no sign of the cube. It must have fallen from the gnome's hand when the sergeant tackled him, and rolled to some corner like a thrown die. He had to find the cube before it consumed them in a fireball.

An idea cut through the cloud of buzzing now kicked up by the insect-device. Moros grabbed the unliving creature by the thorax, and began to wave it back and forth. If the gnome spoke true, the insect would chatter loudly when it drew nearer the cube.

To the right, beneath the overturned chair, the chittering increased, and jumped another order of magnitude as Moros stepped toward it. The wing captain shoved the chair aside. The box was there, radiating from the power of the bouncing atomies within it. Grabbing the cube, he felt it was warm to the touch.

The key was still missing! The insect chattered louder and louder now, its voice a bone-grating buzz that carved its way into Moros's brain. The wing captain turned about, searching for the grayish peg that would defuse the box. He panicked. He couldn't find it!

The sergeant had the gnome in a choke-hold. The gnome was gnawing on the sergeant's knuckles.

Where was that damned key? The clicking grew

louder, faster.

A pudgy hand grasped Moros's wrist, and a second set of fat fingers slammed the gray peg home into its slot in the cube. The chatter of the eager atomie counter subsided at once.

Moros and the innkeep looked at each other, exhaling a single breath as one. Then the fat man let go of Moros's wrist and stepped back, wiping his forehead with his dishcloth. Moros set the cube back on the table, next to overturned mugs of ale.

The sergeant had finally brought his human strength to bear and now stood in the center of the room with his captive, his arms wrapped around the small mad gnome's midsection. The gnome kicked and screamed, but the subordinate stoically ignored both verbal and physical abuse. From the look on his subordinate's face, it was clear that the sergeant thought he had performed a most important task.

Moros brought his face level with the enraged, now-helpless gnome. "Attacking an officer of the Dragon forces is an offense punishable by death," the human snarled. The gnome blanched visibly as the sergeant pulled his blade. "I find you guilty of that charge, and commute your sentence to imprisonment in the mines. Sergeant, lock this one up until the fewmaster comes by with his slave wagon."

The gnome spat a few more curses and threats as the sergeant dragged him outside. The sunlight flashed in a single burst as they passed through the door, leaving Moros and the innkeep alone.

Moros turned back to the nondescript cube. He picked up the device and cradled it in one hand. Already the warmth was gone. The atomie-counting cricket was chirping softly and erratically. Should he turn this over to his superiors along with the gnome? What if he gave it to them and it didn't work?

What if he gave it to them and it did?

He looked at the innkeep, who was watching him warily, intently. "I'm going out on patrol now with Shalebreak," Moros announced. "We're going to check out those tall mountains to the west. I'd better bring the Plus-Gnomium along for safekeeping."

There was a brief silence, then the innkeep said, "You'd best be careful. Those mountains are impassable and uninhabitable. It would be a shame if you happened to lose the Plus-Gnomium while in flight."

"A definite shame," said the wing captain. He looked at the innkeep, who had picked up the piece of raw Gnomite. The larger human was turning the nondescript stone over in his hands, as if his pudgy fingers could unlock its secrets.

"You can keep that rock," said Moros, "as a reminder that you should never listen to a gnome, regardless of how good his offer sounds. Even when he invents what he intends to, he is nothing but trouble. But then, who would believe that such power could be held in a hunk of stone?"

"No one would," muttered the innkeep quietly, slipping the stone into his apron pocket, "and we can thank the gods for that."

Storytellers
Nick O'Donohoe

Night had fallen long since, and the moon — harvest moon, red and full—was up in the mountains to the east. Traders, pilgrims, all manner of travelers had taken advantage of the extra light to make longer journeys, but by now all sensible travelers had made camp or had arrived at inns and homes. Moonlight or no, travel by night could be dangerous.

At the Inn of the Waiting Fire, the logs were blazing and the stew pot already empty. A second crock of cider simmered beside it; the barmaid hurried over, filled a pitcher with several scoops of the huge ladle, and crossed to the tables where tonight's guests took up every bench, talking quietly and finishing the last of the bread.

The barkeep called across to her, "Refill the cider pot, Peilanne." She nodded, spinning nimbly and gracefully as she set the hot pitcher down, carefully out of reach of the little girl gnawing determinedly at the end of a fresh loaf as the girl's mother stroked and untangled the girl's hair.

She stuck another pitcher under the cider barrel and opened the tap. "Are we expecting anyone else, Darien?"

He smiled at her. "You never know." He set ale steins one by one on a large tray. "Though the gods know where we'd put them."

But a breeze shook the lamp flames as the front door opened. A general cry went up: "Shut that door!" "Frosty out there." "Always a latecomer."

As he always did with strangers, Darien eyed them carefully. They were physically unimpressive, of medium height and wiry build. One had black hair, the other brown, and their teeth flashed white as they smiled automatically to the crowd at the tables.

All the same, it seemed to Darien that they passed by the tables with complete indifference, as though they were something apart from the local families, the traders, and the travelers.

He met them from behind the bar, smiling more broadly than the newcomers had. "And what can I do for you?"

One of them spoke. "Is there any supper?"

Darien shook his head. "Long since eaten. Look at this crowd; every bed full, locals in to eat as well. Barely any bread left. Didn't you take food for the road?" He glanced at their tiny packs.

The two looked at each other. The black-haired one said quickly, "We eat where we can, and only take enough for the day. We've traveled quite a ways."

The innkeeper said dubiously, "Traders, are you?" They shook their heads. "Pilgrims?" He added hesitantly, not wishing to be insulting, "Runaway clerics?"

The brown-haired man said, "I'm Gannie and this"— he hesitated slightly—"is Kory. We're storytellers."

Kory added, "We specialize in telling frightening stories."

Gannie glanced around the inn. "This lot looks like they could use the excitement."

"Ah." Darien scratched his head. "So there's a living in telling stories, is there?"

"If you're good at it." Kory looked pointedly at the ale barrel.

Peilanne filled two more steins and drew closer, intrigued. "And how do you make it pay better if you're good?"

Kory said, not entirely happily, "We wager on ourselves."

"My idea," Gannie said proudly.

Peilanne joined the conversation with a laugh, a light silvery sound. "How does that work?"

Kory said unwillingly, "We bet you and anyone else in the room that we can scare people with our story. If we lose, we don't get paid and we don't eat."

Gannie frowned at him. "But we seldom lose."

Kory looked at him glumly. "It could happen."

Darien nodded. "I see. And to win, you have to scare nearly everyone in the dining room."

"As long as they don't turn out to be disguised kenders, or something else without fear," Kory said dubiously.

"Look around you, young sir. That old man, Brann, is a shepherd, with his flock in the cote out back. Young Elinor, making a mess at the table, is from the village, here with Annella her mother. And that fat one is a merchant out of Solamnia, and those others with him, all human—" He leaned forward. "But are you tricking me? Will you scare them just with the story, or with something else?"

"Oh, our stories are good enough all by themselves," Gannie assured him.

Darien settled back into filling an ale pitcher, watching them closely. "And what must I do if you win?"

"You pay us and you make us a meal."

He glanced automatically at the empty stew pot. "Make you a meal?" Darien chuckled. "For now, at least, have the last of the bread. On the house, pending the outcome of the bet."

Peilanne looked at him with surprise and opened her mouth. He shook his head slightly to silence her, then tapped his gold ring against a cup. Eventually the insistent noise silenced everyone.

"This is Kory"—he hesitated, then pointed to the other man—"and this is Gannie. I have a wager with them."

He explained the terms. As he finished, Gannie bowed low and said, "And anyone else can bet, too!"

They looked around at each other. Bet a stranger that they wouldn't be scared of a story? It seemed like sure money.

Kory went from table to table, checking with interested parties, then returned to Gannie. "I hope we have enough if we lose," he warned.

Gannie rolled his eyes at him. "Have we ever lost?" Quickly putting a hand over Kory's mouth, he bowed to the company again. "And now, our story."

"I want one about owlbears," the little girl insisted.

Her mother said quietly, "Hush, Elinor," and looked apologetically at the two young men. "She loves stories."

"A wonderful girl." Kory dropped to one knee. "Sorry, our best story isn't about owlbears. " He glanced at the surrounding company, and said with surprising force, "Can we tell one about dragons?"

The company sat up, startled. Darien and Peilanne leaned forward, concerned.

"Excellent." Gannie put one foot on one end of the bench and leaned over his audience. "Once, not long enough ago, there were two young men, vagabond wanderers. Tale-tellers and inn-hoppers, spenders of money and chasers of dreams. We'll call them"—he pretended to hesitate—"Koryon and Elgan. . . ."

The similarity of names was lost on no one. Brann the shepherd smiled condescendingly, settling back to enjoy a story within a story. Even Elinor looked with sudden interest on the two storytellers, looking from one to the other as if waiting for their real names to shine on their foreheads.

"On this particular morning, Elgan woke . . ."

* * * * *

Elgan woke in the summer sunlight, brushing at his nose. A grass stem was tickling him.

Koryon was holding the stem. "Welcome to morning. Are you all right?"

Elgan wiggled his toes, counted his fingers and finally, with some trepidation, pinched his nostrils and blew his nose. Nothing fell off. "Fine." He disentangled himself from his cloak, crawled to the stream and ducked his face in, drinking deeply.

Koryon said, "Fun night, wasn't it? What nice people."

Elgan glanced down the valley, where smoke from the chimneys came from the cottages and still more smoke floated upward from the hearth of the Inn of Road's Ease. He turned to Koryon. "You really ought to watch yourself more," he said disapprovingly.

"It was just normal entertainment."

"Normal? That trick with the knives? That was reckless."

Elgan grinned. He had palmed a dozen dining knives, one at a time, and made them appear in his hand as he threw them to outline Koryon against the wall.

"And did I hit you with even one knife?"

Koryon, scratching his head, stopped and felt the outline of his left ear. He stared at Elgan accusingly.

"All right, did I hit you with more than one?"

Koryon said morosely, "I ought to be dead."

"Watch what you wish for," Elgan said absently.

"I'm not wishing, simply stating a fact." He quit feeling his ear, but still frowned. "And all those stories about dragon battles—that was simply showing off. I've known you since you were a child—"

"You were a pessimist even then—"

"—and I know for a fact you've *never* been in a dragon battle." He paused. "I don't think you've even *seen* a dragon battle."

"Not true," Elgan said firmly. "You may remember, on the occasion of my older brother's birthday, we both saw a pitched battle involving three armed men and three dragons—"

"Gods, Elgan, that was a puppet show!"

After a moment's silence in the sun, Koryon said, "You haven't said anything about Beldieze."

"Beldieze." Elgan stretched, eyes shut and dreaming. She had walked up to him after the knife throwing, and had stared straight into his eyes. Hers were blue-silver, and caught the candlelight amazingly; that wasn't all they had caught. Her dark hair, long and nearly straight, framed her face until he looked into it and felt he would never break free and get out. And her voice, like bells when she began asking questions. . . .

He started. "She asked me about dragon fights."

Koryon snorted. "And you told stories all night."

By evening's end, the tables had been pulled together

in the middle of the hall, Elgan was standing on the center table, waving a flagon of ale and explaining battles. He had hopped on the back of the strong, good-natured innkeeper, commandeered a broom, and charged about the inn to demonstrate the finer points of lance aiming. At one point, Elgan remembered, he had speared a curtain-ring held by Beldieze.

At a later point, he remembered a great deal of kissing and a walk under the stars.

"Where did you go?"

"Out. First for a walk, and then . . . to see someone."

Koryon frowned suspiciously. He was good at that. "To see who?"

"Someone . . . an authority. He was good with a pen— writing." He squinted, trying to remember. "Late in the night, we wrote something. Together. I wish I remembered what."

Koryon, pausing as he pulled out a clean shirt and glanced down the hill, said, "Why not ask her?"

Elgan bounded to his feet. "Gods. I'm a mess." He snatched the shirt out of Koryon's hands and muttered "Thanks" as he pulled it on. He bounded downhill, remembering that he had thought her good-looking. . . .

Now that he saw her in the sunlight he decided the Inn of Road's Ease must have been dark, or he must have been blind; she was *beautiful*. Beldieze had straight dark hair down to her waist, the figure of a dancer, and a full-lipped mouth that had smiled wickedly the night before. And of course, wonderful large eyes, almost luminous. They were staring at him now, and her smile seemed self-conscious. "Beldieze?" he said, mostly to test how her name sounded in his mouth.

"Elgan. I wasn't sure how you'd be feeling today."

She put a hand on his arm.

Koryon, cloak draped over his bare chest, stood discreetly in the background, drinking from a water jug and making a show of staying out of earshot.

Elgan put his hand on hers, smiling back. "You still like me, in broad daylight?"

"I still admire you," she said immediately. "Your stories about dragon battles impressed everyone. It wasn't just the way you told them"—she stepped back, throwing her arms open—"but the wealth of detail. The swooping and stalling and silent gliding and air currents and lance thrusts—" She mock-thrust, her arms rippling forward. She moved toward him at the same time, until her arms touched his waist.

He blushed. "I didn't mean to brag."

Koryon, nominally out of earshot, snorted.

"It sounded like expertise, not bragging. In fact"— she touched his nose playfully—"I asked you if you would fight a dragon for me, and you said you would. Remember?"

Elgan didn't like where this was leading. "Of course, I might not really be expert enough to fight a real dragon."

She smiled sadly. "I was afraid last night that you'd feel that way later. I said as much. You swore you could and would. We agreed on a binding contract, composed by a cleric, an older man who lives just outside of town." She added, with light additional emphasis, "He's more of a mage, actually."

The hair on the back of Elgan's neck prickled. "Why a mage?"

"So that the contract would bind." She took it out and showed it to him.

"I'm not going to fight a dragon—"

The parchment flickered out of her hands suddenly and materialized around his right arm, tightening itself slowly. He tugged at it. Nothing happened. He took out a knife and cut at it. The parchment wrapped itself tighter.

"See?" Beldieze stood with her arms folded, looking anxiously at the parchment. "It's exactly what you wanted. It does *contract*, and it is *binding*."

The contract pulled still tighter, and his hand turned dark red. Elgan bit his lip, envisioning the cylinder of paper closing on itself until it severed his arm. Koryon looked worried.

Elgan took a quick, shuddering breath. "All right, I'll honor it. For now."

"Good." She pointed down the hill. "Your saddle and lance are at the base of the hill; find your own mount. You have only two days."

She pointed to the parchment, which had loosened but stayed on his arm. Elgan looked at it intently, understanding little of the legal scrawl but recognizing his own signature beneath the words "fight a dragon."

He gave up. "So. Where is this supposed dragon?" he asked skeptically.

Her mouth quirked. "The one named in the contract is Jaegendar."

Koryon, standing presumably out of earshot, made a great sucking sound, and dropping his bottle, doubled over choking.

Elgan ran over and pounded his back—perhaps too fervently; Koryon dropped to his knees, gasping.

"Are you all right?"

Koryon glared. "I'm fine, except for my back."

"You must have choked on something."

"Of course," he said coldly.

Elgan turned back to Beldieze, folded his arms and asked casually, "Why Jaegendar?"

"You've heard of him?"

"If it's the same dragon. For instance, this Jaegendar wouldn't be called Jaegendar the Black? Dark Jaegendar?" He added awkwardly, " 'The Wings of Death?' "

"Also Jaegendar the Wealthy. The one and only Jaegendar. Yes."

Elgan frowned. "Why Jaegendar?"

He expected many things—a tale of tragedy and revenge, a story of human greed and dragon horde, a quest for glory or a magic token. What he did not expect was the sudden shimmer of air and whoosh of wings as her human form vanished and a silver dragon appeared before them.

"If he dies," the silver dragon said calmly, "his stepchild will inherit everything." She looked down at the humans, a fanged smile curving on her face. "Not everyone in the inn last night was human."

Koryon started choking again.

Beldieze laughed, a silvery noise that echoed across the hills, and off she flew.

* * * * *

"And off she flew." Kory paused to wink at Peilanne, who frowned back. The reference to her silvery laugh hadn't escaped her.

Peilanne gathered the dining knives back up and rubbed futilely at the scars in the bread board. In case anyone had missed the parallels between themselves and their story, Gannie had palmed four dinner knives from the table, making them disappear; then, one at a time from an apparently empty hand, he had thrown them at Kory, who caught them on the inn's bread board and returned them, palming them himself a final time.

"So," Peilanne leaned across the bar. "So far we have a greedy, vicious dragon and a young, treacherous, murderous dragon. What's next?"

Everyone in the inn was listening.

"Why do you think so ill of dragons? And why does your friend keep looking out the window?"

Gannie pulled back with a start. "Habit. Sorry." He turned around. "Not all dragons are bad, as our tale will tell you. Why, after Beldieze was gone . . ."

* * * * *

After Beldieze was gone, Koryon walked over to Elgan.

"You," he said with the satisfaction one feels when friends have been foolish, "are in real trouble."

"So we are."

" 'We?' " Koryon looked around in mock confusion.

Elgan looked around as well. "I don't see anyone else."

"Jaegendar," Koryon said firmly, "will laugh until it hurts when he sees you."

Elgan eyed him.

"Us," Koryon added, not happily.

"We'll find a way to beat him. We'll do fine. We're young, smart, clever, coordinated—"

"All that, of course." Koryon shivered. "But Jaegendar!"

"He's just a dragon, right?"

Koryon said in a small voice, "When I was little, my parents used to scare me with Jaegendar stories."

"Me too, if it'll make you feel any better."

Koryon froze, thinking. "Did the contract say 'fight a dragon,' or 'kill a dragon'?"

" 'Fight.' "

"Then there's your answer. We fight for a while, then quit. There's no shame in that."

"There is, actually."

"Maybe so, but I can live with my shame better than I can with my death. Assuming we can even survive a real fight with Jaegendar. Why are you grinning like that?"

"I've got an idea. Dragons are reasonable, right?" He grinned at Koryon. "Most dragons."

"Which reminds me, did you happen to tell Beldieze how you know so much about dragon battles?"

Elgan shifted uncomfortably. "I didn't say I'd actually been in one."

Koryon seemed to melt, his outline blurring, and a dragon stood before Elgan. "So she doesn't know the truth yet."

Elgan, changing his own form as rapidly, sighed. "No. She doesn't."

* * * * *

"I don't like it at all," Peilanne said firmly as she refilled the table. "A vicious, evil dragon, a greedy, murderous, younger dragon, and two dragon-scoundrels." She emphasized the last word. "Besides, this is an awful lot of shape-changing. All dragons don't change shape."

"Some do."

Everyone turned to look at Annella, Elinor's mother. She flinched at their stare but rallied and said, "Red dragons change shape, and silver ones. Black ones don't."

Brann nodded over his stein. "Young Annella's right about everything, including the black ones. Red and silver do, black don't. So they say."

Gannie nodded approvingly. "And the two dragons, Koryon and Elgan, are silver." He folded his arms.

"Besides," Kory said thoughtfully, "other dragons could use magic."

"True." Gannie let grim disapproval enter his voice. "Even a black dragon like Jaegendar could wear a ring of shaping."

The audience was stirring restlessly. They appealed to the innkeeper.

"They're right," Darien said unwillingly. "If a black dragon could find a ring of shaping somewhere, and if he could wear it, he could change to human shape."

"You see?" Gannie smiled brightly at Peilanne. "A dragon could be among you right now, and no one would know. . . ."

* * * * *

Jaegendar was surprisingly easy to find. As Koryon had said gloomily, "Just follow the weeping." There was a fire in the hills, where a farm was burning. Elgan hiked up to it in human form, not wishing to panic any survivors.

A huge black dragon, fully three times as long as Elgan in dragon form, perched on the edge of a roofless cottage, peering in like a carrion crow. He turned a cold eye this way and that as he checked the corners. He peered down at Elgan, who had stopped well back. "Who is it now?"

"Just me, Elgan." He licked his lips, which felt suddenly dry.

"Elgan?" The black dragon looked Elgan up and down, not smiling and not frowning. Jaegendar waved a red-stained claw. "Never mind; it's obvious. You're here to fight me?"

"I seem to have to"—Elgan could feel his ears reddening—"because, well, the other night, I might have said something about knowing how to fight dragons—"

"You were bragging." A noise, half scream and half wail, sounded from inside the cottage. "Excuse me." Jaegendar tracked something this way and that, striking down swiftly like a crane into a stream. There was another scream, and another as Jaegendar thrust his head up and down inside the cottage.

"And I was wondering," Elgan said, suddenly ashamed of himself as he said it, "if, since you might not want a real fight and all, if we could stage just enough of a mock fight to satisfy—"

"Let me guess." The black dragon rose up, wiping his mouth with a claw. "A lady has bound you to fight me. And she wants you to kill me because of my cruel ways, is that it?"

"Well, she has her own motives—mostly monetary—"

Jaegendar smiled, yellowing fangs showing suddenly. "Ah. Beldieze? Why am I not surprised?" There was blood on one of his fangs. Jaegendar said, "Excuse me again." His tongue flickered across the tooth, licking it clean. His eyes half-closed like a purring cat's.

When he opened them again he said, "And I can't dissuade you from this . . . fight?"

Elgan said honestly, "I wish you could."

"Well, let me try." Almost casually he flung a stone the size of a kender at Elgan. As Elgan ducked, Jaegendar threw another, and another.

Elgan scrambled frantically, searching for cover. Moments later, cowering in a ditch and half buried under building stones, he heard mocking laughter and felt a cold wind as Jaegendar rose and flew off.

Something rolled down the pile of stones toward him; he put up an arm to ward it off. The thing that hit his arm was soft, wet and pulpy. Elgan shuddered and struggled under the stones.

Several of them rolled free and Koryon's head appeared. "I saw him fly off. Big brute, isn't he? How did it go?" He cocked his head, sniffing the air. "I smell blood. Are you all right?"

Elgan reached up. "Pull me free. Then let's think of a strategy for tomorrow." He looked at the black dot in the distance. "A very good one."

* * * * *

Elinor had buried her head against her mother's sweater, and was peeking out with one frightened eye.

In a single smooth gesture, before her mother could object, Kory popped Elinor onto his shoulders, grabbed the cider ladle, and charged at Gannie, who flapped his arms in mock panic and fled through the inn. They spun and ducked, making spiral turns and leaps near the fire and quick dives in the cold air near the door. From time to time one or the other of them shouted: "Glide!" "Stall!" "Plunge!" "Loop!" Elinor waved the spoon and tried to hit Gannie. She was very happy.

But Peilanne, Darien, and the customers watched nervously, and nobody missed that Gannie paused by the window to scan the sky intently.

When Kory paused breathlessly by the table and set the girl down, Annella grabbed her and held her tight. Elinor waved her arms enthusiastically. "They know all about dragons!"

"Quite a bit," Gannie admitted. The other adults in the room looked less convinced about this, turning to Darien for confirmation.

"What would I know?" he said irritably. "I run an inn."

After a moment's silence he admitted grudgingly, "But I know a little about dragons—the way a man like myself might hear things—and yes, all the details sound real."

Gannie sat beside Brann, who shrank back from him. "Are you cold?" Gannie gestured at the fire, which was dying to embers. "Soon it'll be covered with gray ash, like someone waking by a burned-out campfire in the morning . . ."

* * * * *

They woke covered with a light pall of ashes, as from a burned-out campfire; they looked down the valley and saw that much of it was hidden by smoke. They washed up quietly, not looking at each other.

They headed downhill slowly, in human form, carrying the lance and the saddle. When they reached the villagers, no one glanced at them or wondered at their load; everyone was burdened.

Some were empty-eyed and blank, some were angry, some weeping. All of them carried trunks, awkward and badly tied parcels, or grain sacks packed hastily. Many of them carried children too young or too tired to walk.

Ahead of them the sign for the Inn of Road's Ease rocked as it flamed, the letters glowing as they burned.

The innkeeper was one of the refugees, half-stumbling as he walked. On his back he bore a rack of pewter ale steins.

He tripped on a rock in the road. Koryon leapt forward to steady his load and hold him upright. "Are you all right?"

The innkeeper looked at him as though he hadn't understood the words. "He burned our buildings, our farms." He pointed to the opposite hill, where the ruins of cottages and outbuildings were visible through the smoke. "He burned the second cutting of hay that we needed for the winter." His brow furrowed. "He said he was warming up for a special fight."

Koryon and Elgan watched him stumble down the valley. Elgan rubbed his arm where the contract still clung.

Koryon stepped quickly behind the ruins of the grain storage and tossed a coin. "Call it."

A moment later he muttered darkly and changed forms. "Put the saddle on me."

Koryon, with Elgan on his back, used the morning wind to drift up the opposite hillside toward the outskirts of the town. A barn, hayrack beside it, blazed in front of them. Elgan tugged on the left rein. "Circle it to the left, hold your wings still to not make any noise, spiral up to the right on the thermal rise from the fire—

"I know how to fly."

Elgan shut up as Koryon dropped toward the blaze. A woman, running back and forth in front of the barn, screamed at the sky, waving a baby aloft. The baby didn't move. Elgan shut his eyes. "Hurry up."

As Koryon glided into the edge of the thermal, his right wing tipped up, full of rising air. He rolled toward it and spiraled up, moving in a little at a time until they were running a tight spiral upward. Elgan checked the lance swivel for the ninth time, looking around constantly. "Koryon?"

"Mmm?" Koryon had his lips pressed tight over the bit, swinging this way and that nervously.

"I think he knows—"

"Of course," a voice beside them said coolly, and Elgan slammed the reins to the left as a dark figure streaked through the space where they had been, claws raking empty air.

"—everything we're going to do." Elgan held the lance close to himself, grateful he hadn't dropped it. As Koryon swung around, he held up a finger automatically, at arm's length like a wing tip, and tested the breeze. It felt cold.

They hung under the cloud cover, looking this way and that, seeking Jaegendar.

Elgan said finally, "What's the classic maneuver out of a failed lunge?"

"Stoop, gain velocity, cup wings at the bottom, slingshot upward, flap hard and find an updraft, rise into clouds"—Koryon scanned the low-lying cloud cover frantically—"where you hide and wait for an advantage," he finished slowly.

"He had to use another updraft. The wind by the

mountains, or—" Elgan stopped as the flaming ruins around them snapped into perspective. "Kory, this place is Jaegendar's playground. He laid out a whole system of updrafts for himself. . . . Get up high, shifting from thermal to thermal, and see if we can fool him."

"I don't think we can fool him," Koryon said gloomily. Clearly they didn't. For his next attack, Jaegendar dropped out of the clouds like a stone, leaving a small jagged hole before the cloud closed behind him, and swerved toward them with barely a flip of a wing tip. Elgan shouted and threw himself flat; Koryon, inelegantly, stalled and let himself tumble.

Elgan hung on desperately. "Get close to the clouds. At least he can't dive like that again."

Koryon flapped up, avoiding the obvious updrafts. The weather was restless; crosswinds shook them and required Koryon to make constant corrections just to stay over the hillside. This far up, their breath came out in white plumes.

Elgan tapped Koryon's side. "Look." Jaegendar, ahead, was moving slowly away at an angle as he scanned the sky below him.

"So, where do we hide?" asked Koryon.

"We don't," Elgan said. "We charge, diving with no wing-noise and lots of speed. Pull out at the last minute. I have an idea."

When he had finished explaining his plan, Koryon said, "This isn't an inn, and he doesn't want to be entertained."

Elgan looked at Jaegendar's effortless flight. "We have to try something."

With a sigh of misgiving, Koryon moved forward, catching a last breeze to rise and then drop, gaining momentum. Elgan watched their target cautiously, ready to call off the attack. He never looked their way. Jaegendar was nearly motionless, wings wide to catch an updraft and spilling slightly when he rose too high. He was a perfect target as he looked intently down at a circular pond, deep and rimmed with steep limestone in the green hills below him.

Elgan looked down as well. The pond was completely calm, untroubled by any ground-level breezes. It was like a mirror—

Elgan saw, to his horror, that both dragons were clearly visible in the pond.

"Break off!" Elgan screamed but he was already pulling the reins in a vicious left. Koryon banked immediately, the steepness of the turn pressing Elgan down into the saddle.

Jaegendar spun, his teeth showing in a terrible smile. He aimed for the point where Koryon would have to pull out of the turn or stall.

Elgan tugged the reins hard to the right. Koryon muttered, "All right," and flipped nearly over, his left wing high where the right had been. Elgan grabbed for the saddle as they spun off in a foolish, energy-wasting, clumsy maneuver that saved their lives as Jaegendar shot past them, his claws close enough to ruffle Elgan's hair.

Elgan said quietly to Koryon, "We're dead."

Koryon agreed. "If we're very lucky."

"Hide in the clouds?"

"He'd only follow us in. He can go anywhere we can." Jaegendar was moving toward them again, gaining speed.

They heard a rumble of thunder. A storm, climbing over the mountains, was dropping in low. The clouds were very dark, ragged underneath with whirling winds.

Elgan leaned down to Koryon and said, "Cloud-suck?"

"What a rotten idea. We'll be thrown around like toys." Koryon added, "No dragon in his right mind— Oh, Right." He turned toward the storm. "Watch my back."

"Aim to the left of the storm, zigzagging."

As they moved directly under the cloud, Koryon quit beating his wings. The thunder was deafening, close, the air rough enough that Elgan had to clutch the saddle swivel and squeeze his legs tight to hold on. The air rushed upward around them. In seconds they were inside the thunder cloud.

They rocked about in darkness, illuminated by flashes. Koryon corrected constantly to stay upright. Elgan hung on, remembering a story in the lore of a dragon who had been knocked unconscious by the buffeting and expelled, head down, from a storm.

A particularly bright flash showed Koryon turning to look back at Elgan. He looked afraid. He said apologetically, "I can't do this forever. I'm getting tired."

"So will Jaegendar, and he's old. Aren't you in better shape than he is?"

"Jaegendar," Koryon said firmly, "doesn't have a rider."

Elgan considered, then spoke through cupped hands over the thunder. "Drift forward, then to the left and down. It's time."

"If we have to," Koryon said glumly.

As they broke free of the clouds, they saw that the burning buildings below them had subsided. Elgan tugged Koryon's right rein, directing him toward the ruined granary where they had left Beldieze.

The wind tore the clouds apart. Elgan said in relief, "We'll have sunshine soon, I think."

"Will that give us some kind of advantage?"

"It'll give someone an advantage," he said vaguely. "Don't go straight to the granary; circle around and check for signs of him. Go leftward," he added hastily. This was not a time to use the classic patterns.

Koryon banked left, then spilled air from his wings to drop. Elgan grabbed the lance pin tightly. "Where are you going?"

Before he could answer, Elgan looked up and said tightly, "Company to our left."

Without waiting to check, Koryon banked dizzily to the left.

Jaegendar swooped out of one of the remaining clouds, then vanished, but there was no question that he must have seen them.

Koryon finished his turn and leveled off. "What next?"

"He's not to either side." The remaining clouds had nearly dissipated except for the thunderhead hanging over the valley.

In full sunlight, Koryon nearly hovered in place, craning his neck up and down.

"Below?" He peered. "Above?" He squinted. "Nope. We lost him, I hope."

A shadow fell on them, growing darker every second. Elgan shouted in sudden panic, "He was in the sun! He was in the—"

Koryon jerked sideways as Elgan brought the lance straight up. Jaegendar, smashing down past them, scraped his left wing on the lance.

But after the shock of impact, Elgan dropped the lance. It passed under Koryon's body and out of sight.

They rose up close to the cloud cover again. Jaegendar slowed and turned, watching them, roaring out as he saw Elgan empty-handed. Koryon, his neck stretched out straight, straining, flapped his wings frantically sideways as fast as possible.

When they looked up, the thunderhead had drifted over the valley; Jaegendar, circling just under the darkest clouds, descended toward them. His black body was silhouetted in the flashes of lightning.

Koryon said in nearly his natural voice, "Oh, good, you made him mad."

*　*　*　*　*

"You made him mad?" Darien said in disbelief, caught up in the story in spite of himself. "What kind of fool's trick is that?"

"A fool's trick," Gannie said grimly. He drifted to the right of the window, peering out without leaving a silhouette. Elinor had fallen asleep on Kory's back; he swooped forward and dropped her into Peilanne's arms without waking the child.

"Still," Gannie said thoughtfully, "An angry enemy isn't a thinking enemy. The one hope left is that you can trick him . . ."

*　*　*　*　*

"He tricked us," Koryon said, scanning the sky frantically. "Where did he go?"

"He dove toward us, then slingshotted back into the clouds while my body hid him from you. He's that good." They dove, picking up velocity.

Koryon flapped forward, dropping slightly to gain velocity from the dive. His body was still rigidly straight. "This is awkward. Do you think he knows you haven't got the lance?"

"He saw me drop it. I'm sure of that." Elgan flexed his empty arms, trying to relax.

The circular pond lay ahead. Koryon banked toward it, spilling air from his left wing to drop as he turned. He watched their shadow on the grass, tracking until he was nearly between the pond and the sun, directly overhead.

In the blinding moment when the pond was a fiery golden disk, Koryon saw, or thought he saw, a second small black dot reflected above them. He hissed to Elgan, "Look up. Now."

He looked. "I can't see a thing—"

"Hold your thumb up, block the sun out with it, and look for wings to either side."

Elgan shouted, "There! Straight up, in the sun, diving for us. He's dropping—closer—closer—Gods, his claws—"

Koryon shouted, "Hang on." Curving the front edges of his wings into his body, he turned his downward velocity upward, a slingshot effect of his own. He clutched his claws tightly to his body as though shielding himself in panic.

Jaegendar, directly over him, flexed his huge claws and roared with anger and pleasure as he dropped—

"Catch!" Koryon lifted his head, revealing the lance he had hidden under his body, and tossed it back to Elgan. Elgan deftly caught it and threw it forward like a spear, using all their momentum and his full strength.

The air whistled around the lance as it struck Jaegendar in the breastbone, sailing in as easily as if it had struck a black cloud.

Jaegendar fell, end over end, slowly, crashing on a pinnacle of rock. The impact alone should have killed him. Koryon dropped lower, grateful that the trick had worked—

* * * * *

"Would a trick like that work, sirs? Specially against another dragon?" Brann was asking for information, not objecting.

Gannie regarded him coldly. "Against a stupid, arrogant one who hadn't been challenged in a long while? It was easy."

Brann subsided quickly, putting a cup to his mouth as much to hide behind it as to drink.

Gannie went on, "Or at least it worked as well as they could expect. Koryon flew low . . ."

* * * * *

Koryon flew low to see if Jaegendar were dead.

His body, on the cold grass, raised a mist like a hot spring or water on a fire. The lance, passing through his body, pinned him to the earth.

"We did it," Koryon said with relief.

There was a rustle as the contract dropped from Elgan's forearm and crumbled to ashes. The breeze caught the ashes and sent them swirling past Jaegendar's nose—

Where they rose suddenly in a quick puff. Jaegendar,

breathing heavily, opened one eye. "Very good," he said coldly.

Koryon and Elgan, on the ground, froze.

"It nearly worked. A better throw and I would be dead"—he glanced down—"instead of in great pain." Know," he said in a low hiss, and coughed. "Know this. I will heal. And I will find you."

Elgan said with barely a tremor, "You'll never find us."

Jaegendar took the lance in his wicked talons and snapped it off, barely above the entry wound. "I will find you, whatever form you take, and I will burn and destroy every place you have been, until the day I catch you. You will wander the earth, and death and misery will follow you nightly."

Elgan opened his mouth, closed it and strode off quickly. Koryon changed to human form and followed. They paused only to pick up their knapsacks before leaving the smoking valley. As he put on his, Elgan looked thoughtfully at the huge black figure. "I wonder how fast he can heal."

The two of them walked down the first of many roads.

* * * * *

"—the first of many roads."

The fire was reduced to embers, the lamps out. The inn was shadowy and seemed suddenly as cold as the night.

Kory finished, "And so the two took on human form and fled from town to town, from inn to inn, seeking to hide among humans and pursued nightly by the healed dragon Jaegendar. And everywhere they went, they were followed shortly by flames and destruction. To this day, wherever they go, few survive."

No one said anything for a long while. Finally, Brann asked in a quavering voice, "And did he ever catch them?"

Gannie, all smiles gone finally, looked out the window for the twentieth time. "Not yet."

"But he's destroyed every place they've been."

"Completely." Kory watched Gannie's expression anxiously. "Not one stone on another. Refugees, blood, and tears.

"So there are two dragons fleeing another, forever?" the herdsman asked plaintively.

Kory spread his hands. In the firelight, the shadows of his outspread arms flickered like wings, hanging over the table. No one moved until he dropped his arms. "I'm afraid it's the end."

Kory coughed discreetly. "If you all remember," he said earnestly, "our bargain was that if our story frightened you, you would pay us." He stared at each of them one by one; several of them flinched. "I think we've earned our reward."

The people paid nervously, digging coins out of pockets, pouches and purses. They dropped them into Kory and Gannie's hands as though making a peace offering or a bribe.

The shepherd pulled out five or six corroded coins, pressing them into Kory's palm. "All I have," he said miserably.

Kory patted his shoulder reassuringly, but took every coin.

Annella took the still-sleeping Elinor back from

Peilanne and cradled her protectively on her way out of the inn. Kory tried to pat Elinor's head, but the mother snatched her away.

One and all, even the long-distance travelers, slipped into coats and fled into the night. Kory and Gannie were left alone with the innkeeper, the barmaid, two hats full of money, and an inn of completely empty beds.

Peilanne, clearing tables, scowled at them. "Was that nice?"

Kory said innocently, "By any chance, do you have room for us to stay?"

"I have all the room I need," Darien said coldly. "Thanks to you."

Peilanne slammed the cups down. There wasn't a coin on the tray; all tip money had gone to the storytellers. "All that looking out the window was a nice touch."

Gannie looked back, all injured innocence. He poked at the fire. "Your embers are dying."

"It will be fine." Darien glared around at the empty inn. "After all, this is the Inn of the Waiting Fire."

"And you still haven't paid us," Kory said flatly.

"And what should I pay you, for having ruined my business?"

Gannie boldly tapped Darien's finger. "That ring looks nice."

Darien looked down at it with amusement. "No, it doesn't. It's worth more than it looks, at least to me. Here." Gannie watched in disbelief as Darien took two gold coins from the till and tossed one to each of them. "Least I could do."

"And now," he added heavily, "If you really can change into dragons, I recommend that you do so."

Now his shadow was large on the wall. Kory and

Gannie shifted uncomfortably. "It's like we tried to explain," Kory said finally, plaintively, "it's just a story."

"Not even that good a story," Darien said conversationally. "It needed a better ending. Would you like to hear one?"

Neither of them said anything. From behind the bar Peilanne, polishing cups, watched closely.

"Once, not long ago, there were two irresponsible young men who told a story slandering two dragons. They made their living retelling this story, frightening people, spreading bias and fear against dragons, and hinting strongly that they were dragons themselves. They also hinted that they were being pursued by a black dragon, because of treachery on the part of a silver dragon, and embellished the story with other details that were almost completely untrue."

Gannie bristled. "We based that story on actual fact."

"You based it," Darien said coldly, "on a real black dragon and a real silver dragon. You made up all the rest."

"What's the harm in that?" Kory said feebly. "A story's a story."

Darien smiled at him. "Not always." He tapped his ring on the bar. "What kind of silly dragon would chase a pair of inn-hopping liars all over Krynn—"

The two storytellers smiled, relieved.

"—when all he had to do was find an inn, and wait there?"

Their smiles faded.

The innkeeper's shadow spread and lowered from the ceiling, and his arms seemed to fade into it, until a black dragon, ring of shaping still on his claw, was crouched in the dining hall. "I haven't finished paying my wager—"

"We forgive you," Gannie squeaked.

"Quite all right, really," Kory quavered.

"Nonsense." He raised an obsidian claw, pretending to think. "Ah, yes. You said I should make you a meal." He smiled down at them, his sharp teeth gleaming red in the firelight. "My pleasure."

From the bar, a silver dragon said firmly, "Not inside, Jaegendar."

Although the window wasn't open, Kory and Gannie heeded her hint. The two dragons followed, pushing aside the shattered casement. The fire died completely as the sound of panicked screams and flapping wings faded in the distance.

The First Dragonarmy Engineer's Secret Weapon
Don Perrin and Margaret Weis

"Steady, steady . . ." Kang cautioned.

The Sivak and Baaz draconians, manning the ballista, waited tensely, eagerly for their commander's order.

Just out of ballista range, the enemy—elven light cavalry—hovered, searching for holes in Ariakas's line of defense. The elf commander was endeavoring to find the weakest spot in the line, an area left unmanned by the notoriously sloppy and undisciplined forces of the dragonarmies.

Perhaps the slimy pointy-ear thought he'd found it. Kang grinned. The elf motioned a section of ten horsemen forward to check the right flank of the enemy lines.

Kang's voice was soft; only his men could hear him at first. "Hold up, steady, steady . . ." He roared the word, "FIRE!"

As the first elf crossed a small, dried-out ravine and began moving to the far right, the ballista sent a giant bolt hurtling toward the second elf in line. The massive missile hit the elf squarely, sending him and his horse crashing into the elf behind them. Elves and horses went down in a tangle. No one stood up. The rest of the elves retreated quickly, taking with them their two dead. The elven scouting squadron retreated back to its own lines.

The weapon's crew yelled a hearty cheer, hoisting their banner and waving for the whole army to see.

Kang, a large Bozak draconian, stood behind the crew

of Baaz and Sivak draconians manning the large, cross-bowlike engine. He crossed his arms across his chest. Kang's grin widened. "Now they know we can hit out to the creek bed. They still don't know we can hit out to the road!"

His men were pounding each other on their scaly backs. Kang gave them a moment to celebrate—the Dark Queen knew there hadn't been many such moments lately. He was about to call them back to duty when a Sivak draconian emerged from the brush, came to stand in front of Kang.

The Sivak saluted. "Sir, Lord Rajak wants to see you in the Battle Tent. Right away."

"Rajak? What the hell does he want?" Kang growled. "We work for General Nemik."

Kang had been promoted to Division Engineer, and reported directly to the Division Commander. Six months before, he had been the Bridge Master of the Bridging Squadron under then Second-Aide Rajak. He and his command had proved, by building this ballista, that they could handle combat engineering. Nemik, one of the few skilled generals left in the dragonarmy, had been most complimentary on the draconians' work and had taken them under his direct command.

It was good, Kang felt, to be appreciated.

Not anymore, apparently. Kang had never liked Rajak, and the feeling was mutual. To Rajak, the draconians were meat to be flung to the enemy until the "real" fighting units—made up of humans—could take over.

"We work for General Nemik," Kang repeated stubbornly.

The Sivak shook his head. "No, sir. Not anymore. Nemik was promoted yesterday to Ariakas's Sub-

Commander, after Boromond was axed last night during the raid. Lord Rajak is now the Division Commander of the First Division."

"By the Dark Queen's eyeballs!" Kang ground his teeth in frustration.

"Shall I tell Lord Rajak you're coming, sir?" the Sivak prodded. "He's waiting."

Kang was on the verge of telling Lord Rajak that he could pull up a chair in the Abyss and get comfortable, when his sub-commander, Slith, drew Kang aside.

"You've got to go, sir."

"The man's an idiot!" Kang fumed. "You know what he'll do with us! He'll put us on point or something equally as dangerous. He's had it out for us ever since that bridge collapsed under him at Verson's Lake. It was his own damned fault. I warned him not to try to bring those woolly mammoths across, but he wouldn't listen—"

Slith commiserated with his commander. "I know, sir, but you've got to talk to him." Slith lowered his voice. "You've heard the rumors, sir. This war's almost over and we're on the losing end. We're still alive, praise Her Dark Majesty, and I'd like to keep it that way. Don't give that bastard Rajak the chance to vent his anger on us before the finish."

Grumbling, Kang was forced to admit that Slith was right. Thanks to the bickering and infighting of the Dark Queen's commanders, the dragonarmies were being driven out of captured territory, forced to fall back on their central city of Neraka. The battles being fought now were not glorious victories, as they had been in the beginning. They were battles of desperation. No one wanted to die for what was so obviously a lost cause. Desertion was rife. Even those who remained loyal to the cause—such as Kang and his men—were reluctant to spend their lives to no purpose. Manning the long-range weapons, which inflicted casualities on the enemy at little danger to themselves, suited Kang fine.

Leaving Slith in charge, ordering the men to have the ballista ready for action on his return, Kang marched down the road toward the Battle Tent. The First Division flag flew in front of the Battle Tent, indicating that the division commander was inside. The human guards came lazily to attention and, though Kang outranked them, they didn't salute as the draconian entered.

"Ah, Kang. Come and sit down." Lord Rajak wore black leather armor, so new that it still glistened. Beside him sat two of the other regimental commanders and a huge minotaur warrior.

"As you no doubt have heard," Rajak continued, "I have been promoted to General, and now command the First Division. I am going to need excellent regimental commanders, and frankly, Kang, that doesn't include you. No offense, but we all know you lizard-boys are a bit thick, eh what?"

Kang's claws itched. It took every ounce of self-control the draconian possessed to keep from tearing off his commander's face and feeding it to him for lunch.

Rajak was continuing. He gestured toward the minotaur. "I want you to meet Tchk'pal. He will be your new commander. Commander of the Third Regiment, First Division."

Kang's anger was momentarily diverted by confusion. "Uh, sir, we don't *have* a third regiment in the division. . . ."

Rajak waved his hand lazily. "My dear draco, *you* are the third regiment—you and your little band of engineers. It has become obvious to me that this army is wasting a valuable resource in you draconians. Engineering is better left to the humans, who have the mental capacities to undertake it. You draconians will now find your true calling, what you were intended to be all along. You will become the main fighting troops of the First Division! Commander Tchk'pal, here, will be given the honor of leading you."

Kang's scales clicked together in alarm. Not only was he being demoted, but he was being sent to the front of the fighting, with a minotaur warrior at the head!

And this was no ordinary minotaur warrior.

"You know Tchk'pal's reputation as a courageous fighter," Rajak was saying.

"I know his reputation, sir," Kang said darkly.

This Tchk'pal was single-handedly responsible for the fact that there were now no minotaurs left alive in the First Dragonarmy. He had led them all to death in suicide charges—stupid, behind-the-lines attacks that had no hope of success. For those under his command, at least. Somehow, Tchk'pal always managed to return.

"You have men ready," the minotaur said in what he took for the draconian language. "Me talk to men."

The dark clerics maintained that Sargas, god of the minotaur, was the Dark Queen's consort. Kang could not approve Her Majesty's choice in companions.

Glumly, Kang saluted, and left the tent.

He ran back down the road to his command bunker. Mud huts formed the sleeping and living quarters of the two hundred draconians under his command. Here, too, was the construction area for the battle engines, such as the ballista. The bunker had been dug into the side of a hill.

Kang pulled open the wooden door, paused to let his

eyes adjust to the cool darkness after the glaring sunshine outdoors.

Slith and the commanders of the seven engineer troops sat around the table waiting for Kang's return.

"That was fast!" Slith said. Noting the droop of Kang's wings, the sub-commander added, "That bad, huh?"

Kang gasped for breath. He wasn't used to running. "We've been turned into the Third *Infantry* Regiment!"

Slith scrapped his claws across the wood table, leaving long scratch marks.

Gloth, one of the Bozaks, and admittedly none too bright, blinked and said, "Infantry! That means the front lines! A fellow could get killed doing that!"

Kang sucked in a breath, about to add the *really* bad news, when it walked through the door.

"Enough talk!" Tchk'pal loomed in the doorway, an enormous battle-axe in his hairy hands. He had a bovine stink to him that was particularly repulsive to the reptilian draconians. "Have all troops form ranks. I talk to lizard-boys about tomorrow's battle!"

Lizard-boys! Kang's tongue flickered out from between his teeth. Gloth, knowing his commander's temper, involuntarily cringed.

Reluctantly, slowly, Kang saluted his new regimental commander. "Yes, sir. Right away, sir."

The rest of the draconian officers slid out of the bunker, ran back to their troops.

The sun was halfway down the sky, slumping toward the forest. The battlements faced east, toward the armies of the Golden General, their archenemy. Her army had dogged them for the last six months, forcing retreat after retreat. Intelligence reported that the Golden General was no longer leading her troops, that she had been abducted by the Dark Queen and that her forces were in disarray.

Kang didn't believe it. If anything, such news would only make the elves fight harder. And their officers at least seemed to be able to work together, were not always backstabbing each other. He had no say in command decisions, however. The First Dragonarmy had been ordered to stop its retreat, to stand and face the elves and knights. The entire First Dragonarmy had dug in, was waiting for the assault.

The two hundred draconians of the Third Regiment lined the mud and wooden ramparts. Seven ballistae were arranged along the defenses, each crewed by a troop of twenty draconians. In front of the ramparts stood Tchk'pal, waving that great bloody battle-axe around.

Kang hoped the minotaur would cut off something valuable.

"Glory is upon you, draconian warriors!" Tchk'pal announced. "Tomorrow is going to be big battle. Many thousands of warriors will die tomorrow. Probably most of you! You die with honor! We not hide behind dirt! We charge forth, meet our enemy, and slice their heads off! We going to find great glory for Queen of Darkness and Sargas, God of War!"

The minotaur ranted on like this for almost an hour. Eventually, exhausting his store of draconian language, Tchk'pal reverted back to minotaur, which few of the draconians understood. They stared at him in bemusement.

Slith stood beside Kang, who was shaking his head.

"You speak cow. What in the Abyss is he saying?" Kang whispered.

"Beats the hell outta me," Slith returned. "Some minotaur battle story or something. He keeps mentioning
glory, death, and honor in the same sentence. And
'jumping into the heart of the fighting.' You know, with
all this talk of fighting, I'm starting to get nervous. Like
Gloth says, a fellow could get killed! And just when I
was beginning to think we might live through this."

Slith edged closer, lowered his voice. "You've heard
the scuttlebutt. So what if this Golden General's been
snatched? They got more generals, don't they? We're
losing and losing badly! Everyone knows it. You know
what I've been thinking?" His red eyes had a dreamy
look to them. "We—you and me and the boys—we get
away from here and we start a little settlement in the
Khalkist mountains. I hear there's hill dwarves living
there. Dwarves are energetic bastards. They grow crops,
raise cattle, haul stone out of the mountains, that sort of
rot. We could raid their villages, from time to time,
whenever we needed supplies. Life could be good. . . ."

Kang regarded his sub-commander with admiration.
"That's really beautiful, Slith."

"Ah, well." Slith shrugged. His tone grew bitter.
"Who am I kidding? We'll never live long enough to see
the Khalkist mountains."

Kang grunted. "We've got to do something about our
new commander, and fast. All this nonsense about death
and glory and honor. We'll be slaughtered and you can
bet that no one's going to sing any ballads for us!"

Tchk'pal ranted on. Many of the draconians, standing
in the warm sun, were beginning to nod off, when suddenly Tchk'pal switched back to the draconian's own
language.

"Here is plan for battle tomorrow. We will seek out

the enemy's strongest point and rush forth to meet it! We will crush all resistance before us! Open up great hole. It will be glorious!"

"Open up great holes all right," Slith said sullenly. "In us! Say, sir . . ." The Sivak edged closer. "What if we paid our commander a little visit in his tent tonight?" The draconian drew his dagger, flourished it.

"What will we do with the body?" Kang asked.

"Roast beef for breakfast?"

Kang considered, rubbing his scaled chin. "No," he decided at last. "I, for one, couldn't stomach him. We'd probably all end up with the heaves and the trots. And Rajak's bound to wonder what happened to his pet cow."

"We could say he deserted."

Kang glanced balefully at the minotaur, who was now describing the best way to slay elves in hand-to-hand combat. "Him? Desert?"

Slith listened a moment. "Yeah," he said gloomily, "I see your point, sir. What do we do then?"

" 'Heart of the battle' . . ." Kang mused. Then he smiled, snapped his teeth together.

Slith gazed at him with hope, mingled with wary suspicion. "I know that look, Kang. I know it well. Either you're going to save us, or you're going to get us killed faster than Tchk'pal can!"

"Slith, at the conclusion of this inspiring speech, I want you to take personal command of Second Troop. Go down to the Engineer Stores, and find the plans for building a catapult. Then get to work. I want one catapult built by tonight."

"A catapult? But, sir, we already have the ballistae . . ."

"Damn it, I know what we have! Do as I tell you. One catapult."

"Yes, sir." Slith was dubious.

Tchk'pal finished his speech with a howl that was apparently some sort of scale-raising minotaur battle cry, at which—Kang supposed—they were all supposed to clash their weapons together and cheer. The cry had one effect at least—it woke up the troops. The draconians blinked and gaped and stared at him.

Tchk'pal scowled. He wasn't accustomed to this lackluster response.

Kang gave a rousing cheer. The rest of the draconians, urged by their commanders, joined in. Tchk'pal smiled, pleased. He was gracious enough to dismiss the troops. The draconians, looking grim, straggled back to their quarters.

Climbing the battlements, the minotaur joined Kang, who said to Slith, "You have your orders, Sub-commander. Carry on."

Slith saluted, and dashed off to the storage sheds to their rear.

Tchk'pal looked after Slith. "What is this all about, draco? I gave that lizard-boy no orders!"

"We have a celebration planned for tonight, sir. It will honor you as our new commander, and prepare us for the glory of tomorrow's battle!"

Tchk'pal's snout quivered with pleasure.

"A celebration? For me? This be excellent! I not expect this. You lizard-boys don't have the proper spirit for battle. This help. But"—the minotaur raised a hand—"no ale or wine or intoxicating spirits of any sort! All troops must have a clear head for the great battle tomorrow."

Kang bowed. "Of course, sir. We have a very special drink. We call it 'hard cider', sir."

" 'Hard?' Why 'hard'?" The minotaur looked suspicious.

"Because it's hard to come by, sir. It's made from apples."

"Apples, huh?" Tchk'pal licked his lips. "Sounds healthful. Apple a day keeps dark cleric away."

"We certainly hope so, sir," said Kang. "You must be certain to take *lots* of cider."

* * * * *

But when the morning sun rose, Kang's heart sank. Tchk'pal—who was supposed to be dead drunk by now—was still standing, still pounding his fist into the table, still bawling out minotaur war chants at the top of his lungs.

"Join in!" he would yell and the draconians were forced to mumble through a verse or two.

Kang eyed the minotaur unhappily. He couldn't believe it. After eight hours of quaffing their best hard cider, the damned cow was still on his feet! He and Gloth had gone through four gallons during the course of the long night. And the minotaur accounted for at least three and a half gallons on his own. Kang was worried. The minotaur looked sober as a Solamnic knight and the cider was running low.

Slith appeared in the doorway leading into the bunker. He motioned quietly for Kang to follow him outside.

Tchk'pal, downing yet another mug of cider, was promising to relate yet another stirring story of battle. He did not notice Kang's departure, nor the fact that Gloth had passed out.

A catapult stood just behind the main ramparts. The main arm was made from a timber over eight inches thick. The beams were over a foot thick, and the ropes were massive.

"Well done," Kang said, adding somberly, "I only hope we have a chance to use it."

Slith looked worriedly back into the bunker. "I thought you were going to take care of our esteemed commander. By the Queen, he sounds like he's ready to lead the charge any minute!"

"I know," Kang said, frowning anxiously. "I have a plan, but he's got to be drunk as a dwarf. And he's slurping up that stuff like it was mother's milk! I'd be out cold for a year if I drank half of what he's downed."

The silver sound of an elven trumpet split the air.

Kang and Slith looked at each other and groaned.

"Maybe he didn't hear it," Slith said.

A scale-clicking howl sounded from the bunker.

"He heard it," Kang said.

Tchk'pal surged out of the bunker, dragging along Gloth. The minotaur stood blinking in the early morning sun. Trumpets from across the field sounded. A second later, alarm trumpets from all over the dragonarmy sounded out.

Across the field, the massive army of the Golden General was beginning to form.

"Quick, Slith!" Kang hissed through his teeth. "I'll distract him. You clonk him on the head!"

Slith dashed off. Out of the corner of his eye, Kang saw his sub-commander pick up a stout tree branch.

"Uh, sir!" Kang yelled, going up to stand in front of Tchk'pal. "The . . . uh . . . enemy is approaching."

So the enemy was, approaching from behind. Slith slipped up behind the minotaur. Using his wings for elevation, the draconian rose slightly into the air and, using the full force of his powerful arms, brought the tree branch crashing down on top of the minotaur's horned skull.

Tchk'pal blinked, rocked a moment on his feet, lifted a hand to rub his head. Then—glaring balefully—he turned around to face the astounded and trembling Slith.

"What in Sargas's name do you think you are doing?" The minotaur glowered. "You trying to knock me out?"

"N-n-no, s-s-sir. It's . . . it's . . ." Slith stammered. "An . . . an old draconian custom, sir! Right before a battle!" He whipped around and brought the tree branch down on the head of the unsuspecting Gloth.

The draconian toppled like a felled ox.

" 'Hit by a tree, your sword will swing free,' " Kang added desperately. "It's an old . . . draconian saying."

"Really?" Tchk'pal looked interested. "Me enjoy learning new customs."

He started to reach for the tree branch. Kang and Slith winced and braced themselves for the blow, when they were saved by the trumpet. The enemy trumpet.

Tchk'pal's ears pricked. "Ah! Battle at last!" he said, and headed toward the ramparts. He halted momentarily when he saw the catapult. "I didn't order a catapult. Have that thing removed. We won't be needing any of these sissy siege engines today. We'll fight those pointy-ears in hand-to-hand combat!"

"Sir, might I point out that it would be better to soften them up first." Kang made a final attempt. "Use the archers and the ballistae and catapult fire to take out as many as we can before we charge. . . ."

"Bah! You sound like General Nemik. What the matter, lizard? Going yellow on me?" Tchk'pal glared at Kang.

"No, sir," Kang said evenly. "Uh, sir, are you sure

you're feeling all right?" He looked hopefully at the minotaur. "You seem a little pale around the snout."

"Never felt better!" Tchk'pal said. "Now, have lizard-boys fall into formation." He placed his hairy, stinking hand on Kang's shoulder. "Glory will be ours today! You know, though, draco, me need more apple juice. Me thirsty."

Kang turned to Slith, who was looking dejected. "Have the regiment form ranks on the battlements, full fighting order. Prepare for hand-to-hand combat."

Slith muttered something in draconian regarding pot roast, saluted and trotted slowly and halfheartedly down the ramparts. He began shouting orders.

Kang motioned to his other officer. "Gloth, fetch the commander another jug of cider. He has to be in fighting shape and he's thirsty! Move!"

"We're about out," Gloth said in an undertone.

"I've got a jug of dwarf spirits under my cot," said Kang in a low voice. "Add that to it."

Gloth returned with a mug. The minotaur drank it in one long, deep swallow. When he was done, he wiped his eyes.

"Great Sargas! That's good," Tchk'pal said reverently, and hit Kang on the shoulder blades, nearly sending the draconian hurtling over the ramparts.

Catching himself, Kang looked out to where the Golden General's army was beginning to close ranks. Heavy cavalry formed in front, ready for a charge. Kang had never seen so many elves. He didn't know there were that many elves in the whole blasted world.

"Here's what I think of you, elf slime!"

Tchk'pal tossed the empty mug out in front of the rampart, sent it smashing on the rocks below. Along with it went the draconians' chances for survival. Kang shook his head and consigned his soul to the Dark Queen.

A shout sounded from somewhere down the ramparts.

"A dragon! A copper dragon!"

Kang groaned. This was just all they needed!

The dragon soared into view. The sun flashed off the copper scales, shone silver on the tip of the terrible weapon known as the dragonlance. The elven cavalry arrayed in front of the draconians took the dragon's appearance as their signal, and began their charge. The ground rumbled with the noise of their horses' hooves. Elven voices raised in an eerie song that set the draconians' teeth on edge.

Tchk'pal looked over to Kang.

"Today is a glorious day to die, wouldn't you agree, draco?"

"A glorious day for *one* of us to die, at any rate," Kang muttered.

"What did you say, draco?"

"I said, I can hardly wait to follow you into the fray, sir," Kang amended.

Tchk'pal smiled approvingly. "At my signal, we will leap from the ramparts and meet them head on, horn to horn, claw to claw."

"Yes, sir," said Kang miserably.

"CHARGE!" Tchk'pal yelled, raised his axe, and fell flat on his face.

Kang stared in disbelief, afraid to hope. He kicked at the recumbent minotaur with a clawed foot.

Tchk'pal answered with a snuffling snore.

"Slith! Gloth! To me!" Kang shouted.

He grabbed hold of his commander beneath his hairy armpits. The other two draconians each picked up a leg.

"Now what?" Slith demanded.

"He wanted to be in the heart of the battle." Kang grunted. "He's going to get his wish! Over there."

The other two looked, saw, grinned. Together, straining with the load, they dragged the drunken minotaur down the ramparts. It took some work, but they managed at last to load him into the bowl of the catapult.

"What a great idea!" Slith was admiring. "They'll find the body on the battlefield, far away from us. Everyone will think he died of wounds received in combat. No one will suspect us of a thing! You're a genius, sir!"

Slith took up his position, holding his sword over the retaining rope.

"Wait for my order!" Kang yelled.

He raced back up the ramparts. The elven cavalry was nearly upon them. "To your posts! Prepare for battle!" he shouted.

The draconians scattered. Crossbow shots fired out all across the rampart front. Ballistae crews manned their weapons.

The main enemy advance hit the second regiment, to the right of Kang's position. He waited. Behind the heavy cavalry, long lines of infantry surged forward. As the elves crossed the dried creek bed, Kang ordered the ballistae to fire. Their effect was immediate. Huge gaps appeared in the orderly lines of the advancing troops. Enemy lines began to waver. The draconians reloaded for a second shot.

But the damage done by the large weapons had caught the attention of the dragonrider. The copper dragon arced overhead and began its descent, diving down to cripple the defenders. The heavy cavalry shifted their attack to Kang's front, and charged.

Kang turned his back on it all. He looked down at Slith.

The Sivak stood ready, sword in hand.

At that moment, Tchk'pal woke up. He stared around, saw himself in the bowl of the catapult. The sight had a sobering effect.

"Sargas take you dracos!" he bellowed, struggling to free himself! "Get me out of this! I'll flail you alive for—"

"FIRE!" Kang shouted.

Slith sliced the retaining rope. The main arm of the catapult straightened, sent the minotaur soaring into the air.

"Charge," said Kang, watching the minotaur fly gracefully over the treetops.

"Abyss take me!" Slith cried, racing up on the ramparts to watch. "Will you look at that, sir!"

The copper dragon had unleashed a stream of acid at a ballista site on the rampart. The weapon exploded, its crew scrambling to get out of the way of the attack. The copper dragon was preparing to pick them off, one by one, when the minotaur, hurtling through the air, struck the dragon squarely in the chest.

"Dark Queen's grace," Kang said, awed. "Sank his horns right into it!" He turned to his sub-commander. "Nice shot, Slith!"

"Thank you, sir," Slith replied.

The dragon and its elven rider and the minotaur fell like so many sacks of potatoes. They hit the ground hard, sending up a great cloud of dust.

"A glorious death," said Kang solemnly.

"And honorable," Slith added. He raised his voice. "The commander's dead! A moment's silence for the dead commander."

After about a few seconds, Kang said, "I don't think they heard you."

Slith shrugged.

Kang turned to his command. "Get those ballistae going! Crossbowmen, fire at will."

The surviving ballistae lashed out at the oncoming elven cavalry, decimating the front ranks. The horses wheeled and bucked and snorted, terrified at the blood and noise. The infantry, coming behind them, stopped dead in their tracks.

"Fire!" yelled Kang.

Ballistae missiles smashed into the enemy.

The elven cavalry routed, turned and ran. The horses crashed through the infantry lines to their rear, killing the elves' own soldiers, and sending them into panic-stricken retreat.

"Let's speed them on their way!" Kang shouted. He jumped down from the ramparts, followed by his men. They were about to chase after the retreating elves, planning on picking off a few stragglers and putting to death the wounded, when—out of the corner of his eye—Kang saw glinting armor.

He was afraid at first he'd made a mistake, wheeled to face this new threat, only to discover that it was Nemik's Death Riders, the First Dragonarmy's senior regiment of cavalry. They charged past the draconians and into the fray, demolishing the forces to their front.

Kang ordered his men back. Their job was done. "Reform!"

The command echoed down the line. Slowly, the draconians formed into battle lines.

This day was theirs. Kang's strategy had worked.

He ordered his troops back to the ramparts. On his way, he stopped at the carcass of the fallen copper dragon.

Tchk'pal lay beside the dragon. The top of the minotaur's head was covered with blood. The two horns were still embedded in the dragon's chest. Kang gazed in silent wonder. A thrown lance might have glanced off the armored beast, but not even the heaviest scales or the thickest hide could withstand the impact of a catapulted minotaur.

The elf dragonrider lay dead beneath the carcass of the dragon. Kang sliced the dragonrider to bits with his sword. The Golden General—or whoever was in command—would know that it was draconians who had killed this officer.

"Where's our fearless leader?" asked Slith, coming up from behind.

Kang pointed. The two walked over to take a closer look at the minotaur's body. They were debating whether or not it would be wise to haul the cow's carcass back to present to Lord Rajak, when the carcass moved.

"Great Chemosh!" Kang's wings flapped involuntarily, carried him half a foot into the air before he recovered from the shock.

Slith stood, frozen with horror.

The minotaur's huge horns were still embedded in the dragon's chest. Tchk'pal began twisting and turning, pushing at the dragon with his hands, trying to free himself.

"Kang! Kang!" Tchk'pal shouted. "I can see you, Kang!"

"We're dead dracos," said Slith in a low tone. "He's bound to remember that we did this to him! Maybe I should just sort of accidentally run him through with my sword, sir—"

A shout arose from behind them.

"Too late," Kang muttered. "Someone's seen us."

He looked back to see Lord Rajak, surrounded by his human bodyguards, touring the battlefield. They had spotted the body of the copper dragon and were coming over to investigate.

Kang saluted and stood at attention.

Covered in gore, Tchk'pal staggered to his feet, reeling and clutching his aching head.

Rajak regarded them with astonishment. "I must say that I'm pleasantly surprised. My new Third Regiment has won the day. You're covered in blood, Tchk'pal. What happened to you?"

The minotaur groaned, scowled, and opened his mouth.

"Sir," said Kang, before the minotaur could say a word, "you would not believe it! Our regimental commander single-handedly slew this dragon. He gored it, sir. An act of courage that, I'll wager, has never been performed by any other minotaur alive. He then took on the whole of the enemy cavalry by himself. He fell on them like a thunderbolt, sir. As if he were dropped from the heavens!"

Slith choked, coughed.

"It was a sight to behold, sir!" Kang continued fervently. "True glory and honor to our commander! Hip, hip! Hurrah!" He gave a cheer.

Slith, somewhat belatedly, echoed it.

Tchk'pal gaped, blinked, dazed.

Rajak walked over to the dead dragon. He could see the holes left by the minotaur's horns in the dragon's chest. Rajak gazed at Tchk'pal in awe.

"By the Dark Queen! I've never seen the like! Well done, Tchk'pal! As the draco said, you have earned great glory and honor. I shall see that you are rewarded. Regimental Commander, you will accompany me."

"But . . . but . . ." Tchk'pal glared back at Kang. "They . . . I . . ."

"Don't be modest, Tchk'pal," Rajak said. "This army needs heroes. You're a tribute to us all. Help him along, there, men."

Two human soldiers steadied the stumbling Tchk'pal, escorted him, staggering and weaving and mumbling to himself, back to the ramparts.

"That was brilliant, sir!" Slith said. "He'll never dare tell the truth now!"

Kang shook his head. "He won't tell Rajak the truth. But wait until he gets hold of us. He's *still* our commander, or have you forgotten?"

Slith's tongue slid out of his mouth, curled at the tip. Together, they strode somberly back to the ramparts. Gloth came up and reported.

"Sir, we lost four men, counting the commander, and one ballista. I've already got third troop working on building another one. What's the matter?"

Kang shook his head. "Don't count the commander. He's alive."

Gloth dropped his sword, narrowly missing his foot. "Alive? How could he have lived through that? Sargas take him and—"

"Attention!" Kang saluted.

Tchk'pal was climbing up onto the ramparts.

"Now we're in for it," Slith muttered.

Kang braced himself.

Tchk'pal walked up to the draconian commander, grabbed hold of him by the shoulders, and kissed him on both sides of his face.

Kang almost passed out from the smell and the shock.

"S-s-sir?" he stammered.

Tchk'pal grinned. "Well done, men. I gain honor and glory in division commander's eyes." The minotaur's own eyes narrowed. He jerked a thumb back at the catapult. "That my idea, you know. Both of you remember that!"

"Oh, yes, sir," said Kang.

"Your idea, sir," Slith added. "Genius. Pure genius."

"Yes, wasn't it." Tchk'pal was smiling again. "And now I have another, even better idea . . ."

The draconians groaned inwardly, waited to hear their fate.

Tchk'pal turned to gaze fondly at the catapult.

"We're going to do that again," he said. "You will fire me into battle on the morrow. Except this time, I want to attain more range and greater height. I want to be able to fly at least twice as high and travel twice as far at twice the speed. Can you handle that, dracos?"

The two draconians looked at each other, and grinned.

"Your next flight will be truly glorious, sir," Kang promised.

"You can bet on it, sir," Slith said.

"Excellent." Tchk'pal put a hairy arm around each of them. "And now, lizard-boys, let's celebrate. Do you have any more of that tasty apple juice?"

Through the Door at the Top of the Sky
Roger E. Moore

He was hurrying home, the comfort of sheltering rock just a hundred and twenty miles straight down, when they caught up with him. Lemborg saw a streak flash across the left rearview mirror, but the word *missile* had not reached his brain when the port hydrodynamic maneuvering tank exploded at the rear of his ship.

Lemborg was slammed between his flight seat and leather seat restraints a dozen times like a rubber ball, ears ringing from the louder-than-thunder bang of the pressurized tank's demise. When his double vision cleared, the diminutive gnome saw the great blue sphere of Krynn shining from his rearview mirrors instead of filling his forward command window. The *Spirit of Mount Nevermind, Mark XXVIII-B* was yawing to the right, clockwise, a miles-long contrail of twisted white smoke falling behind it like the tail of a burning comet.

On top of that, there was a new star ahead among the infinite constellations, a star that did not move with the others. The star was bright and steady, and even a novice wildspace pilot like Lemborg could tell with a glance that it was following him.

They were following him.

Lemborg gasped. His mind overloaded with a thousand unspeakable terrors, the white-bearded gnome grabbed the yellow lever at his side with both hands and tugged back sharply. Metal clamps unlocked with shrieks and groans along the *Spirit*'s stern; warning sirens and alarm bells raised deafening cries in protest. With a jolt that ran the length of the *Spirit* and shook Lemborg right down to his teeth, the entire hydrodynamic maneuvering assembly came free of the ship's fuselage, just as Krynn's vast, white-streaked face drifted back into view from Lemborg's right.

At the very moment the assembly was jettisoned, Lemborg released the yellow lever and reached up, grabbing an overhead handring attached to a thick pin. He jerked down. Metal screamed as a huge spring shot sternward along a track, pulling on the rope to the primary gyroscopic stabilizer. The rumbling whine of the gyro immediately went through the *Spirit*, and the ship's tumbling ceased.

Lemborg fell back into his wool-padded seat, his breath shallow and his wood-brown face pale and streaked with sweat. Glorious Krynn was straight ahead again, a beautiful blue-and-white ball that filled his window and stretched beyond. Sancrist Island and the safety of Mount Nevermind were minutes away. He was almost home. The loss of the maneuvering assembly, which had cost 17,406 steels, weighed two tons, and took three years to perfect, meant nothing. If *they* caught him—only that mattered. The burst tank rendered the assembly both useless and dangerous. It would also slow him down, and speed was Lemborg's only friend.

A flicker passed to starboard, very close by. Lemborg saw the dark streak flash ahead, barely visible against the white clouds of Krynn before it vanished.

They'd missed. That was unusual. It would not happen with the next shot, he knew. It was time to chuck his last cow chip, as his cousin in the Agricultural Byproducts Disposal Guild liked to say.

Lemborg adjusted the gyro using a steering bar, reducing the angle of his dive into Krynn and orienting the ship toward Sancrist Island. He then mumbled a traditional gnomish engineering prayer ("Great Reorx, please do not let this device blow up in an inappropriate manner!"), stood up in his seat as far as the restraining straps would allow, and kicked down with his right boot.

His boot heel thumped down on a metal plate, which gave way slightly. Lemborg heard a scraping sound far behind him. He shut his eyes, gritted his teeth, and forced himself back in his seat as far as he could go.

There was a *BOOM!* louder than the maneuvering-tank explosion, louder than lightning in your own living room, louder than Reorx's Hammer against the Anvil of Creation, forging Chaos into the Stars, the Five Worlds, and Universal Order—or so ran the crazed thought through Lemborg's mind as a beyond-tremendous force slammed him back into the overstuffed pilot's seat and tried to pull the skin off his face. Hot needles seared his eardrums. He couldn't breathe. He passed out.

He involuntarily opened his eyes again to a mad, whirling scene. Wind blasted through the cabin and pummeled his face, snapping the straps against his chest and arms. Clouds raced by the shattered command window, titanic cotton balls and lacy streaks of white hurling overhead against a bright blue sky. The air stank of roasted metal, wood, and paint.

Lemborg lay limp and unmoving in his seat. A headache burned like lava throughout his skull. His orange coverall suit was filthy, his body felt like it had been pounded by giants, and he thought he would soon throw up.

He remembered the emergency button. May as well, he thought through the boiling pain in his head. Be interested to see what happens if it fails. The fingers of his right hand crawled down to the end of the armrest, curled under the knob at the end, and fumbled with the button there.

A shock rumbled through the ship, throwing Lemborg forward into his straps. The chaos of passing clouds slowed down as the ship decelerated, then flew straighter. Lemborg imagined the *Spirit*'s emergency wings cranking outward and locking into place. The drogue chute had likely been torn instantly away, but it had at least slowed the ship down to make it more maneuverable.

The battered gnome's left hand caught hold of a short vertical bar by his knees. He made a slight adjustment to the bar, and the nose of the *Spirit* tilted downward, revealing a bright wasteland of dunes and dark grass roaring by only a few hundred feet below. Almost home. He squinted into the wind, hunting for a makeshift landing strip.

Lemborg then saw that the ship was descending much too fast. His eyes widened with horror. Instinctively, he put out his right hand to deflect the eroded sandy ridge rushing up at him.

The *Spirit* cleared the ridge top. Almost.

A bone-breaking, world-shattering *BANG!* rang through the ship. The *Spirit* rocked madly, slammed port and starboard by ground debris as it skidded across the rock-strewn sands. A thousand banshees screamed from the lower hull. The emergency wings smashed into boulders and were torn off. Dust spilled into the pilot's cabin and blinded Lemborg instantly, filling his mouth and stinging his face.

Lemborg never saw the stone walls ahead, or the archway with its two ancient gates—closed—standing right in his ship's path. The fuselage of the cone-shaped spacecraft smashed the wooden gates into clouds of flying splinters. As the ship skidded through, the outriding port and starboard auxiliary maneuvering tanks at the ship's midsection struck the ancient stonework on either side of the gate and blew up instantly, cutting the *Spirit* cleanly in two and destroying most of the arch as well.

In a shower of bright orange flames, splintered rock, and blackened chunks of wreckage, the forward half of the *Spirit of Mount Nevermind, Mark XXVIII-B* ground to a halt in the center of a long-abandoned desert city, nose tilted slightly upward as it climbed the sandy slope around a dry stone fountain. Falling debris rang off the scorched metallic hull.

Lemborg dizzily opened his eyes and had a brief, blurry view of a huge, grinning monster peering in the ruined command window. This cannot possibly be good, he thought, just before unconsciousness mercifully claimed him.

* * * * *

Consciousness claimed Lemborg back after centuries of bad dreams. He was vaguely aware first of being alive. It was not a wholly pleasant sensation. The skin on his face and hands felt hot and sunburned. He licked his chapped lips and discovered that he was thirsty. Terribly thirsty.

"I offer my greetings." The voice in his ears was resonant,

so deep and strong that Lemborg felt his whole body vibrate. "You must soon explain how you brought your curious device into my city, and whether the manner of your arrival was planned in advance. I was quite impressed, and so will be patient with your response."

The little gnome opened his eyes. He looked dizzily up at a richly painted ceiling that stretched beyond the edges of his vision. Little humans in colorful robes marched in great inset circles above, sounding trumpets and beating drums. Toward the center of the parading circles were figures with outstretched arms, reaching toward a handsome, elaborately armored male human on a throne in the center of it all, who raised a sword in his right hand in a bland gesture of triumph. The ceiling was cracked with age, but the colors had not faded greatly.

Lemborg blinked and tensed his body experimentally. A groan escaped his lips as he squeezed his eyes shut. Every part of him ached abominably. He was little more than a living bruise.

"You have many injuries, but you will live," said the resonant voice in a friendly tone. It did not sound like any being Lemborg had ever heard. The words were clear, but the register was so low that Lemborg knew whoever was speaking had to be huge. An ogre, maybe. With luck, not a minotaur.

"Wa—" Lemborg's parched throat closed off before he could continue. He coughed and raised a hand, and was promptly rewarded with waves of agony through his arm, shoulder, and chest.

Cold water unexpectedly splashed into Lemborg's face. He gasped and half sat up, crying out in pain from the sudden movement. He attempted to lie down again, but it only made the pain worse.

A massive, solid object pushed gently against his left arm. He started to cry out again—but blessed, beautiful-as-spring relief poured through his body. His pain was gone. He thought of a sea wave rolling up a beach to cover the sand with its cooling foam, submerging him as it passed.

He sighed, then took a shaky breath and rolled onto his left side, opening his eyes again. He tried to sit up, with great success.

He saw the dragon.

"AAAAAAHHH!" he screamed as he fell back. The dragon gleamed like a vast mountain of burnished golden hue. Huge dark eyes watched him impassively beneath thick scaled ridges. The monster's head nearly brushed against the distant painted ceiling. A great set of ivory claws rested not two feet away from Lemborg, each of the five claws longer than Lemborg's legs.

"More water?" asked the dragon with concern. The great clawed foot beside the gnome lifted soundlessly away from him, formed itself into a cup, and dipped into a broad metal tub nearby. Water cascaded from the claws as they lifted away again and rushed at the gnome with frightening speed.

He scrambled back but was drenched in a second from head to foot. Racked with coughing, Lemborg flailed his arms hysterically.

He dimly sensed that something very large had moved close to him. The air grew exceedingly hot.

"You will have no fear," said the dragon, quoting a spell. The air around Lemborg burned as if a great oven door had opened. The dragon's words sang through the gnome's body, then came to fiery life and leaped into his mind.

275

Lemborg fell back, arms dropping to the floor at his sides. He coughed a bit, caught his breath, then sat up once more. The dragon had assumed its original position and now watched him with patient eyes.

"No more water, thanks!" the wet gnome shouted quickly. "Feeling just fine now, quite fine. Sorry for the fright show there. Not much chance to see a dragon close up before, not around home, anyway. Just in the books. Obviously, dragons are much bigger in real life. Simply caught me off guard." He glanced behind him to make sure there were no more surprises.

"I am pleased," said the dragon, leaving Lemborg a trifle confused as to just which of his remarks the dragon was pleased about. The dragon turned its head slightly to favor the gnome with its right eye. The gnome thought the gesture almost regal. The dragon never wasted movement, doing only what it needed to do and no more.

"We should be introduced," the dragon prompted. Hot, dry air blew against Lemborg's face. The breeze smelled like burned sand. Lemborg's scalp itched, and he quickly curled his chapped lips inward to wet them.

"Ah. Certainly." The gnome carefully got to his feet, brushed off his orange flight suit, and straightened up to face the dragon. (He had an idea floating in the back of his mind that facing a live dragon was extremely dangerous, but for some reason it didn't seem to be worth worrying about.) "Aerodynamics Guild technician-pilot fourth class Lemborgamontgoloferpaddersonrite. The *short* form of the name, of course, but humans butcher it to Lemborg. If there is just a moment to spare, there is the *longer* short form of it, which should take no more than a half hour, or the full form, which—"

"Another time, perhaps," said the dragon with finality. The gnome fell silent. "Lemborg, you may call me Kalkon, which of course is the short form of my own name. I will not trouble you with the longer form." The dragon lifted its snout the slightest bit. "I complimented you earlier on the manner of your arrival here in the so-called Northern Wastes of Solamnia. The show was pleasingly extravagant, as spectacular as the great sand-devil of 353, which carried off the Great Temple's western tower here. I watched the scene in its entirety from the doorway of the constables' main barracks. A very destructive expenditure of energy, to be sure, and one that required a spell of healing on my part to aid your recovery"—the dragon put emphasis on that last part— "but I do applaud your style. You must be well regarded among your fellow wizards."

The gnome's mouth drifted open in surprise. "What? Oh! Not a wizard, thanks, but rather with the Mount Nevermind Aerodynamics Guild instead. Not a wizard, no, no relation at all. And thank you for the spell. Quite pleasant, actually. Eh . . ." Lemborg turned again to look around the room, a huge empty hall. "Just landed a technojammer here, but . . . um, it seems to have been misplaced just now. Seem to have misplaced the landing zone, too—was aiming for Mount Nevermind. Hope that new-model technojammer isn't lost or . . . anything. Perhaps some light could be shed on just where that silly thing seems to have—"

"You are a tinker gnome from Sancrist, to the west," interrupted the dragon, nodding once with understanding. "Your people build mechanical things that blow up."

Lemborg grimaced. "Well, now, not all of them do, of

course. That is something of a myth because less than ninety percent of all gnomish inventions for the last twenty fiscal years really ever blow up or need to be recalled for catastrophic defects in design or workmansh—"

"You called your flying device a technojammer," said the dragon—Kalkon—patiently. "What exactly does a technojammer do?"

"Oh." Lemborg's forehead furrowed in sudden concentration. He had tried explaining this before to humans, but with little success. It was such a simple thing, too. "Well, that vessel, which of course has been misplaced, is a technojammer, and technojammers fly, rather like birds only without the flapping of wings and feathers and such—more like, um, powered gliding, um, the way that spelljammers fly—or glide, rather—only technojammers, unlike spelljammers, use no magic, only machinery, though both were designed for travel into wildspace—that being the, um, nothing that lies above the world, or around the world, or really *between* the different worlds, and these technojammers can, um—"

"You arrived here on a flying ship that could travel between worlds," interrupted Kalkon. Surprised that the dragon had caught on so soon, Lemborg nodded his head vigorously. "Were you returning from another world, then?"

"Oh, no, took off from *here*, absolutely," said Lemborg. He stuck out his chest a bit and pulled on his short white beard in pride. "In fact, first-*ever* successful flight of an Aerodynamics Guild technojammer! A miracle of modern achievement after only twenty-seven tries, not counting the eighty-six previous programs. Got out and took the old *Spirit of Mount Nevermind, Mark XXVIII-B* up for a spin at dawn this morning and . . ."

Lemborg stopped. His gaze dropped, the color running out of his brown face until he was almost gray.

The dragon waited, watching Lemborg carefully.

Lemborg looked up, licked his lips, and swallowed. "Um, pardon for having lost the thread of the current conversation," he said distractedly. "Perhaps best to exchange names and addresses now and get together again as soon as scheduling allows. Yes. Certainly would be a good thing right now to find the way to that technojammer, if it has indeed been seen, then stay in touch later after the Nevermind Postal Guild strike has been settl—"

"Tell me," said the dragon.

"Tell? Tell what? Oh, the address, it, ah, would be best to mail it over when—"

"Tell me now."

"Really cannot remember it right now, but—"

"No. The truth."

Lemborg's face radiated anxiety. "Ah, nothing, really, just thought that it would be best to go before . . . before the welcome is worn out, and—"

Kalkon's great head darted down close to the gnome, without changing expression except to open its mouth slightly.

"Before they get here!" said the gnome with a shout, stumbling backward and falling on the seat of his pants. His eyes were the size of dinner plates and locked on the dragon's teeth. "Before they get here!"

A brittle silence reigned for a bit. The gnome's hands trembled as he clutched at his white beard.

"They," repeated the dragon, pulling back.

"Really need to go," repeated the gnome urgently, fingers twisting strands of his beard into knots. "Really should go, before the . . . um, before . . . It was the passage device generator, there was never the slightest intention of taking the passage device generator from them, it just got in the way when things got out of hand and the time came to get out of there, quickly, before they, um, got to me, and in all the confusion and running everyone happened to wind up on the bridge, and there was the generator on its mounting, and *bam*, ran right into it, quite foolish of course, and the passage device generator snapped loose and got caught here on this sleeve, right here, and naturally there was no time to remove it or take it back so it came right along back to the *Spirit of Mount Nevermind*, and lucky thing it was quite light as such things go, so there it was, stuck on this sleeve, and it was left behind, back on the ship"— Lemborg paused for breath.—"and doubtless right now they want it back very badly—they must have it, really, or else their passage device is only so much junk, so they'll certainly come for it fairly soon, perhaps only minutes from now as they were quite close when it became necessary to trigger the high-speed solid-fuel propulsion system, and it would be for the best of all to be gone and far away before they get here. *Very* far away. Please."

The dragon looked at Lemborg, who looked back, panting.

"I see," said the dragon, and was silent for a minute more.

The gnome began to fidget, looking nervously around the room.

Without further ado, the gleaming dragon came to its

feet. It was terrific in size. Its wings stretched out for a moment, twin metal fans as large as clouds. Lemborg looked up from the floor in amazement and awe, as well as with a greatly renewed sense of fear.

"Let us go see your ship," said the dragon, leading the way out of the great hall. Lemborg mutely got up and followed. Above them, the armored man on the throne looked down unmoved.

* * * * *

The sunlight outdoors blinded Lemborg briefly, forcing him to feel his way along a wall until he bumped into a marble statue base. He was astonished at the great size of the building he was in, but the actual city itself—once he was able to see again—was grander by far. Domes, towers, spires, columns, and high-peaked roofs surrounded the immense open plaza before him. He and the huge dragon stood at the top of a wide, high set of steps that dropped two stories to the plaza itself, so he had a great view of the abandoned city. Most structures seemed to be of the same washed-out shade of gray or tan stone; only the blue in the sky lent color to the scene. Even so, the architecture was delicate and awe-inspiring, and surprisingly well preserved.

Lemborg quickly focused on the central feature of the open, dune-covered plaza below: the remains of the *Spirit of Mount Nevermind, Mark XXVIII-B.* His gaze ran over the battered, smoldering wreckage for a few moments. Then he sat down on the warm top step with a long sigh.

"Could have been worse," he muttered. "Name is still legible, at least."

281

"Was there any possibility you could have been killed?" Kalkon asked, looking in the same direction.

"Killed? Oh, possible, sure. Everything's possible. Happened on the first twenty-seven attempted missions, certainly." He stared at the wreck, his face reflecting defeat. "Stern is gone. Could be a problem. No landing gear. No maneuvering tanks. Landing wings. Running lights. Steering fins. Drogue chute." He sighed again, more softly now. "Ten, twelve weeks at most at dock number two in the lake yards, then a year for the paperwork."

"At Mount Nevermind," the dragon added.

"Yes," said the gnome, closing his eyes. "Not here."

The dragon waited a moment, then said, "They were trying to kill you."

"Eh?" Startled, the gnome opened his eyes. "Oh, yes, of course. They were—" He shivered violently, wrapping his arms around himself as if freezing. He abruptly stood up. One hand crept to the top of his balding head and gingerly felt the skin there. "Best to be going soon," he said in a low voice.

"Before they get here," supplied the dragon.

"Yes," said the gnome. "Yes. Best to leave soon. Now, perhaps."

The dragon raised its head, its long snout turning up to sniff the wind. It closed its eyes and became motionless for a full minute. Then it lowered its head and looked at Lemborg again. "No one has arrived yet. Nothing has changed. You are safe here with me for the present. Come back inside, and let us consider the situation and the options."

The gnome followed the dragon back into the building. Lemborg looked around as he did, noticing again the profusion of paintings on the walls and ceilings. Much of the metalwork present—stair railings, robed human statues, wall sconces, table furnishings—bore little rust or corrosion, but a layer of grit covered everything. Lemborg's short boots crushed sand beneath them. The dragon's tread was a soft, rhythmic earthquake that rumbled through the rooms and halls.

"Nice home," Lemborg finally said.

"This was the administration building," said Kalkon. "The city was called Lake Cantrios. There was a large lake to the east, against the city wall. The city was a resort for the wealthy of old Solamnia, a place of refuge and amusement. The amphitheater still stands, though the barracks are fallen and the gladiatorial arena is in poor repair. The Cataclysm drained the lake, burned off the crops to the north and south, and broke the irrigation tunnels. There was a windstorm, too, I believe, and the temple is missing a tower, as I mentioned. Otherwise, despite the sand, it is in good order. The citizens have been gone not quite four centuries, but with the dry air preserving the city, it is almost like they left yesterday. Lake Cantrios was forgotten by all until I found it again. That was only . . . only a few years ago."

Lemborg started to frame a question, opening his mouth.

"I rule alone here," said Kalkon. "No other beast or being will trouble us. They are not eager to challenge me for the privilege."

Lemborg stopped walking and stared up at the dragon, mouth still open.

"I do not read minds, really," said Kalkon without turning around, "but I know the mortal mind well enough to predict the more likely responses. Your thoughts are safe."

"Oh," said the gnome. He was silent as he walked into a particularly huge chamber behind the dragon. The dragon trod heavily toward the far end, half-turned toward Lemborg, and settled its great scaled belly on the dusty marble floor. Its tail slowly whipped back and forth through the air before settling to the floor as well.

"Welcome to my throne room," Kalkon said, tossing its head in a gentle arc to take in the whole chamber. The dragon's great voice echoed from the distant walls and pillars. No furniture was present. The paintings were too distant to make out clearly.

"Thanks," mumbled Lemborg. He looked around, still anxious, and licked his dry lips. "Should be about time to go," he added.

"There is still time," said the dragon. "Come closer."

The gnome hesitated, then did as he was told.

"Forgive me," said Kalkon. "There is much I need to know in order to make a proper decision, and my personal method of investigation has always proven to be the best."

"Wha—" said Lemborg.

The dragon uttered a word of power. Its eyes instantly grew in the gnome's vision until they filled the entire world. Lemborg's mind emptied and awaited a command.

"Remember now," said Kalkon. "Think of the enemy. Think of what happened that brought you here."

Lemborg rocked back on his heels but remained standing. His eyes were unfocused and glazed. He had a dream.

The dragon closed its own eyes and saw the dream:
There was fire and thunder, and the technojammer Spirit

was aloft, a vessel that flew without magic. The gnomes had done the impossible. The pilot shouted with joy, pulled metal levers and twisted knobs. The cabin shook, but the sky outside steadily turned from blue to dark blue to black, and there were stars all around, stars like the glowing dust of gems, more stars than grains of sand in a desert. In the window was a vast globe across which blue seas and dark lands passed, and whorls of white turned like pinwheels. The pilot looked down in wonder, forgetful of all but the glory of his homeworld of Krynn.

But the pilot soon saw another ship there above the world, a spelljammer that flew by magic, and it moved faster than did the Spirit. It looked like a huge coiled shell, this other ship, with long straight tentacles reaching forward from the mouth of the great shell, and this ship moved alongside the gnome's ship as crewmen caught it fast with ropes. With dull, lifeless eyes, the same crewmen then caught the gnome and forcibly brought him aboard the coiled ship to meet his new masters.

The gnome pilot had read about this type of ship, called a nautiloid. He had read of its masters and knew certain frightening rumors about them, and the men with lifeless eyes took the little pilot to those masters, who were preparing to eat a meal when their guest arrived.

It was the meal that the gnome pilot remembered most clearly and would never forget, the meal that fought as it was held down. The gnome saw one of the purple-skinned masters silently lower its tentacled face over the screaming man's head and—

Kalkon leaped to all four feet, jaws apart and all teeth bare and gleaming. The dragon's great tail lashed back and slapped a wall, shattering the painted plaster into white dust. For long minutes, the dragon's breath bellowed hoarsely through the building, echoing down every hall.

Pushing aside the repellent image at last, Kalkon looked down at the entranced gnome who gazed up at her with glassy eyes.

He is just a gnome, she thought. *He is like a child in the world, and wicked things are coming for him. But he is not my child. My children are gone. He is a gnome with no one to save him. I could leave him here, and the wicked things would surely find him, and I would think no more about it. I was not there for my own eggs, and a wicked thing took them. I let them be held for ransom, but the promise was a lie, and now my children are lost and gone. I was not there for them. I gave my children into the claws of evil and let them go. He is not my child. He is not my child. But—*

Kalkon heard a faint sound, not one that a human or a gnome would have heard. Kalkon raised her head. Wind blew against a swiftly moving object, a flying object, and she heard it clearly now. It was three miles away.

She looked down at the gnome. "Lemborg," she said. The gnome blinked and stirred, awakening, and raised an unsteady hand to his face. "Lemborg, we must leave now."

* * * * *

It was, of course, too late to leave the abandoned city. The little gnome had been dead right that *they* would arrive shortly in search of him. It was not yet too late to prepare, though the useful preparations were few.

Still, Kalkon was not particularly worried. The brain eaters had their own flying ship, but she was Kalkon, and this was her city. She hustled Lemborg out of the way, hiding him in a basement room that was undoubtedly once a mortuary (but she didn't tell him that). Then she meditated briefly, spoke the name of a spell, and became invisible. That done, she went quietly outside into the noon sun to greet the invaders.

The first thing she noticed upon getting outside was that the invaders were already over her city. That was rather quick, she thought, looking steadily up at the curious device drifting over the stadium. It was just as the gnome had remembered it: a golden coiled shell, set upright, from the mouth of which several interwoven wooden tentacles projected forward, forming a pointed bow. A tall pole with skulls tied to it arose from the middle of the device, and a peculiar sail projected from the back side of the coiled shell. A rudder hung from the bottom of the tentacled hull.

The invaders' ship was quite large. Kalkon eyed the flying ship and thought it was only slightly shorter than her own length of two hundred fifteen feet. She guessed the ship was entirely made of wood. Excellent: If it was wood, it would burn.

She carefully took up a position at the bottom of the steps, facing directly into the central plaza where smoke still rose from the charred remains of the *Spirit of Mount Nevermind*, and waited. She remained there for twenty minutes, watching as the flying ship circled the city. Then it drifted closer, cruising along until it was just over the *Spirit*.

Her mouth opened, preparing for her attack, when without warning the ship shot straight upward into the sky. Kalkon had the shocked impression that the ship had been fired from a bow. She stood there dumbly, looking up in astonishment as the ship became a dot against the blue zenith, then vanished altogether.

She waited in the silent plaza for an hour more, saw and heard nothing, then snorted in uncertainty. She took wing, flew around her city, and saw that it was intact. Dispelling her invisibility, she returned to the administration building to get the little gnome.

"Problem resolved?" the gnome asked fretfully, glad to be out of the basement room. (He had figured out for himself that it had once been a mortuary.)

"It would seem so," said Kalkon easily. She described the ship, its actions, and its hasty departure.

Lemborg listened but wasn't comforted. "A repeat visit might still be forthcoming," he muttered, unconsciously wringing his hands.

"Or it might not," said the dragon. She regarded the gnome in thought. "I am curious to know the nature of this passage device generator that you took from them."

Lemborg sighed and explained. Apparently, each group of worlds and their sun was encased in an unbreakable sphere of unthinkable size. A "door" through this sphere into other spheres could be opened only by using a passage device, and the generator provided the magic to power the device. The creatures who had tried to kill Lemborg could not leave this group of worlds without their generator; they were stuck in this sphere for good, and they were not likely to appreciate that if they had business elsewhere.

Kalkon nodded understanding, though it was just so much garbage to her. A doorway in the heavens—the idea beggared reason. Trust a gnome to believe in such a thing. Still, his story held up so far. She elected to wait before rendering a final verdict on the issue.

That done, she waited a polite interval before asking, "Do you play khas?"

"Khas?" The gnome's hands slowed in their wringing. "There is a khas set here?"

"The best," said Kalkon.

Lemborg soon admitted that, indeed, Kalkon had the finest khas set in Ansalon, so far as he knew. They started a game as Lemborg ate his way through a pouch of dried fruit he had managed to salvage from the wreckage of his ship. ("Certainly looked real, anyway," he commented about the gargoyle statue in the middle of the dry fountain, whose grinning face had peered into his broken command window upon his landing.)

It was during their long game in Kalkon's throne room that Lemborg began to talk. Evening fell as he described Mount Nevermind's gnome-on-the-moons wildspace program to Kalkon in great detail, revealing how tinker-gnome colonies would be founded on every one of the wandering stars in the sky that he called planets, and how gnomes no longer had to rely on balky, unreliable magical spelljammers to enter space, now that wonderful mechanized technojammers could be used instead, assuming that no more of them blew up on ignition.

"Of course," he went on breathlessly, "reports are constantly received at the Bureau of Colonization, Deportation, and Missing Luggage that the gnomes of Mount Nevermind have already established footholds on numerous worlds, in this sphere and others, but future models of the *Spirit of Mount Nevermind* will ensure that this trickle turns into a raging flood, a great storm of gnomish civilization and enlightenment that will transform the spheres. There will be steam-powered refrigerators and whooshwagons for everyone."

"I see," said Kalkon, carefully scooting a blue rook

along the board with a long foreclaw. She examined the hexagonal board with one eye, then nodded approval. She had not a clue as to what the gnome was talking about, but talking seemed to ease his mind.

Lemborg moved a white cavalryman only a second later. "This expansionist phase is beneficial for the gnomes as well as for the future of the spheres, of course," he added, chewing on a dried fig. "Recent demographic statistics indicate that subterranean urban growth at Mount Nevermind is proceeding along an exponential function thanks to the development of reliable hydrodynamic aquaculture and the successful mass production of nonpoisonous artificial foodstuffs like snerg and goofunx and kwatz and—well, no, hoirk still causes twenty percent fatalities, so the bugs are not quite out of that one, but three out of four is still marvelous. The children seem to love goofunx and cannot get enough of it, though it does cause numerous cavities." He shifted in his chair and looked up expectantly at the other player. "Remarkable to find a gold dragon so interested in applied technology."

"Brass," said Kalkon. She hated the way the gnome just moved pieces without thinking about it first. It was driving her crazy.

"Pardon?"

"I am a brass dragon. You thought I was a gold dragon?"

Lemborg's mouth dropped open, and bits of chewed fig fell out. "Ah, many apologies are due," he said with embarrassment. "Appearances were deceiving. A kingly figure, too, for a brass dragon."

"Queenly." The white cavalryman . . . what was the gnome planning with it? She was finding it hard to concentrate on the game. Something the gnome had said. . . .

"Que—a *female* brass dragon?" The gnome was amazed.

"I am a female brass dragon."

"Ah . . . many more apologies are due, then, but nonetheless for one so young as well as a *female* brass dra—"

"Old. A dragon is strongest and happiest when it grows old in its power, and I am very old. We are not like humans, who treasure only their youth."

Lemborg thought there was something odd about the way Kalkon said that. He looked down at the blue-and-white marble playing board. He thought about his next words carefully. "Well, then, obviously life must be at its very best right now."

Kalkon moved a claw anyway, lightly tapped a blue cleric along a row of hexes, and left it in what she knew was a bad spot. It was the only good move she could make. She suddenly lost interest in the game.

Lemborg moved his white queen immediately afterward. The word "check" was on his lips, but the dragon had turned her head away to look at a distant wall.

"Obviously it must be," said the dragon. "Obviously."

Perhaps it was best to change the subject, Lemborg sensed. Home and family were usually safe topics, at least with humans. He looked at the board, coughed, and said "Check" under his breath. Then, more strongly: "Are there any young ones who come here now and then to visit? Any hatchlings happy to see the old home and mother's wings?"

The huge dragon did not respond, but continued to stare at the wall and the darkness.

Lemborg waited until he began to fidget again. He

coughed but got no response. Had this game been played in the Mount Nevermind Academy for the Endless Study of Khas and Nothing Else, Kalkon by now would have had to forfeit the ga—

"I do not know where my children are," said the dragon in a remarkably quiet voice. "They are probably dead, and I can only hope that they are."

No adequate reply came to the stunned gnome's mind. He stared at the dragon. A little time passed.

"I had a clutch of eggs," said Kalkon softly. "Four little eggs. A little less than a hundred years ago, the Dark Queen took them with all the other eggs of our kind, promising their return after the coming war. We feared for our children and swore our neutrality. Then she secretly poured foulness into the eggs with magic. They hatched into draconians, stunted mockeries of their parents. My four children were turned into Baaz, destroyed in body and spirit, corrupted and broken. If there is mercy in the world, they are long dead now. If any of them survive, they would not know me, nor know anything of what I or our kind know. They would be evil and lost to me forever, and if I saw them I would have to kill them, my own children."

Lemborg stared down at the khas board. It suddenly meant nothing to him.

"Forgive my sudden leaving, but I will return in the morning," said Kalkon, getting to her feet. Her great wings unfurled and stretched. "I feel the need for a long flight and a drink from the ocean. My congratulations on your style of play. I must resign the game."

The great dragon left quickly. After a long wait, Lemborg slowly put the game pieces back in their starting places, feeling miserable. It was all his fault for asking about her children. He wished he had been born mute. He slowly unrolled the carpet Kalkon had found for him, wrapped himself in it, and blew out the oil lamp that had provided light for the game. He lay down but found no comfort in the silence and darkness.

* * * * *

Faint red light fell over the plaza. Lunitari was full, the other two moons out of sight, and the sky above full of glittering stars. Kalkon lifted her head toward them and wondered what she had done to deserve this life. She went through the motions of living with nothing behind them. Fleeing to a deserted ruin did not insulate her from the guilt and pain, so she slept and flew and ate and kept her mind as empty as she could. In the end, it did not help. Her children were destroyed, and she was in part responsible.

She swiftly crouched and threw herself into the air, wings unfurling and thundering down in great pumping motions that lifted her into the red moonlight. Her gaze fell upon the great empty city of darkness below. Nothing moved but windblown sand. The city was hollow like her life, dead like her children. Her eyes lifted and listlessly skimmed the rooftops and spires.

An object floated into view from behind the one remaining tower of the Great Temple. Moonlight gleamed from the tall golden shell and the polished wooden tentacles aimed at her.

Kalkon blinked. How did *that* get here?

They shot her five times in as many seconds.

White-hot blows hit her in the neck, right foreleg, and right side of her great scaled chest. She inhaled sharply;

shattered ribs and ballista-launched spears stabbed into her lungs. A sharp blow from a catapulted weight broke the main bone in her right wing. The entire wing folded up as she shut her eyes and roared in agony, rolling to the left and falling toward the abandoned military stables one hundred feet below.

* * * * *

Lemborg sat up, still wrapped in the carpet. The roar and the rumbling sound afterward were fading. An earthquake? He had never heard anything at Mount Nevermind about the Northern Wastes being subject to earthquakes. It seemed unlikely.

He got out of the carpet, unable to sleep. He thought he should go see what was going on, but he dreaded the thought of running into Kalkon after his gaffe during the khas game. He should leave on his own before the brain eaters returned, or before he made an even greater fool of himself before the dragon. Kalkon had rescued him from the crashed technojammer, healed him, entertained him, and he repaid her with this. His face burned with shame.

He could still see a bit in the huge, dark room. After collecting his few belongings, he walked out into a long, high hall, trying to recall the way out. He walked to one end of the corridor, took two lefts and a right, and realized he was completely lost. A window loomed ahead, faint red moonlight shining through its sand-dulled panes. Disgusted with himself, Lemborg dropped his few belongings and managed to pull himself up to the window ledge to look out over the dark city.

He was still on the administration building's third

floor. Lunitari's red light fell over the ruins. Thousands of gnomes would walk on the red moon's surface someday, Lemborg thought. Gnomes would build magnificent cities there, spreading their great inventions across wildspace, and there would be hydrodynamics for all. But it was impossible to care about it now. It meant as little as the khas game. Lemborg blinked back tears and sighed. He dropped his gaze.

A pole rose up right in front of his window, in the middle of the air not twenty feet away. Tied to the pole were human skulls. Holes had been gnawed in their bloodstained crowns.

With a gasp, Lemborg let go of the window ledge and ran the moment his feet hit the floor. He left his belongings where they fell. Behind him, the huge golden coiled shell of the brain eaters' spelljammer rose up and stopped, hovering beside the translucent window like an upright coin. It began to turn, the bow swinging wide.

Lemborg saw a corner ahead. He dove around it as the great window exploded inward behind him. The spelljammer's long bow raked the window from right to left, knocking out hundreds of panes in a glistening waterfall. Before the noise had ended, gaunt human figures in ragged clothes leaped down from the tentacled bow into the corridor. Shards of glass crunched under their bare feet. No one cried out—all faces were empty, even of their purpose. They set off immediately after the gnome.

They are going to catch me, the terrified gnome thought as he ran down a dark hall. They are going to catch me, and then they are going to *eat* me. The certain knowledge spurred him on even faster. He took two rights, a left, and found a spiral stairway down. He descended two floors, turned left again as he left the stairs, then fled down a narrow hall. Footsteps echoed far behind him.

He dodged through a doorway and found himself in a four-way intersection. He went right. Faint light was ahead. He stopped, unsure what it was, then moved forward cautiously to check.

Ahead was an open doorway leading to the night air. He crept close, boots crunching softly on windblown sand, and peered out into the moonlight. The plaza lay before him. The faint smell of scorched paint lingered in the air, drifting over from the visible wreckage of the *Spirit of Mount Nevermind*.

He squinted. Moving around the pointed nose of the *Spirit* were manlike figures in long robes. They did not seem to be walking; instead, they moved as if floating over the ground.

Brain eaters. Lemborg had seen them levitate during the chase aboard their nautiloid spelljammer, vainly trying to catch him. He turned and ran back into the building, through the archway into the four-way intersection.

A four-fingered hand there sank its claws into his left shoulder. Hysterical, Lemborg turned and sank his teeth into the creature's skin. It was cold and slimy like a live eel. The hand jerked away from him instantly. But more hands grabbed him by his arms and clothing, human hands with scarred, filthy skin. He fought them insanely, screaming as he did, but they had him tight and there was nothing he could do. They held him down just as they'd held down the man whose brain was eaten out while he was still alive.

Gently rubbing its injured arm, the brain eater waited

until the gnome had exhausted himself. Then it raised its uninjured arm in the dim light and gestured toward the plaza. The empty-eyed humans who held the gnome nodded and followed their robed master as he left, taking their captive with them.

* * * * *

Three other brain eaters waited by the *Spirit* and the dry fountain, their feet hovering scant inches over the sand. Their robes rippled in a cool breeze. Shivering in the grip of the human slaves, Lemborg recognized the milky eyes and obscene tentacles, writhing like worms, hanging from the mauve horrors that passed for faces among brain eaters. They kept their thin hands hidden within their wide sleeves, arms crossed in front of them as if considering judgment.

The slaves halted before their floating lords. A long moment passed in silence. Then one of the slaves walked over to face Lemborg. He struggled once more to free himself, but could not.

The raggedly dressed human, a woman, looked down at Lemborg. In the red moonlight her eyes were bottomless holes, as if she had died weeks ago and rotted away inside.

"You are the cause of much needless trouble," she said without accent or inflection. She could have been reciting something she read on a sign. "You would have escaped, your deeds unpunished, were it not for the power of our telepathic masters to read the simple minds of vermin like you. You will tell us where the passage device generator is hidden."

Lemborg struggled, even less effectively than before,

before he subsided. The woman was looking over his shoulder, as if listening to something that Lemborg couldn't hear.

"You left the generator inside your ship, beside your pilot's chair," said the woman. "It is unguarded. Does anyone else know you are here?"

Lemborg, breathing heavily, simply stared up at her.

"Only the old female brass dragon," said the woman. She waited, then added, "which is dead. We shot it down with our ship's catapults and ballistae. Two of our masters are examining the body now. Do you know of any other valuables in this city?"

"Shut up!" Lemborg shouted at her in fury. "Shut up, shut up, *shut up!*" Tears suddenly ran down his whiskered cheeks.

"You hide nothing from us. Our masters take the information from your mind as soon as you think of it. They tell me what to say so I may communicate with you. Your thoughts are as simple as those of fish." She paused. "You have not seen any treasure here. As that is the case, our masters have only one more use for you. They are tired and hungry from hunting you down. Our masters will now feed, and they will feed on you last so you will know what is to come." The woman stopped, a puppet hanging on its strings.

One of the hovering brain eaters drifted forward, toward the woman and Lemborg. Its feet touched the ground directly behind the woman. Narrow fingers seized the woman by the arms, long claws digging into her bruised and dirty skin.

The empty-eyed woman sank down to her knees, her head tilting back abruptly. Wide eyes reflected the red moon above. Her pale lips trembled.

The brain eater gently lowered itself over her until the moist tentacles where its mouth should have been touched her face, then stretched out and covered her head from the eyes up, tightening their grip in seconds.

The woman shuddered, then spasmed violently. She opened her mouth and screamed up at the night sky like the damned. Lemborg threw back his head and howled with her, eyes squeezed tight and feet kicking wildly.

A monstrous roaring broke over the city. It drowned out both cries. The roar crashed and echoed through the night, fading into echoes and the howl of distant wind.

Lemborg opened his eyes, gasping and shaking. The other brain eaters now stood on the ground and stared off to Lemborg's right in silence. Forgotten, the woman lay on her side, knees drawn up and hands entangled in her blood-matted hair as she sobbed. Lemborg looked in the direction the brain eaters faced.

There was a low thundering, like a heavy thing running with a strange gait. At the far end of the sand-covered plaza, a huge moonlit shape hurled into view from around a street corner. It quickly turned toward Lemborg and the brain eaters in a loping run, favoring its right foreleg as it came on. It was very fast.

Kalkon. Whatever the brain eaters had done to her, it had obviously not been enough. Certainly, if she could heal Lemborg, she could do something for herself.

It took a moment before Lemborg realized what was going to happen. Escape was critical. Thrashing wildly, he wrestled his left arm free from a distracted slave's grip, whirled, and bit the hand of the slave who held his right arm. The slave let go with a curse. Lemborg fled from the group in panic. Kalkon would not be able to see him in the darkness as she attacked, and he wanted to get as far from the brain eaters as possible.

He was wise. Kalkon did not wait for the brain eaters to display any tricks or talents they had. When they discovered she was alive, the two who were investigating her body had tried to destroy her mind in some excruciatingly painful manner. Their smoking bodies, half sunk in a wide pool of molten sand, now lay together in the street outside the ruins of the military stables.

Kalkon opened her mouth when she was within range of the brain eaters and blew death at them. A roaring jet of superheated air rushed from her jaws. One of the brain eaters vanished into thin air before the blast struck it. The other three and their human slaves were thrown back, smoke billowed from their roasting, dancing bodies. Inhuman shrieks rang out as they quickly fell, limbs jerking spasmodically. Then they grew still, as small flames crackled over their smoldering clothing and charred flesh.

Even as the superheated jet left her throat, Kalkon felt lances of mental force stab her between the eyes and sink deep into her head. It was the same mind-destroying attack the other two brain eaters had launched at her, only many times more powerful and desperate. The lances exploded inside her mind in blinding, agonizing light. The pain was too great to hold in. It tore apart her very thoughts in a second.

Lemborg felt the heat wave engulf him as he fled. The air was scorching, too hot to breathe. He fell and covered his head with his arms, burying his face in the sand. Screams rang from behind him and died. He heard the deep thumping of the dragon's feet, felt the ground vibrations through his flesh. The skin on the back of his neck and the top of his head felt badly sunburned.

The thumping and huffing continued from behind him, in the direction of the wreckage of his ship. Smarting from pain, Lemborg lifted his head and peered around when the heat had passed. Kalkon was there, rearing and stamping the ground. She made bizarre rumbling noises like grunts and whimpers. Her fractured right wing dragged in the sand as her tail whipped around, throwing up a great cloud of sand that slowly filled the plaza air.

A clawed hand dug into Lemborg's shoulder, jerking him to his feet. He looked up. "Kalkon!" he screamed.

The dragon staggered and looked around wildly. The charred remains of the brain eaters and their slaves hung from her claws in shreds. She started forward in Lemborg's direction, favoring her right leg.

I will kill this one if I am attacked, buzzed a voice in her head.

Kalkon jerked back, her eyes unnaturally wide. She shivered and looked for the source of the cry. Fifty feet ahead of her was a brain eater, clutching Lemborg in front of it like a shield.

I will get the passage device generator and leave if I am not attacked, buzzed the voice, which Lemborg as well heard inside his own mind. *I will then teleport again, but this time to my ship and while holding this small one. I will then set the small one free. I will get the passage device generator without interference.*

Finished, the brain eater slowly edged toward the *Spirit of Mount Nevermind,* keeping Lemborg between itself and the dragon.

Kalkon rocked unsteadily, wide eyes blinking twice. "Queen of Darkness," came her low reply, "give back my eggs."

The brain eater hesitated, then continued moving toward the wrecked ship. Half-dragged along by the brain eater, Lemborg reached out a hand to the dragon. "Kalkon," he said. His face was filled with terror.

Kalkon drew back her head, then lunged forward. She covered the fifty feet to the brain eater in less time than passes between two heartbeats.

The startled brain eater shoved Lemborg at the onrushing dragon, then turned to flee. The gnome stumbled and fell. Something heavy and huge came down on his right leg and broke it in four places below the knee with a single loud snap. Wailing, Lemborg rolled on his back, grasping his crushed leg.

A flying thing thumped down on the ground beside him. He saw it, but its meaning did not register through the all-encompassing haze of pain. It was a brain eater's arm, its four-fingered hand still twitching. The rest of the brain eater was not there.

Lemborg felt he was close to passing out. Shock was settling in, and the world took on a decidedly fluffy look. The torrent of pain receded. Dying is not half bad, he thought, if that is what this is. Even the brain eaters' nautiloid ship had a fluffy, dreamlike look about it. It floated like a cloud over the administration building. Rocks and spears showered down from it at Kalkon, who dodged some of the blows and roared back at the ship. She roared and called the ship Dark Queen. Was that the spelljammer's name? Lemborg was surprised she would know this. She was calling everything Dark Queen now, though.

The gnome fell back on one elbow. His leg felt so much better now, even if it was bent strangely here and there. He saw Kalkon seize the grinning gargoyle statue in the empty fountain in one great clawed hand (or perhaps it was a foot—he could not be sure what the proper term was for it) and tear the statue free with one motion. The dragon swung the statue back sharply and threw it spinning into the sky.

Now, what was that for? thought Lemborg. The statue hit the nautiloid with a sound as loud as Reorx's Hammer. It made a rain, a rain of splinters and boards and golden shell broke like a bad egg, a dry rain falling on the dry night sand. He knew he should write this up in his next report to the Mount Nevermind Steering Committee on Raining Things. If he could just find a pen and a fresh sheet of . . .

* * * * *

There was a long time of strange dreams and fever. Pain blew against him, then was gone. He became light as a feather, wind rushing over him like water. He was cradled in a bronze bed, he dreamed, far above the world where the only sound was a slow, rhythmic thunder. He once felt himself rising to the surface of a great sea, the sun's light filtering into his eyes. *Sleep*, said a great, soft voice, and Lemborg slipped back into the depths of the dream.

No time passed at all, and it was night again. Blades of cool grass pressed against Lemborg's hot skin. He could barely move, but it did not seem to matter.

You are home, said the great voice. *I can heal your injuries but not your fever. Your people will find you soon; they may be able to do what I cannot. You must rest until they come. You have nothing to fear now.*

The voice hesitated, then went on. *My mind has healed,*

thanks be to luck and rest, and my wing has healed, thanks be to magic, so I will now return to my people, too. It will be a long flight north, but I believe I am ready for it. There was another pause, a longer one. *I owe you much, Lemborg. I ran from the past but it found me again, and now I can face it and go on. But I will miss your company and your curious style of khas. I am glad that your ship chose my city as its final port. It—and you—brought me what I needed.*

There was silence. Then the wind stirred greatly for a few moments. When it subsided, it was very peaceful and still. All was right with the world.

It lasted for twenty minutes. Then the gnomes found him.

* * * * *

"Rubbish to the twelfth power!" snorted the First Undersecretary to the Aerodynamics Guild Director. He flung the Medical Guild's report to the side, where the thick pages joined a hundred other reports in a large wooden crate beneath a carefully lettered sign that read RECYCLED BOTTLES ONLY. "I can't believe those bedpan engineers would send me such rot. Brain eaters! Spelljammers! A dragon who can play khas! Lemborgamontgoloferpaddersonrite took a bad hit on the head, and that's all there is to it. Same thing happened to my third cousin, the one who was struck by lightning and imagined he was a dragon-fighting hero or some such." The First Undersecretary sighed heavily, looking down at his desktop. "Amazing, though, that he survived the loss of his ship. The technojammer must have gone into the sea right after liftoff. Such a promising start, too. Absolutely perfect liftoff."

"Didn't explode at all," agreed the Second Under

secretary, head bobbing violently as he stood on the other side of the deck. "Always an excellent start to any aeronautical undertaking."

The First Undersecretary grunted, pulling his short white beard thoughtfully. "Perhaps it would be best to have Lemborgamontgoloferpaddersonrite pilot the next mission as well, since he has the edge in experience, delusions or not. His fever's gone, and with a refresher course or two on the next model, he could—"

"An admirable idea, I agree," said the Second Undersecretary, nodding again but with less enthusiasm. "Perfectly admirable except for the minor fact that Lemborgamontgoloferpaddersonrite checked himself out of the Primary Downslope Trauma Center this morning and submitted his vacation request. I am afraid he is already gone."

The First Undersecretary stared at the Second in astonishment. "Gone? He's gone? Where to? Cancel his request! Bring him back at once! He's our senior technojammer pilot! This is mutiny!"

The gnome standing on the other side of the desk winced. He knew this next part wasn't going to be easy. "I agree completely that it is certainly akin to mutiny, as he didn't even wait for the vacation request to go through its normal seventy-eight-week period of approval before he left for the harbor at Xenos, where he has undoubtedly caught a ship by now." He handed his supervisor another sheet of paper, which the First Undersecretary read after locating the spectacles on top of his head. "Perhaps, though, it is for the best, as he still seems to be caught up in his, um, delusions, rather like your third cousin."

The First Undersecretary groaned and let the sheet

fall from his fingers. "Off to the north to the home of the dragons, taking only six changes of clothing and a khas set. I see your point. Very well, call up the dormitory and have the students gather in the auditorium in two hours to pick a pilot for mission number twenty-nine. We'll draw straws, as usual."

The Second Undersecretary shouted, "At once!" and darted from the room. The First Undersecretary glanced at Lemborg's vacation request once more, then wadded it up and tossed it into the crate with the other papers. "We'll get this technojammer thing right eventually," he muttered, and went on with his paperwork.

Aurora's Eggs
Douglas Niles

In an age when stars were born and dreams began, the gods of light and darkness gave to the world their children, the first dragons. These regal serpents soared in the skies over Krynn, numbering but ten in all—five favored daughters of Paladine, and five more bold sons of Takhisis.

The dragons of the Platinum Father were creatures of light and goodness, formed of the metals that brightened and gave strength to the world. They were gold and silver, brass and bronze and copper. Females all, the quintet of serpentine sisters made their lairs in the west of Ansalon and dwelled there for countless eons, singing praises of Paladine among the vast swath of peaks that would one day be called Kharolis.

Arrayed against them were the five sons of the Dark Queen, wyrms of implacable evil arrayed in the colors of their matriarch: red, blue, black, green and white. They spread wickedness and destruction in the name of Takhisis, each serpent a blight of chaos and waste upon a great section of the world. Ultimately, like the daughters of Paladine, these chromatic dragons settled, making their lairs in the great mountains of central Ansalon. This smoldering, volcanic region would later be known as the Khalkist.

For the better part of an era, the number of the ten dragons remained constant. Ancient beings, they did not age beyond their full maturity, but neither did they procreate. Naturally, Paladine and Takhisis each wished for wyrmlings born of their mighty offspring, that all Krynn might be populated with dragonkind.

But for the timeless millennia of prehistory these godly efforts failed, until at last the world came to a cusp of growing history, and ogres and elves came forth upon the land. Each of these folk laid claim to realms, allying with the mighty wyrms or taking them as foes. They worshiped the Platinum Father and the Dark Queen, but called them by new names—Paladine was E'li to the elves, and the ogres knew Takhisis as Darklady.

Ultimately, with the aid of mortal sacrifice and cosmic sorcery, Paladine and Takhisis both discerned the secret of spawning—the creation of eggs. Each of the gods bred with the offspring dragons; their efforts brought forth a clutch from the Dark Queen herself, and a smaller nest from each of Paladine's daughters.

At last the Dark Queen had hope for her ultimate domination—the answer to her schemes would be war! A trumpet call of fury rang through the skies of Krynn, summoning the chromatic dragons to their task. Her foe's descendants would be slain, and evil would rule the world.

In those days the ogres were mighty, and with their help the dragons of Takhisis struck with swift lethality. In short order, the wyrms of silver, bronze, brass and copper were surprised, ambushed, and slain. Knowing that but one of her enemies remained, Takhisis planned for her ultimate mastery. . . .

* * * * *

Everywhere black smoke spewed into the air, dozens of billowing plumes rising from a shattered landscape to form a forest of vaporous, impossibly lofty trees. Tortured, churning trunks merged into glowering overcast, an oppressive blanket shrouding the breadth of Krynn.

At least, across that portion of the world within Furyion's vision. The red dragon flew high, skimming the underside of the heavy stratus, banking easily around the pillars of ash and smoke, riding the expulsive updrafts of heat. The volcanic mountains of central Ansalon were the source of the massive black columns. From his soaring vantage Furyion could see a hundred peaks spewing their fiery guts into the sky.

Deep chasms and canyons scarred the ground. In some of these raged the white ribbons marking turbulent streams, while others glowed dangerously with the crimson fire of flowing, liquid rock. Steep cones rose from lifeless bedrock to form a jagged skyline of darkstone peaks, often clustering in a massif of six or eight well-defined summits, spewing smoke, lava, and steam from an assortment of craters. Other mountains rose far above their neighbors, pyramids of hardened magma surrounding calderas many miles across.

Furyion flew past one such massive summit, skirting the rim of the high crater. With detached interest he admired a gridwork of fiery cracks amid darkened slabs of cooler lava, the pattern that crisscrossed the floor of the vast caldera. In moments the dragon's flight carried him beyond the sight, great strokes of his scarlet wings pressing downward in a slow, measured cadence. Updrafts of scalding heat that would have seared the scales off of Akis, the white dragon, merely lifted the mighty red higher, saving him the straining of his mighty wings.

Now the greatest of mountains came into view, the massive peak dwarfing even the mightiest among the lesser summits. Rising as a cone of massive, primordial rock, this was a volcanic matriarch that could obliterate the entire range if she should unleash her might against the world. Black along the lower slopes, where cliffs plunged into shadowed gorges on all sides, the mighty peak's color merged toward a rusty red on the higher elevations. A series of jagged ledges jutted like shoulders from the massif, barren outcrops on an otherwise sweeping expanse of steep mountainside.

Despite the mountain's great size, the crater at the summit was uncharacteristically small, giving the peak the appearance of a sharp point that nearly grazed the underside of the black stratus. Unlike many of the volcanoes, the crater spewed neither ash, smoke, steam, nor fire from the deep shaft. Yet heat glowed there, the crimson glow of fundamental fire forming a circle of light against the clouds.

Once before, Furyion had actually flown above the great crater to confirm this fact. So intense had been the blistering emanations of raging heat that the ancient red dragon had been forced to veer away at the very edge of the caldera, knowing he would certainly have perished if he flew any farther into the searing updrafts. Yet even in that quick glance he had seen enough to know that this mountain plunged an unimaginable depth toward the heart of Krynn.

Furyion's eyes gleamed as he lighted on a lofty ledge, one of the highest on the cracked and barren mountainside. He spread his jaws, extending a scarlet-scaled neck to its full length before bellowing a great cloud of flame into the sky. Wisps of oily fire scorched the mountainside, hissing and burning with a sound like thunder as the mighty red made bold announcement of his arrival.

The sharp *crack* exploded from a nearby ledge, a perch only slightly lower than Furyion's, and a bolt of lightning speared the sky. Arkan, the ancient blue, uncoiled from his own vantage and dipped his head in acknowledgement of his red brother's arrival. Furyion bowed too, his yellow eyes bright. Jealously, the crimson wyrm eyed the necklace of silver scales gleaming on Arkan's blue neck. It was a trophy, symbol of the blue dragon's triumph over Paladine's dragon of silver.

The stink of noxious gas stung Furyion's nostrils and he looked down to see a greenish-yellow cloud drift along the sloping mountainside. Korril, the wyrm of emerald green, raised his head to regard Furyion. Leathery lids hooded the green's dark, deceptively gentle eyes, and wisps of poisonous breath still rose from the twin gaping nostrils as the green glared impassively at the two higher serpents.

Furyion was further inflamed to see brass scales dangling in a chain around Korril's neck. So the green, too, had met with success in the war against Paladine's daughters.

Turning his eyes to the sky, Furyion sought signs of other arrivals. Next to fly into sight was black Corrozus, gliding around the shoulder of the great volcano to come to rest on a well-scoured outcrop of rock. The black dragon announced his presence with a spew of dark acid, spitting a river of the burning, sizzling liquid that spilled far down the slope of the peak, until at last the churning, corrosive flowage dissolved itself into the porous rock. Even from his much higher perch, Furyion noted that a circlet of copper scales ringed Corrozus's snakelike neck.

Finally Akis, the massive white, came into view, soaring as far as possible from the flaming peaks. As he approached his own ledge, farther down on the mountainside, Akis blew a great cloud across the rocks, leaving them frost-lined and cool. Only then did the colorless serpent settle to his perch. Raising the wedge of his head, Akis blasted another cloud of frost into the air, let the sweep of the breeze carry the chill back across himself.

Bitterly Furyion saw that even the swift-flying Akis, whose discomfort in these hot regions was well known to his cousins, bore a symbol of triumph. His throat was surrounded by an array of bronze scales, proof of another kill.

"Be comfortable, my brother," urged Furyion, more than a hint of mockery in his voice as he addressed the drooping white.

"Bah!" sneered Akis. "The heart of the Khalkists lies too far from realms of ice and snow. You would not speak so—"

"Silence!" barked Arkan, the command echoing across the mountainside. Furyion whirled upon the insolent blue, enraged by the interruption, but the azure wyrm hissed a more compelling warning. "Our mistress speaks!"

The mighty red fell silent, poised to listen and heed as rumbling within the mountain grew to a palpable shuddering in the bedrock. The vibration forced Furyion to grip the outcrop of his perch with powerful talons lest he be shaken from the ledge. Rocks broke free, tumbling from the summit and slopes, but the thrones of the five dragons had been chosen with care. Landslides spilled and roared past each, but none of the rubble flew far enough outward to strike any of the five sons of the Queen.

Smoke and ash abruptly exploded from the crater, billowing into the sky, swirling downward to encircle the serpents nearest the summit. Tongues of fire lashed through the enclosing murk, and bits of fiery lava spattered onto the rocks, hissing and spitting with infernal fire. Again pale Akis spewed his cloud of frost, miserably trying to hold the heat at bay. The other dragons simply squinted against the mild assaults, knowing by the size of the eruption that the summons of their mistress Queen was of tremendous importance.

For a long time Furyion huddled in the haze of ash and smoke, feeling the stinging burn in his nostrils, blinking his leathery eyelids over flakes of powdered rock. He thought with amusement of Akis, knowing that the white must be suffering tremendously—despite the fact that his low perch marked his lesser status, but also allowed him to avoid the worst of the Queen's vented fury.

Finally the ash and smoke gave way to pure fire, a blossom of blue flame shooting straight upward from the volcano's maw. The pillar burned away the clouds, boring a passageway straight through to pale sky, sending waves of shimmering heat rising relentlessly to the heavens. The cloaking overcast surrounded the gap, like a cylinder of murk enclosing a heat-scoured chimney.

The Dark Queen's glory cleansed with its killing heat, sweeping the ash and debris away, raising a mighty wind across the face of the mountain. Still Furyion and his brothers clung to their perches, turning faces away from the stinging gale, looking upward to witness the glory of their mighty mistress.

Only when the fire had nearly burned itself out, when the hole in the dark cloud mass began to close, did the words of the Queen become known to her children.

"Welcome, mighty sons . . . know that your actions have been pleasing to me. Your courage, your cruel and relentless violence shall be well rewarded."

"Greetings, Mother Queen," murmured Furyion, in cadence with the other wyrms. He felt a rush of warmth and affection for the great, chaotic goddess who had given birth to his brothers and himself.

"Our eggs, the precious orbs that each of you has given me, are nurtured in the heart of the Abyss. They thrive and prosper . . . and someday, they will yield handsome offspring. Then shall our children populate the entire face of Krynn."

Furyion shivered in delight at this word of the spawning, and bowed his crimson head in abject worship. "We are unworthy of your grace, Mother Queen," he rasped, spewing steam and fire from his nostrils. "The red dragons shall rule the world in your name!"

"Aye, my boldest, my mightiest son. The wyrms of blue and black, of green and white, shall aid and serve them—but it is my desire that the dragons of fire be the masters of my world!"

Crowing, Furyion raised his face to the cloudy sky, bellowing a great fireball of searing, sizzling heat.

"But know, too, my children, that there is still danger in Krynn." The cautionary words came as the other four serpents regarded the mighty red, their expressions carefully masked to conceal the emotions of envy and displeasure that lurked in their wicked thoughts.

"But mistress—" It was Arkan, the mighty serpent with scales of turquoise blue, who spoke up next. "I myself have slain the silver dragon. See, I bear a necklace of scales, ripped from that wretched wyrm's rotten corpse."

"Aye, my son."

"And I!" Green Korril was not to be outdone. "The wyrm of brass perished in the crush of my bite and the rending talons of my claws. I, too, wear a necklace of hated scales, proof that our great enemy has been slain."

"Hear of my own trophy, Mother!" cried Corrozus, shaking his supple neck and setting the ring of copper-colored scales jangling. "I, too, have slain a wyrm of Paladine."

Next it was Akis who boasted, brandishing his own circlet of bronze scales.

"I see your triumphs, my sons—and my pride showers you like the warmth of fire from the sky."

Four dragons bowed, accepting the praise. Only Furyion looked on, envy and rage vying for mastery of his seething emotions.

"But still there is danger, and it is for this reason that I have gathered you."

"We know that Aurora, the gold, still lives," Arkan assured the Queen of Darkness. "But surely she cannot long evade us."

"No, but there is further danger, my sons. The dragons of Paladine have worked to deceive us—even as they were slain, one by one, by my loyal sons."

"How?" demanded Furyion, secretly encouraged by the suggestion that his brothers' efforts might have resulted in a clumsy failure.

"As her sisters were slain, Aurora herself remained aloof—and all the time she was coiled around the future of her race."

"Mean you that Paladine's dragons, too, have eggs?" Corrozus hissed. The other serpents fell silent, chilled by his suggestion.

"Aye, my black one. They have eggs, and have commissioned Aurora with the task of guarding them."

"Are the spawn in the far plane of Paladine?" Furyion

asked the question, but dreaded to hear the answer. They were so close to ultimate victory, making themselves and their spawn the unchallenged masters of the world. Yet if the Platinum Father was guarding the eggs, much as Takhisis had secured the spawn of evil dragonkind in the Abyss, their plans could yet be thwarted.

"Here they have made their mistake," stated the Queen. "They have allowed the eggs to remain upon Krynn."

"Where we can reach and destroy them!" Furyion pledged, determined that he would gain that necklace of golden scales.

"Yes, my sons. You must slay Aurora, *and* eradicate the clutch of metal eggs. Only then will our future be safe, freed from the threat of Paladine's dragons."

"The gold is a daydreamer—she will be easy prey!" boasted Corrozus. "It shall be my pleasure to rot the gilded scales from her flanks with the spittle of my breath!"

"We fly at once, my Queen!" promised Furyion, with a flexing of his broad, sail-sized wings. The red was annoyed that his black cousin had been quicker with the boastful promise.

"But tell us," inquired Akis. "Where may the eggs of the metal dragons be found?"

"You must search, my sons. They are concealed in the western mountains, and I bid you, all five of my mighty children, fly there, find the clutch, and destroy it—utterly and completely. Succeed, and the dragons of metal shall be forever banished from the world!"

Five proud bellows challenged the sky as the wyrms of Takhisis raised their heads. Jaws spread wide, they spewed deadly breath—fire and lightning, acid and frost and deadly gas, all churning together, rising in a pillar of evil might.

In the sudden silence that descended, Furyion trembled, on the brink of his lofty ledge. The western mountains were far away, across the broad plain that was central Ansalon. Yet he knew that he could cross that distance in a matter of a few days. Once above the distant range, he could use magic, or perhaps merely his keen eyesight, to discover Aurora and the clutch of eggs.

Arkan and Akis flung themselves into the air, crying in martial fury. Furyion tensed, then halted as the voice of his mistress came into his mind.

"Wait, my crimson son . . . I would have words with you, alone."

Tingling, Furyion paused, watching as Corrozus and Korril took wing. He waited, taut with anticipation, as the black and green wyrms trailed their brothers along the swooping gorges leading to the west.

"I desire, Furyion, that *you* shall win the greatest triumph in this battle. All have heard me decree that the red dragons shall be lords of the world—but you need this trophy, this proof, to hold above your brothers, to show them the rightness of my choice!"

"Aye, Queen Mother." Furyion was grimly certain of this same fact—he had already determined that he would do whatever was necessary to slay Aurora himself. "I shall wear the scales of the golden wyrm around my neck, a trophy that will herald my greatness through the ages! My talons, my fangs shall rend her to pieces!"

"Brave words, and true. But heed: Do not make waste of your magic, my son. I have granted you the mightiest of spells, the most potent enchantments within my power. Use them!"

Already the red dragon had pictured the brute violence he would deliver against golden Aurora, but here again he heard the Queen's advice. He would paralyze her with magic, then squeeze the life from the idle serpent of gold before she knew that she was attacked.

With a bellow of challenge and triumph, Furyion spread scarlet wings to catch the upward drafts, leaping into the air and winging westward toward the destiny that would decide the future of the world.

* * * * *

There were no seasons, then—nothing like the passing of months or years. In places the world was cold, and cold it remained; in other realms, warmth was the ruling condition, and such climes held sway with the passing of hundreds, of thousands of sunrises.

Yet still time passed, and one being sensed this more keenly than any other. Like a band of gold she encircled the finger of a spiked mountain peak, following her master's command, waiting with immortal patience through the passing of countless days for the arrival of her sisters.

Still she waited, as time and events took shape upon the world. And at last she knew:

The others would never return.

* * * * *

Aurora coiled near the summit of her lofty peak, holding her golden head upraised, keen eyes searching the eastern horizon as they had searched it for days uncounted. The sky was cloudless, the sun high above, yet no glimmer of brightness speckled along that distant horizon.

The knowledge that she was alone grew in the mighty gold dragon slowly, like a gradual awakening from a deep and profound slumber. When it took solid root, she knew the truth: her sisters were slain, victims of the Dark Queen's treachery.

A lesser being might have given way to despair, even fear; to Aurora this was simply a problem that required her full concentration. Thoughts of many things drifted through her ancient, timeless mind as she turned toward this new, discomforting reality.

For a time her thoughts wandered, as they had done during more peaceful times. In truth, what did it mean to be really, truly alone? Aurora had always been a solitary creature, disdaining the petty concerns of Paladine's other serpents. Brass, copper, and bronze had been full of petty jealousies, even greed, and the impatient silver had been too shortsighted and active for more than a few days' pensive conversation.

Solitary life suited Aurora, for it gave her plenty of time to think, which was her favorite pastime by far. She was content to pass the days with considerations of poetry and history and all forms of knowledge marching in steady progression through her awareness. And of course, there was also the matter of her magic—she delighted in weaving enchantments, and Paladine had bestowed upon her a remarkable gift for arcane power. Already Aurora had mastered many spells, but with sorcery, as with life itself, one could never have too much time to study, to meditate, and to think.

For that matter was she, even now, really alone? In truth, no, for there were the eggs in the great cavern below, secured in the vault that arched over a vast, underground sea. The secret trove lay in the heart of this mountain ridge, beneath a mile of solid rock. It had only one clear point of access—the Valley of Paladine. That vale lay in clear view of the gold dragon's current vantage, where she had remained for an uncountable number of days.

That thought reminded her that she hadn't eaten in some time. She looked for some sign of prey in the game-rich valleys below. Something moved, far down the slope of the mighty peak, and Aurora became more keenly aware of her hunger. Unwilling to waste time in a long pursuit, she decided to use magic in the aid of her hunt. The golden body shifted under the influence of a polymorph spell, shrinking, the metallic scales of her breast merging into the plumage of a proud eagle. Leathery wings of shining membrane became the feathered limbs of a mighty soaring bird. Keen-eyed and shrewd, the gliding predator moved away from the mountain, circling easily, gradually spiraling lower.

The source of movement was clear to Aurora, now—a herd of elk grazed through a meadow of tall grass. The proud bull stood alert while his does nibbled at lush clover. Several of the great, shaggy deer gathered around a small spring, heads lowered to drink.

Diving lower now, the eagle that was Aurora veered to the side, ensuring that the bull did not take alarm. When the tops of the trees skimmed just below the bird's feathered belly, she stroked her wings, speedily approaching the meadow where the herd sought sustenance.

Breaking from the cover of the trees, Aurora shifted into her true shape. Golden wings abruptly cast half the clearing in menacing shadow, and drew a bugling bellow of alarm from the great bull. Immediately the elk stampeded, scattering in every direction toward the shelter of the surrounding woods. But the gold dragon had already selected her victim, a doe with the gray muzzle and stiff, clumsy gait of an elder. The elk limped after the younger members of the herd, braying in shrill panic as the massive, winged shadow eclipsed her flight.

Aurora dropped like a pouncing cat, bearing the elk to earth and breaking the muscular neck with a single, crushing bite. By the time the rest of the herd had scattered, she crouched over the fresh meat, the odor of blood making her belly rumble. The clearing was pleasant, with the fragrance of many blossoms soothing to the gold dragon's nostrils. The pastoral surroundings of lush pines and the placid waters of the spring made a splendid framework for a meal.

But there were the eggs, Aurora's sole responsibility. She could not see the Valley of Paladine from here, so she knew that she could not linger in the pleasant lowland. Seizing the carcass in her jaws, she gave a powerful downstroke of leathery wings, hurling herself into the air. The golden serpent flew at a gentle incline, circling toward high altitude, gradually working her way back toward the lofty summit.

The sun had neared the western horizon by the time she reached the slopes around her peak. The body of the elk dangling from her jaws, Aurora warily looked over the mountain, and the surrounding skies, before coming to rest on the exalted height. Crouching over the still-warm carcass, the gold dragon was about to tear into the meal when she hesitated. Blinking, then staring intently, she detected a trace of movement in the sky, a winged creature approaching from the north.

The flyer was clearly larger than any bird, yet the brownish, indistinct coloring was too dull for a dragon.

Propping the fresh meat firmly between two boulders, the golden serpent lifted her head, squinting into the shadows between the mountains, trying to discern the nature of the approaching creature.

Soon Aurora recognized the powerful body and the broad, feathered wings of a griffon. Because the hawk-faced predators generally avoided dragons, she was surprised to see this one coursing steadily closer to her high peak. She waited with the patience of the near-immortal, watching the griffon strain for altitude, laboring toward the sanctified rocks of the lofty summit. Now she could see the black and white pattern of the griffon's wing feathers, the hooked hawk-beak of the proud face. The griffon's body was like that of a great cat, powerful paws and muscular legs coming to rest on an outcrop of rock a short distance below the gold dragon's perch.

"Greetings, Honored Ancient," declared the griffon politely. The creature spoke in its own language, but Aurora was familiar with the tongue—as, indeed, she understood the speech of every intelligent being across the breadth of Krynn.

"Welcome, Feathered Hunter," the gold dragon replied with formal correctness. She was silent then, patiently waiting to learn the griffon's business.

"The skies are empty, for many miles across the plains," the sleek predator noted vaguely. When Aurora made merely a noncommittal rumble in reply, the hawk-faced creature continued. "I grieve for the loss of your bold sisters."

"You speak with a certainty that goes beyond my own knowledge," admitted the gold dragon—though she had guessed at this truth.

"One by one, the dragons of metal have been savaged by the Queen's wyrms," related the griffon, with a sad shake of the hawklike head. "Now, my cousins tell me that the serpents of Takhisis have taken wing from the Khalkist. They seek the last of their enemies."

Aurora's filmy eyelids half-lowered as she considered this information. The words of the griffon clearly placed a certain urgency on her situation, compelling action. The dragons of the Dark Queen would no doubt move swiftly—she knew that they had little use for a proper interval of meditation and philosophical discussion. And the gold dragon also knew that her enemy's actions must be faced with firm choices and decisive responses of her own. Perhaps the time for thinking was past, at least for now.

With a wrenching twist, Aurora pulled a rear haunch from the elk. She reared upward with the limb in one forepaw, and gestured to the remainder of the meaty carcass.

"You are welcome to food . . . and I thank you for your news," she informed the hawk-faced flyer.

The feathered cat bowed low, wings extended to honor the gilded serpent. "I thank you for your generosity, Ancient One. My cubs have been hungry for some days, now."

"Let them eat well." With a glint of sunlight on golden scales, Aurora took to the air, leaving the pleased griffon to tear the carcass into portable pieces. The dragon circled her lofty peak, studying the skies to east and north, reassuring herself that the wyrms of Takhisis were not yet on her doorstep. In mid-flight, she devoured the haunch of fresh meat, then tucked her broad wings and dove toward the Valley of Paladine.

She steered past sheer walls that plunged thousands of feet into the narrow, shadowed vale—a place inaccessible to landbound creatures, fully encircled by those lofty precipices. At the valley floor, Aurora settled to the ground, tucking her wings to enter the black, jagged opening that gaped in the mountain wall.

The tunnel within extended for a very long distance, but shortly past the entrance it widened dramatically. Again Aurora took to the air, spreading her wings to glide toward the great cavern in the depths of the mountain range.

Arrival always came as a shock—one second she veered through the winding cave, and the next she was in the great chamber. Below her lapped the placid waters of the vast, underground lake. Like an enclosed piece of sky, the vast ceiling lofted far overhead, encircling a body of water so broad that, at some distant point in the future, it would count no less than five teeming cities along its shores. Now it was home only to millions of bats, and to a very precious nest.

The gold dragon's flight was direct and purposeful. She flew toward a lofty pillar that rose from the center of the lake to merge with the high, arched ceiling. Aurora banked, circling the shaft, until she neared a wide ledge in the precipitous surface.

Settling to that platform, Aurora tucked her wings and passed through a shadowy niche barely wide enough for her sinuous form. Within, the moist air of the grotto soothed her nostrils; immediately she felt the sense of benign well-being that was the hallmark of this sacred cavern.

In the center of the circular chamber she saw the nest—a huge, bowl-shaped basket made from an array of massive gemstones hewn together by combined blasts of fire and frost, gold and silver dragon breath. The eggs within glowed subtly, illumination reflecting in myriad facets from ruby and emerald, and from a hundred tiny waterfalls on the grotto walls, where sparkling water trickled down the slick, reflective rock.

Aurora knew that there were twenty eggs here, four of each color—bright spheres of brass and bronze, the deep purity of copper, silver with a shine like pure light, and the perfection of deep, burnished gold. The latter had emerged from Aurora herself; the others had been born of her four sisters, some ageless time before their deaths. Fathered by Paladine himself, these eggs represented the hope for a future that included the metal dragons of the Platinum Father.

How would the world be changed, should the wyrms of Takhisis reach the grotto and destroy this precious clutch? This was a question that Aurora could have pondered for a very long time indeed. Yet she realized, with a glimmer of regret, that the time for philosophizing was past—now, she must be a warrior worthy of her kind. She would rely upon talon and fang, wield her fiery breath and powerful sinew with deadly force.

And meet the enemy with her magic. She knew that the banked fires of enchantment within her—wells of abiding power, capable of great force and violence—represented her best hope of victory.

Emerging from the grotto, flying over the water again, Aurora began to make her plan. She would meet the wyrms of the Dark Queen with her spells, and with all the formidable weapons inherent to her body. She must have discipline and patience, while at the same time her enemies, she devoutly hoped, would be governed by the chaotic influences of their immortal mistress.

Finally she passed through the long tunnel and was outside the mountain again, rising on the evening breezes toward her summit. She settled there at midnight, chilled by a sense of impending danger. Turning her eyes toward the plains, she called upon the power of magic, chanting softly, weaving the spell of true sight.

Immediately she saw them, five specks of evil color, tiny across the northeastern horizon. The white came first, speed carrying him ahead of the others. She could see, too, that the red and black flew as a pair, some miles behind the pale, ghostly serpent. The blue and green strained after, straggling far to the rear.

Aurora moved slightly down the face of her summit, on the slope facing her enemy's approach. Looking over a smooth cliff, she chose a perfect place for her next spell. The mirage arcana was a complicated casting, but the gold dragon spoke the sounds, called upon the magic with precision and care. Following her command, a false picture grew on the mountainside—a scene so real that, certainly, an eager and hasty white dragon might be fooled. Her magical weaving completed, Aurora admired the scene she had created, then climbed back to her summit, curling behind the crest of rock where she could observe the white's approach without being seen herself.

That ghostly serpent winged onward with frantic speed, reaching the foothills of the Western Range before dawn. By sunup, he was visible to Aurora's eyes, even unenhanced by magic. The gold watched carefully, masking herself with an invisibility spell to augment the almost-complete concealment offered by the mountain wall.

The spell proved superfluous, as the white's eyes remained fixed upon the mirage arcana. Silently, pale lips curling into a cruel smile, that evil wyrm tucked his wings, arrowing into a powerful and speedy dive. The creature plunged toward the image on the mountainside, and Aurora could sense the serpent's vicious eagerness as it swept toward the thing that it saw there—the vision of a gold dragon on a wide ledge, slumbering unconcernedly.

So intent was the white on his intended victim that the wyrm never hesitated, diving with long neck outstretched, anxious to drive long, sharp fangs through golden scales. When the serpent met the unseen mountainside he was flying at full speed, augmented by the momentum of a steep dive. Even far above, Aurora heard the crunching of vertebrae and the heavy thud of a massive body, already lifeless, smashing down the length of the smooth cliff.

The gold dragon swept outward, spiraling beside the precipice, sweeping over the massive, pale corpse sprawled across the talus at the base of the cliff. With a deep cry that echoed through the halls of the mountain valleys, Aurora confirmed her enemy's death, then tilted narrow wings to sweep upward.

Climbing above the ridge again, she now saw the red and black dragons, clearly distinct as serpentine, long-winged forms. Farther away, the blue and green strained for speed and altitude over the foothills. Commencing the next phase of her plan, Aurora glided above the highest crest of the Kharolis skyline, in clear view of the Dark Queen's wyrms.

Immediately, the red and black serpents banked toward Aurora. The trailing blue and green, meanwhile, veered along the course of a long, deep gorge—a route that would allow them to circle around the great mountain without climbing to the gold's lofty height.

Aurora's glide carried her toward a southern subpeak of the great massif, allowing the closer pair of her foes to quickly close the distance. Barely a mile separated her from the enemy when she dove, vanishing from view down the western slope of the towering mountain. Her eyes fixed upon the Valley of Paladine, she flew close to the descending ground, veering upward or banking sharply to avoid the outcropping peaks and knobs that rose in her path.

Soon she heard the cries of fury from above, knew that the red and black had crossed the ridge and seen her. Without wasting speed on a backward look, Aurora sensed that they followed her dive—and soon another shriek, considerably closer than the first, confirmed her suspicion.

Pure, unrestrained fury underlay the red's cry. Knowing that her enemy's rage could work to her own advantage, Aurora resolved to be patient, to allow that savage hatred to reach an unmanageable level. This was not the time to turn and offer battle to the crimson serpent, her largest and most powerful foe. Yet the gold dragon knew that, among all of the Dark Queen's wyrms, the red was also the most potent wielder of magic, and that was a threat she was determined to counter immediately.

She held to her plan, finally lighting to the ground before the familiar tunnel mouth. Her heart caught at the thought of the treasure within, but she allowed herself no hesitation as, with a flick of her golden tail, Aurora raced into the tunnel.

Almost instantly she turned, another spell forming in

her mind. She stared at the circle of daylight beyond the cavern, knowing what she would see very soon. Red scales flashed and then the crimson dragon crouched there, ready to pounce after his golden foe.

Aurora spat her spell of the feeblemind, a weaving of magic that struck the red in his seething, magical center. The enchantment rocked the crimson wyrm backward with deceptively subtle force. In the instant of its effect the spell wiped clean the slate of the red dragon's awareness of magic, causing every arcane casting to vanish from the monster's memory.

With a bellow, the enraged serpent instead spewed a crackling, hissing ball of fire into the tunnel. Aurora, who had turned to flee as soon as her spell was cast, was slightly singed at the tip of her tail. Like her blood-colored foe, however, the gold dragon could suffer no great harm from the normally deadly inferno of a dragon's breath.

She raced through the lightless passage with all the speed of long familiarity and keen, dark-sensitive eyes. After a hundred steps she entered the expanded section of the cavern, turning about again to face the narrow bottleneck. She felt the approach of her enemies, evil surging down the narrow cave.

But still it was not the time to fight. Instead Aurora whispered the incantations of another potent spell, felt the magic flow from her body, infusing the very bedrock of the mountain. That surface flexed and buckled, then churned upward from the floor and down from the ceiling, merging to form a wall of stone completely blocking the passage. The gold dragon listened for long heartbeats, hoping for the sound of a heavy body crashing into that wall, that the red's fury and headlong flight would cause it real harm.

Instead she heard a bellow of frustration and felt the wall grow warm under the onslaught of fiery breath. No matter, that—Aurora knew that the wall would withstand any heat the crimson serpent could belch forth.

And two of the Dark Queen's wyrms were thwarted, at least temporarily. The circumstance *might* give her enough time to deal with her other enemies, if she reacted quickly—and was blessed with good luck. Assuming that the green and blue still winged along the deep canyon, Aurora tried to picture their exact location. Her teleport spell was a simple word, uttered sharply, and before the echo returned from the enclosing cavern walls the gold dragon was poised in midair, high above a churning river that gouged ever deeper into the bedrock.

Immediately before her, and some distance below, the green dragon soared on widespread wings, unaware of his enemy's sudden appearance. A quick glance showed Aurora that the blue was far ahead, and, like the green, apparently hadn't noticed the gold's instantaneous arrival. Aurora plunged, wings swept far back for maximum speed—and to minimize the sound of her purposeful flight.

Nearing her target, Aurora saw a spot of pearly light floating above the green dragon's tail, like some kind of large, flying gem. As she opened her jaws for a breath of killing fire, she felt an uncanny tingle of alarm—there was something unnatural about the bauble, something strongly suggestive of magic. Closer still, the gold saw the staring pupil in the circled whiteness of the magical orb, and knew that she'd been observed.

The green's curling turn was startlingly quick, emerald jaws darting back to face the onrushing Aurora.

Warned by his wizard eye, the reptilian flyer twisted through a steep, desperate loop, roaring around as fiery pressure welled in the gold dragon's belly, spewing from Aurora's jaws into a blast of searing, hissing flame. At the same time, she felt a cloud of noxious vapor surround her, toxins stinging the membranes of eyes and nostrils, cutting into tender nerve ends with jarring pain.

Amid the cloud of fire and gas, the two mighty serpents collided. Choking and gagging, Aurora sought to fasten her fanged jaws around the green's neck. Her enemy's charred wings cracked away, turning to ashes under the raking slash of the gold dragon's claws—but then she recoiled in sudden pain as emerald claws ripped her own flesh. Aurora twisted, barely avoiding the rending belly-slash of her enemy's fangs. Finally the golden jaws found their target, closed around the neck, and with a crushing bite, ripped away the green dragon's life.

Releasing the bleeding, charred corpse to tumble toward the river, Aurora extended her wings and stroked for altitude. She blinked remnants of gas from still-bleary eyes, trying to locate the blue. She saw that the azure serpent had wheeled about at the sounds of battle and now winged toward her, closing the distance fast.

Abruptly the blue dragon vanished, and Aurora wondered for a precious second if her enemy had used a spell of invisibility. The truth came an instant later—but that delay was almost fatal. The gold whirled with instinctive speed, seeing that her foe had copied her own tactic, teleporting into perfect attack position. Shrieking at the image of the blue diving straight toward her, Aurora tried to draw a breath through the choking remnant of the green dragon's gas, to again fill her belly with the killing fire of dragonbreath. A spasm of coughing was the only result.

The bolt of lightning spit from the blue's mouth, ripping away a golden wing in a blast of searing, flesh-charring power. Aurora flailed at the blue's tail as the dragon swept past and then immediately banked out of his plunging dive. Canting drastically to the side, the gold instinctively stroked with her good wing—but this only sent her spinning crazily, tumbling out of control into the canyon depths.

Aurora trimmed her wing, pulling the leathery membrane back to her side as she arced neck and tail to bring herself out of the spin. Another spell fell from her lips, a single word of magic, and the power of levitation brought her plunge to a halt. Slowly the golden body started to rise, drifting gently back toward the sky. The blue dragon howled triumphantly, growing larger in her view as he winged straight toward Aurora. Azure jaws gaped, another cruel lightning bolt forming within.

The gold dragon saw utter doom, for herself and for all of her kind, in that merciless maw—and she knew that she could not afford to fail. She had hoped to save her most powerful spell until the end of the fight—or to not use it at all, because it tapped into black reaches that reeked more of the Dark Queen than the Platinum Father. Yet now she had no choice, and with a verbal quickness to match the speed of her decision, Aurora spat a dark and killing word full into the face of the onrushing wyrm.

The death spell seized the blue dragon by the guts, coiling the serpentine body into a wriggling ball. The lightning bolt died, unspat, as the pulse of vitality withered and perished in the azure belly. Plunging downward, the dragon's corpse followed its green brother, vanishing into the raging turbulence of the mountain river.

Forcing herself to ignore the pain flaming through the nub of her left wing, still airborne on the power of the levitation spell, Aurora summoned another incantation. This time the magic brought a gust of wind, swirling air pushing her buoyant body toward the mountain. The gust circled the mighty peak, whisking its mighty passenger toward a high shelf of rock on an otherwise inaccessible cliff.

Coming to rest on the ledge, Aurora slumped to the ground, a momentary wave of weakness spasming through her golden body. Knowing that urgency allowed no delay, she painfully dragged herself across the flat surface of rock toward a jumble of boulders piled against the wall of cliff. Moaning unconsciously, pain wracking her flesh, the gold dragon pulled away huge boulders with her foreclaws.

Soon she had revealed a cave mouth, one of several secret entrances leading to the vast chamber beneath the mountain. Crawling along a rubble-strewn passageway, she soon reached a ledge where dark space yawned into the distance and the waters of the subterranean lake glistened darkly a hundred feet below.

Without hesitating, Aurora dove straight from the ledge, plunging into deep, chill waters. With strong kicks of her rear legs she swam, stroking with her forelegs to steer toward another shadowy passage on the periphery of the vast chamber. Despite the strain of hard, repetitive movement, the cool water felt good against the gold dragon's wounds, and she swam to her destination with unflagging determination.

At the base of the cliff, she rose from the water with the force of levitation magic. Water flowed off her body and back to the lake like a series of waterfalls. As she floated upward, coming to rest at the mouth of a long, familiar tunnel, Aurora could only hope that the wall of stone was still intact, still blocked the red and black from this sacred cavern.

Yet as she reached the access tunnel and started through the darkness, an oily and reptilian scent assailed her nostrils. With a stab of fear Aurora knew the truth—and made up her mind not to waste time going all the way to her arcane barrier. The stench told her that the two wyrms of the Dark Queen had already passed. Clearly they had battered down the wall of stone, and now were somewhere within the watery cavern.

Again Aurora hurled herself into that cold liquid, diving below the surface and stroking toward the center of the lake. She forced herself not to think about the eggs, so vulnerable in their pristine grotto. She reminded herself that the entrance was well-concealed, and she could only hope that the Dark Queen's wyrms had not yet found the treasured clutch.

Finally the great pillar of stone loomed overhead, rising from the lake like a precipitous mountain, merging fully into a dark and jagged sky. Peering through the shadows, Aurora unsuccessfully sought evidence of the black or red dragons. Once more the power of levitation pulled her upward, carrying her past the cliffs of the lofty column as she rose toward the ledge. She drew a breath, felt the fires of killing heat seething within her belly as she pivoted in a spiral, seeking any sign of movement in the shadows. Again she had been forced to make noise, and certainly the evil wyrms must have heard.

Still, the black came at her so quickly that Aurora barely saw the monster against the darkness—only the white teeth, gleaming like bony daggers in a gaping mouth, gave hint of the monster's approach. Her reaction was instantaneous, and the dark space thrummed and boiled, filled with the searing, orange-red explosion of Aurora's breath. Steam hissed, and the black dragon's shriek of pain rang through the darkness, echoing from the far walls around the underground sea.

A stream of searing acid spumed from that fireball, splashing along Aurora's flank, burning and corroding through her golden scales. Veering to escape the crackling fire, the midnight-dark wyrm tumbled below his foe, and Aurora dropped, catlike, onto the creature's back. Swiftly her jaws found the ridged backbone at the base of the neck, and with a crushing, bone-snapping bite the gold dragon severed her enemy's spine.

Leaving the lifeless body to splash into the water, Aurora used her tail to pull her still-levitating body to the edge of the grotto's ledge. Scales flaked off of her side as the acid hissed deeper into her flesh, scoring fiery rivers of pain. Crawling slowly, her left foreleg virtually useless, she poked her head into the softly phosphorescent illumination of the grotto.

She felt weak with relief as she saw, in the center of the circular chamber, that the gem-studded nest was undisturbed, the precious globes of the eggs still gleaming metallic and pristine.

* * * * *

Furyion glided through the vast cavern, soaring near the ceiling. He was enraged by the gold's trickery, the enchantment that had wiped his own arsenal of spells from his mind. Frustration grew within him as he sensed that the nest of metal eggs was close, but remained unable to find it.

Still, he knew now that victory was imminent.

He had seen the white fall, and heard the slaying of the black. From the gold's lengthy absence he deduced that Arkan and Korril, too, had suffered from Aurora's deadly strength.

Yet now the mighty golden serpent was badly wounded—the scent of blood, and of charred, lightning-ravaged flesh, was acrid in the air, clear proof of Aurora's many hurts. She was weakened, vulnerable, and close; he could see her now, stretched exhausted on a narrow ledge, high above the black waters of the lake.

Furyion pictured those golden scales, imagined how the necklace would dance and jangle as his heart swelled with pride, absorbed the many praises of his Queen.

He would wear that trophy around his neck forever, he resolved, tucking his scarlet wings and diving toward the helpless gold.

* * * * *

With pain wracking her crippled limbs and scarred, ravaged body, Aurora turned her gaze outward. She knew that the red could not be far away, and was not surprised as a bellow of fury echoed through the chamber, signaling the monster's approach.

The crimson form, sleek and powerful, unwounded and fresh, plunged toward Aurora from above. Embers of fire still surged in her belly, but the gold knew that against this enemy her killing fireball would have little effect.

Her deadly spells all but exhausted, wings rended and wounds bleeding across her body, Aurora knew that she faced an attack she could not defeat. With a bleak moan she thought of the eggs . . . they were certainly doomed if she should perish and leave the crimson serpent to plunder and kill.

The red dragon bored in, jaws gaping, foreclaws extended to rip into the golden body. In the instant before collision, a plan sprang into Aurora's mind, compelling action without consideration of regrets or misgivings. There was no time to philosophize—she knew what she had to do.

The gold dragon sprang as the red swept to the ledge. Aurora reached out a strong foreleg to clasp her enemy in a firm embrace. The wyrm of Takhisis, not expecting the tactic, smashed violently into his foe, and the two serpents were instantly entangled in a web of tails, talons, necks and legs. They teetered at the brink of the precipice, then toppled toward the water below.

Even as they fell Aurora felt shock and dismay at the red's strength. The cruel wyrm twisted and squirmed, struggling to escape from her clasp—and in seconds he would inevitably succeed.

"You will be *mine*," the red hissed furiously, his tone shrill and commanding. "My trophy! I will wear your scales about my neck!"

Aurora's mind worked frantically. She had but a single spell left. She dared not risk it against her enemy, for success against a squirming, resisting target was far from assured—whereas, if she cast it upon herself the impact would be immediate, inevitable . . . and fatal.

She remembered the red's words—a ring of her scales, he would wear. With a whiplike slash she gave him his wish, wrapping her sinuous neck in tight coils around the crimson throat. Chanting a word of power as still, dark water rushed upward, Aurora felt her consciousness depart, replaced by the bleak coldness of self-inflicted death. Powerful magic coursed through her serpentine body, turning golden-scaled flesh into lifeless, solid stone.

Stiff spirals of rocky tail still wrapped the red's torso, and immovable limbs and neck of solid stone enclosed the evil dragon's throat in a permanent necklace. The golden serpent, daughter of Paladine, had turned herself into immovable stone, useful only as a statue, a decorative structure, a permanent monument . . .

Or, perhaps, as an anchor.

Aurora never felt the cold water surround her, couldn't sense the wriggling, writhing body of her drowning enemy as the two monsters plunged into the lightless depths of the subterranean lake. Nor did she sense the final expulsion of hateful breath, fire sizzling in momentary steam, then doused in chill water. Still squirming, sinking steadily deeper, the crimson serpent at last gave up his own life, joining his foe in a clasp of stony permanence on the bottom of the secret sea.

And even in the lightless depths, its seemed that the stony scales glowed with just the barest trace of gold.

* * * * *

The nest of eggs glowed in the muted light of the grotto. Water trickled down the walls as it had for eons, and would continue for centuries to come.

Within the enclosure of fused gems, the metal spheres shed gentle illumination. The pale wash of light revealed a ghostly figure coiled protectively about the nest. The encircling image was a light, ephemeral form—yet even so, the platinum hue of the smoky surface was clear.

A timeless stretch later, the surfaces of two of the eggs pulsed. A golden membrane parted with a moist rip, revealing a pointed snout of the same color; frantically, a wyrmlike body wriggled through the aperture, blinking and stretching with the awkwardness of first steps.

Soon thereafter, the silver orb ruptured, and another snout pushed forth. Even then the platinum image barely moved, merely shifting a sinuous neck, a vaporous head rising to hover pridefully over the precious offspring.

"I name thee Aurican," whispered a deep voice, the sound coming from a place beyond the world, swirling like a gust of wind around the golden wyrmling. The puff of air twisted next to the silver form, and in another throaty word, tiny Darlantan received his appellation.

And dragons of metal and goodness were born again to Krynn.

If you enjoyed reading *The Dragons at War*, be sure to read these other DRAGONLANCE® saga short story anthologies:

In *The Second Generation* Margaret Weis and Tracy Hickman tell the stories of the children of the Heroes of the Lance. Selections include "Kitiara's Son" and "Raistlin's Daughter" as well as poetry by Michael Williams. Many years have passed since the War of the Lance. Krynn is peaceful, but the future is uncertain. It will take a new generation of heroes to continue the struggle against evil—a darkness that was defeated but never completely destroyed.   (ISBN 0-7869-0260-4)

DRAGONLANCE authors showcase their talents in *The Dragons of Krynn*. This short story collection contains tales of good and evil dragons (and those somehere in between) as well as minotaurs, gully dwarves, gnomes, kender, knights, wizards and draconians. Authors include Nancy Varian Berberick, Jeff Grubb, Richard A. Knaak, Roger E. Moore, Douglas Niles, Nick O'Donohoe, Michael and Teri Williams, and Margaret Weis.   (ISBN 1-56076-830-4)